By *Kris Tualla*:

A Woman of Choice

and

A Primer for Beginning Authors

A Woman
of Choice

Kris Tualla

"Takk du mye!"

Kris Tualla

Goodnight Publishing
http://www.GoodnightPublishing.com

A Woman of Choice is a work of fiction. Names, characters, places and incidents are products of the author's imagination or are used fictitiously and are not to be construed as real. Any resemblance to actual events, locales, organizations, or persons, living or dead, is entirely coincidental.

Published in the United States of America through:

Goodnight Publishing
www.GoodnightPublishing.com

info@GoodnightPublishing.com

ISBN-10: 1451503318
EAN-13: 9781451503319

For my wonderful husband
who supports me
without complaint.

With much love and appreciation
to Candace, Deborah, Denise, Julia, and Nannette,
who have listened to me with great patience.

And to my 4-Ever Divas
for cheering me on.

Chapter One

*T*he dogs wouldn't come back. They yowled and yipped and danced around a muddy heap of fabric lumped beside the receding rain-swollen creek.

"Can't you control those mutts, Rick?" Nicolas Hansen growled. Irritated, he reined Rusten toward the hounds and wondered which particular Cheltenham resident upstream had seen fit to discard their curtains into his creek. But when he got close, his gut twisted.

The heap had hair. Long, black, tangled hair.

Nicolas threw himself from the gelding. "Rick! Get over here!"

He knelt beside the crumpled and filthy form. His knees sunk into the chilled creekside mud and the roar of the tumbling water almost drowned the roar of his pulse. He stretched his hand over the still figure and hesitated, hoping for some sign of life. There was none. He gently turned the body toward him.

She exhaled a faint moan.

"It's a woman, Rick!" Nicolas called over his shoulder. "And she's alive!"

His gaze skimmed the woman's mud-smeared face. Dark brows

slanted from a bruised temple. Their arches flanked a straight nose with a nasty bump. Her lips were blue and the lower one was split and bleeding. That was a good sign. It meant her heart was beating.

"*Å min Gud...*" Nicolas moaned. He yanked his hunting dirk from its sheath and held it over the woman's skirt.

He hesitated again, weighing the ramifications to himself—and her—if he cut away her clothing. But he knew he couldn't balance her on his horse anchored as she was by yards of mud-saturated wool. In Nicolas's personal economy, saving her life far outweighed saving their reputations.

If he wasn't too late already.

Rickard's voice spilled over his shoulder, "Wrap her in this." A blanket nudged his arm.

Nicolas nodded his acknowledgement. He severed the full skirt from her bodice in a few quick strokes. He left her chemise intact and his gaze didn't linger on her bruised and bare legs. He rolled her into the blanket, stood with her cradled in his arms, and faced Rickard.

"Hand her up to me," he said as he transferred the woman into his best friend's sturdy grasp. Rickard accepted the burden without pause.

Nicolas mounted his tall gelding and leaned down to gather the limp bundle. He shifted a bit until he felt both he and the woman were secure on Rusten's back. "Ride ahead, will you? Tell Addie what's coming."

Rickard nodded and turned to his own mount. "Do you know her?"

Nicolas frowned. "No. Do you?"

Rickard prodded his stallion closer and leaned over the unconscious woman. "I don't think so. Hard to tell with all the mud and the bruising, though."

"Hm." Nicolas jerked his chin at Rickard. "Go on, then."

Rickard kicked his horse to an easy canter, waved over his shoulder, and he was gone.

Nicolas followed at a steady walk, afraid to jar his fragile passenger by hurrying the huge gelding. He guided Rusten with his knees while he considered her pale, muddy face.

Lying ten miles southwest of St. Louis, Cheltenham was a small township. Nicolas had lived here his entire life—save for four university years and the year he was obliged to stay in Norway. He believed he knew all of its residents, so he was fairly certain he had never seen this woman before.

And that made her appearance even more puzzling. Where had she come from? Where was she headed? And how did she end up in the creek to begin with? Was she the victim of an accident? Or was something more sinister afoot?

"I suppose if you awaken, you'll explain yourself," he mumbled and shifted her position a little. Her eyelids fluttered and she gave a tiny whimper. But she lay as limp as a drowned cat in his arms.

When he reached the manor, his aging housekeeper stood in the doorway beside Rickard, craning her neck and worrying her apron. His friend stepped forward, accepted the feminine bundle once again, and held her while Nicolas dismounted.

"Thanks, Rick," Nicolas said as he took the woman and hugged her securely against his chest. He faced Addie. "We'll put her in the room at the end of the hall."

She nodded and followed him into the house. "Poor thing," she cooed.

Nicolas topped the stairs without noticeable effort and headed toward the uninhabited room, the furthest one from his. After all, he had no interest in any sort of entanglement and fully expected to return this unexpected and unwanted female to whomever she belonged as soon as she regained consciousness. Once in the room, he laid his mysterious charge on the bed and gave her over to Addie's competent care.

"Rick?" he called down the staircase.

"I'm here, Nick." Rickard stepped out of Nicolas's study and gulped a glass of amber liquid.

Nicolas snorted and started down the steps. "Let's get back to hunting, eh? Before you finish off my best brandy!"

Rickard laughed and set down the empty glass. "You've got more stashed in here than even I could finish and you know it!"

Nicolas reached him, grinned and slapped his shoulder. "Come on, then. If you can manage those dogs, I've a taste for pheasant for supper tonight!"

Chapter Two

April 2, 1819

*T*he frigid liquid world blurred and roared and tumbled around her. Tossed without mercy, she couldn't figure out where up was, where air was, where water wasn't. Hard edges battered her. She was tangled in endless sodden wool. Her limbs chilled, her lungs burned, and she couldn't draw a breath to scream.

Then blackness drowned her senses.

Pain dragged her back toward consciousness. The surge of her pulse slammed her skull with steady sledge hammers. It hurt to breathe. It hurt to think.

Distant voices mumbled through her awareness.

A man, deep and demanding, "Has she awakened?"

A woman, older, "No, not yet."

"Well, what are we to do with her?"

"I'm afraid I don't know."

Had she dreamt it?

Or were they talking about her?

She willed her eyes open and blinked the spinning room into submission. Her blurred gaze staggered over her surroundings and panic squeezed her chest, intensifying the hammers' pounding.

Where am I? What happened to me?

She closed her eyes and inhaled slowly, defying the tenderness in her ribs, and ordered her heart to slow its frantic warning. Then she opened her eyes again and searched for the whisper of anything familiar.

She lay curled on her side in a bed with clean linens. She could see the carved top of the footboard without moving her head, its edges rubbed light by years of use.

Should she recognize it?

Plaster walls hemmed the wood floor of the unadorned room. Finished logs and cross-planks comprised the ceiling. Dank whiffs of wet bark and moldering leaves leached through the open window past blue afternoon shadow-light.

A stone fireplace dominated the opposite wall, beneath a faded medieval tapestry with images of helmeted warriors and carved ships. A plain bedside table and slat-back rocker were the only other occupants of the room. Under the encroaching outdoor scents, she smelled dust and old smoke. Realization squeezed her temples and dug behind her eyes.

No one lived in this room.

She rolled to her back and lifted onto her elbows. A blade of pain knifed up her neck and ricocheted through her skull. Her world went black again.

෫෧ ෬

This time, the room held still. So did she.

The window was closed. A diminutive flame sputtered in the large fireplace, while an oil lamp on the bedside table chased the shadows to the far corners of the chamber. On the seat of the rocking chair, a book waited.

But she was no closer to figuring out where she was.

The door creaked open, pushed by the ample backside of a woman past middle-age. She wore a brown dress, a lace cap and a white apron with the strings tied in a drooping bow. Her eyes remained fixed on her tea tray, which she set on the bedside table. She reached down to pick up the book before easing herself into the rocker. Only then did she look toward the bed.

"Oh, my!" she blurted, her voice loosened by age. "Are you awake, dear?"

Remembering not to move her head, she whispered, "Yes."

"Thank the Lord!" The older woman pushed up from the chair. "I'm so glad to see you finally awake. You were in such a bad way, we weren't at all assured that you'd survive, poor thing!"

She crossed the room with surprising haste and shouted into the hallway. "Maribeth! Come quickly!"

Then she returned to the bedside, moving like a loose bag of potatoes. Rapid footsteps preceded the appearance of a much younger woman, slim and dark.

"Are you hungry, dear? Do you feel you could do with some tea or perhaps some broth? Nothing solid yet! I don't believe that would sit well." Not waiting for an answer, she ordered Maribeth to bring warm broth without delay. "Oh, and find Sir Nicky soon as you're able, and tell him that our girl is finally awake!"

"Sir Nicky?" she croaked. Her mouth was dry, her tongue sticky. She tasted blood.

"Oh, he's not truly knighted." The older woman waved her hand and chuckled. "It's only that I was his nanny when he was just a boy, him and his younger brother, and they loved to play knights and horses and castles and dragons and all. So I started calling his brother 'Sir Gunny' and him 'Sir Nicky' and, well, I reckon I just never stopped."

The woman shook her head. Gray wisps escaped her cap. "Oh, but listen to me go on. You'd believe I've lost all my manners! I haven't even introduced my own self yet! My name is Addie, and that's short for Adelaide, which I feel is much too much of a mouthful for anyone!" She smoothed the covers with her wrinkled hands. "I've been here at the manor almost forty years, now. Why, I nearly raised those two boys myself!"

Addie's verbal deluge drenched her and she felt a wave of panic. So she closed her eyes and tried to sink into the mattress to puzzle things out. If Addie needed to introduce herself, then she hadn't ever been here before. So naturally she wouldn't recognize her surroundings.

But if she doesn't know me, how could she possibly know what happened to me?

Her persistent headache confounded her ability to reason. She heard a bowl rattling on a metal tray and smelled the beef broth. It must be Maribeth who set the tray on the bedside table with an audible sigh.

A shadow blocked the lamplight. "Can you wake up again, dear? Your broth is here," Addie asked.

She opened her eyes and forced a shaky smile, though her sore lower lip stung with the effort. Perhaps broth was a good idea. After all, she had no idea how long she'd gone without food.

"Do you believe you might be able to sit up if we helped you, dear?"

Addie and Maribeth tenderly lifted and tucked until she sat propped against a stack of pillows, though every bit of movement brought new pain to the surface. The room rolled and she swallowed a surge of nausea.

She held out stiff arms and considered the white cotton and lace nightgown she wore. "Are these my clothes?" Her rough voice was unrecognizable.

"Oh no, dearie... Your dress was ruined, I'm sorry to say. A frightful mess, it was, too, what with all the water and mud and being so cut up. Such a shame, since that green color would go so well with your eyes." Addie paused long enough to gently brush a strand of hair from her forehead. "But I cleaned you up. Washed and plaited your hair, as well. And I found one of Miss Lara's best sleeping gowns to dress you in."

Who?

She slid her hands over the finely woven material; it released the faint scents of lavender mixed with camphor.

"Please thank her for me," she murmured. A shadow passed over the housekeeper's face and Maribeth's eyes widened. For a beat, no one spoke.

Addie picked up the bowl of broth and eased her generous bottom onto the edge of the bed. "Let's try this while it's still warm, shall we?"

She managed to swallow most of the broth before hard soles on wood echoed heavily toward the room. Addie rose from the bed and straightened her apron. All eyes turned to the doorway as a man of about thirty years ducked inside. The strong odors of fresh air—and fresh manure—entered with him.

He must be a full hand over six feet.

His broad shoulders and solid build seemed to strain the confines of the small room. If he had not looked so stern, she might have considered him beautiful.

He stopped.

Dark blue eyes raked over her and his jaw clenched. A thin scar on one cheek whitened. Pulling a leather thong from his hair, he retied his shoulder-length blond locks. He released a sigh and approached the bed, frowning.

"So." His uneasy stance and the shift of his feet unnerved her. She looked away, realized she couldn't evade the man, and faced him again. When their eyes met, he asked, "How are you feeling?"

Before she could answer, a shiver convulsed her and her face contorted. Two quick gasps preceded an explosive sneeze. With a grunt and a groan, she put her hands on her temples and slumped over the edge of the bed, vomiting broth onto the floor. Blood dripped from her nose and her field of vision filled with black motes and silver lights.

The burst of activity around her sounded far away. Steel arms lifted her and laid her back onto the pillows. Someone wiped her mouth and nose, and laid a wet cloth over her eyes. She heard the thud of a heavy bucket on the wood planks and the swish of a rag on the floor next to the bed; she smelled the tang of lye soap.

Her face flamed with embarrassment and her lower lip tensed. Hot tears escaped from under the cloth and rolled down her cheeks. Her head throbbed and felt too heavy for her neck.

"There, there." Addie lifted the cool cloth from her eyes and used it to wipe her face. "Don't worry a thing about it, dearie. Happens all the time."

Reassured by the ridiculous claim, she fixed her grateful gaze on the older woman. She purposefully avoided looking toward the imposing male figure, but his stare from the foot of the bed held weight.

Addie rinsed the cloth and pressed it under her nose, then turned with a cocked brow. "Have you forsaken your manners, young man? You have a guest! And a poor injured woman at that!"

The recipient of Addie's scolding slowly straightened and placed his right palm against his chest. Though unsmiling, his hard sapphire gaze met hers and he bowed a little at the waist.

"Please forgive my appalling lack of decorum, madam," he said in a powerful voice that rumbled from the depths of his sizeable chest. "For I was certainly raised to know better by my beloved old, old nanny."

Addie snorted. But she smiled.

"I am Nicolas Reidar Hansen, owner of this estate, your humble servant, and deeply honored rescuer."

Rescuer? From what?

Confused, she tilted her head back and held the cloth firmly beneath her nose. "I ab berry pleased to beet you, Bister Hadsend. By nabe is…" She stopped, her mouth still open.

The cloth dropped to her lap.

"M-my n-name is…" she tried again, but only murky water swirled through her wits. The salt of sweat pricked her skin. Nicolas and Addie exchanged unsettled glances.

"My name is—!" She exhaled the words as though, if said with enough intent, the statement would complete itself.

It did not.

Oh, merciful God; this must be a nightmare!

With a mournful wail of denial, she curled into herself in the center of the bed. *Why don't I wake up?*

"What is it, dear?" Addie touched her shoulder and she recoiled from the very real contact.

"I don't remember my name!" She gulped air. Dread pummeled her aching ribs and made it harder to breathe. "And I don't know what happened to me!"

Neither Addie nor Nicolas moved.

"What!" Nicolas thundered.

"You don't remember aught, dear? Not anything at all?" Addie's gentle tone squeaked.

Drowning in disbelief, a small shake of her head was all she could manage.

℘ ℭ

Nicolas burst into his study, reaching the massive oak desk in two strides. He jerked the top drawer open and grabbed a flask of brandy. He downed two healthy gulps before slamming the pewter flagon on the oak.

"*Hva i helvete!*" He pounded the abused desktop with his other fist. "*Skitt!*"

Rickard leaned against the mantel, half empty crystal glass in hand and his mouth curving in a confused smile. "What's got you so twisted, of a sudden?"

"She doesn't know who she is!" Incredulous, Nicolas turned to face him full-on. "She doesn't *Gud forbanner* know who the *helvete* she is!"

Rickard sank in a nearby chair. "Our mystery woman?"

"Who the *helvete* else, Rick?" Nicolas yanked the leather thong from his hair and dragged his hand through its tangles. "*Skitt!*" he griped again. "What am I supposed to do with her now?"

Rickard's eyes narrowed. "What occurred up there?"

Nicolas swallowed again from the flask. The brandy's familiar burn heated his chest and curled through his belly. It took a moment to force the words.

"That *Gud forbanner* busybody dressed her in Lara's night dress."

"Oh." Rickard slumped deeper in his chair.

Nicolas pressed the backs of his thighs against the sturdy desk. He stroked the cool pewter flask with his thumb, warming the smooth metal.

Rickard's low voice held a determined edge. "It's more than five years now."

His words lit the fuse that Lara's nightgown had set and the brandy had fueled; Nicolas felt like a cannonball about to fire. "And what? *Gud forbanner det!* Do you expect me to forget?"

Rickard rose and faced him; they were nearly the same height, and Rick was apparently unfazed by furious Norse cannons. "Of course not! She was my sister, remember."

Nicolas turned away from his friend's fearless stare. "What's your point?" he snarled.

Rickard gripped his shoulders. He swung his gaze back to Rick's, the set of his jaw deliberately defiant. His eyes narrowed, daring with an unsubtle threat.

Rick's words were sharp steel sliding between his ribs. "Don't you see? If you won't put her to rest, then I cannot put her to rest, either?"

Nicolas swayed at that cruelest of cuts as his last ally finally turned from him. Rickard pushed him into a chair. Pulling up an ottoman, Rick sat and leaned into his face.

"We need to move forward, Nick. It's past time."

Nicolas's hand tightened around the pewter flask. He glared at Rick and refused to surrender.

Rickard shook his head and reached for the flagon, saving it from strangulation. He took a long drink and capped the flask.

"Well, if she doesn't remember, then what do you reckon happened to her?" he asked. "How did she end up in your creek?"

Nicolas knew his friend well enough to understand his maneuvering. For now, he said, "I don't know, but I don't believe it was an accident."

"Because no one came after her?"

"Exactly."

Rickard straightened and stretched his arms overhead. "If you've no objection, I believe I'll pay our resident stranger a visit," he offered.

Nicolas rasped his palms over a couple days' worth of stubble. He smelled the manure on his boots and decided to go outside to clean them.

"Do what you want," he grumbled. He looked up only when Rickard didn't leave.

"I'm curious, Nick. After Addie got her cleaned up, did she turn out to be pretty?"

Nicolas snorted and rolled his eyes. Only Rick.

He shrugged; he truly had not paid any attention. "She may be passable. After the bruises have faded."

ဆ ᘒ

"Good candlelighting, madam…"

With a telltale rattle of her china teacup, she turned toward the unfamiliar masculine voice. Addie was not in sight so the man in the doorway obviously took it upon himself to make his own introduction.

"May I help you?" She realized it was a silly thing to say, but it was the first coherent thought that struggled beyond her oppressive headache. The second involved the enormous improbability that more than one very tall, very beautiful man lived in this house.

"I've come to meet the mystery woman." He smiled as he approached her bed, all wavy auburn hair and sparkling light-hazel eyes. "I'm gratified to see that you're in much better condition than when we fished you out of the creek!"

She regarded him curiously. "We?"

"Nicolas and myself. I'm Rickard Atherton. My land lies to the south, along the Hansen estate." Rickard gestured in what she presumed must be a southerly direction.

"I'm pleased to meet you," she said in a hoarse whisper and extended the hand that didn't grip the teacup.

Rickard accepted it with long, warm fingers and raised it to his lips. His fascinating eyes never left hers, and curvy locks of hair fell forward over his aristocratic brow. He gave her a sultry smile that warmed her deep inside.

"I-I wish I could introduce myself to you," she began. Unwelcome tears threatened at the thought, but she batted them back. "Mr. Hansen didn't explain how you came to find me. Would you be so kind?"

"Of course! May I?" At her nod of assent, Rickard pulled the oak rocker closer to the bed.

With her freed hand she tugged the edge of the blankets over her chest. Entertaining a man in her bedroom wasn't exactly acceptable, but her current circumstance was unorthodox at best. Besides, the door stood wide open and Addie would return at any moment. At least the gown she wore was modestly cut in spite of its delicate beauty.

"Go on then," she encouraged. Rickard smiled at her again and her heart thumped.

"Well, Nick and I were out hunting when my hounds caught your scent. I thought they were merely distracted, so I whistled for them to come back. When they wouldn't, we had no choice but to follow. Nick reached you first, on the edge of the creek. When he turned you over, you moaned. Then we knew you were alive."

"You thought otherwise?" she whispered.

Rickard nodded, his expression grown solemn. "Nick brought you here. Then Addie took full charge of you."

Her thumb traced the curlicued handle of the teacup while she struggled to make sense of why she would have ended up in such a place and in such a condition. But no light shined, no door cracked open; she was still lost in the dark.

"How long—I mean, when did you find me?"

"Yesterday, late in the afternoon."

"And where are we?"

Rickard paled a bit. "Cheltenham. In the Missouri Territory."

She silently scrutinized her gut's reaction to that statement. It didn't seem quite right, somehow. But she had no other recollection to align it with.

"You have very beautiful eyes," he said.

The empty teacup clattered in her lap.

"Do I?" She skimmed her fingers over her face, their weightless touch cataloging the cuts and swelling. "I must look dreadful! Might there be a mirror?"

Rickard shifted awkwardly. His gaze dropped aside, and then returned to hers. "I'll find you one on the morrow," he promised. "When the light's better."

At that, they both glanced at the oil lamp, still faithfully banishing shadows from the room, and she realized that she must look truly horrible, indeed.

Chapter Three

April 3, 1819

*S*he scowled as the room brightened, glowing red inside her eyelids. Through one squinted eye, she watched Addie open the window. Bright sun splashed onto the floor as dust motes danced to the beginning of a new day.

Her knees felt like rusted hinges bolted to heavy planks, and her arms were supple as dried twigs. Her bruised ribs held her nearly immobile, like thick tree bark. She was surprised her body didn't audibly creak and crackle when she carefully stretched her healing limbs.

"Good morning, dearie!" Addie chirped, approaching the bed. "How are you feeling this morning?"

"Stiff," she answered, her voice thick with sleep. Her belly rumbled. "And hungry."

"Oh, that's wonderful! It truly is! I'll go downstairs right quick and make you a bite. Not too much, mind you, you haven't eaten solid in a while." Addie reached under the bed and lifted a blue and white enameled container.

"Might you need to use the chamber pot? And if I help you to the chair, do you feel you can manage on your own?"

"Yes, thank you." She had no idea if she could.

Maribeth, wearing what seemed to be the same dark gray dress but with a clean apron, carried in a ewer of hot water, a basin, and a towel, all of which she set on the bedside table.

With the women's support she eased herself from the bed,

putting weight gingerly on one leg, then the other. It made her dizzy, but the pounding in her head had lessened. Once she was settled in the slat-backed rocker, Addie and Maribeth left her alone.

Curious, she lifted the hem of the nightgown and gaped in stunned disbelief. Her pale legs were splotched with maroon and purple bruises. She pushed back her lace-edged sleeves to reveal more of the same on her arms. The extent of her injuries alarmed her. She had never seen a body so beaten that still lived.

"Father God," she breathed. "Thank You for my life."

Her chest tightened with a dreadful consideration. There was no way around it but to discern the answer for herself; Lord knows, she didn't want anyone else to do it! She slid tentative fingers under the gown and up the length of her legs to the cleft between her thighs. She pressed, tested, explored. She found no swelling or tenderness there.

Dammed breath left her in a gush of relief. At the least, she wasn't violated.

By the time Addie returned with a tray of food, her toilette was complete. She sat straight in the chair, the nightgown tucked protectively around her legs. Breakfast was a small bowl of oatmeal, a poached egg and a pot of hot tea. When the aroma of the food reached her, her mouth began to water and her stomach growled again, loudly.

"We'll get you all fixed up right quick," Addie approved. "There's nothing like a healthy appetite to encourage a body to mend!" She set the tray on the table. "Eat up now! I've some things to attend to, but I'll be back presently."

The food, though simple, tasted better than any banquet she could imagine. In the silent room, sun spilling everywhere, her skin caressed by the exquisite cotton nightgown, she was briefly content in spite of her confusion.

More than halfway through her meal, she caught movement out of the corner of her eye. Turning to the door, she saw half-a-head of tousled auburn hair, one shoulder, and a small fist clutching the edge of the door frame. And whose child might this be?

"Hello, there," she murmured.

The auburn hair moved sideways until one bright blue eye appeared. Rickard's hair. Nicolas's eyes. No help there.

"Do you want to come in and meet me?" she asked.

The hair bounced up and down in a shy nod.

"Well come on, then," she coaxed. "I fear I don't look very friendly right now, but I promise that I am."

At that, both blue eyes emerged. A young boy moved into the room, methodically placing one heel in line with the opposite foot's toes. His wide gaze was nailed to hers.

"How old are you?" she asked him.

He spoke quietly and held up a fistful of splayed fingers. "Five."

That was surprising; she would have reckoned him to be seven by his height.

He brushed his hair from his eyes with the heel of one hand. "The white cat had six kittens yesterday."

She was charmed. "Really?"

He nodded emphatically and his hair flopped back in his eyes. He traced a finger along the worn side of the rocking chair.

"She was in the stable and I watch't her. John told me not to touch her or the kittens 'cause she might bite. The cat lick't them all clean and then they started drinking her milk. 'Cept for one, it was real teeny." He held up two pointer fingers close together to illustrate. "She lick't it and lick't it, but it didn't breathe."

An unexplained stone lodged low in her belly and her brow twitched. "I—I'm sorry to hear that."

"John and I dug a grave and buried her. I made a cross with sticks." The boy's hands dropped to the rocker's arm and squeezed the wood in an awkward massage.

She pressed ahead with her questions, and her breakfast, ignoring the presence of the stone.

"That was very thoughtful of you. Who is John?"

"He's married to Addie. He doesn't talk much 'cause he says she does 'nuff talking for both of 'em."

She gave him a small smile, careful of her broken lip, and nodded her understanding. They were quiet for a moment, and then she needed to ask. It was not the first time—and didn't look to be the last—that she must face her odd situation. She drew a bracing breath.

"What's your name?"

Beneath the unruly canopy of auburn curls, his summer-sky eyes glowed in the morning sun. "Stefan."

And after the expected pause came, "What's yours?"

Seizing on a sudden inspiration she suggested, "How about if you try and guess?"

Stefan's brow furrowed. His fingers gripped the wide arm of the oak rocker as he tried to drill one foot into the wood floor.

"Go ahead," she encouraged. "I'll finish my breakfast, while you try to guess my name." She spooned her last bite of oatmeal and leaned back in the chair.

"Stefan! What are you doing in here? Have you had your breakfast?"

Nicolas ducked through the doorway. His booming bass voice had substance and it pressed against her chest.

Stefan shrank under its weight. "Yes, *Pappa.*"

"Have you done your chores?"

His chin dropped. "No, *Pappa.*"

"Well, go! Get on with them, then."

Without a backward glance, Stefan ran past Nicolas and out the door.

Pappa. So the boy was his. Curious, she looked up at Nicolas.

"I apologize for that. Was he bothering you?" Nicolas didn't seem to notice that she was out of the bed and eating solid food. Almost.

"No. I heard about the kittens born in the stable yesterday. One died."

Nicolas nodded, but she didn't believe he was really listening. She tried a new tack. "I owe you an apology."

Nicolas did look at her now, his navy eyes wide. They were Stefan's eyes. "For what?"

"I didn't thank you for saving my life."

"Oh, that. Well." Nicolas shrugged.

"Rickard told me the story last night. It's clear I owe my life to you. And you've been so kind to provide for me here. I want you to know how much I appreciate it."

"You're quite welcome, madam."

She did not know what else needed saying. Silently she pleated the fabric of the nightgown between her fingers and wondered how he got the scar on his cheek.

He rocked on his heels, hands clasped behind his back. "Do you know yourself today?"

Defeated, her shoulders collapsed and her gaze dropped to her fidgeting fingers. She shook her head cautiously, not wishing to prompt a recurrence of yesterday's pain.

Nicolas cleared his throat. "You've need of a name then. We must call you something. Have you any ideas?"

"Well… when Stefan told me his name, something about it seemed familiar," she offered, grateful for the distraction. "I believe it's possible that my name begins with an 'S' as well."

Nicolas didn't speak. One brow arched, the other dipped.

Unsettled by his severe and intensely focused attention, she picked up the cooled cup of tea, and pressed it against her chest to keep her hands from shaking. She pulled her feet deeper under the nightgown, resting them on a higher rung of the rocker. Why was he staring at her like that?

"You're not a Sarah," he declared suddenly and with some certainty. "Nor a Susan, I don't believe… Sybil?"

She wrinkled her possibly broken nose, regretting it immediately. "No."

"Sabrina? Sigrid? Sophie?"

Easing her grip on the cup, she slid two fingers over her nose and explored the injury. "I don't believe so. Do you?"

"I suppose not." His long arms swung out from behind his back and folded over his broad chest creating a formidable barrier as he considered her. "There's always the obvious choice, of course. Could it be Stefanie?"

"I confess I thought of that straight away, but it didn't feel right. Besides, if I bide here for any length of time—" Horrified, she stopped. The skin of her cheeks tightened, burnt by the rigor of her humiliation.

Nicolas scrubbed his blond-bristled jaw with both hands as if to erase any sign of his reaction. After an eternity, he spoke again. "Stefan and Stefanie in the same household could be bothersome."

"Thank you," she breathed. Her relief was so strong that her hands tingled.

Though Nicolas stood before her, his mind was clearly elsewhere; his unblinking blue eyes looked right through her. Even so, she felt herself sinking into their ocean depths.

Then he spread his hands wide and tilted his head.

"Sydney."

"Sydney?" Surprised, she rolled the possibility around in her mind. Finding no objection, she tried it again. "Sydney. It's unusual. But I can bide."

"Alright, then. Until we know better, you shall be called Sydney." Nicolas appeared quite pleased with himself. And quite unburdened. "Well, Sydney, I must go now. Rickard and I have work to do. I expect I'll see you later, around candlelighting."

"Thank you again, Mr. Hansen, for your kindness and hospitality."

Nicolas waved his hand. "You may call me Nicolas."

She dipped her head in acknowledgement. "Thank you, Nicolas."

He turned to leave and was at the door when she remembered and called out to him. "I nearly forgot! Your wife, Stefan's mother; is her name Lara? I've not yet met her, and I want to thank her for loaning me her nightgown."

Nicolas turned halfway toward her, his ruddy cheeks stiff and his ocean eyes now devoid of light. Then he disappeared through the doorway without a word.

ଚ ଓଷ

True to his promise, Rickard arrived at Sydney's room later with mirror in hand. When she saw it, apprehension tempered her welcome. Rickard sat on the rocker and laid the ornate accessory on the bedside table. It silently screamed at her, *pick me up and look.*

"Nick informs me that you have a name," he began.

She forced herself to regard the man, and not the mirror. "I'll be called Sydney, though I don't believe it's my given name. But I couldn't go nameless in the meantime."

Rickard tilted his head. His hazel eyes caressed her, claimed her. "I believe it might suit you."

Unsettled by his nearly wicked proximity, Sydney glanced at the screaming object on the table. "You brought a mirror."

"I did. Are you prepared to look?"

She hesitated. Then, "I believe I am."

Rickard handed her the mirror. Smothering it facedown on the bedclothes, she slid her fingers along its silver-edged back, tracing the curves and crevices of the cool metal handle. Her heart stumbled.

Would she recognize herself? Or did she forget that, too?

Then she squared her shoulders, sucked a resolute breath, and faced the glass.

She gasped at the wide-eyed reflection she met there.

Her eyes looked more gray than green. She touched the purple bruise over her right temple, the swollen left eye with the russet gash above it, the greening bump on the bridge of her nose, and the black split in her lower lip. An uneven palette of terrible color. "Oh my…"

"It is getting better," Rickard offered.

Sydney's sideways glance and one lifted eyebrow spoke loudly; she was not pleased.

"Is this what I look like? I cannot believe this is my face," she moaned. "What will I look like when it heals?" Her eyes rounded. "Will anyone recognize me?"

"It's distressing, to be certain." Rickard ran his knuckles along her arm. "But I expect you know that bruises do get darker before they fade, don't you?"

Sydney was intent on the multicolored horror framed by the beautiful mirror. The image was not that of a lass; somehow, she knew she was thirty.

"Darkest before the dawn, eh?" Her wry smile was one-sided to protect her cut lip.

Rickard laughed.

He had a wonderful laugh. Sydney dragged her gaze from the mirror to meet his, warm and playful. He leaned closer.

"I still believe that you have beautiful eyes. And I'm able to see the shape and color of your lips." His eyes dropped to them, and they parted without Sydney intending them to. "You have nothing to worry about, Sydney. Trust me. You'll heal splendidly."

Unconvinced, she handed the heavy mirror to Rickard. The nearness of his sculpted and completely non-battered features stirred something unfamiliar in her. His voice was smooth and rich, like dark chocolate. And his chameleon eyes; were they honey with flecks of green? Or green with flecks of amber?

And why was she even thinking about them?

Sydney adjusted her bedclothes, scrambling for a diversion. She settled on, "I met Stefan today. But I haven't yet met Lara."

The ploy was successful. Rickard leaned back in the chair, his mood abruptly altered. His reply was flat. "Lara is…" he cleared his throat and rubbed his eyes with his fingertips for a long minute. "Well she's… dead."

"Oh!" Sydney's hands covered her mouth as if she could stuff her careless words back in. It was no wonder, then, that Nicolas looked at her the way he did. And to compound her embarrassment—and his pain—she was wearing the dead woman's nightclothes. His dead *wife's* nightclothes. This situation could not be more mortifying.

"Poor Nicolas," she crooned. "And Stefan as well. He's growing up without a mother."

Rickard's jaw rippled. His gaze slipped past her and he nodded slowly. His cheeks paled and caved in on themselves. "Lara was my younger sister," he whispered.

It just became more mortifying.

Sydney's shoulders slumped and her face burned. "I'm so very sorry."

Rickard combed his fingers through auburn locks that shimmered in the lamplight like molten bronze. His sculpted features looked like fine Italian marble. Even in his sorrow he took her breath away.

"Did she favor you?" she murmured.

He nodded, absently. "Both of my sisters look just like me. And we are all the spit of our mother."

"That explains Stefan's hair," she observed quietly. "The rest is clearly his father."

"Yes. That it is."

The two sat in silence. Then Sydney tilted her head and considered Rickard. "Are you married?"

"Me?" Rickard eyebrows shot upward into his tumbled hair and he leaned back in surprise. He wagged his head. "No! Oh, no. Lord, no!" Rickard's chuckle started deep in his chest. "Fortunately, I've been able to avoid that particular estate."

He charmed Sydney with a wink. "Not for lack of opportunity, mind you! I've been chased by some rather determined fillies. Almost got caught by one or two of them, I must admit. But this particular stallion can run fast!"

Sydney laughed at the unexpected hubris of his analogy.

Stallion, was he? It struck her so funny that she could not stop, in spite of her embarrassment, bruised ribs and split lip.

"I can just see you!" She waved hands in front of her and tried without success to keep from breathing too deeply. "Running like a hunted fox with a pack of howling girls chasing after you!"

"A very quick fox!" Rickard added, grinning. He shook his head and considered Sydney with narrowed eyes and puzzled brow. "I believe you're the first woman I ever met who would laugh at the idea of a man of my position avoiding matrimony!"

Still smiling, Sydney shrugged; truthfully, she had no idea of his position. But he was warm and sensual and easy to be with, and his presence made her forget her circumstances, if only for an hour.

She held out her left hand in the steady light of the oil lamp. "Look at this. Are you able to see the ridge on this finger? It's quite faint, but it causes me wonder. Do you suppose I wore a wedding ring?"

Rickard took her hand and inspected it. Her heart skipped at his touch.

"I can't say for certain that it was a wedding ring. It might have been any sort of ring. But it does appear that you wore it for some time."

Sydney stared at her hand, trying to divine knowledge from her pale fingers. "I wonder what happened to it. Do you believe I might have been robbed?"

"That might explain why someone left you for dead," Rickard posited. Sydney stared hard at the line in her skin and tried without success to purge its silent secret.

"If I am married, shouldn't someone come looking for me?" she asked the obvious question.

"I can say, with absolute certainty, that I would," replied the adamant bachelor.

Chapter Four

April 4, 1819

*O*n the third morning after her rescue, Sydney announced to Addie that if she didn't get out of that little bedroom, she would certainly lose what small part of her mind she still owned. Addie set down the breakfast tray, rested fists on ample hips and cocked her head.

"Well, you can't go traipsing around in your nightclothes, and that's a fact! Let me see what I can find around this place that might fit you."

Sydney clasped her hands in gratitude. "Addie, you're a jewel."

The housekeeper blushed. "Oh, go on with you! Eat up, now. You need your strength if you plan to go gallivantin' around this place. I'll be back to get the tray!" Addie hurried out the door, head bobbing and elbows pumping.

Sydney chewed her last bite of honeyed biscuit when Addie returned. The housekeeper carried a long-sleeved bodice of gray linen trimmed with black piping. The coordinating linen skirt was burgundy with three black box-pleats in the front, and three in the back.

Sydney held the skirt up to her waist. It was a little short for her, but she didn't care. She would have gladly worn burlap feed bags to be able get out of this room. She assumed the answer before she asked the question, but asked it anyway.

"Where did it come from?"

Addie wiped her hands on the ever-present white apron, her

expression pensive but guarded. "Lara had a few dresses made special."

The skirt grew heavy as iron and Sydney fought the urge to throw it on the floor. "Addie, I can't wear this. What will Nicolas say?"

Addie's lips twisted. "Nicky's a man. He's never seen those dresses and isn't likely to consider where they came from. You go ahead. It's needful and I insist."

ଋ ଔ

It proved a glorious day.

First, she got out of the nightgown and put on the dress; that simple act made her feel human again, in spite of her repaired chemise and battered corset.

Second, Addie brushed and replaited her hair. Sydney willed herself to ignore the bruises on her scalp and allowed herself to thoroughly enjoy this bit of luxury.

And third, she walked out of the small bedroom to explore her strange, new world.

The wide hallway outside her door breathed through large open windows at either end. The cool spring breeze, heavy with new growth, brushed past her. Spotless wood floors reflected light. Sydney crossed the hall to a closed door that faced her room.

It was locked.

Undaunted, she turned around and followed the polished stairwell railing to the room beside hers. She reckoned this was the room where Rickard stayed. She smiled at the memory of his chocolate voice, chameleon eyes and melted bronze hair. The room fit him; it was adorned, but not at all feminine.

Next was Stefan's room. Several wooden toys were stacked neatly—a little too neatly, she thought—on shelves under the window, and a model of a tall navy war ship reigned on a higher shelf. A braided rug in blues and reds brightened the room; Sydney decided that must have been Addie's touch.

Only the door at the head of the stairs remained.

Did she dare?

Curiosity knocked against her, rudely shoving her forward. Holding her breath, she pushed the half-opened portal and peered cautiously into the dim, silent chamber.

Nicolas's bed was so enormous that there was a stepstool on the floor beside it. He was an exceptionally tall man, to be certain, and a broad man as well; this bed was obviously built to ensure his comfort. The foot-thick mattress sat on a platform that rose at least two feet off the floor. A feather bed added another half foot. The massive headboard and footboard were carved of cherry wood.

Even though she was barefoot, Sydney tiptoed inside, afraid to make any sound. The furnishings, like the man himself, were well-made. Utilitarian. Masculine. Clean.

A door beyond the hearth faced the locked room. That must have been Lara's dressing room. *Of course it's locked.*

She glanced, again, at the oversized bed.

Unable to stop herself, she stepped on the stool and sat on the edge. Nicolas's musky male presence was strong here. Sydney closed her eyes and breathed it in. She skimmed her hands over the coverlet and pictured the huge man who slept in this huge bed all by himself.

From what she'd seen of him, he seemed reserved and serious and so different from the warm, seductive Rickard. But something about the stoic widower gripped her and she felt his unexpected pull, strong as steel to a magnet.

She resisted.

Afraid Nicolas might return and find her there, Sydney garnered her diminishing strength and departed. She descended the stairs, inspecting portraits that hung along the wall. The people in them were clearly related to Nicolas judging by the features the artists were able to capture. Some of the older subjects appeared rather royal with their ermine collars, brocade jackets and ornate jewelry.

At the bottom of the staircase was Nicolas's study. An ancient oak desk held court over several unmatched chairs, scattered randomly by their most recent occupants. The aromas of brandy and cigar smoke permeated that space.

"Nicolas's bedroom might have tolerated a wife at one time," Sydney whispered. "But not this room."

The drawing room was across the entrance hall on her left. Sydney sank onto a comfortable, cushioned settee in front of a large window framing the front yard. Leaning back, she succumbed to the demands of her weakened body and closed her eyes for just a moment.

She awoke not remembering where she was. Panic shot lightning through her veins and her heart tried to climb out of her throat. Only when her frantic visual search caught the painted portraits in the stairwell did she remember Nicolas. And Addie. And Stefan.

And Rickard.

Forcing herself to breathe slowly past her bruises, she closed her eyes until she could regain her equilibrium and stop trembling.

"I wonder how long this blasted muddle will last," she grumbled.

When she felt steady enough, Sydney pushed herself up by the arm of the settee. Then she followed the scent of food past the formal dining room, toward the kitchen, Addie, and lunch.

❧ ❦

At seven o'clock that evening, Sydney sat alone at the dining table and waited to have dinner with Nicolas. Addie explained that every night Nicolas ate his dinner with a book, its characters his only companions. He would love to have her company.

"I'm not at all certain that's true," Sydney objected.

In the four days she had been at his estate, he only deigned to speak with her twice. He obviously held very little interest in her company.

But Addie couldn't be dissuaded. So here she sat.

She drummed her fingers on the tablecloth while she waited for her stern host. She smoothed the linen and brushed away imaginary crumbs. She moved her wine goblet a little to the right. She put her napkin in her lap, and then refolded it and set it next to her plate. She lifted a spoon and examined the ornate engraving on the handle.

Was that an H? It looked like an F.

The old silver was worn to a hazy patina. While she pondered how many generations might have held that particular spoon, Nicolas appeared. He filled the doorway, dressed in a clean cotton shirt and nankeen breeches. Sydney smacked the spoon back into place harder than she intended.

Nicolas carried a thick, leather-bound tome with an incongruently feminine crocheted bookmark dangling from its center. Sydney stood awkwardly, her recovering muscles stiff from sitting still so long.

She tried to think of something to say but her mind continued its inconvenient rebellion. Her mouth opened and closed and she couldn't conjure a greeting.

"I wasn't aware that you were joining me for dinner," Nicolas said.

Sydney's face heated. "If it's bothersome to you, I'll eat in the kitchen," she managed.

"No. Uh, no. Not at all."

Nicolas shook his head and glanced at the book in his hand. He set it on the sideboard and walked around the table to hold her chair.

"Please, sit."

Sydney sank back into the carved maple side-chair. Nicolas sat opposite her. He silently considered her over his long, interlocked fingers.

She shrank under his intent scrutiny. "I'm afraid I look rather gruesome."

Nicolas blinked. "On the contrary. You seem to be mending rather quickly," he countered.

Rescued by the arrival of Addie and dinner, Sydney realized she was ravenous. She cut into a roasted chicken breast. It was savory, smoky, succulent. Delicious. She took another bite. And another.

"You must have labored quite well today," Nicolas declared. "Either that or you bore a mighty grudge against that particular chicken."

Sydney froze. Her cheeks roasted with embarrassment. She set the fork on her plate. Her hands dropped to her lap, and her gaze dropped to her hands. She wished to be anywhere else at that moment. Joining Nicolas for dinner was proving a bad misjudgment.

"I—I'm sorry, Sydney. I meant it to be funny."

She wove her napkin through her fingers. Her throat tightened and she couldn't swallow the bite of chicken resting on her tongue. She wanted to get up and leave the room, but her legs weren't cooperating.

"The truth of the matter is..." Nicolas paused and pulled a breath. "I've not shared a meal at this table with an attractive woman for several years."

Attractive? Sydney saw herself in the mirror today. She snorted her dissent.

"Sydney? Would you be polite enough to look at me?"

Sensible that Nicolas had indeed saved her life and was being quite generous in her unusual circumstance, she daren't refuse. Determined to claim any dignity she might still possess, she sat tall, straightened her shoulders, lifted first her chin, and then her eyes. His lonely soul surfaced in the deep sea of his gaze.

Sydney could not have looked away even if her life was at stake. She swallowed the bite of chicken.

"I've grown unaccustomed to the common niceties. I'm afraid I don't know the appropriate words to say anymore." Nicolas leaned back in his chair, his expression gone dark and unreadable. "In truth, I don't recall if I ever did. I knew Lara all of her life. We grew up together. I didn't have to say things to her; she already knew."

"Of course," Sydney whispered, still transfixed.

"Will you accept my apology?" Nicolas looked so uncomfortable that Sydney couldn't help but give him ease.

"Of course," she said again.

"Good." Nicolas punctuated the word with a brief nod of his head, and then took a substantial bite of his chicken. He refilled her wine glass without her asking, and handed her a basket of warm rolls.

The couple ate without speaking. Silver on china rattled the silence. Sydney wanted to ask him about some things that niggled at her, but the longer she hesitated, the harder it became to force her voice across the widening void. As Nicolas neared the end of his meal and her opportunity faded swiftly, she squared her determination and jumped into the chasm.

"Nicolas, what year is it?"

Her question obviously shocked him. He frowned and his lips parted, then pressed together. Sydney noticed and her expression tightened. Any friendliness that might have sparked between them appeared doomed; she was the resident oddity once again.

"I had no idea it was that bad, Sydney. I should have thought to say. It's April fourth of 1819."

Sydney nodded, her countenance clamped in concentration. That seemed about right to her. Distracted, she sipped her wine.

Nicolas continued, "We're in the township of Cheltenham in the Missouri Territory. The closest city would be St. Louis. It's about ten miles northeast of here."

"I recognize all those names, and Cheltenham seems important to me for some reason. But I'm fairly certain it's not my home."

Nicolas nodded and speared his green beans. "I've never seen you before, so it's likely you're right."

Sydney swirled her wine glass, watching the pale, honey-colored liquid coat its sides. "What other towns are nearby?"

Nicolas rested his elbows on the rounded arms of his chair and steepled his fingers. He looked toward the ceiling. "Let's see. There are Wellspring and Elleardsville to the north." His gaze dropped to her in silent question. She shook her head.

"To the west are, Fairview? And Rock Hill?"

Sydney shook her head again, and sipped her wine; its flowery bouquet floated pleasurably past her palate. It was a pleasant counterpoint to her growing frustration; maybe she should refill her glass with the chardonnay and drown in it.

"…and Webster Grove?"

"Webster Grove!" Sydney perked up. "There's something in my life concerning Webster Grove!"

"Do you live there?"

"I don't know, but there must be some connection. What other places are near?"

"To the south of us are the townships of Carondelet and Oakville."

"Yes! Yes!" Sydney grew excited. "I know both of those names!"

Nicolas smiled.

When he did so, his blue eyes twinkled above an expanse of straight white teeth. The sight of it made Sydney's heart dance. She decided he really was beautiful, after all.

"That gives us a place to start, at any rate! I'll send word to the squires of those towns to see if anyone's missing a—" Nicolas stopped.

"Wife?" Sydney completed his thought, suddenly less optimistic. She set her glass down with enough force to throw wine over the rim. "Or sister? Certainly not 'mother' I wouldn't imagine; I don't believe I could forget that." She blotted the spill with her napkin.

"No, I don't believe you would," Nicolas agreed. He wiped his plate with the last roll. "I'll write out the notices tonight. John can take them into town tomorrow, before I go to Rickard's place."

"Rickard's place?"

"We finished shearing my sheep today and Rick went home directly afterwards. That's why we've been spared his company at the table."

Sydney caught the jibe and gave him a half-grin. "How long will you be gone?"

"Five or six days. He has more sheep than I do." Nicolas popped the roll into his mouth and wiped his hands on his napkin.

What are we to do with her?

Echoes of the overheard conversation pushed into Sydney's awareness. She gripped her wine glass so hard she was in danger of shattering it.

"I hope you're not overly concerned with my presence here while you're gone. After all, you don't know aught about me." She granted the goblet a reprieve and shoved her fists into her lap.

Nicolas waved his hand dismissively and shook his head. He reached for his own wineglass and drained it.

"It's no problem. You're not a bother to me, at all. And Addie is beside herself to have someone to care for." He rubbed his jaw; smooth, tanned and clean of whiskers. "Perchance you'll remember something while I'm gone, eh?"

Chapter Five

April 5, 1819

*W*ashed and wrung out from a long day of wrestling irritated sheep and their squirming offspring, Nicolas trudged behind Rickard into his parlor. Lily waited there, her nose hovering over a book.

A book? Nicolas chuckled softly and bit back any comments.

Lily Jane Atherton was beautiful, headstrong and, in her own words, deservedly spoiled. At the spinsterhood-threatening age of twenty-three, she seemed to have tired of playing with the boys in the Territory and had set her sights on him. Her dead sister's husband.

He wasn't certain how he felt about that.

Lily was dressed for dinner in a cornflower blue gown that enhanced her aquamarine eyes and rich auburn hair. She ran her finger along the neckline that plunged between her breasts, drawing his eyes to that well-rounded valley. After allowing him time for a sufficient view, Lily turned as though surprised by his very welcome presence.

"Nicolas, darling!" she cooed, dropping the book to her lap. "How wonderful to see you again! My brother should have told me you were joining us for dinner so that I might have dressed properly."

"There's no need to put yourself out for my sake, Lily." Nicolas swept her with a knowing glance. "What you have on is perfectly adequate."

Lily's pleasant expression didn't alter but he saw her jaw ripple briefly. "I'm afraid I lost track of the time. I've been sitting here reading for quite a while."

She batted her lashes as she glanced down, smoothed her skirt, and then blinked her gaze back to his.

"Is that so, Lily?" Rickard grabbed the book from his baby sister's lap. "And at what point did you become interested in *Castration Techniques for Horses?*"

Nicolas snorted and turned aside to hide his grin. Lily's wrath might be merely the tempest of a woman, but there was no need to provoke it any further. Lily stood erect, ignored her elder brother's jibe, and floated to the parlor's arched doorway.

"I'll check on our dinner's progress," she said, her tone calm and controlled. "Rickard, would you please pour us all some wine?"

Lily sat across from Nicolas at dinner. He owned an unobstructed view of her abundant attributes, and was the recipient of her unslippered toes tickling behind his knees. Neither the view nor the tickling was in any way unpleasant.

"So, Nick. How do you suppose our mystery woman is progressing?" Rickard prodded.

Nicolas frowned at his friend; what was his game? They already talked about Sydney today and what might be done for her. In the process, it became quite clear that Rickard was rather taken with his sudden houseguest.

"Mystery woman?" Lily pounced like a barn cat on field mice. "We have a mystery woman?"

"Nick does," Rickard said; his voice exuded mischief. "Found her in his creek."

Lily rested her heavily demanding gaze on Nicolas, who shrugged it off. He was puckered by Rickard's teasing and decided to ignore the gambit. He stuffed a roll into his mouth and chewed slowly. Very slowly.

Lily withdrew her toes.

"Took her to his house. Half-naked, as a matter of fact," Rickard cut a bite of roasted beef. "Well to be fair, she was, at one time, fully clothed. Until Nick cut her skirt off." He forked the morsel into his mouth.

Lily's eyes rounded and her mouth slammed open.

Unaccountably angry, Nicolas shook his head and concentrated on his meal. But Rickard's life was looking to be shorter with every word that fool uttered.

"Who is this woman?" Lily demanded of Nicolas, flinty eyes shooting blue sparks.

Nicolas slid his chilly gaze from sister to brother. He swallowed his roast and sipped his wine in silence. Rickard dropped the last card.

"Sleeps just down the hall from him."

"Nicolas Reidar Hansen! What precisely is going on?" Lily screeched, her cheeks flushing crimson. "And why haven't you told me?"

Nicolas shot Rickard a look that only a lifelong friend could ever be forgiven for. He leaned back in his chair, picked up his wine goblet and swirled it in the light. He sniffed the bouquet, took a sip, held the cabernet in his mouth, and then swallowed. Only then did he deign to tell Lily the story.

"She claims she can't remember anything?" Lily scoffed, rolling her eyes. "Ha! That's a new trick!"

Ignoring her outburst, Nicolas continued. "I sent letters to nearby squires informing them that we rescued a woman, and asked if anyone has gone missing from their townships."

"Oh, Nicolas," Lily scolded as if he were an errant child. "You don't truly believe anyone has, do you? This woman is quite obviously up to something."

He struggled to remain calm in the face of her condescension. "And what might that be, Lily? To beat herself severely and leave herself for dead in the hope that someone would find her? That's all to pieces a considerable risk!"

"She's hiding something, I tell you," Lily stated with certainty. "She's most likely some spinster who's trying to coerce a charitable soul into supporting her in her old age!"

A significant look passed between Nicolas and Rickard. Lily caught it.

"What is it? Tell me!" she squealed.

Rickard shrugged. "I have to admit that I believe any number of men would be willing to support this particular soul until she reaches old age."

Lily paled and her shoulders wilted. "Why?"

The old friends locked eyes and dared the other to speak first.

Lily slapped the tabletop with an open palm. "Why? Nicolas! Is she comely?"

Nicolas heard panic in her tone. Lily was certainly overreacting; he hadn't encouraged her flirtation, so why would she think he was interested in *any* woman?

Then the two men answered in unplanned unison.

"She's beautiful."

ℰ ℭ

Nicolas shut the door of his room at Atherton's and leaned his forehead against it. He remained motionless for several minutes, unhappily aware of the spinning sensation that made it clear he had too much to drink at dinner. Sunrise sheep-shearing was not going to be pleasant.

Skitt.

He straightened and walked purposefully to the bed as he pulled off his clothes and dropped them on the floor. How much wine did Lily pour for him? And the brandies after dinner; was it three or four? Five?

Nicolas fell naked onto the mattress.

Lily was not subtle in her quest for his attention, and Nicolas was no fool. At first, he dismissed her overtures, assuming them to be a passing fancy; but Lily was not easily dissuaded. She wanted him and he knew it well.

Nicolas brushed the back of his hand across his lips, still able to feel her mouth against his. Her lips were soft, her tongue hard. She guided his hands to her breasts, encouraging intimacy. Her fingers stroked his thigh and he roused, unable to avoid it. That traitorous and self-serving part of him was quite willing. But he couldn't reconcile the fact that Lily was Lara's sister.

Oddly, though, that was a factor in her favor.

While he ached without respite for his dead wife, Nicolas saw much of her in Lily. The physical resemblance was strong and there were moments when Nicolas could convince himself that it was Lara, not Lily, he was looking at.

"But Lily is not Lara," Nicolas mumbled to the dark ceiling and sighed his weariness. Did that truly matter?

ɛⱺ ⱷȝ

Nicolas was gone, so Sydney explored his land without fearing his disapproval. The Hansen estate proved modest, the slate-roofed stone manor its anchor. Behind it at a short distance was the stable, its bottom level also of stone. Sydney found two large storerooms inside, a double row of four stalls each, and hayloft above.

Outside were a corral and paddock for the horses. In the woods behind the stable was the keep for the small flock of sheep. The brood sow and her current crop of piglets were penned between the garden and the root cellar.

The chicken coop was downwind of the house; so was the privy.

As she wandered the grounds, Sydney searched for anything that might prompt a memory: a smell, a color, a sound, a texture. The new leaves on the maple tree? The tang of pine sap or the call of a hawk? The chuckle of the creek? But nothing provided the key that would unlock the mystery of who she was, nor shed any light on what calamity befell her.

Frustrated, she rested on a log, and threw whatever handy forest object she could reach as hard—and as far—as her bruised muscles would allow. Tears muddied the dust on her cheeks. She walked purposefully down the road away from the estate, but stopped because she didn't recognize anything.

And until she did, she had nowhere else to go.

Defeated, Sydney plodded back to the house, kicking every loose pebble unfortunate enough to lie in her path. Her situation pressed against her. She was furious and frightened, confounded and contradictory. And just flat out mad.

Addie's husband, John Spencer—a quiet, weathered man in his late fifties—was working in the yard behind the manor. Sydney stopped to watch him. She had nothing else that needed doing, after all.

John had assembled a tall wooden tripod in the grassy lawn. From it, he hung a huge copper pot. Stefan helped him fill the pot with water from the pump, warmed by the fire they built under it. A smaller iron pot sat nearby on the ground.

"What are you doing?" she finally asked.

"The wool Nick 'n Rick sheared needs cleaning," John said.

"Oh." Sydney waited, and wondered if the process would look familiar or spark a memory.

While the water heated, Addie and Maribeth began to spread sheared wool on a platform of narrow slats. They pulled the fleece apart, releasing the twigs, pebbles and other detritus the sheep picked up in the woods. The women lifted the loosened wool into the copper pot, where its oil kept it afloat.

Sydney hated feeling so purposeless. So, ignoring her wobbly condition, she began to help with the smelly, greasy, gritty job.

Addie objected to her exerting herself, but not too long nor with too much vigor. Maribeth smiled her silent thanks. Stefan hunkered in the garden with a pail.

As the water boiled, the wool sank and its oil rose to the top. It smelled tangy and not unlike a wet dog. Addie ladled the fat into the iron pot on the ground.

"I'll render the wool fat one more time before I use it," she explained. "It's good for salves and soap. But I'm sure you already know that."

Lips pressed to retain an unkind retort, Sydney wondered if she did.

The three women worked through the morning, dripping with effort in spite of the cool spring day. Addie served a cold lunch in the kitchen before she and Maribeth spread the boiled wool in the afternoon sun to dry. At Addie's powerful insistence, Sydney went upstairs to rest.

She felt stronger at that moment than she had since Nicolas found her. She climbed into the bed, relishing the feel of the smooth cotton sheets against her skin and the down pillow that cradled her head. The satisfying ache of effort drained her limbs, and pressed against her eyes and lower back. The darkened room lulled her into a dreamless sleep.

But that evening, when Sydney went down for supper, she felt ghastly. Every one of her thirty years weighed down her limbs. Her aching back wouldn't support her, her head pounded, and her gut was trying to turn inside out. The pain made her skin overly sensitive; even the touch of her clothes caused gooseflesh.

She eased herself into a chair at the kitchen table. A shiver of nausea wiggled through her.

"Addie, might you have some willow bark for tea?"

"Did you over-do yourself today?" Addie turned an evaluative eye on Sydney's clammy skin and hunched stance before rummaging for the medicinal bark. She set the teapot on the cast-iron Franklin stove.

"No, it's not that." Sydney pressed on her abdomen. "My flow has started."

"Ah, the cramps then."

"And I'm afraid I don't have any rags. I didn't pack adequately before falling in the creek, it seems."

Addie smiled at the feeble joke. "Maribeth has a supply in her room. I'll go and get them."

Sydney rested her overly-large head on folded arms until she heard Addie return. Addie handed her the clean stack of rags.

"Thank you," Sydney murmured. She couldn't muster the strength for full voice. Picking two of the rags, she shuffled out the back door to the privy. When she returned, the water for her tea was ready.

"Is it always this bad for you, dear?"

Sydney shrugged. "Most likely. I don't remember."

Addie smacked her forehead with her palm. "What am I asking? I swear this old mind isn't as sharp as it once was!"

Sydney accepted a mug of hot water and put the bark to steep. She stirred milk and honey into the bitter brew and drank it in the comforting kitchen, relaxing while Addie made dinner. Still nauseated, she declined food. After two more cups of tea, she crawled back into bed.

℘ ℭ

While her mornings were spent cleaning fleece, Sydney found herself drawn to the stables in the afternoons. She spent several calming hours there, talking with John.

"How did you and Addie meet?" Sydney asked, picking up a curry brush.

He spoke from the other side of a bay gelding. "She was housekeeper here when I was hired on."

Sydney moved the brush in a circular motion over the coat of the matching mare. "And you fell in love?"

John leaned around the gelding's rump. His warm brown eyes

sparkled amongst his copious wrinkles. "I did. Took her a while, though. Ten years."

Sydney laughed. "Ten years! When were you married?"

"In ninety-two. Nick was five and Gunnar was 'bout three." He disappeared behind the rump again. "Never had children of our own, so she's fierce over them two."

Only a couple more afternoons passed before Sydney took over the grooming altogether. She found the repetitive action of currying the horses soothing, as was the tolerant company of the large animals. They didn't care what her name was or where she came from. And when she was with them, she forgot to worry about not knowing.

Cajoling Addie with common sense, Sydney talked the housekeeper into procuring her a shirt and pair of breeches to work in.

"I only have a couple of borrowed dresses to wear," she reminded Addie, "and I don't want to ruin them."

Even Addie couldn't argue that point.

April 11, 1819

Nicolas returned home late in the afternoon of the sixth day, weary but excited about his new acquisition: the feisty stallion tethered to his saddle. Tall and muscular, the horse's dappled gray coat darkened to charcoal at mane, tail and cannons. The points of his ears nearly touched, and his black muzzle was unexpectedly delicate for such a large animal.

Nicolas called for John as he rode into the yard. John came out of the stable and someone in dusty breeches and chambray shirt followed. Who might that be?

"John will you open the gate?" Nicolas asked. He untied the lead from his saddle and led the stallion into the corral, loosing him there. Freed from restraint, the horse shook his head and trotted around the perimeter of the fence, snorting and prancing, his black tail a high flag.

Nicolas stared at the curvy, dark-haired figure by his foreman's side. "Might you bring me a halter, John?"

"Even so, Nick." John headed back into the stable.

Sydney stood her ground as Nicolas approached.

"What *i Gud's navn* are you wearing?" He tilted his head. "Have you suddenly remembered you're a man?"

Sydney laughed. The delightful sound of it vibrated through his chest and settled low in his belly. Very low. She tossed her head back; her green eyes twinkled and her cheeks bloomed soft pink.

"I bade Addie to find me some work clothes. I've begun helping John with the horses and I didn't want to ruin the dresses I've borrowed."

Nicolas had to confess, he saw her logic straight off. Besides, she looked quite fetching in the unconventional outfit. Rather than appearing manly, the breeches accentuated her womanly shape. Her mane of dark brown hair, tied back with a leather thong like his, glimmered in the waning sunlight.

He thought of Lily in all her carefully arranged glory. The contrast between the two women was marked; and he found one preferable. John handed Nicolas the halter.

The stallion trotted back and forth in the corral, snorting and tossing his head, his tail whipping the air. Agitated at Nicolas's approach, the horse broke into a tight canter, tracing a figure eight in the fenced pen. His jerky movements intensified until, without warning, the gray gathered his haunches and launched himself over the railing. Once free, he ran between the stable and the corral right past Nicolas.

And straight toward Sydney.

Nicolas spun around as his world shifted into dream-slow motion. He struggled impotently to shout a warning, but couldn't get sound past his constricted throat.

Horrified, he watched Sydney plant herself in the path of the oncoming horse. Her arms were straight in front of her, palms forward, fingers splayed. The huge gray skidded to a stop, chunks of dirt and bits of grass thrown in the air as his huge hooves pushed backward to reverse his momentum. He reared up, squealed his threat, and pawed the air above the tiny human in front of him.

Sydney didn't move.

The stallion dropped to all fours, snorting and tossing his mane in protest. He squatted on his haunches, but did not rear up again. When the human didn't retreat, he backed up and pawed the ground, sending more mud and leaves in all directions. He vocalized in grunts, snorts and squeals, ears pinned back and tail whipping the air.

Nicolas gaped at Sydney, his frenzied pulse slamming through his body. He had no idea what to do to save her.

She lowered one hand. Fisting the other, she offered it to the stallion while she talked nonsense in a calm, singsong rhythm. The stallion's ears flicked forward and back with cautious curiosity. As Sydney continued her soothing monologue he remained in place, blowing heavy breaths through flared nostrils and stomping his iron-shod feet.

Nicolas was afraid to move. He prayed John stayed still as well.

Sydney allowed the stallion to assert his physical superiority for several minutes, neither challenging him nor backing down. He tentatively pushed his head forward toward her outstretched fist, then jerked it back. Twice more, he repeated the movement, each time making a show of displeasure with snorting and tossing and stamping. Finally, he sniffed Sydney's knuckles.

Sydney eased forward until she could touch him. Her hand moved over the animal's sweating neck, ears, cheek and nose. Without turning her head, Sydney held her other arm out to Nicolas.

"Give me the halter."

Said in the same singsong tone, Nicolas didn't realize Sydney was talking to him. He was entranced by her actions and the stallion's reaction to her.

"Nicolas, give me the halter."

Startled into movement, but retaining enough presence of mind to do so cautiously, Nicolas handed her the tack. Sydney rubbed the halter against the animal's neck, and then moved it over his cheek and down to his nose. She slid it onto his head, and rubbed his ears as she slipped it into place. Grasping the leather straps, Sydney used her body to urge the horse back toward the corral.

"John, would you bring him a treat?" she asked in the same calm voice. The huge animal allowed her to lead him into the enclosure. John appeared a moment later with a bucket of oats with molasses and set it inside the fence. The gray pushed his nose into the container, snuffled loudly and devoured the sweetened grain.

Consumed with fear and fury, Nicolas tightened his jaw, narrowed his eyes, and headed toward his dangerously rash and reckless female guest.

Chapter Six

*S*ydney heaved a sigh and slipped between the corral's railings. She wiped sweat from her forehead on a sleeve and fanned the front of her shirt. Nicolas strode toward her, shaking his head, the thin scar on his cheek screaming a warning.

"What the *helvete* was that stunt?" he bellowed.

Sydney froze.

"Are you completely out of your *Gud forbannet* head?" The fists at the end of his twitching arms clenched, unclenched, and re-clenched. He looked nearly apoplectic.

"Wh—what?" she stammered.

Nicolas waved his arms in circles around her. "That cursed beast might have killed you!"

Facing down Nicolas, the same way that she faced down the other stallion, Sydney's deliberately calm voice belied her tattered nerves and watery gut.

"I don't know."

"What the *helvete* do you mean, you 'don't know'?" Nicolas's face was scarlet. His snorting breaths sounded like the gray's.

Sydney lifted her chin. "I paid it no mind. I simply did it."

"Of all the—" Nicolas stomped away, and then back. "If that wasn't the—" he sputtered and his face paled beneath his sunburn. "*Skitt*, Sydney!"

Then a loud, "*Gud forbanner det!*"

And an even louder, "*Gud forbanner det all til helvete!*"

Nicolas yanked the leather thong from his hair. His long locks caught on the breeze and circled his head like yellow flames. He took several deep breaths, glaring at her with midnight eyes. He was more magnificent than the horse; fierce and glorious in his anger. Facing her imperious host, Sydney stood silent, defiant, unmoving.

"*Skitt*, Sydney!" he roared again.

Her lower lip betrayed her. Pulled tight against her teeth, it still found strength to tremble. Her cheeks blazed. She blinked away moisture. Maybe he wouldn't notice. But Nicolas's eyes flickered over her countenance and his shoulders relaxed a little.

"I feared for your safety, Sydney. I thought he had you for certain." Worry was foremost in his voice, but she detected an undertone of respect.

"I gotta say, that was some fine horse-handlin' right there," John spoke up behind him.

"Indeed it was," Nicolas admitted. He shook out his fists and rested his hands loosely on his hips.

John slapped his thigh with his hat. "Never saw such a thing in all my born days!"

"I'm forced to confess, neither have I." Nicolas paused. His lips twisted. "I don't believe I could have done as well."

Sydney grew uncomfortable in their praise and felt self-consciously on display.

"It wasn't all that impressive!" she blurted. "My father raises horses. I've seen it done a dozen times before."

No one moved.

No one breathed.

"So you remember that?" Nicolas asked sharply.

Sydney blanched. For a split second, she had seen her life.

"My father raises horses," she said slowly. "In Kentucky, I believe…"

"And you worked with him there?" Nicolas prodded.

She frowned, staring at nothing. "Yes."

"Can you recall aught else?"

Sydney shook her head, flooded with disappointment and buoyed by hope. True, the tantalizing images had retreated beyond her reach, but the fact that they appeared showed improvement. Soon, perhaps, she would regain what she had lost. Sydney regarded the two puzzled male faces in front of her and wished she had more to tell them.

Nicolas turned to John. "Well? It's a beginning."

Throwing his arm around Sydney's shoulders, he squeezed her briefly to him. "And that was a task well accomplished, Sydney. Your father would be mighty proud of you this day."

Dropping his arm, he looked back at John. "I'm about to starve. Let's go see if that wife of yours has got our supper ready yet!"

෫ ஐ

Nicolas considered the woman whose chair he held. No longer dressed in the manly work clothes, she swept into the room wearing a gown he'd never seen.

"I'm sorry! Were you waiting long?" With a flip of her wrist, her napkin plunged to her lap.

"No." He took his seat across the table.

The gray fabric of her gown made her eyes look like clouds before a twister and the black edges matched her straight, dark hair. Her bruises were fading and her skin looked like fresh milk. He wondered how to describe the color of her full lips. They were like a ripe peach. A very ripe peach.

"The language you used so emphatically today?" Sydney asked. "If I were to guess, I would say that you were cursing with rather an abundance of flair."

Nicolas grinned, a little embarrassed. "You were able to discern that, were you?"

Sydney grinned back. "Was that German?"

"It was Norse. I'm of Norwegian descent."

"Oh. Do you always curse in Norse?"

"I grew into that habit." Nicolas selected a warm roll and handed the basket to Sydney. "My wife was delicate in character and cursing made her uncomfortable. If I said it in Norse, she didn't find it so offensive."

Sydney fixed him with the wink of one gray-green eye. "While I'm quite sensible that it's not ladylike, I must say few things in life are as satisfying as a well-placed curse word."

Nicolas chuckled at her unexpectedly bawdy response. "So you understand, then."

Sydney served herself potatoes. "Where did you get the stallion?" she asked.

"He was Rickard's. He purchased him from a breeder down

south of here." Nicolas helped himself to the meat. "He's got decent bloodlines. There's some Arabian in him; you can see it in his ears and the angle of his tail."

Sydney handed Nicolas the bowl of potatoes then forked roast beef onto her plate. "But there's something else. He's quite large and his nose doesn't match the Arab profile."

"He has some Percheron. That's where the size comes from..." He set the potatoes down and looked at Sydney with new appreciation. "But the breeder thought it would be a good mix—"

"The intelligence of the Arab combined with the strength of the Percheron?" Sydney correctly completed the sentence. She pushed the gravy boat toward Nicolas.

Nicolas nodded, pondering his dinner companion. Perhaps she did know horseflesh after all. That was a useful revelation. He stared across the tabletop with his knife and fork in hand, standing like sentries alongside his plate.

He surprised himself when he admitted to Lily that Sydney was beautiful; until that moment, he hadn't consciously thought about it. To look at her this evening by the soft light of the oil lamps, there was truly no denying it. But she was quite different from Lara.

Helvete, she was different from any woman he'd ever known. Her actions today made that undeniably clear.

Sydney pointed her knife at him. "Does this beast have a name?"

Startled out of his reverie, Nicolas nodded. "Rick called him 'Grayson.' But I reckoned that since I planked down good money for him, I've the right to change his name. So now he's *Fyrste*. It's Norse for prince."

"You bought him?"

"I did. Rickard couldn't sit him. He even had his best groom work with the animal, but without much progress."

Sydney frowned. "What possessed you to want him, then?"

"Well, I was hoping John might have better luck with him. If not, I'll try him as stud. With those bloodlines, I'm curious to see what he can get." Then with a shrug, he mentioned the final possibility. "And if neither of those works, I can always geld him."

Sydney looked down at her plate and seemed focused on cutting her meat. She didn't have much to say through the rest of the meal and wouldn't be drawn into conversation. Nicolas wondered why their new camaraderie suddenly evaporated. Had he said something inappropriate again?

Sydney sipped the last of the wine from her crystal goblet and set it down to her left, then moved it to her right. Nicolas lifted the wine bottle in silent question, but she waved it away. She slid the tines of her fork across her plate, making patterns in the remnants of gravy. Then she pleated her napkin. Her silent restlessness exasperated him.

"Sydney! What thought is pestering you so?" When she didn't answer straight away, he softened his tone. "Is there something of importance on your mind?"

She nodded.

He made an effort to sound encouraging. "Would you care to tell me what that is?"

She stared at him. Her pupils dilated, eliminating the green from her eyes. She had no hint of a smile. He held his breath in anticipation without thinking about it.

"Allow me to train him."

Staggered by her preposterous suggestion, Nicolas scrambled in disbelief for a response.

"Well, certainly! And why not stand naked on the roof and catch flaming arrows with your teeth, while you're about it?" he scoffed.

Her stormy eyes narrowed. "What?!"

Nicolas leaned forward over the table. "No, Sydney, absolutely not!"

"And *why* not, might I ask?"

Nicolas was appalled. Was she daring to defy him? Perchance she simply didn't understand the danger. "That beast stands at the least sixteen hands—"

"Seventeen," Sydney corrected him.

Outraged, Nicolas gawked at her. "It's far too dangerous a task for a woman!"

"I handled him today."

"That proves nothing!" Nicolas declaimed. He knew well that it probably did, but he wasn't about to admit that now. "He's bested men twice your size!"

Sydney leaned toward him. "But I know what I'm doing."

"And so did they!" Nicolas roared and pounded his fist on the table. Silverware scattered for cover. Lara never spoke to him in such a way! Who did this impudent woman believe herself to be?

"You saw what transpired today, Nicolas."

He pulled a deep breath and forced his hands to unclench. Though she pushed him hard, it wouldn't do to strangle a woman whose life he had just saved. Instead, he shook his head and asserted his position.

"I'm the head of this household. As such, you'll do as I see fit, Sydney. And that's how it shall be."

"I'm not truly a member of your household, sir."

Nicolas sat back, stunned into silence by her effrontery. It was obvious he was not making his position clear. "But you are my guest." He leveled his sternest gaze at her. "And as such, your welfare is my responsibility."

"I am your guest, Nicolas; that's true," Sydney conceded. "And you've been a very generous and gracious host. That's true as well."

Somewhat placated, Nicolas continued to press his perspective. "And what if I agreed to this most unreasonable request? What will I say, then, when some poor gentleman shows up here looking for you?"

Nicolas waved his fork over his forgotten meal. "Shall I have to tell him that you've been trampled by a horse—a stallion nonetheless—that I foolishly allowed you to handle?"

"No." Sydney's eyes darkened under black-lashed lightening. "You shall tell him that I'm in the paddock, riding that same stallion, and I'm perfectly fine, thank you!"

Nicolas glared at Sydney. His jaw tightened. His pulse pounded. He knew with certainty that, as head of the estate, he could declare how things would be and that would end the discussion. He was sorely tempted to do so.

What stopped him?

Perhaps it was the way she handled the stallion today. After all, he planked down a substantial sum for the animal, and in ten minutes Sydney gained more control over him than Rickard ever had.

Perhaps it was the fact that she was bold enough to ask to take on the task. And she didn't back down when he railed at her. He had to confess, he respected her for that. She had considerable grit.

And perhaps it was because he didn't want to disappoint her.

That possibility confused him most of all.

Sydney's voice softened. "I know how to do this, Nicolas. It's the one thing I know for certain about myself. If some other danger dropped me here, well, this thing is certainly less dangerous than that."

When he didn't respond, she reached for his hand. "Please, Nicolas. Please let me try."

When Sydney's hand touched his, Nicolas felt a jolt through out his frame and his heart somersaulted in his chest. What was this about? A beautiful, headstrong woman took his hand and he, at thirty-two years of age, reacted like an inexperienced adolescent?

Skitt!

For a pace, they faced off in silence, eye to eye and unrelenting.

Then, with a sigh of resignation, and completely against his better judgment, Nicolas nodded his assent.

Sydney jumped up and sprinted around the table. She threw her arms around Nicolas's shoulders, erasing any rejoinder from his astonished mind.

"Oh, thank you! Thank you so very much!" She straightened and grinned. "You won't be sorry, I give you my word. And I'll begin first thing on the morrow!"

Nicolas watched Sydney sashay back to her chair, skirt swirling and braid bouncing. Though frowning, he was... happy. Pleasantly satisfied. When did he last feel like this? And why was he so delighted to be bested in a contest of wills with this strange and perplexing woman?

Helvete if I know.

April 16, 1819

Nicolas finally found time to go to the corral. He grew curious how Sydney fared with training the stallion. All he knew thus far was that she appeared each night for dinner without any fresh injuries.

He eyed the sky as he walked across the yard, always wary of too-dark clouds or a sudden shift in the wind; twisters were a serious concern this time of year. But the scudding clouds overhead appeared innocuous. So far. He turned his attention back to the small woman and huge animal in his corral.

Sydney walked around the enclosure and Fyrste obediently followed her. When she stopped, he stopped. When she started, he followed once more. Every few minutes she reached into her pocket and slipped the huge horse a bite of something.

It wasn't until Nicolas reached the fence that Sydney saw him. Her face split into a wide smile that suffused his chest with bubbles.

"Did you see?" she called out.

"I did!" he answered, climbing into the enclosure.

At the sound of his voice, Fyrste spun around. His ears flicked forward and back and he tossed his head. Sydney led him to where Nicolas waited.

"I'm so proud of him. He's a smart one, he is."

Though she patted the stallion's neck, Fyrste's tail swished mightily and he snorted several times. Sydney snickered. "If I didn't know better, I would say he's jealous!"

"He's displeased about something, that's for certain." Nicolas warily eyed the gray.

Of a sudden, Fyrste's ears laid back and he swung his head toward Nicolas, clipping him squarely in the brow with the hard bones of his nose.

Spun around by the blow, Nicolas grabbed the rails of the corral and in one seamless move was over the fence. He staggered then, hand to his forehead, and turned to face Sydney and the stallion. Blood streamed down his face as curse words and threats poured from his mouth.

"You filthy bastard! *Skitt!*" he bellowed. "I'll geld you yet, bloodlines or no! *Gud forbanner det!*" Filled with sudden panic, he waved Sydney toward him. "Look sharp, Sydney! He may turn against you, as well!"

Sydney shook her head. "He won't hurt me."

Her hands stroked the trembling beast. Speaking in the nonsense singsong that calmed him, Sydney stepped close enough to nestle her head in the bend of his neck. Only the exaggerated flicking of his ears and tail betrayed his unsettled demeanor.

Nicolas swore again and, seeing blood on his shirt, promptly sat down hard on the ground.

"'Twas my last clean shirt, you mindless mule!" he muttered as the world tipped a little.

ℰ℃ ℭ℥

"Let me see," Sydney urged.

Wet tea packets soaked the cut above Nicolas's left eye. Head tilted back, he lifted the leaf-filled gauze to let Sydney see the split. He felt blood pooling under his eye.

"It needs to be stitched."

He groaned. "It's that deep? Well, tell Addie. Let's get it over with."

Addie brought her sewing basket and clean rags into the kitchen, along with a flask of brandy. She handed the flask to Nicolas and he took several healthy swallows. He hated being stitched. It hurt.

"Have you ever stitched a wound before?" she asked Sydney while she threaded a needle.

Sydney was clearly fascinated. "I don't believe so."

"Well it's not so much different from sewing up a tear in some heavy fabric, except you can't pull too tight or you'll cut the skin." Addie motioned Sydney close. "Come watch."

Nicolas moved his chair next to the window where the light was good. Though not particularly pleased to be a tool for teaching, he determined to be strong during the operation, in spite of his discomfort. But with the first insertion of the needle, he grew lightheaded. Ragged gray edges invaded his vision.

Nicolas grabbed the windowsill. "I believe I need to lie down."

Addie had Nicolas lay on the kitchen table. His knees bent over the edge and his toes touched the floor. Sydney knelt beside him on a chair while Addie continued her stitching and instructing. Nicolas was brave by dint of will alone. His jaw clamped shut. Sweat beaded on his upper lip. He clenched his fists. And his legs twitched each time the needle went in.

The torturous task at last completed, the women sat Nicolas upright on a chair. He stayed seated until he felt recovered enough to stand, all the while taking relieved draughts from the brandy flask.

Sydney inspected his repaired injury with interest. "We shall be a sight at Lily's dinner party tomorrow night."

"Oh, Lord. Is that tomorrow?" Nicolas had completely forgotten about the invitation. It arrived the day after he returned home from Atherton's.

Her mouth curved up on one side. "Perhaps we can say we understood it to be a costume dinner and wear masks!"

"You look well, Sydney. Your bruises are nearly gone," he countered. Her face was so close to his, he could have... what?

She sat back on her heels. "Yes, nearly. There are only the lovely greenish-yellow tinges left. And the pink scar by my mouth. And above my eye."

"So you've made good use of the mirror, then?" Nicolas put the cap on the flask. He felt vaguely disappointed but could not imagine why.

"Only every day since the invitation arrived." Sydney smoothed her nankeen breeches with her palms and didn't look at Nicolas. "At the least my gown might cover the rest."

"I doubt that the fair Rickard will even notice." Nicolas closed his eyes and placed the teabag over the stitches.

After a moment she said softly, "I had best go change and wash up for dinner."

Nicolas listened to her fading footsteps and chided himself for that show of peevishness. He couldn't pin down the reason for it, but he was feeling a bit proprietary about Sydney. Perhaps he just didn't want her to be hurt. After all, she hadn't yet regained her memory. And Rickard's unruly past with women was notorious.

Truthfully, though, there was more. Sydney was different since she started working with Fyrste. When she first woke up without a memory, she was quiet and uncertain. Now she displayed the confidence that had been missing. That must be the real Sydney coming out. He liked it.

A lot.

As that thought crossed his mind, an unforgiving paroxysm of guilt blasted through his soul. *Lara*. Her name echoed in his memory, driving out thoughts of anyone else.

Chapter Seven

April 17, 1819

*A*ddie seemed to be everywhere in the small room as she helped Sydney dress for the dinner party at Atherton's. She spent hours washing, brushing and arranging Sydney's hair, though it would have gone faster if Sydney had not continually demanded a less elaborate style. All the while, Addie kept up her commentary.

"This will do fine, then, dear. Your hair's so soft and it shines just like satin! You could wear it hanging down loose and look more elegant than that Lily Atherton any day of the week, if I do say so myself! But are you certain I can't put a few more ribbons in? Weave them in through here and here? Perhaps tie this part up?"

"It's perfect the way it is, Addie. I assure you!" Sydney confined the older woman's busy hands in her own. "I love what you've done. Thank you."

"Well, if you're certain." Addie bit her lower lip and tilted her head to the side. "Couldn't I just—"

"Addie?"

"Yes, dear?"

"Am I going to the dinner in my chemise?"

"Oh, my heavens, no! Of course not! I'll go get your dress straight away! You just sit here and relax. I'll be back off the reel!"

Sydney waited in the rocker in her repaired shift and salvaged corset. Her bare feet tapped a cadence on the wood floor and her fingers drummed a counterpoint on the oak arms. She was nervous, though she knew Rickard's sister planned tonight's occasion out of kindness. The invitation read:

> *A dinner party in the honor of Mistress Sydney,*
> *houseguest of Mister Nicolas Hansen,*
> *for the purpose of introducing her to Cheltenham society.*

But to be put on display for the township to gawk at was definitely daunting.

Both her salvation and anticipation lay in the scrawled note at the bottom: "Sydney, I am looking forward to our evening together with great expectation. Rickard."

Addie re-entered the room, buried under a pile of the most beautiful emerald green velvet Sydney had ever seen.

"I picked it for your eyes." Addie shook out the dress and held it up for Sydney. "Isn't it grand?"

"Oh, yes," Sydney breathed.

Addie lifted the dress and Sydney dove under the pool of fabric, re-emerging through the neckline. Three-quarter sleeves covered the worst of her fading bruises. Cuffs of white lace drew attention to her pale wrists and hands. The neckline was square, cut low enough to show the upper swell of her bosom. Vertical insets of lighter green in the bodice accentuated the curve of her waist. Once laced, the dress fit as though it was created for her.

"Addie, this dress is absolute perfection. Thank you." Sydney hugged the older woman with such force that she almost pushed her over.

"Go on with you." Addie blushed. "You just go and have a good time, dear. The good Lord knows, you deserve it!"

Downstairs, Sydney waited in the entry, feeling as though a nest of hummingbirds had hatched in her belly. Their beating wings vibrated in her chest and dared her heart to keep pace. It was trying to.

Then she heard Nicolas's bedroom door open.

As Nicolas descended the stairs, Sydney reminded herself to breathe. She had only seen him in work shirts, breeches and dusty boots; and even then had thought him beautiful.

This evening, he wore a dark blue velvet frock coat that hugged his broad shoulders and matched his eyes. A brocade waistcoat and white lace shirt complemented his sunburned face, and tight fawn-colored breeches outlined powerful thighs over tall black Hessian boots. His shining blond hair hung loose on his shoulders.

With his towering frame he seemed an ancient Nordic god arrayed in modern attire. His only flaws: the gruesome multicolored stitches, and the blackened eye over one high cheekbone.

His gaze undressed her. Twice. Did he recognize the gown? He swallowed audibly and offered his arm, his expression unexpectedly resigned.

"Are you ready?"

"I am." Sydney slipped her arm through his and felt a slight tremble. "Let's go, Sir Nicky!"

He stopped and tossed an accusing glare at Addie. "No one may call me that unless they've changed my diaper clouts. And you, madam, are much too young, and much too beautiful, to have ever contemplated such an unpleasant task!"

Sydney found his unexpected playfulness delightful. She laughed and squeezed his arm, and he led her out to the waiting shay.

&) C8

The Atherton manor glowed like a rich man's jack-o-lantern. More than twice the size of Nicolas's, it stood three stories high. Carriages of various styles pulled up to the expansive front porch and spewed well-dressed guests. They ascended the spotless steps, and crossed polished wood planks to the open front door where Rickard greeted each of them.

Nicolas stepped from his shay and then offered Sydney his hand. She gripped it, and stepped carefully to the ground. Her gaze widened as it skittered over the manor and the crowd, then met his. He had no idea what she was thinking so he turned, tucked her hand in his arm and led her up the steps to the front door.

"Nick! Welcome, brother." Rickard shook his hand and slapped his shoulder. When he faced Sydney his expression transformed into such a set that, for a moment, Nicolas thought him addled.

"Sydney." He gave a little bow.

"Rickard," she returned.

He lifted her hand to his lips. "You look beautiful."

"Thank, you," she whispered. Nicolas watched an irksome flush bloom on her cheeks.

"Nicolas, darling! There you are!" Lily stepped to the top of the stairs. She began her gliding descent, her modulated voice loud enough to be heard over the affable din. "I was beginning to believe you had left me to fend for myself this evening."

Lily's voice was teasing and her laugh coquettish. But when Nicolas turned to fully face her she recoiled, losing all her aplomb.

"What happened to you?"

Nicolas bowed in Lily's direction, his mouth curved in a half-smile. He cast a sideways glance at Rickard. "Good evening, Lily. I was accosted by the demon horse your esteemed brother forced into my possession."

"Rickard? What's he talking about?"

Rickard didn't appear to hear a single word. He tucked Sydney's hand into the crook of his arm.

"Welcome to my humble home. I hope everything tonight is to your liking."

"I'm certain it will be, Rickard," Sydney murmured. And, as she smiled for the first time since they arrived, he led her toward the drawing room.

"Allow me to begin the introductions."

Nicolas stood with Lily in the entryway, abandoned. He grunted his unexamined irritation and lifted his bent arm to Lily. She accepted it, though her eyes were on Sydney.

"I believe I should be introduced to the guest of honor!" she hissed. "If Rickard doesn't keep her all to pieces to himself!"

Nicolas understood the lightly disguised command and obeyed, simply for the lack of a reason not to. He guided Lily to Sydney's side.

"Pardon me for interrupting." Nicolas stepped between Sydney and Rickard and turned his back on his friend. "Sydney, I'm afraid I've been lax in my responsibilities. May I present the mistress of this estate and our hostess for the evening, Miss Lily Atherton?"

Lily extended one manicured hand. "I'm so pleased to meet you, Madam—do you have a last name?" Her wide, innocent eyes went to Nicolas.

"No, I'm afraid not," Sydney answered for herself. "In truth, Sydney is just the name Nicolas gave me so he had something to call me."

Lily's eyebrows arched at her familiar reference to Nicolas. She offered Sydney a condescending smile and the modulated tone was back in place. "Well, then... just plain 'Sydney' it is! Welcome to our home."

Plain? Most assuredly not the word Nicolas would have chosen to describe the woman. Even with the still-healing cuts and bruises Sydney presented a striking figure, her vitality and grace evident in the unconcerned way that she moved.

He didn't know where that green dress came from, but he'd burn it if he could. She looked more beautiful, more tempting, more desirable tonight than he wanted to acknowledge. But he mustn't forget. He must never forget.

Sydney dipped her chin. "Thank you, Miss Atherton."

"Please. Call me Lily." The younger woman's lips smiled.

Her eyes did not.

ⅎ ⅓

Rickard stepped decisively around the broad blond obstacle and took Sydney's elbow once again. Though he pulled her away, she peered over her shoulder at Lily. Maybe that's what Lara looked like.

Were her greenish eyes mixed with brown like Rickard? Or with blue, like Lily? Clearly the wavy auburn hair bred true. Stefan was proof of that.

Sydney saw something else that shocked her: Lily clearly had set her cap for Nicolas. No woman dressed that way and held a man's arm like that, unless she was trying to attract and claim him. Lily fawned, rubbed, giggled, and pressed.

And what about Nicolas? Truly, she hadn't known him for long. But she credited him with enough sense to know that courting his dead wife's sister wasn't a good idea. Sydney watched his lingering gaze caress the swells of Lily's pale pink breasts, jammed high enough above her décolletage to choke her.

Nicolas was all male, that much was certain.

"Sydney?"

Her attention jerked to the couple Rickard intended to introduce. "Yes? I'm sorry. I'm very pleased to meet you—"

"Margaret Brown." The slender blond woman was in her mid-thirties. She reached for a man with black hair, also in his mid-thirties, who stood nearby engrossed in a conversation concerning Missouri's pending statehood. "This is my husband, Jess."

Jess's gaze swung around to Sydney and his dark brown eyes swept over her. "It's a pleasure, Madam."

Rickard led Sydney to another couple. "And this is my good friend, Lee Matthews, and his beautiful wife, Fanny."

When the very pregnant Fanny turned to face her, a bottomless sadness infused Sydney's core. She forced a pleasant expression. "I'm pleased to meet you, Mrs. Matthews. When is your confinement expected?" The words echoed in a hollow spot below her breastbone.

"Sometime next month, we believe." Fanny blushed and looked adoringly at her much older husband.

"This is our first." Lee slipped his arm around his wife's enlarged waistline.

Sydney touched Fanny's arm. "I pray it goes well for you."

"Thank you." Fanny's chin dipped.

As Rickard moved Sydney away, he whispered, "She was one of the most determined fillies." Sydney clasped a hand over her mouth to keep from hooting out loud.

Seating at dinner was a masterpiece of Lily's planning. Rickard was at the head of the table with Sydney seated at his right, where a wife would be. At the opposite end sat Lily with Nicolas by her side, hinting at the same relationship. Lily stood to get everyone's attention.

"I want to welcome Sydney, and all of our guests, to our home." Lily started the polite applause herself. "There's a very important reason why Rickard and I wanted you to meet Sydney tonight."

Sydney stiffened in her chair, shouldering the weight of multiple curious stares. Beneath the table, Rickard's hand slipped over hers and gave an encouraging squeeze.

"You see, this poor woman, in truth, isn't named Sydney at all. She's the victim of either foul play, or a very brutal accident. So brutal, in fact, that it's caused her to lose..." Lily paused and placed a hand over her heaving bosom. "...all of her memory!"

A buzz of disbelief filled the room.

"All of your memory?" exclaimed John McGovern.

"Well not quite, John," Rickard stepped in. "She obviously knows how to walk and talk, things like that!"

"Then what did she lose?" asked Beth McGovern. In her late fifties, she was his slightly younger wife.

"I don't know my name or where I live," Sydney spoke up. "And I don't remember what happened to me." That prompted a louder buzz.

Lily quickly clarified her own role in the evening, "So I—that is, *we*—invited you all here tonight with the hope that one of you might recognize her."

Silence.

Uneasy glances.

Sympathetic glances.

Helpless glances.

Humiliating glances, all.

Beth McGovern reached her hand toward Sydney. "I'm sorry, my dear. I'm certain something will turn up."

"Thank you." Sydney managed a small smile.

A man in his forties, Humphrey Sinclair, nodded enthusiastically. "A looker like you, miss, won't be alone for lo— ouch!"

He shot an angry look at his chubby wife, Erma. "What'd you do that for?"

As things were about to unhinge, Rickard addressed Lily, "Is dinner prepared?"

Lily clapped her hands. Well-dressed Negro slaves carried platters into the room. The aromas of roasted lamb and freshly baked bread mingled midair with conversation and relieved laughter.

Ashton Caldecott was the first to suggest the sensitive topic of Missouri Territory's application for statehood. "Have you heard what Tallmadge introduced in Congress?"

"Dashed New York Republican!" Lee Matthews blurted, then turned to his young wife. "Pardon my language, dearest. I don't mean to upset you."

Fanny blushed and patted her husband's hand. It was obvious she thought her husband incapable of doing aught inappropriate.

"Yes, I've heard." Rickard kept his eyes on his meal.

"I haven't." Humphrey Sinclair looked from one to the other.

"He asked for an amendment to restrict slavery in Missouri as a condition of statehood!" Tremors of approval and dissent rumbled around the table. "The amendment also calls for emancipation of slaves' children when they turn twenty-five."

"We shall be ruined!" Hannah Caldecott fanned her middle-aged body.

"It's not as though this year isn't shaping up to be hard enough as it is!" Humphrey jabbed his fork at Ashton. "For every last one of us!"

That caught Sydney's attention. What did he mean by that? Might it have something to do with her own situation? She resolved to ask Rickard or Nicolas as soon as she had the opportunity.

Fanny turned wide eyes to her husband. "Can they really make that a condition?"

"The Ohio River is the accepted boundary between the North and the South," Nicolas interjected. "Most of Missouri does lie north of the Ohio River."

"And states north of this line have either abolished slavery or adopted emancipation policies!" Jess Brown pointed out.

Nicolas addressed Ashton. "Have you heard how the voting went?"

"The House approved it, but it was defeated in the Senate," he replied. Another, stronger tremor of approval and dissent shook the room.

Lee Matthews shook his head. "This is going to be an ugly battle."

"It will pit brother against brother." Rickard said. He did not look at Nicolas.

And Nicolas did not look at him. Sydney hadn't thought about it until that moment, but there were no slaves at the Hansen estate. Another thing she resolved to ask Nicolas about.

"Come now, gentlemen. I'm quite certain Congress will come to their senses and realize that our life in this wilderness necessitates slaves." Lily batted her eyelashes and looked bored. "Might we find a topic of conversation less upsetting to the ladies?"

Stuart McAvoy called to Nicolas from the other end of the table, his Scots brogue flavoring his words. "So! What's happened to you, Hansen? You've quite a trophy there on your brow!"

"Rickard sold me a demon stallion. He didn't take a liking to me."

"Which one, then? Rickard or the horse?"

Good natured whoops erupted from the men. Grinning at the joke, Nicolas made eye contact with each one until he had the guests' undivided attention.

"Sydney's breaking him for me."

Sydney's eyes widened in surprise and she sucked an audible breath. What was he doing? Why was he telling them that? She glared down the table.

"Nicolas!" she barked.

His uninjured eyebrow arched. "What?"

"Well, I'll be dashed!" Rickard sat back in his chair and gaped at her.

Everyone at the table now faced Sydney, astonished expressions to a man. Her supper roiled in her stomach and considered leaving. Her face grew hot. Her palms were wet.

She could not think of one thing to say.

Bewildered jokes concerning Nicolas's prowess as a man, and complimenting Sydney's as a stallion breaker, abounded with double entendres and redirected the dinner crowd's attention. Rickard's ability to judge either women or horses was also the subject of good-natured jibes as everyone enjoyed themselves at their affable host's willing expense.

Everyone except for Lily, whose dour expression made it clear she had been completely upstaged.

When the evening finally ended and Nicolas brought her home, Sydney undressed and sank into her soft bed, glad the night's prickly ordeal was over. All she wished for was to escape into sleep. In the morning she would eat breakfast, help Addie in the kitchen, and then work with Fyrste. It was as close to normal as her life could be for now.

As her dreams took over, midnight eyes and afternoon hair floated through her mind. Thunder whispered her name and rumbled ominously between her thighs.

Chapter Eight

April 18, 1819

*A*fter nearly six years of dining alone, Nicolas feared Sydney's constant presence might wear on him. Instead, he found that he looked forward to their conversations. Because she had no memory, there was engaging unpredictability in every thought she expressed. And because she was close to him in age, her easy companionship relaxed him in turn.

When they finished supper the night after Lily's dinner party, Nicolas invited her to join him in his study. "The fire is comfortable and I've a bottle of port wine if you'd prefer that to brandy," he offered.

He wasn't certain what prompted him to do so; Sydney was the first woman he ever entertained in his masculine sanctuary. Even Lara avoided the room.

"Will you tell me about your and Rickard's estates?" she asked, accepting a glass of port. "He has slaves and you don't. Is his property that much bigger?"

Nicolas paused. Was she comparing the wealth of the two men? And for what purpose? Lily's suggestion of a contrived rescue wafted through his contemplation. Nicolas eased into his large stuffed-leather chair, deciding to begin at the beginning. First, he took a slow sip of brandy.

"It started when my father and Rickard's father applied for land grants back in eighty-two. When they saw maps of the plots, neither one was particularly pleased. Rickard's father, being English, wanted farm land. And my father, being Norse, wanted forests for hunting."

Nicolas gestured with his brandy glass. "Now, these men had never met before, but they sized each other up and struck a bargain, settling their hash right there in the grant office. They took adjoining grants of five hundred acres each, and re-drew the boundaries according to the lay of the land."

Sydney nodded. "And they both procured what they wanted."

"They did, mostly. As it turned out, there was more farmable land than they originally thought, so my father leased two hundred acres back to James for as long as the Atherton family desires to farm it."

"So Rickard has slaves to work the fields and run the house?"

"It's a bit much for Lily." Nicolas buried his nose—and his grin—in his brandy glass. The image of Lily lifting a delicate white finger in any sort of menial task was impossible for him to imagine.

Sydney smiled. "Were your parents already married?"

"No, but the land grant did it. My father went back to Pennsylvania and told my mother that he was moving to the Missouri Territory and would she please come with him. She said 'yes' and they married in August of 1782. They moved to this land that same month."

A wistful expression settled over Sydney's features. "Your mother must have truly loved your father."

"She did indeed, much to the consternation of her parents. Miss Kirsten Sven was their only child and they were not well pleased to have her go traipsing off to the unsettled wilderness."

"My parents felt the same way when I moved to Missouri." Sydney's wide eyes jerked to Nicolas's, angry frustration now etched on her face. "And how can I know that, but have no idea *why* I came here?"

He shrugged, helpless. "It seems to come in small bits, when you're not thinking about it."

"How can I make that happen?" Sydney groaned. "How can a body think about not thinking about something without thinking about the thing they don't want to think about?"

Nicolas opened then closed his mouth, still disentangling her words. She sank back into her chair.

"Go on with your story," she muttered with a sullen flourish.

He chuckled in spite of her frustration. Sydney was so animated that he found her quite amusing. Beautiful and funny? An unusual—and powerfully attractive—combination.

"Where was I? Oh, yes. My father built a small cabin and they survived that winter on what game he could kill. Then he built this estate over the years, but he never had slaves. He didn't feel comfortable owning another man. Norway's not like England. Besides, we aren't farming for profit."

Sydney stared into the fire. "And what about you?"

"What about me?"

She turned to face him. "Are you comfortable with owning another man?"

Nicolas waved his hand. "Look around, Sydney. Do you see any slaves?"

"So the answer, then, is no?"

"The answer, then, is no."

"What if you were farming for profit? Like Rickard?"

Nicolas narrowed his eyes. Was she challenging him again? For what purpose?

"I've given that idea some thought. But I couldn't bring myself to such a situation."

Sydney turned away. "But your conscience allows you to accept profits from land worked by slaves."

"It's not a perfect world, Sydney. What else am I to do? Let the land lie fallow?" Stung by her words, he stood to pour another brandy. "At the least, I know Rickard doesn't mistreat them. In fact, he cares for them very well."

"That's some comfort, to be certain."

"Have you owned slaves?" Nicolas pressed unkindly.

Sydney frowned. "I don't believe so. But of course, I can only assume which side of the issue I stand on." Nicolas lifted his brandy in chagrined, wordless acknowledgment. Sydney sighed and sipped her wine.

"Where are your parents now?" she murmured.

Nicolas gazed into the waning fire. "My mother died of pneumonia in the winter of 1812. She was sixty-two. My father died the following year at sixty-nine. As oldest son, I inherited this estate from my father. And as oldest son of an only child, I inherited my mother's estate as well."

"So you have the inheritance from both your parents, plus the income from the lease?"

"Yes." Nicolas stepped behind his chair, unconsciously placing a barrier between himself and what he anticipated her next query to be. He rested loose fists on the chair back and decided to take the offensive.

"You could say I'm wealthy, by Territory standards."

"But you don't live like a wealthy man." Sydney shook her head, her expression puzzled. "I reckon what I mean is, you work hard, Nicolas. And you don't shy away from dirt."

Somewhat placated, he leaned his elbows on the chair back and eyed the brandy glass. Its facets glinted in the firelight, sending shards of light through the amber liquid.

Shards of life glinted through his soul. How might he explain what he felt?

"It—it feels very good to work."

Her voice was soft. "Tell me about work, Nicolas."

His gaze lifted to hers. Was she serious? In the firelight, her green eyes were bottomless. Her full lips parted, relaxed. She was guileless, open, allowing him into her. And demanding nothing in return but what he would freely give.

"Well…" He cleared his throat and searched for words. "It feels good to stretch, and pull, and lift. To swing an axe or a hammer. Or a sheep. There is something deeply satisfying about working your body so hard that you drip sweat, your legs burn, your arms shake. But you can see that new building raised. Or that pile of firewood on the porch. Or draw cold, clear water from that new well."

Sydney rolled her wine glass between her palms. "I feel some of that when I work with horses."

"Yes!" Nicolas pointed at her. "I would believe that you do." He walked around the chair and sat again.

Sydney stared at the deep red liquid in her glass. "Nicolas, might I ask you about something I heard last night at dinner?"

"Of course."

"What did Humphrey Sinclair mean when he said this year is shaping up to be hard enough for every one of us?"

Nicolas drew a deep breath. "There seems to be a sort of financial panic spreading across the country right now."

Sydney frowned. "What's happening?"

"Agriculture prices are falling, so farmers have less money. They can't frequent businesses, so they shutter their doors. Then mortgages are foreclosed on. Once this sort of thing starts, it's mighty hard to stop." Nicolas desired to change the subject before Sydney asked about the impact on his own financial situation. "Have you any more questions about the Hansen dynasty?"

Sydney thought a moment. "Are any of the people you're talking about in the portraits by the stairs?"

"Of course. Would you care to know who is who?"

"I would love that!"

Nicolas warmed to her interest; family pride ran strong in his veins. Years had passed since he had a guest who didn't know the paintings well. Sydney was already climbing the stairs. He followed and called her back down to the lowest painting.

"This is my great-grandfather Christian, uh, 'Fredriksen.' He was Danish, in actuality. But he spent much of his life in Norway." The man in the painting wore a curled gray wig and a faint smile. His hand rested on a bejeweled cane. His clothing was heavily brocaded.

"He's rather regal!" she opined.

"He was not well-liked."

Nicolas guided Sydney to the next step. "And these are his children, Frederick and Marit Christiansen, when they were in their adolescence." Frederick bore a striking resemblance to his dark-eyed father, but Marit looked like Nicolas. Clear blue eyes and abundant blond hair framed an impudent smile.

"She's your grandmother? There's a strong resemblance."

"That there is. The next painting," they climbed two stair steps, "is the wedding portrait of her with my grandfather, Henrik Canute Sven." There was a determined edge to Marit's gaze in this portrait, but her smile still held the hint of humor. Blond and green-eyed, Henrik towered over Marit.

"How tall was he?"

"In his youth, I believe he topped six foot seven." Nicolas straightened unconsciously. "They moved to Philadelphia the year after their wedding. Marit did not get along with her father, and she had some rather strong reservations concerning her brother!"

Nicolas chuckled and shook his head. "But that's a very long story for another day. We are on to my parents."

Up another two stair steps. "This is my father, Reidar Magnus Hansen and his bride, Kirsten Christiansen Sven. This painting was done about six years after they were married, two years before I was born. My grandparents commissioned it on one of their trips back to Philadelphia from the Missouri Territory."

Reidar Hansen was tall, gray-eyed, with light brown hair. Kirsten was blond with light blue eyes. They were a very handsome pair. The couple held hands and their bodies faced each other as they gazed out of the painting. They looked happy. Nicolas turned away from the portrait and rubbed a knuckle over his lips, his jaw flexing. He, too, had been happy once.

He directed Sydney to the last picture.

"And this is my father's father, Martin Gunnar Hansen. Born in Norway and emigrated to America at age twenty-seven. He met a good Norse girl on the ship and they were married by the captain. By the time the ship docked in Boston Harbor, my father was a month past conception!" Nicolas smiled a little, then.

They returned to the study and Sydney raised her wineglass. "Thank you for the tour of Hansen history. I give you your ancestors: may mine be half as interesting, and fully as legitimate!"

Nicolas chuckled and lifted his brandy. "*Skåle!*"

Sydney drained her glass. "So you and Rickard grew up together."

"We did. And if our fathers knew but half the things we planned to do with these lands, they would have lived to be a hundred just to stop us!"

Nicolas leaned toward her and dropped his voice. "There was gold to be had, if we dug deep enough in the right spot. Of course, digging all the way to China was another perfectly reasonable plan, in case the gold didn't make an appearance. Not to mention the idea of re-routing the Mississippi River so the trade barges would come to us, instead of us going to them!"

Sydney whooped with delight at that one.

Nicolas shook his head. "Ah, the follies of youth!"

"It sounds as though you had a happy childhood. I wonder what my own story is." She sat back, bit her lower lip, and squinted at Nicolas.

"What?"

"Stefan."

He frowned. "What about Stefan?"

Her voice was soft, like steel. "I'm only wondering... Will he have memories like yours?"

Nicolas's jovial mood dissipated into a somber air of regret. He looked away from her and gulped the rest of his brandy. He pulled a breath, released it, and stared at the empty glass.

"I don't see how that's possible," he whispered.

&) C&

Every other Sunday there was church in Cheltenham. The traveling pastor came to the building that was school during the week and led the faithful in solid Lutheran worship. Nicolas went often enough to placate God and his neighbors, but not every time the doors were open.

Because Nicolas had a mighty large bone to pick with God.

It wasn't a question of faith. Nicolas was certain there was a God; his belief in that fact could not be shaken. He just wasn't certain what good thing God had in mind when He took Lara and the boy twin, leaving him to raise Stefan by himself. On many a long night, alone in his bed, he asked God that very question. But thus far, God had not produced any answers. So anger kept Nicolas away from church. But the fear of not getting into Heaven to see Lara and the babe, kept him coming back.

On the next Sunday morning after Lily's dinner party, Nicolas got up early, saddled Rusten, and rode into Cheltenham. He tried to corral his thoughts, focusing on the forested beauty that surrounded him. Sunlight pierced the leafy ceiling and fell in hazy shafts to the pine-needle carpet. Birds twittered and squirrels answered. Gray-bottomed clouds floated through a bowl of pale blue.

He went into the church alone, nodding a silent greeting to his neighbors. He sat by himself in the back pew, as was his habit, and pondered this new path that God had diverted him onto.

What was he supposed to do with the woman?

Nicolas was at a loss and he hoped God would give him some ideas regarding Sydney. After all, it was He who dropped her in the water but kept her from dying before Nicolas found her.

Now what?

Nicolas considered his unexpected houseguest. A skillful and intelligent woman, her conversation was pleasant. And she was very attractive as well, there was no question about that. Nicolas had to confess he enjoyed their time together. And she made him laugh.

But she belonged somewhere else, didn't she?

And to someone else?

"Min Far i Himmel, vis meg hva til å gjøre," Nicolas prayed. My Father in Heaven, show me what to do.

Chapter Nine

April 21, 1819

*S*ydney? Is that you? What on God's earth are you wearing?"

At the sound of Rickard's voice, Sydney spun to face him. Her face burst into flames. Of all the people she did not want to see her dressed this way, Rickard topped the list. What was he doing in Nicolas's stable?

"G-good morning, Rickard. I wish I had known you were coming, I would've changed clothes." With hands she prayed he could not see trembling, she smoothed her breeches. And her shirt. And her hair.

Rickard grinned and ran a fingertip along her cheek. "Don't distress yourself, Sydney. You look fine. And your face has healed beautifully, by the by."

Sydney's embarrassed gaze flitted around the stable, landing everywhere but on him.

"Might you explain your fashion decision?" Rickard asked in his chocolate voice.

Sydney tried to sound offhand. Confident. Logical. "It makes sense when I'm working with the horses."

"Ah." He nodded. "So, how are you faring with Grayson?"

She looked at him now. "You mean *Fyrste*. Nicolas changed his name. It's Norse for prince."

"Is it now?"

"Come on, I'll show you." Sydney motioned for Rickard to follow her, and walked out of the stable without waiting to see if he did so.

At the paddock, Sydney blew a chirping whistle, and the gray's head popped up, ears twitching. Another whistle brought Fyrste trotting to her, sniffing for the treat Sydney always had. She slipped through the rails.

Rickard leaned on the fence and watched. Sydney walked around the paddock while Fyrste followed, stopping and starting with her voice commands. Then she faced him and, with a combination of voice and hand signs, got him to back up.

"I'm very impressed, Sydney!" Rickard called to her. "Have you sat him yet?"

"No." Sydney led Fyrste to where Rickard stood. "But soon, I hope. I believe he trusts me now."

Rickard squinted into Sydney's eyes. "You are some unexpected sort of woman, do you know that? I don't believe I've ever met anyone like you before."

Sydney leaned on the other side of the fence. She could smell his cologne and was painfully aware of the manure smeared on her boot. She wiped it against the grass.

"I wonder if I was always of this temperament," she contemplated as she checked her boot. "Or have I changed since I cannot remember?"

Rickard smiled softly. His chameleon eyes were greenish-buckskin in the morning sun. Hanks of burnt copper curled around his ears, having successfully escaped their restraint. "That's an interesting question. I reckon we'll have to see if a body steps forward to claim you, and find out!"

"Hmph. Like my husband?"

Rickard was already close to her, but he leaned closer. "If he exists, and he doesn't claim you, then he certainly doesn't deserve you," he whispered.

Rickard's lips demanded Sydney's attention. She stared at them and imagined how they might feel on hers. They advanced. Her eyes closed. They brushed hers, sending a shiver through her core and gooseflesh down her limbs.

Before he could kiss her properly, a loud and intentional throat-clearing blew them apart. Nicolas frowned as he approached the couple.

"Hello, Rick! What brings you here today?"

"An invitation." Rickard faced Nicolas, noticeably unperturbed. "Lily wishes you and Sydney to come to dinner tomorrow evening. It's not a party, just the four of us this time."

Breathless and a bit disoriented, Sydney blinked and focused on Nicolas. Wordlessly she waited for his response.

"I've no objection. Sydney, would you care to go?" His sarcastic tone made it quite clear he considered the question unnecessary. Why was he irritated? What had she done?

"I believe that would be lovely." Sydney faced Rickard. Her face was on fire again. "Please thank Lily for me."

Fyrste grew restless. He snorted, shook his head and trotted to the opposite side of the paddock. He whinnied from across the enclosure. Sydney watched him for a moment, distracted.

"Oh my!" She turned to Nicolas.

"What?"

Her expression shifted to one of disbelief. "I believe he's afraid of you!"

"Who? The horse?" Nicolas looked at Sydney like she was juggling snakes. Rickard sniggered and ran a finger across his upper lip, masking his grin.

Nicolas scowled at him, then slid his gaze back to Sydney. "How can that be?"

"I don't know." Sydney shook her head. "But, Nicolas you're a very big man and you have a very big voice. And you carry yourself with quite a lot of authority," she offered.

Nicolas looked from Sydney to Fyrste and back again, his blue eyes buried under lowering brows. He jerked his fingers through his hair.

"I've never heard of anything so preposterous!" he boomed. From across the enclosure, Fyrste neighed and snorted, tossing his head in response.

The corners of Rickard's eyes crinkled with mischief. "Is it as preposterous as, oh, someone losing their memory after a horrifying experience, would you say?"

"Pah!" Nicolas scoffed. "Why don't you go deflower someone?"

Rickard laughed his delightful laugh and slapped his thighs.

Nicolas's voice hovered somewhere between derision and resignation. "So, what are we to do?" he asked her. "If you're correct, I mean."

"I'm not certain. But he needs to become accustomed to you." Sydney looked at the nervous animal, her assurance disappearing. Why did she have to suggest the unconventional idea? Why couldn't she just keep quiet? "Perhaps you could spend some time at the corral while I'm working with him?"

Fyrste looked Nicolas in the eye and his ears flicked back in a brief threat. Nicolas stood his ground and spoke to the horse in a low voice.

"*Hvorfor er De redd av meg, eh? De er stor og sterk...Har den liten kvinne sjarmert De?*"

The stallion seemed to find the natural rhythm of the Norse tongue soothing; it was similar to the patter Sydney used. He still bobbed his head, but he did not stamp his feet.

"What did you say?" Sydney asked.

Nicolas gave her a crooked grin. "You are big and strong. Has the little woman charmed you?"

She smiled.

Then he waggled a finger at Rickard. "How you got me to take that cussed beast off your hands is a mystery to me."

April 24, 1819

Two days after the supper at Rickard's, Nicolas barreled into the backyard with his arms waving wildly. "I just met a rider from Atherton's! He's had a rider from Sinclair's! A twister's headed this way!"

Sydney turned to John, horrified. She remembered twisters.

"Help me secure the animals!" he shouted.

Sydney quickly led Fyrste into the stone stable and tied him in his stall. Then she helped John with the other livestock. He jerked his head toward the manor.

"Take Stefan to the cellar. I'll finish here."

Sydney grabbed Stefan's hand and they ran up to the house. The clouds above were already changed, darkening and swirling ominously. Addie stood beside the root cellar door and motioned them inside.

"Where's Nicolas?" Sydney asked over the rapidly rising wind.

"Shuttering the house. You and the boy, get inside now."

Maribeth was already cowering below, fear staining her plain face. Moments later, John climbed into the subterranean storeroom. Only Nicolas was missing. Sydney sat on a bench and nervously lifted Stefan onto her lap. He didn't object.

The wind outside grew stronger, bragging with keening moans. Light faded as black clouds moved overhead. Addie climbed down the ladder and let the door fall shut, but she didn't yet latch it.

"Where is he?" Sydney shouted to be heard over the howl of the wind. Certainly they wouldn't leave him outside!

Addie looked at John, who shook his head.

"We must go get him! And quickly!" Sydney was on the verge of panic. She slid Stefan off her lap and stood. John stood as well and grabbed her arm. His grip was stronger that she expected.

"No." His tone was as controlling as his grasp. "Once inside, no one leaves until the twister's gone."

"But—Nicolas!" Sydney looked back and forth from John to Addie. By the grim set of their mouths, this was not a negotiable point. Her knees bent like spring saplings and she gripped a shelf for support.

Then the wind outside stopped; the sudden quiet was neck-prickling eerie. The air grew thin as if some deity sucked it all away and the hair on their bodies lifted. Sydney's nerves tingled. John and Addie exchanged worried glances.

"Oh, dear God! What's happening?" Sydney blurted.

The cellar door flew open and Nicolas, sweating and windblown, jumped the seven feet to the dirt floor without using the ladder. He fell to his hands and knees, gasping loudly to catch his breath. The door crashed closed behind him and John slipped the sturdy cross-plank into its guides.

Sydney cried out her relief.

The wind returned with such vengeance that the noise deafened, even underground. The cellar door rattled as though a horde of demons were demanding entrance. Sydney felt Stefan's arm around her leg. She sat down on the bench and pulled him onto her lap again. His sturdy little arms slipped around her neck and he huddled against her. She held him tightly in return and rocked him without thinking about it. Nicolas stared intently at the two of them from his spot on the floor.

His expression was odd; Sydney couldn't begin to guess his

thoughts.

Then the lone candle in the cellar blew out.

Now in complete darkness, and with raucous winds screaming outside, there was nothing to do but wait. The manor house should survive; it had already weathered nearly forty years of twisters. But tornadoes were capricious in the destruction they left behind. There was no way to predict what would still be standing when they emerged from this dark womb.

Sydney comforted Stefan, rocking and humming to him, and wondered how he got through previous storms. Addie, most likely. Or maybe Maribeth. She couldn't imagine it was Nicolas.

The wind shrieked its fury. Broken branches banged against and then scraped away from the cellar doors. Each hit jolted through Sydney like lightning. Thunderstorms terrified her. Twisters made her wish to die. But for Stefan's sake, she swallowed her fears and concentrated on reassuring him, calming him. Holding the boy close anchored her in a way that she didn't expect.

And it didn't hurt that Stefan's father was by her side. She couldn't see him, but she felt his presence. She felt heat radiate from his body and smelled his sweat. The bench she sat on wobbled when he shifted his weight against it.

It was close to an hour before the winds evaporated. Pale daylight seeped around the cellar door. Their eyes, accustomed to the dark, could see clearly now. Nicolas remained on the floor, leaning against the bench that Sydney and Stefan sat on.

"What do you think, John?" His introduction of speech jarred as it rent the sudden silence.

John nodded, lifted the plank from the braces, and then used it to push the cellar door open. Light flooded the space, causing everyone to squint. Stefan stirred on Sydney's lap. He had fallen asleep after half-an-hour in the dark and his weight caused her legs to go numb.

"Might you lift him for me?" she asked Nicolas. "It seems my legs have lost feeling."

Nicolas unfolded slowly from the floor. He lifted his sleeping son from Sydney's embrace, and woke him in the process.

"*Pappa?* Is the twister gone?" Stefan rubbed his eyes, his voice raspy from the short nap.

"It is. Let's go see how bad things are."

He set Stefan on the ladder and boosted him into the world. Then he turned to Sydney. "Are you coming?"

She rubbed her legs. "In a minute. I hate this feeling, as though I am being stuck all over with pins!"

Nicolas came over and knelt next to her. He massaged her calves through the breeches. His strong hands were warm and efficient. She was steel again, drawn to his seductive magnet. She resisted less this time.

"That hurts and tickles!" she laughed.

"Might you walk now?"

"I believe so."

Nicolas offered Sydney his hand and helped her up the log ladder. Then he followed her out of the cellar and closed the door behind him.

The only visible damage was to the surrounding forest. Limbs were scattered everywhere, a few dead trees were broken off, and a couple younger ones uprooted. But the buildings remained, apparently with roofs, and that was good.

"John and I will climb up to check shingles tomorrow. And it looks like I've plenty of wood to chop." Nicolas turned to Sydney and smiled, his relief clear. "We've survived yet another one!"

Chapter Ten

April 27, 1819

The dry goods store in Cheltenham was unremarkable, carrying the usual notions and staples that Sydney expected to find there. The proprietors, Jess and Margaret Brown, were happy to see her again.

"You look well, Sydney," Jess said. "I trust your injuries have healed?"

"Yes, sir, they have. Thank you for asking."

"And your memory? Is there progress?" Margaret looked hopeful.

With a deep breath, she retreated behind a polite smile. "No, I'm sorry to report there's been no improvement in that area."

"Oh. I'm sorry. Well, then..." Margaret rearranged a perfectly orderly stack of homemade jellies.

Sydney put her hand on the woman's arm. "Don't concern yourself, Margaret. I'm certain it'll come in time. At least, that's what I tell myself every night."

Margaret offered a kind smile. "And it shall, no doubt."

"Have you a list, Addie?" Jess reached for the paper in Addie's hand. "Sugar, flour, coffee... I'll get them together for you. Jasper? Come give me a hand!" A lanky teenager crossed the back doorway.

"So, Margaret, what have you in stock that's new?" Addie asked.

Margaret's eyes lit. "A trader came through and brought us

limes."

"Did he now! Well, that might do. What do you think, Sydney?"

"Pie."

"What's that, dear?"

Sydney faced Addie, but gazed deeply into a hazy watercolor fog beyond the store's walls. "I know how to make lime pie."

"That sounds delicious!" Margaret enthused. "Will you give me the recipe?"

Sydney returned to present company. "If it turns out to be edible, I should be happy to."

"Limes it is, Margaret!" Addie smiled at Sydney. "Shall we try it this afternoon?"

"We also have pecans," Margaret tempted.

Addie raised an eyebrow at her. "You're a sly saleswoman, Margaret! You know well my John's weakness for pecans!"

Margaret put the limes in one bag, the pecans in another. Then Addie led Jess outside to show him where John left the wagon, while Sydney explored the rest of the store.

The front door opened and Miss Lily Atherton sashayed into the building. Sydney sighed and donned invisible armor. Her expression grew deliberately bland.

"Well, look who's here!" Lily cooed. "My darling Sydney, did Nicolas trust you to leave his property?"

Sydney tightened her armor. "I beg your pardon?"

"Are you certain you remember how to get back to his estate?" Lily looked at Margaret with wide, innocent eyes. Margaret's mouth dropped open, then bounced closed. She glanced uncomfortably between the two women.

Lily sniggered, her grin triumphant.

Sydney's fists clenched while she fought the urge to take Lily down a peg. Or perhaps ten. She smiled tight-lipped and said nothing. She gave Lily her back and feigned intense interest in a bolt of fabric until Addie re-entered the store.

"Addie, I'm going to walk back."

The housekeeper looked surprised. "Oh? Is everything well?"

"Can you find the way?" Lily taunted.

Addie shot her with a look. Sydney ignored her.

"It's a beautiful day, and I feel like a walk." She grabbed the sacks of limes and pecans. "Thank you, Margaret. I'll tell you if the pie turns out. Please give my best to Jess."

Head high, she stalked past Lily and out the door.

Once on the road, Sydney walked at a pace that suited her. She tilted her face upward and let the warmth of the sun erase her irritation with Lily. The aromatic spring growth in the forest renewed her. Birds gossiped in the branches while squirrels scattered in their relentless search for food.

It only took a quarter hour at her brisk pace to walk the mile to the Hansen manor. Sydney tucked the pecans safely on a shelf in the root cellar. After she closed the cellar door and opened the kitchen door she heard... music?

Inside the manor, the strains of a violin were unmistakable. Sydney set the limes on the table, slipped off her shoes and tiptoed down the hall toward the sound. What she saw confounded everything she thought she knew about Nicolas Hansen.

Nicolas was in his study, his back to the open door, playing the violin with his whole body.

Sydney held still as a statue, sculpted by astonishment. With a clarity whose origin she could not fathom, she suddenly understood her host. He was the locked room upstairs. Profound pain preserved behind an impenetrable barricade. Don't let anyone in. Don't let the memories out.

Sydney felt his soul escape its prison through the plaintive tune, enticing hers to join in. She leaned against the doorjamb and closed her eyes. The legato tones of the song swirled over her, around her and through her.

And came to an abrupt halt.

Sydney's eyes opened and met Nicolas's intense blue stare. He stood entrenched. His right hand held the bow poised over the silenced strings, the violin tucked under his strong jaw. Then everything about him tumbled.

"I wasn't aware anyone was here."

Sydney glanced at the violin case on the oak desk. "I'm sorry, Nicolas. I didn't mean to intrude. I was attracted by the music."

Nicolas shook his head and moved to encase the instrument. "I'm out of practice."

Sydney put out her hand. "Please don't stop."

Nicolas eyed her with one brow arched, the other dipped.

"What were you playing? It was lovely."

He hesitated. Then, "An old Nordic lullaby. My mother sang it to us."

"Will you play it for me?"

Nicolas considered her, confusion coloring his countenance. "Why?"

Sydney crossed the study and rested her hands on the top of his leather chair, forcing him to turn his back on the violin case. "Because it stirred my soul to hear it."

"Madam, your soul apparently requires very little to excite it."

"Please?"

Nicolas sighed loudly enough to express extreme irritation. Even so, he nested the violin under his chin. He flexed his wrist and fingered the bow until it settled in his hand. Then he put it to the strings. Eyes closed, he played. His body swayed with the swells of the melody and his elbows danced with the rhythm. Sydney watched, entranced, as his long, strong fingers flew over the neck of the fiddle.

When the last note died, neither of them moved.

"Thank you," Sydney whispered.

Nicolas lowered the instrument. "Did you enjoy it, truly?"

"Oh, yes. Why wouldn't I?"

Nicolas shrugged. "That hasn't been the universal response."

"Be assured, you may play for me anytime."

Nicolas placed the violin in its case. Until then, Sydney hadn't seen its elaborately painted design, inlaid with mother-of-pearl.

"It's very beautiful." She moved closer to touch it. "Is it Norse?"

Nicolas nodded. "It's called a Hardanger fiddle."

"I have no way of knowing if I've ever heard of that!" Sydney laughed.

Nicolas raked one hand through his mane. "It's the most common musical instrument in Norway. And it's only to be found there."

"Is that so?" She wanted to keep him talking, infinitely more fascinated by her new vision of the man, than by the instrument he held in his hands with such uncommon reverence.

Nicolas warmed to her interest. "The Hardanger fiddle is different from the ordinary fiddle because it has sympathetic strings,

and a less curved bridge and fingerboard. See?" Nicolas held the
fiddle up for Sydney and pointed out what he described.

"Yes, I see."

"It's played on two strings, instead of one, most of the time.
That's what gives it such a mournful sound, rather like a bagpipe."

Sydney nodded her understanding.

Nicolas grinned, enjoying a private joke.

"What?" Sydney asked.

"If I were asked, I'd say it was an involuntary choice of style."
Nicolas held up his left hand, fingers splayed. His palm measured at
least four inches across and five inches in length, and the thickness
of his long fingers was in proportion.

"When a race has hands of this size, playing on one string alone
does present a bit of a challenge!"

ℰ ℭ

The invitation to John and Beth McGovern's annual May Day Ball
arrived a little over a week after Lily's formal dinner party and was
considerately addressed to both Nicolas and Sydney. Addie
commented on how nice that was and weren't the McGoverns such
nice people to think of Sydney specially and perchance there was
time to make her a new dress this time and what color did Sydney
believe she should wear to go best with her fair skin, green eyes and
dark hair and did Nicolas have an opinion?

Nicolas gave a non-committal grunt; a generous response
considering Addie was instructing Sydney on the removal of his
stitches during the discussion.

"I don't much care," he growled. "As long as your stitching
involves something other than my head!"

As Sydney dressed for the Ball in the re-created gown she and
Addie worked on together, she pondered what it meant that not one
single whisper of a response was generated by Nicolas's inquiries
on her behalf. It was a full month now, and she fought a burgeoning
depression.

Certainly someone should be missing her! She belonged
somewhere, and to someone, she was certain of that. The strain of
trying to live each day as though she had purpose, while all the
while wondering if she was at odds with whatever purpose she

previously lived for, drained her.

What also drained her was her growing attraction to Nicolas.

Her intent to resist his pull had evaporated.

Every night after dinner it became their habit to enjoy long conversations in his study over glasses of port wine and brandy. By default, most of the topics concerned Nicolas and his life, but Sydney did have opinions and observations of her own. One observation she didn't share was how cathartic these discussions seemed to be for Nicolas. Every night, he grew a little more relaxed, a little more likely to laugh, a little less guarded. The door to his silent room was inching open.

Now and again Sydney convinced him to play the fiddle. That was not an easy battle, for Nicolas resisted mightily.

"I'm not talented, I don't read music well, and I'm out of practice. Which fact will you accept?"

"Not a one."

Nicolas lifted his hands in the air as if to say the matter was out of his control.

Sydney leaned toward him and waited until his gaze shifted to hers. "I've heard you play, Nicolas. And I liked it fine. If it was torture, I most certainly wouldn't be begging for more."

Nicolas considered her; squinting, deciding. "I play by ear, mostly. I only have music for a few pieces. The rest I've worked out on my own. Or create as I go along. So none of it's…" He left the sentence hanging.

Sydney leaned back in her chair and was silent for several minutes, staring into the fire. Then she turned to him again.

"Nicolas, would you please do me the honor of playing your Norwegian Hardanger fiddle for me?"

Nicolas smiled in spite of his declination.

"The most popular instrument in Norway?" she pressed, the corners of her mouth lifting. "The one on which you play two sympathetic strings at one time?"

"You're one persistent body," he complained. But he rose from his chair and retrieved the fiddle case.

He opened it, caressing the ornate instrument as he lifted it from its velvet cradle. He tuned the fiddle, though it didn't need it, and tucked it under his chin with exaggerated shrugs and head wags. Then he placed his fingertips on the neck. The bow hovered over the strings, vibrating with anticipation.

Nicolas laid the bow on the strings and drew it across.

The lone note hovered in the air, clear and strong. Soon joined by others, they danced together in a reel that tugged at Sydney's heart. Nicolas's body swayed with the rise and fall of the melody. The longer he played, the more he relaxed. Sydney closed her eyes and allowed the music to tell her all about the man.

When the song ended, Sydney opened her eyes. Nicolas's gaze was fixed beyond the study. He began another tune, and this time, she watched him play. As his body moved in time with the music, and the music moved in time with her heartbeat, Sydney found the experience so deeply intimate that she had to look away. She warmed in ways that were not familiar, and she didn't know what to think about it.

Only that a Hardanger fiddle was a mighty powerful instrument of seduction.

"Dash it," Sydney muttered as she continued to get ready for the evening event. Without knowing who she was, she wasn't free to fall for anyone. But she was made of flesh, not stone. And Nicolas was so handsome, so smart, so right in front of her every minute, and so very, very lonely.

℘ ℭ

Nicolas Hansen was a man tightly wound and he knew it. It was intentional.

He hadn't always been this way. In fact, before Lara died he was more like Rickard: loose, outgoing and spontaneous. But the night his wife died, he locked himself in the room with her body, numbed by disbelief. He asked her why—why she had to leave him. Didn't she know how much he needed her? How much he had always needed her?

He told her of his long-held dreams that were now undreamable. He cursed his inability to raise a child without its mother. He breathed the terror of living the rest of his life in solitude, without her predictable presence. He stayed beside her, moaning his sorrow until he was limp, completely spent. Until there were no tears left unshed, no words left unsaid.

When morning appeared, a tragically redefined Nicolas Reidar

Hansen stood beside the cold bodies of his life-long beloved and his stillborn son, and locked in his feelings. Then he unlocked the door, and walked out to begin existing in a life he never planned to live.

Nicolas always believed if that lock was breached, the resulting explosion of emotion would destroy him and anyone near to him. What worried him at present was how close Sydney was coming to doing precisely that.

She had quite literally dropped into his life, unbidden and through no fault of her own. As her injuries healed, her physical beauty was undeniable. But it was her inner beauty that pulled him. And her strength. Not just with Fyrste, but with her circumstances. How many women had he met in his thirty-two years who could face a situation as daunting as hers and function as well as she was? Nicolas admired her intelligence, her unique sense of humor, her willingness to help on the estate, her sincere interest in Stefan. And as they spent time together, a true friendship grew between them.

Dressing for the Ball, Nicolas saw the potential for so much more hovering on the horizon.

He wanted more.

And that scared the piss out of him.

Chapter Eleven

May 1, 1819

*N*icolas decided that he and Sydney would pick up Rickard and Lily in the Hansen landau, driven by John Spencer, and they would ride to the McGovern's May Day Ball together. That way, he could keep an eye on Rick.

Nicolas was under no misdirection as to why he and Sydney were invited so often to dine with Rickard and Lily: Lily wanted him and Rickard wanted Sydney. The problem was Nicolas didn't want Rickard to have Sydney. Truthfully, until her situation was revealed, no one should have Sydney. And that resolve was how Nicolas got through each blessed day in her company.

What surprised—no, *irritated*—him was how willing Sydney was to go. Lily's disdain was not even thinly veiled. Her jibes and cuts were rude at best, and often cruel. Of course, all of her words floated on honeyed tones and were punctuated by overly innocent smiles and batting lashes. Nicolas could only wonder how Sydney managed not to scratch the girl's eyes out.

When they reached the McGovern estate, Rickard stepped out first and handed Sydney down. Nicolas watched Rickard's eyes sweep over her perfectly fitted, seductively red dress with its low bust line and corseted waist. Sydney slipped her arm through Rickard's.

"We'll meet you inside," Rickard said, his attention never leaving Sydney. Tucked close beside his shoulder, he led her up the path to the brightly lit manor, alive with festively dressed

Missourians.

Nicolas stepped out of the landau and offered his hand to Lily while his cool gaze trailed after the other couple. When she didn't take his hand, he looked back to see what was amiss.

Lily narrowed her turquoise eyes as she poised in the doorway of the landau. Laying her small hand in Nicolas's much larger one, she didn't let go once she reached the ground. Instead, she looked up at him and squeezed her elbows inward, causing her dress to gape, and her already displayed cleavage to deepen. She lifted her hand for Nicolas to kiss.

"Shall we go in?" she purred as she snuggled under his arm.

Silent and unsmiling, Nicolas escorted Lily into the Ball.

๛ ৪

In the brightly lit ballroom, Sydney saw the men of Cheltenham huddled in one corner loudly discussing the economic climate of the country to the obvious dismay of the women they brought. Nicolas and Lily stepped close to where she stood with Rickard. His expression was lethal and she wondered why.

Ashton Caldecott was once again the source of current news. "It's now officially called The Panic of 1819. Land values are dropping everywhere. In Pennsylvania, they've gone from one hundred and fifty dollars an acre to just thirty-five now!"

"Have you still got land there, Hansen?" Lee Matthews asked.

"I do. But I've no plans to sell it." Nicolas raised one eyebrow. "Perhaps I should buy more, eh?" A few of the men chuckled.

Ashton shook his head. "In Lexington, factories worth upwards of half a million dollars are standing idle." Several men began to mutter at that.

Hearing the name 'Lexington' thrummed a chord in Sydney. She closed her eyes and tried to pin down the elusive wisp of knowledge, but it evaporated before she could grasp it.

"Sydney?" Rickard whispered. "Are you ill?"

She opened her eyes and forced a smile while her gaze shifted to Nicolas and back. "I'm fine. The news is distressing, however."

Rickard pulled her away from the group. "Let's get some punch, shall we?"

Once Rickard and Sydney broke away, other women retrieved

their men and put a stop to the dismal conversation. The general mood lifted over punch and food. A string quartet tuned up to play.

The May Day Ball evolved into a sensory kaleidoscope of color, music, food and drink. By now, most of the landowners from Cheltenham's surrounding estates had heard about Sydney's unfortunate situation. Guests greeted her, introduced themselves, and expressed sympathy along with hopes for the recovery of her memory.

Sydney was surprised to find she was a celebrity of sorts. The toasts to her health alone were taking their toll on her sobriety and she wondered if she would make it through dinner.

Rickard never left her side, always touching, reassuring or steadying her. Feeling giddy, she grinned into his amazing eyes and leaned up for a spontaneous kiss from his perfect lips.

"Madam, you're drunk," he murmured in her ear. The heat of his breath shivered down her neck and warmed her chest. "Let's step outside for some fresh air, shall we?"

Sensible that a break from the toasting was needful, she stumbled when she stepped from the paved walkway onto the manicured lawn. Rickard caught her. She sank gratefully onto an ornate iron bench and took deep breaths of the outdoor air. Rickard sat close beside her.

"Lord, you're beautiful." He nuzzled her hair.

"So are you," Sydney responded, lifting her face to his.

Rickard's lips met Sydney's in a languorous, sensual kiss that melted her insides like butter left in the hot sun. Then they moved down the trail laid out before them: throat, neck, collarbone, cleavage. Sydney hummed a sigh as his tongue tickled her skin, and she contemplated what she might do if he pressed his suit more aggressively. But to Rickard's great credit, he straightened and leaned back.

"Would you care for some fruit punch? Or perhaps tea?" His eyelids drooped and his voice was delightfully husky-sounding.

Sydney gripped the wrought iron vines that formed the arms of the bench, relieved but not a little disappointed. "Tea, please. Strong tea. Black. Thank you, Rickard."

He stood, kissed the top of her head and returned to the house.

৪০ ৫৪

Nicolas stood at the other end of the garden and watched everything that took place between Rickard and Sydney from the shadows. The longer he watched, the angrier he became, though he refused to think about precisely why that was.

Lily came up behind him and startled him out of his discontented contemplation.

"A girl might begin to believe she was forgotten," she said with a pout. "Why are you out here all alone?"

He looked down at her. "I felt the need for air."

Lily walked a slow circle around Nicolas, trailing her fingers along his waist. "Nicolas, do you find me repulsive?"

Nicolas made a face. "No, Lily, of course not!"

"Dare I hope that you might find me attractive?"

"You know—and well—how beautiful you are." Irritation defined his tone. "What game are you playing, now?"

Lily blinked rapidly and her lower lip trembled.

"Game? You call my feelings for you a game? How could you be so mean to me, Nicolas?" Lily presented her back to him, her face turned in profile. "All I want, all I've *ever* wanted, is to have the chance to make you happy."

She paused a beat. "The way Lara did."

That carefully aimed arrow struck true and Nicolas deflated with the hit. The woman in front of him was the same age as, and looked so much like, his beloved Lara when she lived, that he found it impossible to stay angry with her.

He gripped Lily's shoulder and turned her to him. "I'm sorry, Lily. I'm just not myself at the moment."

"Why, Nick? What's bothering you?" Lily leaned closer, looking up at him with full, inviting lips.

At that moment, Rickard re-emerged from the house carrying a cup. The movement diverted Lily's attention to her brother until he joined Sydney, sitting on the bench across the way. Then she rounded on Nicolas.

"Her? Her! Is that it?" Lily shrieked. Her delicate fists thumped Nicolas's chest without effect. "How could you do this to me?"

"Lily, I—"

"What do you know about her anyway? She says she doesn't remember a thing, but how do you know for certain? No one around here has ever heard of such a thing before!"

Lily warmed to her argument. Her voice grew louder and higher in pitch. "Perchance she's hiding something! Perhaps she's in trouble with the law!"

Nicolas put up his hands to quiet Lily as she spewed loud possibilities; it didn't sway her.

"Perhaps she stole something! Perhaps she killed somebody!" Lily rested one fist on her hip and jabbed Nicolas's chest with a stiff finger. "Perhaps she's a prostitute and a customer got too rough! Perhaps he dumped her in the creek afterward to hide the evidence! Did you ever think of that?"

Nicolas snorted his disdain for all of those possibilities, though he truly had no argument against them. "Lily—"

She began to cry in earnest, wiping tears with a lace-gloved fist. "Here I am, Nicolas Reidar Hansen, right in front of you! You've known me all my life. You know my whole family. You married my sister, may her soul rest in peace." Lily sniffed loudly. "There are no questions about who I am or what I've done!"

Seeing his wife's apparition so distraught broke Nicolas. He opened his arms and Lily fell against him. She hugged him tightly and stifled her sobs in the folds of his linen shirt. Nicolas didn't speak; he was rapidly sinking in quicksand and he didn't trust any of his emotions to be real.

He patted Lily's back and mumbled nonsensical phrases in a soothing monotone while his mind battled his heart. He knew she was Lily, not Lara, and his emotional response to her was a reflection of his love for her dead sister. But the quicksand was deftly swallowing the difference. He had to find a way out of it.

He wanted a drink.

He needed a drink; strong brandy and lots of it.

∞ ∞

Sydney sat in silent shock as she and Rickard overheard Lily's strident speculations.

"I'm sorry, Sydney," Rickard said after they were gone. "Lily didn't mean all that."

Sydney raised her chin and looked down her nose at him. "Yes, Rickard, she did. The question is: do you share her thoughts?"

Rickard slid off the bench onto one knee in front of Sydney. "I pledge this to you, Sydney of Cheltenham. I will uphold the rectitude of your name…" He shrugged at that, one side of his mouth curling. "Against any who would try to besmirch it. Even my baby sister. Or perhaps, especially my baby sister."

Sydney intended to remain aloof but Rickard's antics were too endearing. And he looked so handsome in the lamp light. And he smelled so good. And he brought her tea. She reached out one hand and tapped him ceremoniously on each shoulder. "Arise, Sir Rickard the Sibling Slayer. Save me from besmirchers!"

Rickard stood and pulled Sydney up beside him. He kissed her parted lips very, very well. His tongue twisted around hers and invited a response which she willingly gave. Her head was already spinning, but now she felt she was floating. Unearthed. He pressed the length of his body along hers, and she felt his strength and his dangerous sensual charisma.

When the kiss ended, he rested his forehead against hers while she caught her breath. And remembered where she was.

"Shall we dine, milady?"

"Lead on, gallant knight," she whispered.

Sydney was determined not to think about Lily. She lost herself in the food, the dancing and the wine, relishing a wide variety in all areas. Though Rickard tried to monopolize her, she accepted other dance partners. And she watched Nicolas.

He moved with unexpected grace for such a big man. Sydney closed her eyes and imagined it was his hand on the small of her back. She saw his dark blue eyes smiling down at her and she smiled in response, encouraging partners who assumed her smile was for them. Though she waited between musical pieces until the last moment, Nicolas was the one man in the room who didn't ask her to dance.

She couldn't help but notice, though, how heavily he drank. It didn't seem to affect him as much as she thought it would. Still, she noticed a bobbled step now and then, and an unfocused gaze when his attention went unclaimed.

On the other hand, Sydney was undoubtedly feeling the effects of the wine. But she didn't care. Tonight, Nicolas or no, lost memory or no, she pretended that everything in her life was perfect.

She accepted another glass of cabernet from Rickard and gulped it down before leaning into his strong, protective arms and allowing herself to be swept onto the dance floor for the last cotillion that night.

Riding home in the landau, Rickard sat close to Sydney. His thigh pressed along hers, his booted heel wedged between her feet. He leaned a little forward so that his shoulder pushed back against hers, and his arm brushed her breast with every jostle of the ride.

Rickard's casual possession of her was intoxicating, and Sydney was already quite far down that particular path. She closed her eyes and leaned into him, breathing the very male mixture of cologne, brandy and cigars. She smiled.

Chapter Twelve

*N*icolas sat across from Sydney, glaring at her, keenly sensible of Rickard's flirtation. He knew well Rickard's history with women and he was mad as *helvete* that his charms seemed to be working on Sydney. He wanted to wring both their idiotic necks.

Nicolas felt like Sydney belonged to him. It required every scrap of his precarious self-control to keep from reaching across the carriage and pulling her into his own lap. But Lily sat close and silent beside him; her hand grasping his arm the inescapable weight that held him down.

Nicolas considered Lily, then. Her half-open lips demanded his ministrations and her hand dropped from his arm to his lap. Startled by her boldness, he felt the heat of her palm and responded immediately. He shifted in his seat to adjust his suddenly uncomfortable breeches. Then he closed his eyes and kissed her, taking his time about it.

But he was imagining a red dress and dark hair.

The carriage slowed to a stop in front of the Atherton manor. When the door opened, Nicolas lumbered out and offered his hand to Lily. He helped her down and walked her to the front door. There, she turned to face him and leaned against him, slipping her hands under his frock coat and waistcoat.

Nicolas lifted her delicate face in his hands and kissed her hard. He slid one hand around her back and down to her hip. He pulled her into him as the urgency of his arousal besieged them both.

Lily pulled away from the kiss. "Nick, no."

Nicolas let go as though she burned him. He swayed in front of her with alcohol, jealousy and arousal screaming through his veins in equal portions.

"I'll not be toyed with, Lily," he growled. "Remember that!"

Seething, he turned and marched back to the landau. Throwing the door open, Nicolas bounded in and dropped heavily on his seat. Rickard broke away from their kiss. He pushed Sydney upright, away from his lap.

"Goodnight, Milady." Rickard kissed her hand and backed out of the carriage.

Both Nicolas and Sydney were silent on the ride to the Hansen manor. Nicolas stared out of the landau and nurtured his indignation. When they arrived at his home, he climbed out, helped Sydney down, then whirled and thundered into the house.

In his study, with frock coat and waistcoat successfully wrestled to the floor, Nicolas jerked open the top drawer of his desk. He grabbed the pewter flask and cursed under his breath as he uncapped it. He swallowed one healthy gulp before Sydney caught up to him.

He turned to her, vexed curiosity sloshing out of him. "Yes?"

Sydney drew a deep breath and grasped the doorjamb. "I'm leaving."

Nicolas froze, flask halfway to his lips. "What? When?"

"Tomorrow."

That made no sense. The flask lowered. "Where'll you go?"

She shrugged and didn't look at him.

"Why?" Nicolas did not feel particularly well-spoken at that moment.

Sydney swayed forward and gripped the back of a chair. "I'm in your way. Yours and Lily's. It's best if I get out."

"Mine and Lily's?" Nicolas repeated. He shook his head. Preposterous.

"I did not stutter," she enunciated.

He snorted. "Mine and Lily's! *Gud forbanner det!*"

Nicolas downed another unneeded swig of brandy. "*Hva i Guds navn* makes you believe that has anything to do with you?" He was not aware he mixed languages.

"My presence here makes it difficult for you to be with her..." Sydney's voice trailed off. She blinked slowly.

Nicolas thrust the silver flask at Sydney to punctuate his words, baptizing the rug with alcohol.

"I'll be with whomever I wish! And your presence won't stop me!" he bellowed, knowing it was a complete lie. Good God but he sounded like an ass.

Then another possibility crossed his mind and pierced his heart. The blow jolted him.

"Is it Rick?" Nicolas demanded. "Are you saying this so you can run off to be with Rick?"

"What!"

"Is that it?" Nicolas sloshed more brandy from the flask as he waved it at her. "Rickard?"

"I, as well, can be with whom I want!" she shouted.

"And you want to be with Rickard, is that it?" Nicolas slammed the flask on the desk with a clang of metal and a splash of amber liquid. "I saw how he said his goodnight to you in the landau! Indeed I did! *Gud forbanner det all til helvete!*"

"And I saw how you wished to say your goodnight to Lily!" Sydney glanced pointedly at Nicolas's groin.

They glared at each other with jaws jutted and fists clenched. Nicolas's tone was intentionally icy. "If you want Rick, go to him. I'll not stop you."

Sydney's lower lip began to quiver and Nicolas noticed even through the brandy haze. He frowned, puzzled at her response.

"And then you can have Lily." Sydney voice was oddly pinched. "That's what you want."

That was the end for Nicolas.

The lock was breached.

The explosion came.

"Damn it all to hell, Sydney!" he roared in English for her benefit. "Blasted, bloody hell!"

Nicolas began to pace back and forth, wall to wall in his study. His refuge felt like a cage. "*Gud forbanner det! Skitt!*" He stopped in front of her, towering over her. "*Helvetet med det*! I don't want Lily!"

Sydney held onto the chair and didn't cower as he expected her to. Instead she tilted her chin even higher in overt challenge. "Truly? That's most assuredly not how it appears!"

"Why *i Guds navn* would I be interested in a silly, conceited little girl?" Nicolas was so angry he was shaking. His arms waved wildly around Sydney and his voice expanded, filling the room. "I'm not looking for someone! I don't need anyone!"

He moved back a step and jerked his hands through his hair. "*Skitt!*"

Sydney looked angry enough to claw his face. She tightened her grip on the back of the chair, her whitened knuckles nearly breaking out of her skin. Her jaw clenched. Her bosom quivered. She didn't speak.

"I don't want another wife! But if I did, I'd want a strong woman! A capable woman! An intelligent woman!" Nicolas hollered as he leaned toward Sydney again. One stiff finger escaped his proffered fist. "Fully grown, beyond all the games! *Skitt!* Do you believe that sounds like Lily? Well? Do you?"

Sydney flinched at the enraged power displayed just inches from her. Nicolas noticed and retreated. He raked his hands through his hair again; frustration consumed him. Why was she so *forbannet* confusing?

In his mind he saw Sydney prancing around in those blasted breeches, her arse clearly on display. He saw her dark brown hair hanging loose to her waist before she braided it in the morning. He saw her smile, heard her laugh. He looked into her gray-green eyes.

He knew what he wanted and was absolutely terrified to say it.

Trying to both avoid and force the issue, he repeated the question, "Do you wish to be with Rickard?"

Infuriating woman that she was, Sydney turned the question around. "Are you truly claiming you *don't* wish to be with Lily?"

Nicolas stepped around the chair and grabbed Sydney by the shoulders. His fingers dug into her arms. He stared into her eyes, jaw clenched, lips pursed until he could force the words out.

"No, Sydney! I don't wish to be with Lily!" Nicolas pushed the strangled words past his aggravation. He hated that she was making him say it. Couldn't she see? Didn't she know?

"I want—no. I don't want," he faltered and willed her to read his mind.

Sydney's expression was a cross between fear and confusion. Her eyes speared his and held them.

"What I mean is, I desire—" Nicolas stopped and took a deep breath. His mouth hung open. It was his last opportunity to turn back. Powerless to do so, he was swept forward by the breach.

"—to be with you."

"Wh-what?" Sydney's knees buckled and Nicolas held her up. "Me?"

"Yes, _Gudshjelp meg._" Nicolas's anger fell away with the confession. He was an open wound, desperate for healing. "I want you, Sydney."

Nicolas bent his head to hers. Her face lifted to meet him.

The kiss distilled his world to a pair of hungry lips, and it was a larger world than he could have imagined. He had no idea how long it lasted, but it was an eternity just the same. Sydney wrapped her arms around him. She pressed her body against his and released possibilities that engulfed him.

Nicolas dropped to the carpet in front of the fireplace and pulled Sydney down next to him. His bulk dwarfed her, but he disappeared inside her embrace. His hands scooped her breasts from her dress and he lowered his mouth to cover one, then the other. Sydney wound her fingers through Nicolas's loose hair to hold his head. She moaned softly. It sounded like heaven.

Sydney raised Nicolas's lips to hers once again. As he slid his palm under her skirt, Sydney opened to allow him access.

"Oh, Sydney, _Gudshjelp meg..._" Nicolas breathed when his fingers found her. Sydney whimpered and arched her back. Her fingers plucked at his sleeves.

Nicolas rose on one elbow. Pausing in the remnant of firelight, the question was clear; his need and desire stood between them, straining against his breeches. In urgent answer, Sydney tugged at the front of her skirt, lifting it out of his way. Nicolas knelt between her legs, his shaking hands worked at unfastening his flies. Sydney reached up to help, and then she guided him, iron-hard, into her.

Nicolas filled Sydney completely with his first tentative push and he felt a quake of response radiate through her body. She lifted her hips, asking for more.

He did not need to be asked again.

Cautious at first, Nicolas soon gave himself over to the inexorable joy of joining with this particular woman. Sydney squirmed under him, meeting his movements with her own. Her breathing came in short gasps culminating in a cry as her body stiffened against his and her fingernails dug through his shirt. Nicolas let himself go then. A guttural grunt rumbled through his chest and left his body in a long, satisfied groan. He collapsed on top of her and held her in a hazy fog of bliss. For several minutes, their mingled panted breaths were all he could hear.

Then Sydney began to cry.

Small sniffles soon grew to deep, gulping sobs.

Nicolas was terrified that he had been too rough; uncaring in his desperate urgency, had he hurt her?

"Sydney? What've I done?" he rasped. "Did I harm you?"

Sydney shook her head, but she didn't stop crying. Nicolas gently pulled away from her; it almost hurt, like rending his own body. He examined the petticoat that lay beneath her. The lack of blood confirmed what he thought was true.

"You weren't a virgin," Nicolas whispered as he lay down beside her. "Did you believe you might be?"

Again Sydney shook her head. She put her arms around him and pulled him close, tucking her head under his chin. Her cheek rested against his still-hammering heart. He held her until her diminishing sobs allowed her to speak.

"I never—I mean—it's never been like that before."

Nicolas didn't move, didn't register his surprise.

"What do you mean?" he asked, though he was fairly certain he knew.

"At the end. That, that…" Sydney's face burned hot and damp through his shirt front.

"Are you saying that you never 'finished' before?" Nicolas kept his voice gentle and matter-of-fact. Sydney nodded and Nicolas hugged her closer.

"Are you certain?" he prodded. "What I mean is, you don't remember being married, do you?"

Sydney heaved a ragged sigh and her body shook with it. "No, but I can tell you this with absolute certainty: there are some things a body may not remember, but there are others that are unforgettable. If I had ever experienced that before, I would know it."

Nicolas and Sydney lay on the floor and held each other. He was unwilling to let go, lest their fragile bond be broken. When the fire finally died, he helped her to her feet in the dark, cooling room, then led her to the stairs. At the top, he hesitated, glancing at his bedroom door and then down the hall to Sydney's.

She made the decision for him. She pulled Nicolas past the room with too many memories, to the one that held no memories at all.

80 03

Nicolas awoke before dawn. He was curled around Sydney, both of them naked. He closed his eyes and thought back a few hours to the second time.

With the pounding urgency of deprivation behind him, he was able to take more time with her. They stood in the middle of her room, illuminated by fading moonlight through the opened shutters. He undressed her slowly, kissed her skin as it was exposed, and raised gooseflesh on her healed body. He let her undress him, surprised when she caressed him boldly in return.

He carried her to the bed and laid her on the white sheets, her dark hair spilling in all directions. Nicolas could see her in his mind's eye; the dark circles of her bosom and the darker thatch at the inner angle of her thighs. With slow, maddening deliberation they touched, teased and tarried, until neither one could hold any longer. Their mutual culmination left him feeling breathless and boneless, unable to move. They stayed connected, drifting into satiated sleep.

Aware he mustn't be found in her room, Nicolas pulled himself away from the warmth and comfort of her slumbering body. He felt the hollowing loss immediately. He fumbled for his discarded clothing on the floor, closed the shutters on the graying sky of dawn, and padded down the hall to his room. He dropped his clothes on a chair and climbed into his bed, idly fondling that part of him that woke up early every day.

"I should believe you would sleep late this morning," he mumbled, smiling at his joke. But his smile faded as he considered what to do next.

Making love to Sydney was not the wisest thing he had ever done, that was clear enough. While he desired her, he wasn't in love with her. Certainly she was beautiful. And she was interesting to talk with. Nicolas truly looked forward to their conversations after dinner each evening. And she possessed an admirable skill with horses, plus the confidence to wear those ridiculous breeches and still maintain her femininity. She was undoubtedly different from any woman Nicolas ever met.

But love her? No. He wouldn't love again. He couldn't. That was too big a risk.

The other, larger, reason marched in and sat heavily on his chest: Sydney might already be married. If that was the case then they had, in their alcohol-loosened arousal, just committed adultery.

Twice.

But, if she was married, why had a month gone by with no response to his inquiries? Perhaps her husband was dead. That idea hadn't occurred to him before. Had it occurred to Sydney?

Or what if he simply didn't want to be married anymore? Could he possibly keep quiet and hope she would never remember him? No. That was, in all nature's wrath, a crazy idea.

But if she didn't remember, how would she get out of this limbo?

Nicolas rubbed his eyes as the determined headache of his overindulgence lodged there. The only thing he could do was ask Sydney all these questions and see if she possessed any answers. They must talk today, and settle on how things would be between them after last night.

Nicolas rolled onto his stomach and pulled the covers over his nakedness. It was then he realized that, all the while he made love with Sydney, he had not thought of Lara once.

Chapter Thirteen

*S*ydney uncurled under the covers. She drew a deep breath and stretched like a spoiled housecat, relishing the sultry caress of the cotton sheets against her naked body.

Naked body?

Memory slapped her awake. With a cry, Sydney rolled over and threw her arm to the other side of the bed; but she was alone.

"No. Oh, no. Oh, God, no."

Please make it not be true.

The blunt, persistent pounding in her head reminded her of the dinner party and the copious amount of wine she enjoyed. The damp stickiness between her thighs reminded her of what happened later.

What have I done?

Sydney slid her fingers to her tender quim, remembering. Beautiful beyond language, desperately needful, giving and gratified, Nicolas carried her outside herself and showed her a place she had never been. It was unexpected, ethereal, consuming her in such a way that she was more whole afterward than she could have ever imagined.

But it was a mistake.

A very big mistake. She rubbed herself hard and tried to stop the wanting. She must never do it again.

Sydney considered hiding in bed and not facing him. She wondered how many hours it would take for Addie to come looking for her. Maybe she could sneak away from the estate and—what? She had no place to go.

After a quarter hour, Sydney heaved herself out of bed and collected her ball gown from the floor. With the cold water in the bedside ewer, she washed away all the physical reminders of last night's bliss. She welcomed the chill and gooseflesh; shivers of discomfort, not arousal.

The emotional reminders would require much deeper cleansing. They were branded on her soul.

Sydney dressed in the breeches and work shirt. Then she plaited her hair, squared her shoulders, and lifted her chin. With a bracing sigh of resignation, she went down to breakfast.

Nicolas sat at the table in the kitchen and he looked rough. Bloodshot eyes rose to meet her as she came through the door. The cadence of her heart missed a beat. It wanted to sprint into his arms. She had grossly underestimated the impact of facing him again.

He glanced a warning toward Addie, back turned and cheerfully chatting while she cooked the eggs.

Eggs. Sydney's stomach rebelled at the thought. She poured herself a mug of coffee and added a little milk. Ruffling Stefan's hair, she sat down next to him.

"What are your plans today, little man?" Sydney sipped her coffee and avoided Nicolas's eyes.

"Clean the chicken poop."

"You mean 'coop'," Nicolas corrected. Stefan scowled at his father.

"Chickens don't coop, they poop!" he corrected right back. Sydney laughed out loud, nearly spitting coffee.

"You're right, Stefan," Nicolas acquiesced. "My mistake."

Stefan attacked his eggs with satisfied energy. Sydney made deliberate small talk with Addie who wanted to know all about the party, relaying as much detail as she could stand to. Or remember. Nicolas rested silent at the other end of the table, mechanically forking food through stiff, colorless lips.

Sydney rose from the table, her nerves frayed like a worn rope tether and even less reliable.

"Have a good day, Addie." She patted Stefan's shoulder. "You, too, little man."

She hurried out the back door without a word to Nicolas.

∞ ∞

Nicolas half-stood, shoveled the last bite, gulped his too-hot coffee and followed Sydney out the door. He approached her in the stable while she bridled Fyrste. A saddle was on the floor at her feet.

"Do you have it in mind to mount that beast today?" were his first incredulous words to her since last night. It was not at all what he intended to say. His stomach threatened to throw his breakfast at him.

Sydney shot him a challenging look.

"Perhaps," she responded in the same tone. "Perhaps I wish to mount something myself!"

Nicolas's face grew hot. Even after what they shared last night, she was still challenging, infuriating, confusing. And he was convinced this was not how this conversation should go. Frustrated, he sat down hard on a bale of hay and dropped his thick, aching head onto the heels of his hands.

"I'm sorry, Sydney."

He heard tack jangling. "What are you sorry for?" Her tone had softened a little.

Nicolas raised his head and stared at her, his thoughts unformed. What was the right answer? When he didn't speak, Sydney faced him again. He examined her countenance and tried to gage her mood.

"It wasn't my intent to snap at you."

Her shoulders relaxed. "Apology accepted," she whispered. She rubbed her palms against her thighs. Fyrste snorted and shifted his weight.

Relieved, Nicolas pulled a deep breath and blew it out through loose lips. He managed a weak smile.

"Let's begin again."

Sydney looped Fyrste's reins around a stall latch. Then she dropped, cross-legged, in front of him. Nicolas offered one hand and she took hold of it. That was a good start.

"Last night," Nicolas began, "was..." and he fumbled. Fear squeezed his ribs and he fought to inhale.

"Wonderful," Sydney picked it up. But before he could speak, she added, "And horrible."

Nicolas held his inhaled breath, cushioning his struggling heart.

He wasn't sure what he felt.

"Well put," he finally admitted. It was, at the least, honest.

"We cannot do that again," Sydney stated with determination. "We must not do that again."

Nicolas didn't respond. Trepidation hollered at him to put distance between himself and this woman, and quickly. But longing, desire, and need pummeled his gut, bruising him toward foolishness.

"No," he pretended to agree. "Not again." He couldn't look at her. He couldn't lie, looking into her eyes.

They sat silently, holding hands. Her fingers stroked his. He wanted to kiss them. Instead, he asked her the question that occurred to him early this morning.

"Sydney, do you believe you could be a widow? That whatever—or whoever—nearly killed you might have killed him?" Nicolas watched intently as Sydney turned the idea over in her mind.

"I don't know," she admitted. "It's possible. Or I could be a run-of-the-mill adulteress." Her wry smile negated the sting of her words.

Nicolas's faint smile echoed hers. "No one's responded to the notices. It's been a month, now. Perhaps you truly don't have anyone."

Sydney's expression sank below her cheeks, pulling down the corners of her mouth. "Or perchance, whomever I had no longer wants me."

Nicolas was surprised that her thoughts followed the same line as his. He wanted to comfort her, but had no idea how. He tried, "In either circumstance it appears you have the opportunity to begin a new life."

Sydney stared at him, her brows drawing together over diluted gray eyes. "Does it?"

Startled, Nicolas realized that he was on the verge of suggesting more than he intended. He stopped and regrouped. "Of course, I've no experience to draw on… It only seems…"

He shrugged.

Sydney faced the floor. A drop of moisture darkened her nankeens. She wiped something from her cheek. She spoke so quietly, Nicolas could barely make out what she said.

"I reckon I should consider that. But I'm not certain that I'm ready just yet. I feel I must give it more time."

"How much more time?" he asked. Once again, he realized that his words hinted at things he didn't feel. Panic prodded him and he reworded his question. "I mean, how much time do you feel is right? What terms can you bide?"

"At the least three months, I believe." Sydney met his gaze with gray pools of hopeless depth. "Assuming I still remember naught, of course; and that's a truly large assumption."

"Three months," Nicolas repeated, then clarified. "You intend two more, then?"

"I'll find a way to repay you for all of this, Nicolas," Sydney said with a level of confidence her countenance did not begin to reflect. "For everything that you've done for me."

Nicolas waved his hand in a gesture of dismissal. "Sydney, that's not on my mind. Don't let it concern you. It's been my honor to assist you."

Visibly relieved, Sydney said, "Two more months, then. If I don't have answers by the first of July, then I'll begin a new life as Sydney... Something-or-other!"

Nicolas chuckled. There was that delightful sense of humor again.

"But in the meantime." Sydney paused and tightened her grip on his hand. "We truly mustn't be together again like last night. It wasn't right."

Wasn't right? Nicolas wanted to shout that it was the epitome of right! The way their bodies melded, responded; it was positively glorious! Even now he could smell her hair, taste her lips, feel her hand on him. He dove into her completely and she surfaced with him, bursting through earthly boundaries. His manhood stirred, eager. He pulled his knees together.

"Yes. We must be wise," he rasped. And he thought he couldn't lie and still look at her.

Sydney reached up to stroke Nicolas's cheek. He laid his hand over hers, and turned to kiss her palm. Then she pulled her hand from his, unfolded from the ground, and led Fyrste out of the stable without looking back.

Nicolas slumped against the stable wall. Living with her now was going to be hell.

Rickard stepped through the Hansen's kitchen door. "Hello! Is anyone at home?"

"*Onkel* Rick!" Stefan hopped off his chair threw his arms around Rickard's legs. Then he leaned way back to look up at his tall uncle. "Did you bring me somethin'?"

"I brought you this," Rickard grabbed Stefan around the waist, lifted him upside down, and slung him over his shoulder.

Stefan giggled wildly. "What else?" he squealed.

"This!" Rickard tickled his nephew. He squirmed and wiggled and his infectious laugh filled the room, all the while safe in Rickard's strong grasp.

"I—w-want—c-candy!" Stefan gasped between spasms of laughter. Rickard flipped him back over and set him on his feet. Dizzy from the sudden movement, Stefan dropped on his bottom and grinned expectantly at his uncle. He lifted open hands. Rickard reached into his pocket and pulled out a piece of peppermint.

"Finish your lunch first, understand?" Rickard admonished as he handed the treat to his sister's son. Stefan climbed back into his seat. He set the candy carefully by his plate.

"What do you say to your *Onkel* Rick?" Addie prompted.

"Thank you." Stefan's blue eyes did not leave his sweet.

But Rickard's hazel eyes shifted to Sydney.

When he appeared so unexpectedly at the door, Sydney's nerves snapped to awareness, sending urgent messages to pertinent parts of her body. The first message entailed how intimately he said goodnight to her the evening before last. The second message concerned what happened between her and Nicolas immediately afterward.

Sydney felt her gut warm and her cheeks blaze.

Rickard pulled out a chair and sat at the table. He turned to Sydney and lifted one corner of his mouth in a perfectly adorable grin.

"And how are you today, Madam? Any 'besmirchers' in sight from whom I, your humble and obedient servant, might protect you?"

Sydney conjured what she hoped was a convincing smile, and shook her head. Her mouth was glued shut by a sudden lack of moisture.

Since her appallingly wonderful night with Nicolas, Rickard was the farthest man from her mind. Sydney had not taken time to consider how her horrific actions might affect their burgeoning relationship. Flirtation aside, one thing seemed clear: Rickard was romantically interested in her. And while she hadn't professed any particular feelings for him—how could she in her situation?—at the ball she kissed him quite warmly and more than once. Of course he would be encouraged.

And now here he was, unbidden and unexpected, dribbling chameleon chocolate bronze all over her.

Skitt.

She decided to ask Nicolas to teach her to curse in Norse. It was needful.

Sydney glanced out the kitchen window and prayed that a deadly, black, screaming twister might manifest itself and provide her imminent rescue. Lacking that, she sat squarely in a tangled mess of inappropriate attractions and unknown ramifications. What sort of horrible woman might she truly be?

No wonder no one wanted her back.

Sydney looked down at her bowl of soup. Breaking off a piece of bread, she dipped it and put it in her mouth, chewing slowly.

Rickard ruffled Stefan's hair, lips pressed and brow lightly creased.

The room did darken, but it was Nicolas who manifested in the doorway. Sydney looked up from her soup and gasped.

His shirt was slung over one broad shoulder and his muscular body was slicked with sweat. Tiny wood chips covered his hair, and stuck to the skin of his arms and the blond fur of his chest. The waistband of his breeches sagged so low that the line of darkening hair, which pointed from his flat stomach downward, was clearly visible.

Rickard or no, Sydney could not look away.

"*Pappa* you been choppin' wood!" Stefan laughed. "You look like a woodchucker!"

"I have and I'm mighty hungry." Nicolas frowned as he glanced from Sydney to Rickard. "Has your *Onkel* Rick left me any food?"

Rickard stood quickly and indicated that Nicolas should take his seat. "I just stopped by to say hello. Go ahead, Nick."

Nicolas sat at the table. He glanced at Rickard as Addie set a bowl of the meaty soup in front of him, but Rickard watched Sydney. She looked away and could not force herself to watch him back.

Then Nicolas looked at Sydney. She slid the loaf of bread closer to him. Eyes now fixed on her meal, she ate another bite of soup-sopped bread, though her stomach was strongly disinclined. But she was at a complete loss for any other course of action in the inconceivably awkward presence of these two particular men.

The silence between the three adults was as taut and noisy as Nicolas's fiddle strings.

Stefan, on the other hand, thoroughly enjoyed his peppermint.

Chapter Fourteen

May 12, 1819

*B*y the end of the week, Fyrste wore a saddle and allowed Sydney to ride him in the paddock. She broached the idea of taking him for a ride around the Hansen property.

"Not alone, you're not!" Nicolas blustered.

Undaunted, Sydney suggested, "Fine, then. Come with me."

"Can I come?" Stefan asked, obviously eager to get away from his chores.

Nicolas waved his hand. "I can't, Sydney. I've a lot to accomplish today."

"It needn't be a long ride," Sydney pointed out. "And you have to eat sometime. Addie could pack us a lunch to take with us, couldn't you Addie?"

"Even so," Addie agreed.

Nicolas leaned back in his chair and cradled his coffee cup with both hands. He stared at it as though it might speak. When it declined, he shifted his gaze to Stefan.

"Perhaps another time, eh? We need to give Fyrste a chance and he might not behave."

"Please, *pappa*?"

Nicolas shook his head. "I can't take you, Stefan. If there's a problem with Fyrste, Sydney may have to ride back with me on Rusten."

"Fyrste will be good. Sydney will make him be!" Stefan insisted. "Please?"

"I said not this time!" Nicolas barked. "Don't ask me again!"

Stefan shrank and didn't provoke his *pappa* any further.

Just after noon, Nicolas saddled his sorrel gelding and packed the lunch in his saddlebags. Sydney tied a rolled blanket behind Fyrste's seat.

"Where would you care to go?" Nicolas asked once they were mounted.

Sydney shrugged. "The property line between your estate and Rickard's?"

"We shall only bide as long as you're able to control that animal. Agreed?"

"Agreed."

Nicolas rode in front. He sat straight but relaxed, reins in one hand, the other resting on his thigh. His hair was tied, as usual, but Sydney imagined it loose in the breeze. He turned to look at her. His eyes out-blued the sky even on this perfect day.

She smiled, content.

"How's he doing?" he asked. His voice wasn't chocolate. It was an earthquake. And it shook her core.

"I think he's happy," she answered. *So am I.*

In truth, Fyrste did seem as glad as she to be out of the enclosures. Head up, tail high, his ears flicked forward and back as he took in every detail of the wooded landscape. The sun darted through branches above them and played peek-a-boo with the leaf-mulched forest floor.

Comprised of ancient trees that topped forty feet or more, the forest smelled old. Under the sun-warmed aroma of young sprouts, lurked the thick reek of rotted leaves and decomposing wood. In the hollows, fungi flourished, releasing invisible spores that colored the scent of the air. New sap leeched from the bark of pine trees, adding a fresh tang and a reminder of winter.

Soon Sydney rode abreast of Nicolas. They didn't talk much, other than Nicolas pointing out the occasional landmark. But something about him was different. There weren't lines on his face today.

That was it. No tired lines. No irritated lines. No worry lines. No anger lines.

No laugh lines.

Nicolas led her to his estate's border, and they followed it along the edge of the forest. A field of ridges, with tiny green fingers stretching out of the dark earth, came close to the forest rim.

"This is the leased land," Nicolas explained. "Looks like corn this year."

Sydney's stomach growled assertively.

"Did you say something?" he teased.

Her cheeks warmed. "I reckon I didn't have as big a breakfast as I thought."

"The creek is up ahead to the left. There's a likely spot for a picnic."

When they reached the clearing they hobbled the horses. Nicolas pulled Addie's provisions from his saddlebags while Sydney spread the woolen blanket on the ground. They ate without much conversation, and then Sydney asked the question that gnawed at her.

"This isn't the creek you found me in, is it?" She looked skeptically at the idyllic brook that gurgled down the gentle slope.

Nicolas nodded and gestured with a nearly naked chicken bone. "It is, but you were upstream a ways, closer to town. Don't be fooled by how it looks now, Sydney. With the winter melt and spring rains this creek gets very nasty."

"And cold," Sydney remembered.

"And cold."

Her vocal stomach now quieted, Sydney lay back on the blanket. She watched the leaves overhead, costumed in multiple shades of green, dancing with the breeze. Nicolas tossed the chicken bone into the water, and stretched out on his back next to her. He sighed deeply and rubbed his belly.

"Lying here this way makes it seem as though time has stopped," Sydney whispered.

Nicolas rolled on his side to face her and propped his head on one elbow. "That it does."

Sydney was sensible of Nicolas's vibrant masculinity lying only inches from her. The space between them was charged, like the air before a lightning strike. Desire eddied low in her belly, and sent out ripples.

She needed a distraction. "Tell me about something."

"What do you wish to hear?" How could an earthquake be so soft and so devastating at the same time?

Sydney couldn't think of an answer. Her thoughts brimmed with how much she desired to pull Nicolas to her and do again what he did the night of the ball. She turned her face to his. Her lips parted—hoping for words—but none came out.

Instead, Nicolas kissed them.

His mouth was inquisitive at first, and then deliberate. She answered him eagerly, rent by the implicit lightning into two women. One recoiled in disgust at the wantonness of her behavior; the other knew she'd die without his touch. That need overshadowed all else.

Nicolas's arm reached to pull her closer when he halted in mid-kiss. His lips abandoned hers. He leaned back, incredulous, and looked over her shirt and breeches.

"Are you wearing a corset?"

A dousing of icy water would have been slightly less effective in killing the mood.

"Ohhh!" Sydney groaned. "Don't you believe in allowing a woman at least a modicum of dignity?"

"I—I'm just surprised," Nicolas stammered. "Taking into consideration what else you're wearing."

Sydney sat up, rested her elbows on her knees and covered her face with her hands. She could not imagine ever being as humiliated as she was at that moment. Would that dashed tornado never appear when she needed it?

"It's necessary for support," she explained from behind the stiff bars of her fingers. "I took the corset I was wearing when you found me and cut the bottom off at my waist."

When he didn't respond, Sydney glanced back at Nicolas through her splayed fingers and, seeing the confusion on his face, shook her head.

"You've never had a bosom, have you?"

Nicolas's mouth popped open, but his astonished expression didn't require explanation.

"Well, as attractive as they may be, they're rather heavy. And riding horseback is hard when the front half of you 'gees' and the rest of you 'haws'!"

Nicolas stared at her in wide-eyed shock.

And then he burst into thunderous laughter. He laughed so hard, he couldn't stop; his raucous guffaws echoed through the forest. He sat up to catch his breath, but still he laughed. He held his sides until tears ran down his cheeks, and still he laughed. He rolled to his hands and knees, pounding the blanket with his fist.

And still he laughed.

His enjoyment of the moment was so infectious that, despite her embarrassment, Sydney couldn't help but laugh with him. She wiped her cheeks on her sleeve and giggled without control.

"What a delight you are!" Nicolas wheezed. "Gees and haws! *Å min Gud!*"

And he was off again, his face red, his body shaking, tears streaming. And the more he laughed, the more Sydney laughed.

Nicolas lumbered to his feet, his laughter as yet undiminished.

"Please excuse me, madam, I must visit the trees," he managed before staggering several yards off. Sydney could hear him chortle in the distance, as well as his substantial stream splattering against dry leaves.

"Gees and haws!" he whooped again. Sydney grinned.

Nicolas returned and dropped to the blanket, still unable to regain complete control.

"Oh, Sydney—I'm sorry to have attacked your dignity." He wiped his eyes. "But I have not laughed this way in years!" And he sniggered again.

Smiling, Sydney considered the huge man sitting in front of her. His face was a mess of laugh lines now, grooved into his sunburned features. Unrestrained joy replenished as soon as he wiped it away. His navy eyes sparkled. Sydney's heart tumbled into the chasm of his delight.

Nicolas was completely at ease for the first time since she met him. She saw the man that hid behind the long-held façade of pain. For a moment, the door was wide open and his silent room blazed with light.

And then, without forethought or warning, she loved him.

The day shattered into a million blades of brilliant ecstasy and brutal agony. Her joy and horror at the realization burst outward, and neither could be contained. She felt cut to ribbons by their intensity.

Thankfully, the earlier sensual mood had now dissipated beyond recall. Sydney and Nicolas repacked their picnic, but she couldn't look at him. She knew he would see, and he mustn't see.

He mustn't be allowed to know how her world had shifted so tragically.

℘ ℘

As they continued their ride, they neared the Atherton manor. Nicolas shot Sydney a conspiratorial look.

"Would you care to show Rickard that you can sit that beast? It might be amusing."

Nicolas had so many ulterior motives in that suggestion, they could scarce be counted. Let Rick see his own horsemanship bested by this woman. Let Rick see Sydney dressed in her dirty breeches and riding astride, and perchance shock him out of his interest in her. Let Lily see that Nick didn't pine for her, but instead he relished Sydney's easy company. Let them both see how glorious Sydney looked in spite of her apparel, and let everyone see what an amazing woman rode this huge stallion by his side.

A shadow passed through Sydney's expression, but she nodded.

When they rode into the Athertons' yard, Rickard threw open the door and stepped out onto the porch. Nicolas noticed signs of Fyrste's discomfort, presumably at seeing Rickard again. Sydney dismounted quickly. She stood still on the lawn and kept a firm grip on the stallion's reins. Nicolas tied Rusten to the hitching post and took the porch steps two at a time.

"Rick!" He held out his hand. "We've missed you! We decided to come by and say hello!"

Rickard shook Nick's hand but he stared at Sydney. He turned disbelieving eyes to Nicolas.

"Can you fathom the progress she's made with that beast?" Nicolas waved a proud hand at Sydney. "I scarcely can, and I see it every day!" He thumped Rickard on the back.

"Nicolas! I thought I heard your voice!" Lily danced out the front door. She wore a rose colored dress and matching slippers; her copper-streaked auburn hair was tied in a blue ribbon that matched her eyes. She beamed up at Nicolas.

"What brings you—"

Lily stopped and faced Sydney in the stained breeches and dusty work shirt. Her jaw opened in a silent shout, then wiggled its way around to an enormous grin. And then she began to laugh.

In fact, she pointed and laughed until tears ran down her cheeks. She fanned her face, wiped her eyes and gripped her waist, gasping against her corset. That recalled to Nicolas's mind Sydney's unique, though unseen, garment.

Twice today Sydney's unconventional attire had inspired the same response, but on this occasion she did not join in the revelry. In fact, she frowned intently at the clear sky, as though she expected a storm.

"Oh my!" Lily gasped. "In all my born days, I've never seen the likes! What in heaven's name are you wearing?"

Sydney glared at her. Then she glared at Nicolas.

Rickard didn't speak. Nor did Nicolas come to her defense. He glanced from one woman to the other as his mouth flapped impotently. He finally faced Rickard, who appeared as inept as he felt.

Sydney stepped forward and deliberately tied Fyrste's reins to the hitching post. She climbed the porch steps with straight-backed, high-chinned dignity and stopped in front of the three adults.

"Good afternoon, Lily. Rickard." Her voice drooled honey. "Nicolas and I haven't seen the two of you since the May Day Ball, so we rode over here to invite you to dine with us tomorrow night. Will you come?" Sydney directed a dazzling smile at Rickard.

Rickard's gaze melted over Sydney. "We would love to! Isn't that so, Lily?"

Lily frowned.

Nicolas was surprised by the invitation. He deduced that whatever dampened Sydney's spirit the last time she saw Rickard, was now behind her. That deduction blew a cannonball hole through his belly.

He was also surprised that Lily was not as pleased by the invitation as he would have expected. While that was puzzling, it was of no consequence.

"Wonderful!" Sydney oozed. "We shall expect you both at candlelighting tomorrow, then."

"I am—that is, we're looking forward to it." Rickard returned Sydney's smile.

Sydney turned and walked regally down the porch steps to the hitching post.

Nicolas followed her willingly, though a scowl pressed his

brow down. This visit did not end in any way in the same manner it began. What flipped it around?

Fyrste was skittish, not pleased with being mounted again. Sydney bent over and checked his shoes. She raised her face to his.

"May I ride with you, Nicolas?" Her eyes begged him for an affirmative answer. "It seems Fyrste has picked up a stone."

Without a word, Nicolas jerked a nod and gave Sydney a leg up into his saddle. He looped the stallion's reins around Rusten's saddle horn, and then mounted behind Sydney. He forced a pleasant expression and tone.

"See you tomorrow night, then!" He waved at the pair on the porch. Sydney waved as well.

Nicolas urged Rusten to an easy canter across the green manicured expanse. Once out of sight of the manor, Nicolas slowed the horses to a walk.

"So, do you mind telling me what the *helvete* that was all about?" he demanded.

Sydney presented a tentative profile. "Uh, which part in particular?"

"Let's start with the invitation to dinner."

Nicolas entertained the uncomfortable notion that Sydney manipulated the afternoon to end up this way, so she could arrange time with Rickard. Never mind that the visit to the Athertons' was entirely his suggestion.

"Lily humiliated me and I felt the need to redeem myself. All I could think of was to turn the other cheek. Inviting them to dine with us was the first idea that came to mind."

"It's not your place to do so."

The profile was replaced by a black braid and a stiff back. "Well *some* one needed to do *some* thing."

Nicolas clenched his jaw. Embarrassment washed through him; an emotion he was unaccustomed to and didn't know how to deflect. He reviewed the conversation until he unearthed his failure.

Lily's attack. He didn't defend Sydney. And to make it worse, he mistrusted her motives.

But he didn't know what to say to her.

"I'm sorry, Nicolas, if I did overstep."

Her brusque apology startled him out of his mortified silence.

"No, Sydney," he said in her ear. His lips brushed against her neck. "I'm the one who must apologize. You were right to act the way you did." He tightened his hold on her waist. "I'm sorry."

After a minute or two, she relaxed against him. "Accepted," she whispered.

He enjoyed the feel of her weight against his chest. "Did Fyrste really have a stone?"

The words poured out of her. "No. He was tired of being ridden. And I believe he got nervous when he saw Rickard. But after what occurred with Lily, I couldn't bring myself to say that I wasn't able to ride him. So I concocted the stone story."

Sydney twisted around and looked Nicolas in the eye. "If you wish to put me down, I could try him again."

"No, it's quite alright. We're almost halfway home. We'll give the poor animal a break; after all, he's had a big day."

"You don't mind?"

"Not in the least."

Besides, Nicolas could think of nothing more pleasant than riding on a beautiful afternoon with this particular woman's bountiful arse planted firmly between his thighs.

Chapter Fifteen

May 13, 1819

*A*ddie ordered Maribeth to butcher three chickens and check the vegetable garden for ripe produce. She sent Stefan into the woods to find mushrooms for the sauce and wildflowers for the table. John was to bring up three bottles of the best wine from the root cellar.

Sydney stared at the mirror, squinting, evaluating. Tonight, she needed to be absolutely incandescent if she hoped to erase yesterday's humiliating portrait. The mirror agreed that her dark hair, paired with a low-cut black velvet bodice, provided a striking contrast for her fair skin. And her eyes glowed more green than gray next to the black. She laced the burgundy and black skirt, pinched her cheeks and bit her lips. Then, she shifted her bosom in her shortened corset to create higher swells and deeper cleavage.

This thing with Lily had become war.

Sydney heard Nicolas greet their guests. Borrowing the trick Lily used, she hesitated before descending the stairs. The amazed looks on both men's faces confirmed that her efforts had not gone to waste. And if they hadn't, the combustion of dismay on Lily's said it all.

Sydney crossed to Rickard and extended her hands. She greeted him with a warm kiss on his cheek before turning to Lily.

"I trust you find my attire tonight suitable to the occasion?" Her voice evidenced amusement. "And I must say, you look lovely yourself, Lily."

"Yes. I m-mean, thank you," Lily stuttered.

Addie's table was beautiful, her dinner delicious. Nicolas was generous with the wine and Rickard effused over the vintage. Sydney's conversation captured both men's attention. By the time dessert was served, Lily sat silent and scowling in her chair.

"It's decent weather out, Rick. Shall we enjoy our brandy on the porch with a couple of cigars?" Nicolas suggested.

"You know me well, brother. After you?"

Lily remained seated, a pleasant look now smeared on her face, as the men ambled out of the dining room. Sydney helped Addie carry dishes to the kitchen. When she returned, Lily's pleasant look was gone.

"What do you think you're doing here?" The battle had begun.

"Why, whatever do you mean, Lily?"

Lily tossed the first missile. "I suppose you still 'do not remember' your name?"

"No. Why do you ask?" Sydney deflected.

"You still 'do not remember' where you live?"

"No. I don't."

"And, I suppose you'll claim that you 'don't even know' if you're married!"

That grenade landed true. Sydney flinched inwardly and her gaze faltered but she shook her head, no.

Lily stood and walked around the linen-topped battlefield, stopping in front of Sydney. One hand rested on her hip, the other stabbed the table with a bayonet-finger.

"I don't believe that 'lost memory' story for a single dashed moment. What are you really after?"

"Nothing!" Sydney cried. "What do you believe I'm after?"

Lily wrinkled her nose in a disgusted pout. "Nicolas, of course! Or perchance his money?"

Sydney was incredulous. "Are you, in all seriousness, suggesting that I nearly killed myself in order to be noticed by Nicolas? For the sake of money?"

"It would be worth it, if you got what you came for."

Silence your weapons, foolish girl. "I had never once heard of Nicolas Hansen until the day I woke up in this house."

"Oh really, madam?" Lily's sarcasm blazed. "And how do you know?"

"It's God's truth. Ask Addie! She had never seen me before!"

"That signifies nothing, and you know it well!"

Sydney's fuse was very close to Lily's fire. "Lily, what is it that you want?"

Lily stepped back, surprised. "I want what's rightly mine!"

"And that is?"

"Nicolas!"

"And in what manner am I preventing you from having him?"

Outflanked by the question, Lily blinked blue sparks at Sydney. "You, you are... here. You're living in his house!"

The fuse leaned toward the flame. "And?"

"And—and who knows what temptations you are dangling in front of him!"

The fuse caught.

It smoldered, slow and dangerous. Sydney stiffened and looked down at the younger woman. "Listen to my words, Lily, and listen well. Nicolas is a grown man with a fine, strong mind. He has given no indication that he has any interest in anyone. But if it comes to that, be assured he shall choose whom he pleases. But I warrant you this..."

Sydney burned closer and Lily cowered. "You would do well to stay out of my way, Lily. For aught you know, I could be hiding something."

Her eyes narrowed. "Perchance I'm in trouble with the law; perhaps I'm a prostitute?"

Her palms moved to her hips. "Perhaps I stole something; or perhaps..."

Sydney's bomb exploded. "I killed someone."

It was a perfect hit. Lily's face paled and she fell back. The hand that covered her mouth trembled.

Sydney straightened and smoothed her skirt. She smiled at Lily with her lips, but not her eyes. "I'm going outside to join the men. Are you coming?"

Sydney twisted slowly and quit the battlefield, triumphant.

May 16, 1819

Sydney rode Fyrste bareback across an expansive, moonlit meadow. He galloped with a slow, easy rhythm that rocked her forward and back. His mane, his tail and her long black hair whipped around her in the breeze she knew was there, but couldn't feel. She was naked.

Sydney looked down, and it wasn't Fyrste, but Nicolas below her, on his back. Her hands no longer held reins, but were palm-to-palm with his, their fingers intertwined. Her knees didn't grip the flanks of the stallion, but Nicolas's instead. He moved below her in the same slow rhythm, rocking her forward and back as he pushed himself fully into her.

Sydney pitched the bedclothes off, panting, her body filmed with sweat.

This sparse room was now her prison. Since May Day, shades of Nicolas tortured her every time she slipped into sleep. She imagined that she could feel his breath in her hair. His mouth on her skin. His heaviness pressed into her.

She touched herself there; her body was damp and eager. Her belly quivered deep inside, and tendrils of desire unfurled outward, grasping, hungry. If she had known what exquisite pleasure he offered, might she have chosen differently that night? Knowing, but not having, consumed her. Is this how Eve felt after biting the apple?

If only she were still ignorant.

Sydney climbed out of bed and opened her door. Tiptoeing into the moonlit hall she met silence, no one else stirred. Relieved, she descended the stairs, quick and silent on bare feet, and eased out the front door. Wearing only her chemise, she stepped into the cool night air. She crossed the porch and leaned against one of its stone columns.

Sydney raised her chin to face the night breeze as it lifted the ends of her hair and enticed them to dance wickedly around her shoulders. The stone floor was cold and she curled her toes against the chill. She waited for the night to absorb the heat of her arousal.

She was doomed.

Nicolas resided in her heart. He didn't wish to be there, and she hadn't invited him in. But there he was. She had no family, no income, no home. If she left him, how would she live?

Father in Heaven, what am I going to do?

She gazed at the yard, blue and frosted silver by moonlight. The surrounding forest was black with shadow. Leaves whispered to each other as the breeze danced with them as well. The ghostly call of an owl preceded the dry, grassy swish of its attack. As the predator flew by the house, prey dangling from its beak, Sydney felt an uncanny kinship with the doomed rodent.

An earthquake rattled the night: "You were unable to sleep as well?"

Sydney spun and crossed arms over her bosom. "Oh, my Lord! Nicolas! You frightened me!"

"Forgive me, Sydney. It wasn't my intent. Are you ill?" He sat in a large wooden chair tucked close to the house. He, too, was barefoot and wore only loose drawstring breeches.

Sydney shook her head, feeling her heat rise again. "No. I had a dream that… woke me up."

"About your life? About who you are?"

"No, nothing of that sort."

"Ah." Nicolas gazed at an empty crystal glass in one hand. With a deep sigh, he set it down on the floor, and stood.

Sydney's gaze caressed his strong shoulders, powerful chest and broad waist, all painted pale indigo by the moon's reflection. Nicolas stopped in front of her. Sydney turned her back to him.

"It's a beautiful night." She was completely unnerved by his nearly naked proximity. She clenched her fists, pushing nails deep into her palms for penance.

"That it is."

He was so close she could smell the brandy he had enjoyed and the sunburn on his skin. There was something else, an earthy male scent that churned the depths of her. She recognized it; she smelled it in his bedroom.

The breeze flirted around them. It playfully disheveled their hair, molded the inadequate fabric of their clothing to them, and then plucked it away again.

Nicolas combed his fingers through Sydney's mane. "Your hair is beautiful. It shines even in the moonlight."

Stop that. "It's too straight."

"Straight and heavy, dark like Fyrste's tail. When you ride him, you look like part of him." As Nicolas described the imagery from her dream, Sydney half-believed he could read her mind.

She knew full well all the reasons why she should resist him. Nicolas didn't care about her, and she'd be foolish to think he did.

Opening herself to any possibilities with him could only hurt her.

And she wasn't a virgin; she had lain with a man before. If she trusted her gut, that man would have been her husband. Who was he? More importantly, where was he?

And what about Rickard? They called each other 'brother.' She mustn't come between them.

Nicolas continued to stroke her hair, causing her skin to pucker with pleasure. *Please, stop that.*

"You're beautiful in the moonlight," he whispered.

Sydney looked over her shoulder. His navy eyes were black in the dark. His silvered hair was tucked behind his ears. He was inches from her. She was powerless to stop herself.

Sydney uncrossed her arms as she slowly turned around. Nicolas encircled her and his lips possessed hers. He lifted her and she wrapped her legs around him. She felt his hardness through flimsy fabric. Terrified, she broke away from the kiss.

"Nicolas, we cannot. We mustn't. We mustn't join again."

His answer was to kiss her again. His mouth held the intoxicating taste of the brandy and her head spun in the most distressing and pleasant manner. A remnant of sanity punched her in the chest.

She stopped him again and stammered her protest. "We're not married... I mean, I might be married... But we're not married... to each other."

Nicolas set Sydney down. Amazingly, her legs held her up. He rested one hand on the pillar and leaned over her, a seductive canopy. She felt his warm breath in her ear and the heat from his body burned her cheek.

"Would you prefer me to leave you alone, Sydney?" he rumbled.

She faced the ground. "I believe—I believe you should."

"That's not what I asked you."

Sydney winced, fighting with any defense she could rally. "It's not right."

"Why?"

"It might be adultery."

"And it might not be."

Sydney's resolve was crumbling under his onslaught.

"At the very least, it is fornication," she whispered.

Nicolas's lips brushed her ear in answer.

"Please, Nicolas," was all she could manage.

"I'll not force you, Sydney. I'm not that sort of man." He inhaled deeply; the tip of his nose tickled her temple. "But I do desire you. I'm certain that much is quite evident."

Sydney couldn't breathe and she was afraid she might faint. Or worse, give in. She put her hands on Nicolas's chest and pushed past him. She ran to the front door, yanked it open, and escaped through it.

ℰℴ ℭℬ

Nicolas heaved a deep sigh and ran his hands over his face and through his hair. He pushed her too hard. He knew it, but he couldn't stop himself. Memories of their night filled his dark hours and he ached to have her again, right or wrong.

Padding across the porch to pick up the brandy glass, he went to his study and generously refilled it. He was a lightning bolt ready to strike; he needed the alcohol and cool air outside to diffuse him.

The brandy was gone when the front door opened again. Nicolas lifted a guarded gaze to the woman who stood in front of him. Pale skin, white shift, a shroud of black locks; her eyes absorbed the moonlight and gave nothing back.

She was not smiling and she did not speak.

Nicolas stood slowly, afraid she would leave again. "We don't need to join," he offered.

Her head tilted. She was listening.

He stroked her arm with his knuckles. "There are other ways."

Her head tipped back and she frowned. "Other ways?"

He waited.

"What other ways?"

"I'll show you." He reached for Sydney and her arms welcomed him once more. Their kiss triggered his lightening. He needed to stay in control, or he would destroy her.

Nicolas sat on the bench and effortlessly pulled Sydney across his lap. His mouth went to her bosom through the thin cotton shift, leaving wet circles. His hand slid between her legs.

Nicolas knew well what he was doing. His work-calloused hands were capable of very tender touch. Sydney breathed a long moan. He kissed her, his tongue imitating his fingers.

Soon, Sydney gasped and squirmed in his arms. Her hips jerked and pressed against his hand. With a choked cry, her body stiffened. She tightened her arms around Nicolas as the explosion of pleasure shook through her. When she collapsed, limp in Nicolas's cradling embrace, her breath came in uneven bursts.

"Was that satisfactory?" he whispered.

Sydney's face was pressed against his neck, her arms still looped around his shoulders. She nodded.

Her words tickled his throat. "What about you?"

Sydney must feel his hardness beneath her. He felt ready to burst.

"Another time," he replied, and gave her a little shove. "You go on up now." Sydney slid off of his lap. "Good night, Sydney. Sleep well."

"Are you coming in?"

"In a bit. You go on ahead."

Sydney leaned over and kissed Nicolas, then slipped back into the house. After a few quick strokes, Nicolas finished. Relief loosened him, but satisfaction eluded his grasp.

He went inside, to his bed, alone.

Chapter Sixteen

May 22, 1819

*L*ast week's midnight tryst with Nicolas didn't help matters in the least. On the contrary, it made Sydney want him, and what he could do for her, even more than before.

Furious at both her yearning for Nicolas and her weakness in seeking him out, Sydney sat by a window in the upstairs hall and took out her anger on the wool she carded. Her vigorous strokes of the hatchel tore at the washed fleece again and again. Her muscles burned with the deliberate self-flagellation. She sweated with the effort in spite of the cross-breeze that made her choose this particular spot for her task.

Sydney paused, panting, and looked out the window. Nicolas strode toward the house. In one hand he carried a milk bucket, and in the other he cradled what appeared to be a large ball of dirty fuzz. Curious, Sydney set the wool aside and skipped down the stairs. She reached the kitchen in time to see Nicolas set the bucket of milk on the table. The fuzz turned out to be a tiny lamb. Nicolas looked up when Sydney bounced into the room.

She gasped, alarmed to see blood on Nicolas's shirt. "What's happened? Are you all right?"

"I'm fine. But a wolf got this one's ewe." Nicolas looked blankly around the room, then pulled a handkerchief from his pocket. "His pelt will bring a good price, however."

"Poor wee thing," Sydney murmured as the frightened lamb bleated weakly.

Nicolas sat at the table and dipped his handkerchief in the pail of milk. He pushed it into the lamb's mouth. Confused at first, it mouthed the fabric and found food. He began to suck. Nicolas repeated the process, holding the baby on his lap. Sydney watched in fascination as the huge, bloodied predator nurtured the tiny, helpless creature. The contrast grew sharper when Stefan appeared at the back door.

"*Pappa!* A baby lamb!" he exclaimed, his eyes wide. "Can I keep it? Please, *pappa?*"

Stefan leaned against Nicolas and petted the lamb. His earnest blue eyes searched the adult pair they echoed.

Nicolas dipped the cloth again. "Stefan, he may not live. Cow's milk isn't meant for sheep."

"I know, *Pappa*. But he will."

"Stefan." Nicolas paused and looked into his son's eyes. "He's food."

Stefan frowned. "What?"

"Why do we have sheep, son?"

"For wool." Stefan focused on the lamb in his father's lap. He did not face his father.

"And?"

Stefan's lower lip stuck out and the corners of his mouth dipped.

"Stefan? Look at me." Nicolas's deep voice was unusually gentle. Somber blue eyes rose to his. "Can you answer me?"

Stefan's voice was barely audible. "For food, *Pappa*. For the people."

"That's right."

Both were quiet. Nicolas looked at his sad son. Then he looked at Sydney.

Confusion and helplessness defined his expression, as if he wanted to give in to his son but didn't know how. What could she say to him? The decision wasn't hers to make. She shrugged and tried to convey her support with a small smile.

"But…" Nicolas paused. He frowned.

Stefan picked at his father's sleeve. "But what, *Pappa?*"

Nicolas shook his head slightly, then continued. "If you want to take care of him, and be serious about it, I reckon I could let you try."

"Really?" Stefan began to bounce.

"Listen to me, son."

Stefan's eyes locked on his father's.

"We won't try to save this one's life because he's a cute baby animal that we want for a pet, but because he's our livelihood. We'll get wool from him, and we'll either let him service the ewes or we'll butcher him for meat. Do you understand?"

"Yes, *Pappa*." The bouncing increased.

"If he lives, we can decide later."

Stefan nodded enthusiastically, sending his wavy auburn hair flying everywhere.

"It won't be easy, now," Nicolas cautioned. "There's a lot of work to do, caring for an orphaned animal."

"Show me."

"Sit down on the floor."

Stefan dropped cross-legged in the middle of the kitchen and Nicolas settled the lamb in his lap. He set the milk bucket next to Stefan and handed him the handkerchief.

"Soak it in the milk, and then give it to the lamb to suck on. Be careful to keep it wadded up so he doesn't swallow the fabric and gag on it. Do you understand?"

Stefan was the epitome of responsible concentration as he followed his father's instructions. After a few tries, he accomplished it very well. Nicolas stood and turned to Sydney, who remained quiet by the kitchen door so as not to disturb the atypically tender father and son interaction.

"I need to skin the wolf, and butcher the ewe. Tell Addie there'll be fresh chops for dinner."

"I shall," Sydney assured him.

With a wink, Nicolas disappeared out the back door.

May 27, 1819

The sound of his bedroom door as it creaked open, then clicked closed, woke Nicolas from a dreamless sleep. He opened his eyes to see a white ghost with long dark hair float around the foot of his bed. He rolled onto his back and watched the apparition.

Outlined only by starlight that ventured through his bedroom windows, the ghost hesitated, and then slid onto its knees over the covers of his bed. As the wraith moved closer, its warmth belied its spectral appearance. A catch in its breathing made Nicolas reach out to it.

"Is something amiss, Sydney?" he whispered.

He felt her shake her head. Her hot cheeks were damp.

"Sydney? What's happened?" Nicolas sat up as alarm shot through him. "Have you remembered something?"

She shook her head again. Nicolas relaxed against the headboard, bemused. He fumbled in the dim light for her trembling hand, and waited for her to tell him.

She cried quietly. One arm moved in constant wiping motions timed by regular sniffs. Quivering gasps marked the minutes.

Nicolas's concern deepened. He cared for Sydney; there was no point in denying that. She was now a fixture in his days. Her presence at meals and in his study at night became pleasant interludes in a life that had been devoid of pleasantry for a very long time. Her wordless tears warned him that things were about to change. And change scared him.

"What sort of horrible wanton must I truly be?" she croaked suddenly.

"Wanton?" Nicolas repeated, confused. "What are you talking about?"

She sniffed and wiped again. "To come crawling to your bed, unbidden, of course."

"Is that all it is?" Doused by equal parts relief and arousal, the contrasting emotions battled for dominance.

"How can you say that? Don't you understand?"

He squeezed her hand. "No."

"It's so completely wrong!" Sydney blurted.

She attempted to pull her hand from Nicolas's but he held tight. He had no answer to that. And his rampant desire for her was not helpful.

"And I'm all to pieces ashamed that I'm not able to keep myself from doing so!" Sydney disappeared inside a cacophony of shoulder-shaking sobs. She was broken, beaten by the sensual need he had unwittingly awakened.

It wasn't his fault; their assignation was unplanned. And even so, how could he anticipate her unusual response? Nicolas pulled her close, using physical strength to align her resistant body along his. He tucked her head against his shoulder and rested his chin on her hair to keep it there. He waited for her to tire of fighting him. He waited until she succumbed to the inevitable.

"It's a powerful thing, Sydney," he whispered. "Not everyone experiences it, you see; not even all husbands and wives." He winced, but Sydney did not respond to that unintentionally revealing statement.

After a long shuddering pause, she murmured, "I don't know all about myself, that much is true. But I do feel certain that I'm not the kind of woman who beds multiple men on a regular basis."

Nicolas nodded against her head. After her reaction to their first copulation, that was a very safe bet.

Sydney's voice was muffled as she curled against Nicolas. "I can't imagine what you must think of me."

At that, Nicolas retreated and rolled on his side to face her, though it was too dark to see her features.

"What I think of you?" He unerringly brushed tears from her cheeks. "My dearest Sydney, I think—no, I *know* that you're a warm, passionate and caring woman. You were created to love and be loved. I don't think badly of you at all."

"But, Nicolas, that's intended for marriage."

"Consummation is intended for marriage, I'll not argue with you there. We did err in that, to be certain."

They rested for a pace, quiet again. His body, pressed solidly against hers, seemed to calm her and he thought she had finally stopped crying.

"But what you did on the porch that night; that wasn't consummation," she ventured.

"No."

"And it wasn't fornication?"

"No. How could it be? I didn't enter you."

Sydney whispered, "But it was quite intimate."

"Very." Nicolas smiled at the memory. His arousal, dimmed by Sydney's tears, brightened again.

Sydney drew a deep breath. "Was it a sin, Nicolas?"

Nicolas thought about that for a while. "I don't know for certain, Sydney. To some it might be. But if I was to be honest? I would say it was an amazing gift."

Sydney melted against Nicolas. His words hung in the air

between them, full of opportunity. She began to comb her fingertips through the curls on his chest, raising gooseflesh. His desire for her set his skin on fire.

Nicolas spoke his impending nightmare into Sydney's ear. "I won't touch you again, if that's what you prefer."

Moisture on his shoulder indicated she might be crying again. "I'm so confused, Nicolas. I want... what I don't want... to want."

Nicolas kissed her forehead. A compromise might help. "Would it be easier if, on occasion, I paid a visit to your room?"

Sydney hesitated.

He knew a 'yes' meant she held every expectation that she would be physical with him again. Could she admit that? Or was he pushing her too far? And what would he do if she said 'no'?

He'd spend a lot of nights out on the porch with his prick in his hand.

At last, her nod bestowed his relief.

"I'll not press you, Sydney, should you ever say 'no.' And I promise we won't join again. Will that do?"

Sydney hesitated, then nodded again.

Relieved, Nicolas slipped his hand to that most desirable of places; with a throaty hum, she opened for him. Suffused with her sensual warmth, he did not have care about what anyone might think about it.

May 28, 1819

"I need to go to church."

Nicolas turned to Sydney, eyebrows raised in surprise. "Do you? All right." He handed her a glass of wine. "The preacher comes this Sunday, in fact."

"What sort of church is it?"

"Lutheran." Nicolas sat, as always, in his favorite leather chair. Habits kept him from having to think about his life.

Sydney contemplated the deep burgundy wine. "I'm Catholic."

Nicolas leaned back and considered her. "You're a Papist?"

"I believe so."

"Hmm." Nicolas sipped his brandy, careful not to reveal too much of what he thought about that.

"Do you believe I could go anyway? To the Lutheran service, I mean?"

"Well, seeing as how it's the only church in the township, they cannot be exclusionary about who attends, then, can they?"

"I reckon not."

"Very well, we'll go on Sunday."

"You'll go, as well?"

Sydney's surprise was unexpected and Nicolas took a bit of offense. "What's that meaning?"

"I didn't mean aught by it. It's just that, well, have you gone lately? I mean since you found me?"

"Once. The Sunday after Lily's dinner party. The preacher comes but every other week, after all, and I didn't go the morning after the May Day Bal—" Nicolas clipped the word short and wished to God he could pull *those* particular words back out of the air.

"I'm sorry, Nicolas, I wasn't aware." Sydney blushed, her cheeks matching her wine.

Nicolas waved his hand as if to erase the comment. "It's all well and good, Sydney. We'll go this Sunday. Together."

"Do you believe the preacher would hear my confession?"

Nicolas spit brandy. He pulled his handkerchief from his pocket, wiped his shirtfront and looked at Sydney like she had just asked if she might set his hair on fire.

"Do you know anything about the Lutherans?" he asked, incredulous.

"I'm not certain…"

"Have you heard of Martin Luther? His 'Ninety-five Theses on the Practice of Indulgences' against the Pope?" Nicolas expounded.

Every inch of Sydney looked so stricken that he immediately regretted the way he responded. He tried another tack.

"Sydney, anyone is welcome in the church, but there are some Papist practices that Lutherans don't hold to."

Sydney dropped her eyes to her wineglass. She didn't ask which practices those might be.

"But if you have concerns, I'm certain the preacher will talk with you and pray for you," Nicolas continued, hoping it was helpful. She nodded. Apparently it was.

Chapter Seventeen

May 30, 1819

*S*ydney stood outside the schoolhouse-cum-church staring at the door. Panic gripped her and she had no idea why. The building felt dangerous, as if it waited for her to enter to destroy her. Her pulse sped up and she had the urge to bolt.

Bunkum. It's naught but wood and shingles.

She took a deep breath, tightened her grip on Nicolas's arm, and walked inside. The room looked familiar; but then it looked just like every other territorial meeting room, she reasoned. So why wouldn't her heart slow down and give her some peace?

Nicolas escorted her to a pew in the rear. She sat next to him with her back straight, stiffened against the unexplained threat.

"I wonder if the service will be familiar to me?" she murmured.

He shrugged.

Still, she couldn't shake an oppressive inkling of illicit sexual activity. It must be her own guilt over Nicolas, she decided. This was a children's schoolhouse, for Heaven's sake.

To her great relief, Sydney enjoyed the service. She closed her eyes and lost herself in the hymns, the prayers and the message. And she enjoyed Nicolas's bass voice singing harmony beside her. The earthquake had a fine sense of pitch.

When the service ended, several parishioners made a point to greet Sydney and express their pleasure at seeing her again. Lee Matthews was among the last to say hello. Fanny rested in the pew, her hand on her abdomen. Sydney approached her.

"Hello, Fanny. How are you feeling?"

"Not very well, I am afraid," Fanny winced.

Some certainty inside Sydney slipped into place. "Where does it hurt?"

"Here," Fanny held the bottom of her swollen belly.

"May I?" Sydney rested her hand on Fanny and felt her stomach tighten. Fanny whimpered in response.

"Fanny, what you're feeling are birth pains."

Fanny's eyes slammed wide open. "Now? Here? Oh, my Lord!"

Sydney leaned toward Fanny and waited until the girl's panicked eyes met hers.

"There's nothing to be afraid of. I'll tell Lee to take you home and have Nicolas fetch the midwife."

Sydney had no idea if that was possible, but it did calm Fanny. She hurried over to Lee and whispered in his ear. He sprinted to his wife's side, his face gone white as a full moon. Sydney joined Nicolas and the pastor.

"Hello, Miss Sydney. It's a pleasure to meet you." Pastor Fritz Mueller was a trim man in his mid-forties. His gray hair had almost completely disappeared, but a few hardy strands held their ground. "How might I help you today?"

"Well first off, I must ask Mr. Hansen to fetch the midwife for Mrs. Matthews."

Nicolas spun around as Lee helped Fanny through the church door. His cheeks retreated into his jaw and his face paled to match Lee's.

"Nicolas?"

Nicolas shifted his dark gaze back to Sydney. "What?"

"Her pains are quite strong and Lee is taking her home. There is a midwife in Cheltenham, isn't there?"

Nicolas nodded.

"Might you fetch her?"

"No. No, I can't." He looked around the remaining church crowd. "Is Rick here?"

"I believe he left... Nicolas? What's going on?"

"I can't go for the midwife. Send someone else."

Sydney's jaw dropped. "Are you serious?"

Nicolas's stony expression was as serious as she'd seen it. "Jess! Margaret!" he called out.

The Browns crossed the emptying room. "Hello, Nick. Sydney," Jess nodded in greeting.

Nicolas sat down hard on a pew. "Fanny Matthews needs the midwife."

A puzzled Margaret looked to Sydney. She relayed her brief conversation with Fanny to the couple, ending with her offer to send Nicolas for the midwife.

"Oh! Of course, Nick. I'll go fetch her off the reel." Jess tugged Margaret to the door and they were gone.

Sydney stared at Nicolas. His sculpted features were set hard; his skin had gone from pale to flushed. She sat on the pew beside him. Something was very wrong.

"Go talk to the pastor," he growled.

She rested her hand on his arm. "Are you ill?"

"Go. I'll be fine." He pushed her decidedly away from him.

She squelched her exasperation for the moment. After all, that was her reason for being here.

Fritz Mueller listened while Sydney confessed her transgressions during the past two months. He expressed concern at what he heard, but the confidentiality of his position prevented him from interfering. Then he bowed his head, rested his hand on Sydney's shoulder, and prayed with her.

Nicolas waited in the pew where she left him. "Have you finished here?" he asked when she approached.

"We have." Sydney faced Pastor Mueller. "Thank you, Father."

"God bless you, Sydney."

Nicolas didn't speak at all on the ride back to his estate, giving Sydney far too much time to wonder what in particular had unnerved the man so.

June 14, 1819

June sauntered in and the weather grew steadily warmer and wetter. Fanny delivered a healthy boy but Nicolas never mentioned his odd reaction when he gave Sydney the news. She didn't press him on it. It was too hot to risk starting any argument.

He was able to ride Fyrste now, and she had to let him. Deprived of her regular task, she wandered somewhat aimlessly around the Hansen grounds, and searched without success for a reason to get up each morning.

Stefan's lamb lived. He named it Wolf because it survived the attack on its mother. The lamb did not thrive on cow's milk, so Nicolas bought a nanny goat from Rickard. Now healthy and growing, Wolf followed Stefan all around the estate, his tail wagging a frantic salute. Watching the unlikely pair was one thing that did make Sydney smile.

Unfortunately, there was still no word from any quarter concerning a missing woman, and no significant gains in her memory. Her life had no direction and she floated through her days adrift as a rudderless ketch. The situation so depressed her, that Sydney took to her bed and slept through the hot, humid Missouri afternoons. She felt sluggish and unwell. Even Nicolas commented that she looked pale and her appetite was quite diminished.

One night at dinner, he presented an idea.

"St. Louis?" she repeated. "Why do you wish to take me to St. Louis?"

"Well, I haven't been there myself in quite a while and I believe it might be a good diversion. We could buy supplies for the estate, go to dinner, perchance there'll be a play or an opera. What do you think?"

Sydney considered the excursion truly might lift her from the funk she'd fallen into. "How long would we be gone?"

"Well, it's just over ten miles, a two-hour carriage ride, or so. Two, perhaps three days, if we see a reason." Nicolas reached out to take her hand. "Are you up to it, Sydney? I'm a bit worried about you. You haven't been yourself lately."

Sydney didn't jerk her hand from his grasp, though his thoughtless words made her want to tear around the room, naked and screaming. Of course she hadn't been herself! Didn't he understand? She didn't know who 'herself' was!

Instead, she inhaled a steadying breath, determined not to verbally eviscerate her benefactor. At least, not until after the proposed journey.

"A trip to St. Louis sounds wonderful. I only have one request."

"And that is?"

"Might we take the wagon instead of the landau? I don't believe I could stand two hours in this heat in a closed conveyance." It made her nauseated just to consider it.

"That's fine with me! It leaves more room for supplies. And I believe the weather should hold."

"Thank you." Sydney lifted her wine glass. "What day shall we leave?"

"There's no time like the present, is there? Let's go tomorrow."

Sydney's eyes rounded and her glass hit the table. She didn't notice the spillage.

"Tomorrow!"

Nicolas grinned wickedly. "Do you have so much to pack that you need more time?"

"Aren't you so very amusing!" she snipped.

Then she consented to smile; his rare jest *was* funny. She hopped up and ran to the kitchen door, almost leveling Addie.

"We're going to St. Louis tomorrow! Can you please help me get ready?" she squeaked.

"Tomorrow is it? Well, I suppose so." Addie smiled at Nicolas. "That sounds like a wonderful plan!"

Sydney was halfway down the hall to the stairs when she stopped and turned around. She hurried back to Nicolas, still sitting in the dining room. She threw her arms around his shoulders and planted a solid kiss on his cheek.

June 15, 1819

Stefan asked if he could go to St. Louis as well, but Nicolas told him no.

"What would Wolf do without you here?" Sydney attempted to soften his disappointment. "You have to take care of him."

"He could come, too," Stefan suggested.

Sydney shook her head and volleyed a warning look at Nicolas, whose mouth sprung open to chastise his son. He snapped it shut.

"Hotels don't let lambs sleep in the rooms," she explained. "And they don't let little boys sleep in the stable." Sydney had anticipated Stefan's next point with accuracy. He snapped his mouth shut in uncanny imitation of his father.

After breakfast, Nicolas hitched the wagon to the matched set of bays. In the back was Sydney's borrowed satchel, along with several bags of wool and the wolf pelt. Sydney donned a wide-brimmed gypsy hat, courtesy of Addie, and tied the ribbon under her chin.

Nicolas occupied well over half of the wagon seat with his wide stance. While the road to St. Louis was oft-traveled, that didn't make it smooth. Sydney tried to stay on her side of the bench, but every time they hit a bump she slid into Nicolas.

"You can fidget for the next two hours, or you can relax against me," he said. "I don't mind the relaxing, but I'm afraid the fidgeting will begin to wear on me!"

Relieved, Sydney did relax against him. His solidity was such a comfort, even though his body was rock hard.

It was time to stop that particular train before it went too far. She cast about for a topic they hadn't already discussed to death. "Tell me about your schooling, Nicolas. What was it like out here on the edge of civilization?"

He pulled a face and glanced sideways at her. "What?"

"You know what I mean," she scolded.

He chuckled. "Do you mean how could us bumpkins learn our ciphers and letters without city folk to keep us straight? "

Sydney stuck her tongue out at him and he laughed.

"My mother taught Gunnar and me until I was seventeen," he began, still grinning. "That's how I learned Norse. Then she sent me to Pennsylvania to her parents. I studied at a college in Philadelphia for two years, and then I went to Norway for a year."

"A year in Norway? How exciting!"

Nicolas raised an eyebrow at her. "That's one way to view it, I suppose."

"You had the opportunity to explore your heritage, a chance to know your history. To meet your distant family! That must have been wonderful, wasn't it?"

"In actuality, it was they who wanted to know me. It was a journey of obligation, you might say."

"Obligation?" Sydney was confused. "How were you obligated?"

Nicolas waved his hand. "My mother's relatives were concerned about her inheritance. I suppose they wanted to assure themselves that I wouldn't mishandle it."

"And did you survive such scrutiny?"

"Apparently so, in that I did inherit without a word of objection from them."

"Did Gunnar go to Norway as well?"

"No. He joined the navy when he was nineteen. Been there ever since."

Sydney adjusted her straw hat as the wagon and the sun changed angles. "What did you study at the university?"

"Latin, literature, world history. And I had classes in business, law and a bit of engineering. At any rate, I knew where I would live and what my life would be like, so I studied whatever suited me at the time."

Sydney thought about that. "I wonder if I went to school."

"Well, do you know about Plato? Or Socrates?" Nicolas quizzed.

"Yes."

"How about Leonardo de Vinci? Michelangelo? Shakespeare?"

"Yes."

"Can you speak Latin?"

"I understand the Mass." That statement was made without pause. It was one more confirmation about her identity.

"Greek? French?"

Sydney laughed. "I doubt it…"

"Do you know about the war against England in 1776?"

"And crazy King George? Yes, I do."

"The Renaissance? The Middle Ages? The Dark Ages?"

"Yes, yes and yes."

"Well, you're not ignorant." Nicolas scratched his head. "And you speak intelligently. It's my opinion that you were schooled somewhere, and schooled well at that."

Sydney warmed inside; Nicolas's honest evaluation of her as an intelligent and educated woman pleased her. She suddenly realized that she wanted a man to be attracted to her mind, not only her gender. Had she always felt that way? That was a revelation with ramifications she would ponder later. For now, she relaxed against him a little more.

The ride was long, and quite warm, much of it drenched in dust and midday sun. Sydney felt light-headed, and she told Nicolas so. He pulled the wagon off to the side of the road and opened a flask of water for her, which she gulped down gratefully.

"Can you rest on my leg?" He slid to one side of the bench seat.

Sydney leaned over and rested her head in Nicolas's lap. It

wasn't perfect, but it helped. She nodded to Nicolas and he slapped the reins, urging the horses to move forward again. Sydney closed her eyes. Nicolas's hand rested comfortably on her hip. The creaking of the wagon and the rhythmic clomping of eight iron-clad hooves replaced their conversation.

As the wagon crossed into St. Louis, Nicolas woke Sydney. There were houses and businesses and people and horses and wagons and noises everywhere. The air was dustier than in Cheltenham, and carried the busy scents of smoke, hot tar and hot humanity. She sat up and stretched, stiff from sleeping in the awkward position.

Nicolas turned their wagon around the corner of a large warehouse and she saw the vast Mississippi River, its surface studded with a myriad of diamonds sparkling in the sun. She smelled water and fish and mud. The calls of the dock workers echoed off the warehouse walls.

"I'll settle the horses and wagon at a livery, and then we'll go eat lunch," Nicolas said. "I'll have our things sent ahead to the hotel."

At that moment, Sydney realized she was starving.

"I am glad to hear it. Do you like fish?"

∞ ∞

Nicolas, with Sydney on his arm, entered his favorite St. Louis establishment. It was a tavern that sold what he felt was the best fried catfish in the world.

Sydney covered her nose the moment they entered the front door. She pulled back and shook her head. "I'm afraid some of the fish has gone bad. Something doesn't smell right at all."

Nicolas sniffed the air. It smelled fine to him; strongly fishy, to be certain, but that was expected. Disappointed, he offered, "My second favorite establishment sells barbeque."

"That sounds better."

Inside that tavern, Nicolas and Sydney sat at a table by a window. The place was crowded, much more so than the fish place. Sydney said that was an encouraging sign. Nicolas ordered beer for them both while they waited for their food. Sydney sipped hers and watched the rush of people outside. She looked happy and Nicolas was pleased to be there.

His contentment was short-lived however, when a buxom woman of his age, whose mode of dress left no doubt of her assets, plopped down on the bench next to him.

"Nicky!" she squealed with delight. "Where've you been? I've missed you mightily!" She snuggled closer. "You know you're my favorite! God love a big man!" Her hand dropped to Nicolas's lap and grabbed that big part of him.

Sydney arrested the mug of beer halfway to her lips, and stared saucer-eyed and gape-mouthed at their overly familiar intruder.

Surprise, followed by recognition, followed by realization, followed by dismay shot through Nicolas's awareness in as many seconds, ending with the heat of embarrassment that shamed any sunburn he might ever have had. Nicolas looked frantically between the two women, desperate for something to say.

Sydney slammed her mug on the table and extended her right hand. "I'm Sydney. I'm Nicolas's houseguest."

"Pleased to meet you, Sydney." The woman was forced to let go of Nicolas to shake Sydney's hand, much to his relief. He crossed his legs and dropped a protective hand into his lap.

"I'm Rosie, Nicolas's—"

"ROSIE!" Nicolas bellowed to stop her from finishing the incriminating sentence. "It's—uh—very nice to see you, as well. How long's it been?"

He immediately regretted asking that question.

"Months! Not since you last came to sell pelts! What was that, March?" Rosie counted on her fingers. "You were always so regular!" The implication was his condemnation.

"That must be my fault, Rosie. I arrived at Nicolas's home on the first of April." Sydney smiled oh-so-sweetly at the squirming object of the unwelcome attention.

"Yes, well, I haven't had to get away, I mean, had a *chance* to get away, since then. This is my first trip to St. Louis since March." Nicolas wondered why he felt the need to explain anything to either one of them.

"Oh." Rosie's gaze trickled over Sydney, slowly and thoroughly.

In Rosie's profession, understanding men was a necessary skill. Nicolas reckoned she put it together that he was getting his urges satisfied elsewhere, and that 'elsewhere' was sitting across the table from her right now. Never known to burn bridges, especially ones that paid well, Rosie rose to her feet. She patted Nicolas on the shoulder.

"I hope you enjoy this trip, Nicky. Come see me again when… things… are finished. It was a pleasure, Sydney." With a wet, tongue-tipped kiss on his cheek, Rosie sailed out of the tavern in a colorful cloud, leaving a wake of lustful looks.

"Not one word," Nicolas warned.

Sydney shook her head in acquiescence and lifted her mug to her grinning lips. Salvation arrived in the form of a large platter of tender barbequed meat, a loaf of warm, yeasty bread and another pitcher of cooled beer.

Nicolas leaned back in his chair, quite satisfied with the meal, and scratched his belly. He pointed Sydney toward the privy and stood to stretch. Handbills posted by the front door showed a company of actors was performing *Taming of the Shrew* in a theater not far from their hotel. When Nicolas walked Sydney to their hotel, he asked her about going to the play.

"I love that play!" Sydney slipped her arm through his. "That sounds wonderful!"

Good. Forgiven for Rosie.

Chapter Eighteen

June 15, 1819
St. Louis

*S*ydney and Nicolas strolled along the river. In spite of the depressed economy, Nicolas received acceptable prices on both the wool and the pelt, so he was in a very good mood. They rounded a corner by a stable and discovered what appeared to be an auction. Curious, they ambled down the rows of livestock. They didn't find aught that interested them until they reached the last row.

"Oh, Nicolas, look at her!" Sydney breathed.

Before he felt her let go of his arm, Sydney stood beside the tall filly. Nicolas reckoned her to be nearly sixteen hands.

Sydney let the horse sniff her fists. "Isn't she beautiful?"

A glossy dark brown, the filly had a blaze of white down her scooped nose. Her feathered fetlocks were white as well. The tips of her ears almost touched as she considered Nicolas with intelligent eyes.

"She's got Arabian blood," he observed.

"Yes," Sydney agreed. "And my guess is Clydesdale by her size and coloring."

A nearly bald man limped up to the two of them. "Aye, you're both right. She's a beauty, no?"

"What made you choose this mix of breeds?" Sydney asked.

"I didn't choose it, her Jezebel of a mother did! Some black-hearted stallion wooed her and she gave in. Never did know where he came from or where he got to after."

"How old is she?"

"Three."

"Is she saddle-trained?"

"Not yet. I hoped she'd grow big enough to work the traces with my Clydes, but..." he shrugged.

Sydney ran her hands over the filly's sturdy legs, chest and flanks. She smiled up at Nicolas, nearly blinding him. "Wouldn't she make Fyrste a fine wife?"

"How much are you asking for her?" Nicolas queried.

"I can't sell her outright. I've had a couple o' others askin' about her, so she's to the block for certain."

Nicolas turned to Sydney. "Looks like we're staying for the auction."

As though she already knew, the horse nuzzled Sydney and rested her head against Sydney's shoulder. Sydney leaned her forehead against the filly's in response. Nicolas vowed right then and there to outbid any other interested parties for this particular animal.

And he did. Nicolas went to plank down the considerable payment. He returned and handed Sydney the ownership paper.

The filly was in her name.

Sydney looked up at Nicolas and frowned. "Why did you do that?"

"She's yours, look at her," Nicolas answered with a satisfied shrug. The filly was resting against Sydney's shoulder again.

Sydney pushed the paper toward him. "I can't accept a gift like this! It's not appropriate."

Nicolas pushed her hand back. "Sydney, if you start a new life, you'll need a horse."

"But..."

Nicolas raised both hands indicating the matter was closed.

Sydney's voice was oddly pinched. "Thank you, Nicolas."

She threw her arms around him and hugged him, her body pressed hard against his. Then she tilted her head back and looked at him with such tenderness that—for a moment—his heart softened and all the possibilities that she embodied surged in. Bright as a midsummer's dawn, they dazzled him with hope. He had forgotten hope. But hope was a lie. So he hardened his heart once more.

"We missed the play," he deflected.

"That's fine," Sydney assured him. "We can go tomorrow. I'm quite exhausted."

He took her hand and they walked back to the hotel. "What will you name her?"

"Fyrste means prince. What is 'princess'?"

"*Prinsesse.*"

"Then I'll call her Sessa. She looks royal, doesn't she?"

Nicolas smiled at the note of pride in Sydney's voice, delighted to be the man that put it there.

"That she does."

June 16, 1819

Nicolas awoke with the first light of day. He lay in bed and thought about Sydney. There were just two weeks until July first, her self-appointed 'new beginning' day. It dawned on Nicolas at that moment that he, too, would need to make choices concerning her future.

With that unconsidered realization, his heart somersaulted and he broke a sweat. He struggled to breathe, pulling deep gulps as unexpected panic hurtled through him. He had stopped making any sort of plans nearly six years ago. Moving habitually through his life, and enjoying the unusual diversion of her company, he had not given any consideration to what came next.

What would he do?

More to the point, what would she do? Would she leave Cheltenham? Would she leave him? He didn't want her to go. But he couldn't ask her to stay unless he offered her a reason. Unless he offered her hope. Unless he offered her love.

How could he offer something he couldn't risk having?

Nicolas rolled out of bed and relieved himself copiously into the chamber pot. That mundane act helped to restore his equilibrium. He sat on the edge of the bed until he felt like himself again, unaware of how much time passed. Then he dressed.

When he knocked, Sydney opened her door while brushing her dark, glorious hair. She wore a deep pink cotton summer dress. He liked that color on her very much. She smiled up at him.

"Good morning. Did you sleep well?" she asked. She set the brush down and twisted her hair into a topknot.

Denying the panic of his earlier revelation, Nicolas nodded. "I did indeed, madam. And yourself?"

"I slept as though I were hibernating! But I'm starving now. Do you realize we never ate dinner last night?"

"I suppose we forgot with the auction and all."

"You may make it up to me now." Sydney grabbed the gypsy hat and stepped into the hallway, closing the door behind her. "Feed me, Nicolas! Please!"

In the hotel's dining room they feasted on freshly baked biscuits and gravy, eggs, ham, grits and coffee.

Nicolas leaned back and grinned at Sydney.

"I have always admired the way you can eat," he commented, that being an honest accolade in his estimation. She raised one eyebrow at him.

"Hm. So, I eat a lot, I look good in breeches and I ride astride? And to make the situation worse, you gave me a name that could also be a man's." Sydney shook her head. "These aren't your typical compliments, sir. Should I be offended?"

Nicolas laughed. "No, Sydney. You aren't a typical woman."

Seeing her momentary frown, Nicolas clarified, "And that, rest assured, is the greatest compliment of all!"

Nicolas and Sydney wandered along streets and explored different shops that Nicolas wanted to visit. He stocked up on a number of supplies that they didn't grow or make for themselves at the estate. He also asked Sydney's opinion on quite a few purchases until, horrified, he caught himself. He must stop thinking of her as permanent.

They chose a quiet tavern near the theater for a late midday meal. As they talked, Nicolas glanced at a table across the room where two men in their twenties alternated between very private conversation and staring intently at Sydney.

Nicolas could stand it no longer. "Might you know those men?"

"Which men?" Sydney followed his gaze. The men avoided hers. "Not that I can recall. Why do you ask?"

"They keep looking at you." Nicolas lifted his beer to his lips and watched over the rim of his glass. "The dark skinny one in particular."

Their meal arrived and Sydney helped herself to a sizable portion of meat and potatoes.

"I do have quite an appetite, don't I?" Smiling, she broke a chunk of bread from the loaf.

"Well, I'm glad to mark it. You seemed off your feed before we came."

Her shoulders drooped. "I was so depressed, Nicolas. It's impossible to describe how it feels not to know yourself."

She laid her hand over his. "Thank you so much for bringing me here."

Nicolas glanced again at the two men. When Sydney touched him, they appeared very surprised, exchanging shocked glances and furtive whispers. Something quite odd was afoot.

He leaned toward her, working up his best love-struck expression. "Play along with me for a moment, will you?" He lifted her hand to his lips and kissed her palm.

Sydney smiled awkwardly, then looked down and feigned shyness. "Who are we acting for?"

"Your two men."

"*My* two men?" Her skeptical look was hidden from them as she pushed a strand of hair from her eyes.

Nicolas leaned close and brushed her lips with his. Though he knew he was play-acting, it didn't lessen the bone melting impact of that intimate contact one bit. He closed his eyes and did it again, for the moment forgetting the other reason.

The two strangers stood and hurried out of the establishment. Nicolas paused for a heartbeat, and sauntered to the tavern door. He pretended to look at the handbills posted there, then leaned outside and looked up and down the street. The two men had effectively disappeared, so he returned to the table with no more knowledge than he started with.

Sydney asked, "Do you believe they knew me?"

Nicolas continued his meal and explained between large bites.

"Sydney, I saw two things. First, the dark skinny one had his eye on you from the minute we walked in. Almost as though he was seeing a ghost."

Nicolas gulped a large swallow of beer to wash down the meat. "Perchance he knew you before and thought you were dead."

"Then why wouldn't he say something to me?" Sydney's expression screamed her frustration.

"Perhaps he knows your, uh, husband and believes you're

having an affair of the heart? Or perhaps he believes you staged your disappearance? Or even your death?" Nicolas posited.

"If so, perhaps he'll get word to this—husband—that I'm quite alive and well." Sydney appeared inexplicably glum at the suggestion. "What was the other thing?"

Nicolas glanced around at the surrounding tables. "The other thing could get them life imprisonment."

Sydney's eyes widened. "Life imprisonment? For what, Nicolas?"

"Well, that's in Missouri. It would be castration in Virginia." Nicolas took another bite of meat.

"What on earth are you talking about?"

"Sodomy," he said with his mouth full.

Sydney's mouth crashed open. She slid her glance to the vacated table. "How do you know?"

"A man doesn't run his foot up the inside of another man's leg, unless he has it in mind to share quite a bit more than a meal," he stated matter-of-factly.

Sydney's face went white. She pushed her plate away

"I don't feel well."

Her eyes rolled back and she slipped out of her chair while Nicolas jumped to catch her. He lowered her to the floor and cradled her head in his lap. His gaze ricocheted around the tavern searching for help. The barmaid scurried over and began to wave a wet cloth over her.

After mere seconds, Sydney's eyes fluttered open. The barmaid still waved the towel; Sydney reached up to stop her.

"What happened?" She searched for Nicolas's frowning eyes.

"You fainted."

The barmaid tried again to revive her by brandishing the towel.

"Would you stop that!" Sydney snapped. Offended, the girl turned and stomped off.

"I'm sorry, Sydney. It was insensitive of me to mention such a subject to you at all, much less while you were trying to enjoy a meal," Nicolas apologized.

"Sodomy isn't a pleasant subject, Nicolas, but I assure you I'm not that squeamish." Sydney rubbed her forehead.

Nicolas helped her back into her seat and poured her another glass of beer. "Then what happened?"

"When you said what they were doing, I felt this blackish cloud surround me…" She mimed her words with splayed hands. "It pressed against me and there was no way out." Her eyes met his. "The next thing I knew, that girl was flapping that smelly towel over my face."

"And you are certain you didn't recognize either of those men?" Nicolas prodded.

Sydney closed her eyes and sat still for a pace. "No. No, I don't think so."

She opened her eyes. Spying her plate of food, she pulled it toward her.

"Waste not, want not," she quoted as she forked a bite. "That Ben Franklin was a wise man."

Nicolas sat back in his chair and shook his head, absolutely baffled by the beautiful changeling in front of him.

ജ ോ

Nicolas escorted Sydney to their box for the performance of *Taming of the Shrew*. As she sank into the padded chair, Sydney seemed to vibrate with excitement, her eyes green as new pine needles. The deep pink of her dress matched her lips.

Nicolas wanted to pull her into him and feel those soft lips part, feel her tongue tangle with his. He settled for sitting close beside her; his long legs straddling her chair.

He leaned close, inhaling the rosy scent of her hair. "I know. You don't recall if you've ever attended a play before."

"On the contrary! I know I have! My father took me to plays in Louisville twice a year, when he went to sell horses."

"I give up," Nicolas muttered, with a crooked smile. "Your memory is a mystery to me!"

Sydney laughed, resting her hand on Nicolas's thigh. "Rest assured, it is to me as well!"

Her hand felt like a branding iron and he fought the urge to jerk away. How did she do it? How did she rouse his basest urges with nothing more than a brush of her fingers? He shifted his weight in the smallish chair.

Sydney sat up straight and grabbed Nicolas's arm. "Look, over there," she pointed with her chin. "Is that the 'dark skinny' one?"

Nicolas leaned to the side to get a better angle. Sure enough, sitting in the front row of the audience, looking—eager? nervous?—was the same man that stared at Sydney in the tavern.

"Perhaps it was one of the actors he was having lunch with," Nicolas suggested. "You know, there's a commonly held belief regarding artists, actors, that sort of man."

Sydney pinned him with a mischievous grin. "That they better stay out of Virginia, apparently."

Once the play began, any doubt about Nicolas's theory being true was dispelled. Dark Skinny was literally on the edge of his seat whenever the actor playing Lucentio appeared on the stage. And the actor was indeed the same man whose foot slid up Skinny's leg under their lunch table. In turn, Lucentio seemed to drift toward that side of the stage whenever the scene allowed.

"They had best be careful," Nicolas whispered to Sydney. "It's a dangerous game."

They turned their attention back to the play, though other than Lucentio, most of the actors were mediocre at best. The surreptitious interaction between Skinny and Lucentio was infinitely more entertaining.

When the play ended, Nicolas rose from the tiny chair and stretched, reaching high over his head. Taking Sydney's elbow, he turned and shot one last look at Skinny.

Skinny was staring right at him.

ఖ ☞

Assuming the sharp knock at her door was Nicolas, Sydney opened it without asking. Mr. Skinny stood in the hall. She jumped back in surprise and he walked right into her room.

Skinny's brown eyes drilled into hers. "Why are you following me?"

Sydney quickly surmised that the truth—that she didn't know him, or aught about him—wouldn't be satisfactory. So she took a different tack.

"Why should I tell you anything?" she taunted with falsified confidence and prayed she was convincing. "Why is it any of your business?"

"It is if I am your business!" he sneered. "Did he send you?"

"What if he did? Is there something he should know?" Sydney bluffed. An inspiration lit. "Or perhaps something he shouldn't know? Is that it?"

Skinny flinched as though he'd been struck. He looked scared. Perhaps even terrified. Who was this 'he' person, and what power did he hold that frightened Skinny so thoroughly?

"Does he suspect something?" The sneer was gone. Clearly, Skinny was regrouping. He wiped his mouth with a trembling palm. "What might you tell him? You've no evidence."

"Really?" Sydney decided to take a very large gamble. "There were caresses under the table this afternoon. Something like that could get you both in a lot of trouble."

The resultant horror on Skinny's face was quickly replaced by fury. He grabbed Sydney's arms and pushed her deeper into the room. His snarling face closed in on hers.

"Be careful what you say!"

Sydney winced. "You're hurting me!"

"Wouldn't he like to know the game you're playing? Who's the big Swede?"

"Norwegian," Sydney spat without thinking. She tried to wrestle free, but he held her in a bruising grip. "Let me go!"

But he held her close. "You're no paragon of virtue yourself! When he finds out, he'll kill you. Again."

"Let go of the lady." Nicolas's deep voice carried the threat without effort.

Skinny spun around to face the huge and irate Norwegian. Nicolas leaned on the doorjamb, arms crossed and a pistol tucked in his breeches. While Nicolas's stance appeared casual, there was nothing relaxed about him.

"I suggest for your own safety that you leave this hotel immediately. I also suggest that you don't return."

Skinny tossed a nervous glance back and forth, then pitched a warning glare at Sydney.

Nicolas did not move out of the doorway, he just dropped his hand to the pistol. Skinny was forced to turn sideways and slip out beside him. Nicolas turned his head to watch Skinny leave. He waited another minute, and then stepped into Sydney's room and closed her door.

Sydney breathed a sigh of relief. "That was perfect timing!"

Nicolas propped one foot on a chair and leaned his elbows on his knee.

"It wasn't an accident, Sydney. I was listening to everything from the moment he knocked on your door. What was he talking about?"

Sydney threw her hands up. "I've no idea. I don't even know who he is! But I got the distinct feeling that he wasn't going to believe that. I was hoping I could draw some answers from him if I went along with him, but that didn't work."

She sat down on the bed, shoulders slumped. "He definitely knew me, and apparently we both know... someone. He's afraid of that person, and he's hiding something, and he believes I'm going to tell that someone what he's hiding. And, to make things interesting, he apparently believes I'm hiding you from that someone as well!"

Sydney looked up at Nicolas. Frustration burned in her eyes and her hands fisted in her lap. "Only, I don't know who I'm hiding you from, what I know, or whom I might tell! *Skitt!*"

Nicolas stared at her.

"Sydney?"

She heaved a deep breath. "What?"

"He said 'kill you again'."

She looked at him, shocked that she had immediately forgotten such a horrific revelation. The black cloud was back, trying to smother her, but she fought against it. "He did, didn't he."

"It would appear that what happened to you was no accident."

She blinked hard to disperse the cloud. "It would appear..."

"Are you... have you told me everything?"

Sydney wasn't certain how to answer that. "Nicolas, I've told you everything that I know, as little as that is. Do you mistrust me?"

"Uh, no." Nicolas scrubbed his jaw with one palm. "No. But it does appear that you might still be in danger."

Sydney nodded toward the pistol. "I saw the rifle in the wagon. Where did that come from?"

"It's just a little something I like to take on trips away from home." Nicolas pulled it from his breeches and held it out in front of him. Lamplight slid along the barrel. "It comes in handy when I need to make my presence known."

At his explanation Sydney allowed a small smile. When was Nicolas's hulking presence ever a *secret?*

She stood and moved across the room. He straightened as she approached. She frowned into his dark blue eyes.

"Might we go home in the morning?"

Nicolas brushed his knuckle along her cheek. "We'll leave right after breakfast."

Chapter Nineteen

June 17, 1819

*S*o," Sydney began once the wagon cleared the city. "Tell me about Rosie."

Nicolas hesitated and his scar rippled.

"No."

Sydney sat back, surprised. "No?"

Nicolas didn't respond, didn't turn his head, didn't acknowledge the question. He just kept driving.

"Why not?"

Nicolas slipped her a sideways glance, and then refocused on the road.

"What is there to say, Sydney? She is what she is and I visited her for only one purpose." Nicolas's voice was jagged and the scar outlined the blade of his jaw. "I'm a man with needs. You of all people know that well enough."

Humiliated by the hazardous turn of the conversation, Sydney twisted away from him to look at Sessa, stepping along behind the wagon.

"You have needs, as well," he cut. "And I believe we're both fully aware that you do!"

"Nicolas!"

"What?"

Storm clouds on the wagon's bench mirrored ones forming in the morning sky overhead.

"You needn't be cruel!" Sydney's words dropped in the chasm

between them. Her interlaced fingers didn't hold still. A pair of hot tears left dark dots on her skirt.

She was deeply ashamed of her desire for Nicolas. She tried, she honestly did, to stay clear of him. But his potency overpowered her. Sensual, sexual, taking, giving, lifting, drowning, wanting, needing. He consumed her. And she loved him in spite of it.

What was it he said? *It's a powerful thing. Not everyone experiences it, not even all husbands and wives.* Sydney felt certain that, married or not, she had never shared this sort of passion with any other man.

A sudden thought shocked her: was Nicolas revealing secrets about his own marriage? Had Lara been less—responsive?

She couldn't think about that now. She purposefully tucked the possibility away to ponder at another time.

Because tonight when Nicolas handed her the papers for Sessa, Sydney's heart exploded all over him. That he would give her such a gift was beyond her comprehension. Certainly he must feel inclined toward her; hadn't she seen it in his eyes when she hugged him? Another tear dropped and Sydney heaved a patchy sigh.

Her fists pressed against her belly. *Dear Father, what will I do on July first? What will happen to me?*

Nicolas drove the team in unwavering silence for another mile. Then he covered Sydney's fisted hands with his. Gently, he worked his fingers between hers until he could take hold. Though she resisted at first, she knew he was trying to make amends in his wordless male way. She relaxed and let him, accepting his tactile apology with a squeeze of her own. Nicolas lifted her hand to his lips and kissed it in acknowledgement.

Then he looked up at the sky. "I am afraid we're in for it, Sydney. We're bound to get soaked."

ରେ ଓଃ

Nicolas pulled off his shirt with the first drops and stuffed it under the tarp that protected their supplies. The first grumble of thunder was followed hastily by a second. The pewter ribbon of sky visible between endless trees was filled with heavy clouds, charged and murky. Lightening blinked.

Sydney slid closer to him.

"Are you afraid of thunderstorms?" he queried.

Sydney shook her head and waved her hand. But at the next blaze of light and its simultaneous roar, she squealed and curled into his lap. He stopped the wagon.

The *plith-plith* of gentle rain gave way to the deafening smack of weighty drops thrashing the leaves around them. Nicolas urged the horses off the road into the protection of the forest as the clouds breached. He checked the tarp and made certain Sessa's lead was secure; the filly's ears twitched in the storm as she pranced and pulled against her tether.

Another flash-boom combination threw Sydney off the bench and into him. She buried her face against his chest and slid her arms around his waist. Nicolas bent his head over hers. His hair hung in dripping strands around her face.

With his arms still around her, he led her deeper into the trees to a large flat rock where they sat together in the cooling rain. Sydney huddled against him, her head under his chin and her face pressed against his shoulder. Conversation was impossible, as lightening and thunder argued vehemently and shot water bullets all around them.

Nicolas liked protecting Sydney.

He liked it because it was unexpected.

He thought her fearless. The way she faced her situation. The way she faced Fyrste. Even the way she faced him. All depicted an intrepid member of the gender that she redefined as definitely not weaker. But now she looked to him for comfort.

He wondered about the man who had her first. Had that man comforted her? Had he cared for her? Did he understand her? Was he worthy of her trust? Obviously not.

If he was, Sydney wouldn't be in *his* arms now.

The storm slowly calmed to a steady rain, but it was still too wet to drive.

Sydney relaxed a little and looked up at him. Her eyelashes were spiky and black with rain, and water dripped off her nose. Nicolas smiled and wiped the drip away. Then he noticed a drip on her chin and slid his finger along her jaw to catch it. Water ran off her eyebrows. He leaned over and kissed the drops away.

Sydney brushed heavy strands of wet hair from his face, and tried to tuck them behind his ears. Giggling at the failed attempt, she stood and faced him. Using both hands, she tried again to get his abundant locks to stay out of the way, but the rain thwarted her attempts.

"I give up!" she laughed. She leaned over and kissed the water drops from his cheeks. Then she kissed them from his eyelashes. Then from his upper lip. And then his lower lip.

And she waited.

Nicolas pulled her to him, slippery with rain as his mouth claimed hers. Her hands swiped his back, shoulders and arms as the cloudburst rewetted every inch of his skin. Her mouth traveled down his throat and along his collarbone. He groaned his craving.

He worked his fingers through her hair and pulled it from its constraints. It clung to her neck like a black vine, heavy with rainwater. He slid off the rock and she leaned against his chest. The downpour slicked their bodies as warm tongues tasted cool rain-washed skin.

A loud nicker from Sessa brought them back to awareness. The rain had slowed to a drizzle. Nicolas wound Sydney's hair around his hand and pulled her in for one long, bottomless kiss. Fulfillment would have to wait, however, for another time and place.

Nicolas handed Sydney up to the wagon bench, then adjusted his breeches with an acknowledging grin and climbed up next to her. Clucking to the team, he shook the reigns. The bays strained to pull the wagon from the roadside mud. Sydney settled under Nicolas's arm as the team gained purchase and headed toward home.

"Nicolas?"

"Hmm?"

"Might I ask you a hard question?"

Dread nudged him, spoiling his contented mood. "Hard for you, or hard for me?" he teased, buying a little time.

"You, I think." There was no humor in her tone.

He nodded. "I suppose I owe you that."

Sydney didn't change her position and he couldn't see her face. So he knew she couldn't see his. He waited.

"Why wouldn't you fetch the midwife?"

Nicolas's world went flat. He didn't know she could knock him senseless without laying a hand on him. Though he intended to, he couldn't force himself to say the words out loud because every time he did, Lara died again.

Sydney pulled away and faced him. Her eyes were enormous. Gray like the storm yet green like new life. She didn't blink.

"Nicolas?"

His brow twitched and he shook his head erratically.

"Was it Lara?" she whispered. "Is that how she died?"

"Yes," he rasped.

"But Stefan lived."

"His brother died. They were twins."

"Oh."

"That's why, you see? The babies were too much for her." Nicolas pressed his eyes with his thumb and forefinger. "It was my fault."

Sydney gripped his arm and pulled it away. "How? How could that be?"

Nicolas frowned at her. Wasn't that answer obvious? "I married her. I laid with her. My lust for her killed her."

Her brow lowered. "You don't truly believe that."

Of course he did. *It was the truth.* "That's why, Sydney."

"Why what?"

"Why I can never do it again. Ever."

Sydney's chin lifted. Her stare was intense. "Do what?"

"Love. Marry. My turn has passed."

Her countenance shifted. Her mouth opened. She turned away from him, her arms flailing as she scrambled from the moving wagon. Nicolas yanked back on the reins and booted the brake hard.

"Sydney! What are you doing?" he yelled.

She didn't answer him. She fell to her hands and knees on the sodden forest floor and vomited. Nicolas leapt from the wagon and knelt at her side. He held her hair and rubbed her back, and when she sat up on her heels he fished his damp handkerchief from his wet back pocket and gave it to her.

Sydney wiped her mouth, her face flushed, then pale, then flushed again. "Breakfast was too greasy, it seems. Sat in my belly like a rock…"

"Is that all it is? Are you certain?" he demanded.

"Yes." She staggered to her feet and wobbled back to the wagon.

"Sydney!" he called after her. He followed when she ignored

him.

He lifted her back to the bench and climbed up next to her, sliding all the way to one side. "Rest like you did the other day," he suggested. He patted his thigh.

She said nothing, and she didn't look at him. But she curled on the bench and laid her head in his lap. She closed her eyes.

"Not much of a traveler, are you?" he said softly. When she didn't respond, he rested his hand on her hip and slapped the reins.

He welcomed her silence right then. Something was niggling at him and he needed to figure out what it was. For the next hour he rethought his words and tried to discern why they didn't feel as they always had. Their flavor was different. The saltiness of his sorrow had turned bitter. But he couldn't explain how, exactly.

When they reached his estate, Sessa was tucked in her new stall and then Sydney was tucked in her bed. Nicolas retreated to his study to have a brandy or two and ponder the odd sensation. When he saw his violin case on his desk, it stopped him sure as a bullet. Clarity shot through him.

He opened the case and lifted the unique instrument. He ran his fingers over the elaborate mother-of-pearl inlays. He inhaled the sharp aroma of the wood and lacquer. He slid his palm along the narrow neck and his fingers over the taught strings.

This Hardanger fiddle was a work of art. And very valuable to him besides; not only because of the extraordinary craftsmanship that went into it, but because it was a gift from one of his older cousins, given to him over a decade ago when he stayed in Norway.

When he played it, he experienced music and it stirred his soul. Just like Sydney said.

And what if this fiddle was taken from him and destroyed?

If he said that his instrument was gone forever, and music was no longer in his life, he would be understood. Empathized with. Certainly not expected to play again.

But if he walked into his study one day and another fiddle lay on his desk—what then? It could never be the same as his beloved Hardanger. It would feel different in his hands and tucked under his chin. It would sound different. Make different music.

For nearly six years, he had stoically shouldered the burden of loss. However, when he spoke to Sydney today, his rhetoric sounded more like he was stubbornly prolonging the pain of his loss. To make his situation more complicated, he had a suspicion that a new fiddle might be sleeping in the room upstairs right now.

"*Skitt.*" Nicolas gulped a large glass of brandy. He poured another.

ℰ ℭ

Sydney went down to supper at seven. A long nap had served her well and she was ready to face Nicolas again.

"Are you better?" he asked when she entered the dining room.

"Yes, thank you." She sat as he held her chair. "I'm afraid I didn't sleep much after that horrible encounter last night. Every time I closed my eyes I saw him again." While Nicolas moved to his own chair she continued, "I think the lack of sleep, combined with those fried eggs and that greasy bacon, did me in."

Nicolas unfolded his napkin and laid it in his lap. His brow ebbed and his sea gaze washed over her. "Are you certain, Sydney? There's nothing else?"

"Yes, of course." She stared back at him. "What else could it be? I'm fine."

After they helped themselves to supper, Nicolas told her, "Addie said I had a visitor while we were gone."

She paused, her knife hovering over the roasted lamb. "Who?"

"The Cheltenham schoolteacher. Said he was going to homesteads in the area to see if he had any new students coming in the fall. Addie told him I wasn't here and he should come back."

"Has Stefan started school yet?"

Nicolas cut a precise piece of lamb before he answered. "I had thought to send him away to a military school."

That was a surprise. "What on earth prompted you to choose that path?"

He frowned. "I don't consider myself able to educate him."

"Don't you like your son?"

Nicolas slammed his silverware on the table. "What sort of question is that?"

Sydney looked him hard in the eyes. "I only want to know why it is you don't want him around."

Nicolas's brow pushed down and his face reddened beyond his perpetual sunburn.

"Is it because he reminds you?" she pressed.

Nicolas's expression transformed into shock and unmasked anger. Pain in his soul escaped through dilated pupils turning his eyes nearly black. He didn't move, but Sydney saw a tremor in his hands. The scar on his cheek rippled and paled.

"You have overstepped yourself, Sydney!" he warned.

She dipped her chin. "If I have, then I apologize."

Nicolas looked away and cut another morsel of uneaten lamb.

"But am I right?"

"*Gud forbanner det!*" he shouted. "What are you trying to do?"

"I'm trying to make you think before you make a decision you might regret!" she declared.

"It's none of your affair!" he declared right back.

Sydney folded her arms. She lifted one brow. "That is why you should listen to me. I'm impartial."

"Oh! Is that so?" Nicolas scoffed. He leaned on his elbows. "Then what, pray tell, would you have me do?"

"Perhaps he could learn some basic things here first," she proposed in a measured tone. She leaned forward and spoke across the white linen divide. "At home. With his father. Who loves him."

Nicolas glared at her. But he didn't argue. He seemed to be considering her words, so she pushed on. "You could still send Stefan away at a later date, should you prefer. When he's older, of course."

Nicolas faced his dinner plate and ate without answering. Sydney heard the force of his breath and saw the jerk of his hands. His silverware scraped the china, squealing through their brittle silence. Sydney had just about decided to retire to her room and leave him alone to his brooding when he cleared his throat. She met his gaze, glad to note the ocean was visible in his eyes again.

"I suppose I could consider it. If the teacher comes back, I'll hear him out. After all, as you said, other decisions can be made if it comes to that."

Chapter Twenty

June 21, 1819
Cheltenham

The schoolteacher was medium. Medium height, medium build, sandy brown hair and medium brown eyes. He was so non-descript as to be markedly so. He shook Nicolas's hand with a medium grip.

"How do you do, sir? My name is Devin Kilbourne. I'm the teacher here in Cheltenham," he said in a medium voice. "I understand you have a son who'll be starting school soon?"

"Perhaps so." Nicolas waved Mr. Kilbourne to a seat.

"Perhaps so?"

"I'm a widower, Mr. Kilbourne, with an estate to care for. I haven't time to see to my son's education. My plans are to send him to military school when he turns seven."

"I see. And how old is he now, might I ask?"

"Five. Six in September."

The teacher's eyes flickered around the room. "And has he had his basic instruction yet?"

Nicolas frowned. "What precisely do you mean by his basic instruction?"

"Can he count?"

"Yes. To ten."

"But no farther?"

Nicolas shook his head.

"So he has no skills in arithmetic?"

"No."

Mr. Kilbourne tilted his head. "How about his letters, sir? Does he know the alphabet?"

Nicolas cleared his throat and shifted uneasily in his chair. "Um, no, he doesn't."

"So he's not able to read at all?"

Nicolas shook his head again. He was getting a disturbing view of Stefan's deficiencies, along with the realization that he, by his neglect, was the one to blame for them.

"If he doesn't know his letters, then I don't imagine he can write? Or can he write his name?"

Humbled by this nondescript entity, Nicolas shook his head for a third time.

Devin Kilbourne leaned back in his chair and fixed Nicolas with a pleasant gaze. "I can help you, Mr. Hansen. Regular classes don't begin until September, so I have time to tutor your son— what's his name?"

"Stefan."

"I can tutor Stefan for the next couple of months and help prepare him for whatever school you wish to send him to."

Nicolas leaned forward and fixed a narrowed eye on the teacher. "What will this cost me?"

Kilbourne chuckled. "Well of course, a man has to eat." He mentioned a number.

Nicolas countered.

Kilbourne accepted and with a handshake the deal was struck. "Shall we go meet the student?"

Nicolas led the teacher out the back door. "Stefan has chores to do, so he's most likely in the stable with John Spencer, my foreman."

"Chores are important. They build character and responsibility," Mr. Kilbourne approved. Why that comment vexed Nicolas was beyond him.

❧ ❧

Sydney was working Sessa in the corral, dressed as always in the stained breeches and oversized chambray work shirt.

"Sydney!" Nicolas called. "There's someone present you need to meet!"

She turned toward him and he saw her shoulders fall. Her cheeks splotched a vivid red. She ambled toward him, Sessa in tow. Her chin dipped as if she had pulled an invisible hat brim low over her forehead.

"Sydney, this is Mr. Kilbourne, the Cheltenham school teacher. He's going to tutor Stefan." Nicolas grinned, confident she'd be pleased.

"Nice to meet you." Sydney didn't smile. And she didn't meet the man's eyes.

Devin sent an awkward glance at Nicolas then jerked his chin in a semblance of a nod. "Madam."

Nicolas grew annoyed by her unexpected rudeness. "Have you seen Stefan?"

"I believe he's cleaning stalls. If you'll excuse me?" She turned, put Sessa between her and the teacher, and crossed the corral.

Nicolas resolved to take her to task for her discourtesy later. For now, he led Mr. Kilbourne toward the stable. He noticed the teacher stared over his shoulder at Sydney, presently hidden behind the filly. Considering her unusual mode of dress, that wasn't surprising.

They found Stefan feeding Wolf, and Nicolas introduced him to Mr. Kilbourne. "He's going to be your teacher. He's going to teach you about numbers and letters. You'll learn to read and do arithmetic."

Stefan looked up at the teacher, then at his father.

"Why?"

Nicolas wasn't prepared for that particular response. Before he could concoct an answer, the teacher knelt so his eyes were at Stefan's level.

"Someday you'll be the man at this estate, Stefan. I'm going to teach you some things that you'll need to know in order to take care of it."

Stefan seemed unconvinced. He looked back up at Nicolas with a confused expression.

"This is important, Stefan. So important, that... um... I'll do some of your chores so you have time to learn from Mr. Kilbourne," Nicolas offered.

That offer obviously held some weight. Stefan turned back to the teacher. "Do you have candy?"

"Yes."

"All right."

And that was the end of the discussion.

ℰ ℭ

Nicolas sent the teacher on his way after agreeing to a schedule for Stefan's tutoring. When there was a knock at the front door, he assumed the man had returned for some reason. Instead, he was surprised to find Lily Atherton standing on his front porch, her carriage and driver in his yard. Of late he had forgotten about her and her seductive pursuit of his attention. That recollection now slapped him across the face with her expensive perfume.

"Nicolas! How I've missed you! I haven't seen you in weeks." She stood on tiptoe to kiss his cheek and pressed her body to his.

"I've been very busy," he demurred, setting her away from him. "What can I do for you?"

"I brought you a present," she cooed, undaunted. She twirled her finger in circles against his chest.

He tried not to visibly recoil. "Oh?"

"It's outside."

At her insistence and with his eyes closed, Nicolas permitted Lily to lead him outside, down his porch steps, and around the front of her carriage. She adjusted his stance to face just the right direction. After so long a pause that he started to object, Lily gave him permission to open his eyes. Resting on a wooden trestle in front of him was the most unique and beautifully crafted leather saddle he had ever seen. He was stunned.

"Lily, it's beautiful!" Nicolas ran his hands appreciatively over the intricate woven and hand-tooled design. "I've never seen such a thing! Where did you get it?"

Clapping her hands together, Lily hopped from foot to foot. "A trader came to the house and he had it in his wagon. He got it from another trader who got it from a Cheyenne Indian chief! Do you really like it?"

"I do, I really do." Nicolas could not take his eyes off the unusual design of the seat and pommel. "But what's the occasion?"

"Do I need an occasion, Nicolas? Aren't we closer than that?" Lily leaned into him. "We haven't seen each other for so long and I wanted to let you know that I was thinking of you."

Nicolas was torn from top to bottom. One side of him wanted to accept the saddle, intrigued by its distinctive design. The other warned him that Lily's price might be higher than he was willing to pay. Without intending to, he parroted Sydney's words to him concerning Sessa.

"I can't accept such a gift, Lily. It's not appropriate."

Lily's lips pulled down at the edges. "Nicolas, you mustn't be so mean."

He spread his hands. "I don't intend to be mean, Lily..."

She stomped one tiny, satin-slippered foot. "But I was so excited to acquire this for you!"

"And I do appreciate the thought..."

"Nicolas Reidar Hansen! I declare! If you won't accept it? Well—I don't know what I'll do!"

"I could purchase it from you," he offered.

Her mouth slammed open and tears splashed from her blue-green eyes, instantly wetting her cheeks. "I swear! You are the most heartless, unfeeling, and selfish man in the entire Missouri Territory!"

Chagrined by her accusations, Nicolas wrapped guilty arms around the young woman he'd known since childhood. "I'm sorry, Lily. I didn't consider your feelings. Thank you for the saddle. It's the handsomest piece of tack I've ever seen, much less owned."

Lily lifted her bowed mouth, her pink cheeks glistening with tears.

Nicolas—in equal parts gratitude and guilt—obliged her with a satisfactory kiss. Then he carried the saddle to the stable, thrilled to own it in spite of the thump in his chest warning him of unseen strings attached to its stirrups.

Lily waited for him in the drawing room. When she didn't make any move to leave, he realized the timing of her visit was intentional. Cornered, he invited her to stay for supper and escorted her to the dining room. They sat at the table and made small talk, waiting for Sydney. When she didn't appear, Nicolas asked Addie about her.

"She took a plate to her room. She said she was tired, poor dear. She did look a bit peaked."

"Did she? She wasn't feeling well the other morning, either.

Lily, will you excuse me a moment? I'm going to check on her." He was gone from the table before Lily could object.

Upstairs, Nicolas tapped on Sydney's door. Then he tapped again, a little harder.

She didn't answer.

So he opened the door and walked in.

Sydney sat on the rocker, a plate of untouched food on the table beside her.

"That door is in need of a lock," she said in a voice like ice.

Nicolas closed the door behind him and walked halfway across the room, stopped by the steel of her stare. "Sydney? What's wrong?"

She looked at him as if he had just asked her if she felt gravity was important, or might he shut it off.

"What's wrong?" she repeated. She held up one finger. "Let's begin with: someone tried to kill me—probably my husband—and if he finds out he didn't succeed, he might try again! And I can't remember any of it!"

She held up another finger. "Next: that teacher upset me. Look at him—he's not exactly a frightening man, but when he came near me, I couldn't breathe. And before you ask me, no. I don't know him and I don't know why!"

Nicolas tried to corral her tirade. "Do you think he knew you?"

"How should I know?" she huffed. "He said naught to me!"

Nicolas reined in his irritation. She was being so—female. "I'm only trying to understand, Sydney."

Her tone was deliberate and condescending. "And if I understood it, then I'd explain it to you. I would use very short sentences, with very small words."

Time for a different tack before he exploded. "Are you ill?"

She narrowed her eyes. "I. Am. Fine."

He waved his hand in question toward the plate of food.

She shrugged. "I didn't feel like eating with Lily."

That was surprising. Not wanting to share a meal with Lily was understandable; the girl was outright rude. But, "You knew she was here? How?"

"I saw her. When she gave you the saddle." Sydney's pewter-green gaze slithered toward the door and coiled there. "And I saw how you thanked her."

"I was only being polite."

Sydney struck him with a look that poisoned his words. Then she rose. She held up a third finger and stepped toward him. He resisted the urge to back up.

"Third. I gave the man I love the most intimate gift I could give him. In truth, the only gift that is mine to give." Her arm swung wide and she jabbed a finger at the window. "And then he stood in front of his house and kissed another woman because of a gift that *she* gave him. A woman, I might add, in whom he fervently stated he has absolutely no interest!"

Her arm fell to her side. "My gift, therefore, must be of no more consequence than hers."

Nicolas was thunderstruck. Lightning tingled his extremities.

Sydney's lower lip began to tremble, her eyes now a watery gray. "I'm not made of stone, Nicolas. And I cannot pretend the things you do don't hurt me."

Nicolas moved toward her bed as if in a nightmare. He sank on its edge. "You said the man…" He couldn't finish the sentence and he prayed she wouldn't repeat it.

Sydney's breath caught as she surrendered. With shoulders slumped she blasted open the doors of his purgatory.

"I do love you, Nicolas Reidar Hansen. Not that you deserve it."

Nicolas gawked wide-eyed at her. The only parts of him that moved were his clenching fists. He didn't even blink. *Ignore that. Change the subject.*

"I hurt you?" he managed.

Sydney sat back in the rocker. Her bravado dissolved as he watched her.

"It's true, Nicolas, you've never voiced any words concerning your regard for me. But you seem to say so much in other ways. The way you talk to me. The way you touch me."

This was precarious. Nicolas's pulse pounded so hard he could barely hear her.

"I don't understand. Am I misled? Do I imagine these things?" she asked.

Nicolas shook his head slowly, eyes now fastened to the floor. He couldn't speak. He was trying to keep breathing.

"Tell me the truth. Am I another 'Rosie' to you? Is that why you bought me the horse? As payment?"

"No, of course not!" he declaimed. Iron bands of terror squeezed his torso. He wanted to tell her that he did care about her; but he swore he'd never again open that door. The bands tightened.

"Because in spite of what's passed between us, I'm not that kind of woman, Nicolas. I haven't—I don't—"

"I KNOW!" He stood as the words exploded, filling the room with anguish. He swam through them, feeling he might drown.

"Then what am I?" Sydney's somber face lifted to his.

"*Gud forbanner det all til helvete!*" he swore. He stomped across the room and scuttled his hands through his hair. Then he turned back to challenge her.

"You're married."

"You don't know that for certain." Sydney's tone betrayed her doubt.

"And you don't know that you're not!"

They stood still, entrenched across the room from each other. Nicolas was angry. Frustrated. Scared. But he refused to be the first to look away. Sydney held her ground, her expression unchanged. Sorrow and supplication led him into unfamiliar realms. It required several minutes of silently attempting to master his unruly emotions before he could speak.

"I'm sorry… that I've hurt you, Sydney. My actions were selfish and unthinking. I beg for your pardon."

At Sydney's nod, Nicolas asked, "You'll not hold it against me, then?"

"I can't," she murmured.

That was odd. "Can't?"

Sydney leaned back in the chair and shook her head. "I—I misspoke. I meant shouldn't. Because I owe you too much. And I don't know how to start my life over without your assistance. Legally, I mean. What must I do?"

Not certain how it came about, Nicolas was too relieved at the shift in their conversation to question it. He stood by the fireplace and leaned on the mantle while he considered the query.

"I'm not assured that I know." He scratched his chin, rasping this day's whiskers. "But I could write my lawyer in St. Louis and ask him what needs to be done."

"That would be helpful. Thank you, Nicolas."

He offered penance for his earlier transgression. "In fact, if it would give you ease, we could write him tonight, as soon as Lily leaves."

Sydney looked hopeful. "Could we?"

Nicolas snorted. "I bet old Nelson Ivarsen never saw a question like this in his whole sixty years! This ought to keep that old codger busy."

Sydney flashed a rueful smile. "I'm so glad I could be of help."

Nicolas winked his appreciation of her sarcasm. He moved toward the chamber door. Then he faced her, leaned forward, and pinned her with one lifted brow.

"And, for your information, madam; the horse was most assuredly *not* 'payment'!"

Chapter Twenty One

*I*t was well past midnight and the moon leaned far to the west. Unable to sleep, Nicolas sat on the porch and nursed a large brandy. Another habit that defined his carefully regulated life.

He learned something disturbing about himself tonight. He hurt Sydney. He didn't mean to. He did it by not considering her. Nicolas realized that he was quite accustomed to considering only one point of view, that being his own. Unconcerned about others' actions, he assumed no one cared about his. The idea that those around him might care what he did kept him from slumber.

Nicolas sipped the brandy and held the glass up. He turned it and watched the moon's reflection slide from facet to facet. In the silver light, the amber liquid looked dark, sinister. Nicolas dropped his hand into his lap and rested the glass on his thigh. He needed to face the question searing his conscience.

Had he considered Lara?

Nicolas loved her from childhood on, and there was never any question they would marry. But in that knowledge, had his adolescent flirtations caused her pain? What about those times he kissed other girls behind the schoolhouse? Or danced with anyone willing while Lara waited for him to choose her? Or tried to see how bold he could be, how far he could go with older girls—or women—who taught him how to kiss, where to touch, how to please.

Where was his consideration of Lara, then?

Once married, Nicolas only remembered telling her his ideas, his goals. He told her what their life would be like, but he never asked her what she thought about it. Lara adored him, she needed him, she supported him without question. She always did what he told her was best.

A crooked smile formed on Nicolas's face as he swallowed the last of the brandy. He could not imagine Sydney ever being so compliant. And that was precisely why he was out on the porch. Because Sydney let him know tonight in no uncertain way that his actions, actions he considered meaningless, were not meaningless to her.

Nicolas leaned his head back and considered Lily's viewpoint. He was fairly certain that she didn't find his kiss meaningless.

Skitt.

What about Rosie? He'd shared her bed once a month for a long time. Even if she had sex with men for a living, might she harbor special feelings for him?

Nicolas turned the situation around, and thought of how he felt when Sydney spent time with Rickard. If she loved him as she claimed tonight, then her time with Rickard was, in theory, meaningless. But it didn't feel meaningless to Nicolas. It dug into his gut and twisted his mood.

And then the light of realization dawned, full and bright.

Nicolas understood.

June 25, 1819

"Mr. Kilbourne said that Stefan is doing quite well with his lessons," Nicolas handed Sydney the emptied glass of lemonade. He was chopping wood, shirtless in the summer heat. "He wants to have a recital of sorts."

"Oh?" She poured him another glass from the pitcher.

Nicolas leaned on his axe and wiped his brow with a cloth that hung from his drooping waistband. "I agreed. It's today at candlelighting."

Sydney nodded, smiled blandly, and handed him the cooled beverage. If she showed any interest, Nicolas might ask her to attend. And the last place in all creation that she wanted to be was any confined space with Mr. Kilbourne.

Nicolas drained the glass again, handed it to her, pulled up his sagging breeches and swung the axe into position. "You will be there, as well."

"Stefan is your son, Nicolas. It's your presence that's required, not mine," she demurred.

The axe came down in a muscle-jolting stroke that echoed through the forest. Nicolas hefted it back to his shoulder and shot her a sideways look that brooked no argument.

"You will be there," he repeated.

The axe came down again, and she felt its repercussions shake her soul. "I don't believe—"

"But I do."

He straightened and turned his face toward her. Sweat dripped down his cheeks. His hair was tied back, but loose strands stuck to his neck. Salt water flowed through every sun-reddened hill and valley of his magnificent frame. The dampened breeches sagged lower.

Sydney fervently wished he would take her right then, right there. On the grass of the yard in the shade of the forest. Under the canopy of blue sky that lit up his eyes in a way that made her gut tingle. She could not have denied him any more than she could have denied herself air.

"You will be there."

Defeated, she nodded.

"Good." He turned and gripped the axe.

She collected the glass and pitcher. Walking back to the manor, her pulse kept sending extra heat to her nether parts. If she hadn't been carrying the lemonade, she would have rubbed herself hard, hoping to stop the need he always fired. Damn the man.

She descended the stairs later that afternoon after changing from her work clothes into the pink cotton dress. Because Sydney could not discern what precisely about Mr. Kilbourne bothered her, it had proved easiest to avoid him altogether. She had done a fine job of it until tonight. She prayed the presentation would be short.

Sydney entered the drawing room and took her seat next to Nicolas. She smiled at Stefan and avoided Mr. Kilbourne's gaze. When Stefan grinned back at her, she immediately regretted her reluctance to be there.

"Thank you for taking the time to attend this humble recital; our young man here," the teacher gestured toward Stefan, "has been working quite hard these past days and is ready to demonstrate some of his new skills. So Stefan, would you please start by counting to one hundred?"

Nicolas's eyebrows arched. Sydney leaned forward in her chair. Addie came to stand in the doorway, wiping her hands on a towel. Stefan stood.

"One, two, three, four..." his voice was clear and confident.

"Twenty-three, twenty-four, twenty-five..." Nicolas sat straighter in his seat and smiled.

"Thirty-eight, thirty-nine, um..." Stefan twisted his mouth and looked at the ceiling. "f-f-f-f...i-i..."

Nicolas drew a breath, but Sydney smacked him squarely in the chest with the back of her hand, startling him to silence. From the edge of her vision she saw him look at her, but she didn't look at him.

Instead, she spoke slowly and clearly. "I'm sorry, Stefan. You were about to say what comes after three... I mean thirty."

"Three?" Stefan frowned, then enlightenment lifted his countenance. "Four-ty! Forty-one, forty-two..." He was on his way once again.

"...Ninety-eight, ninety-nine," Stefan drew a large, dramatic breath, "One hundred!"

Sydney jumped to her feet and applauded while Stefan bowed repeatedly in exaggerated thanks. She intentionally bumped Nicolas's arm as she stood, and now she kicked his foot. Belatedly catching the hints, he rose and clapped for his son. Addie applauded from the hallway.

Mr. Kilbourne waved his hands and encouraged them to sit. He handed Stefan a slate and chalk.

"Stefan, would you please write and recite the letters of the alphabet?"

With his face scrunched in concentration, Stefan wrote the alphabet in capitals and named every letter. He stumbled on a couple but, under the threat of another beating, Nicolas did not intervene.

And this time, Nicolas jumped to his feet without prompting. Stefan blushed and tried to screw one of his feet into the carpet.

"Mr. Kilbourne, my sincerest accolades to you, sir! You have accomplished quite a bit in a short time," Nicolas complimented.

"Well, it's easy work with such a bright and capable young pupil," he demurred.

Sydney hugged Stefan. "I'm so proud of you, little man," she whispered in his ear. "Now go hug your *pappa*."

Stefan wriggled over to Nicolas and wrapped his arms around his father's powerful thighs. Nicolas reached down, lifted the boy and settled him on his hip so they were eye-to-eye.

"You did well tonight, son. I'm proud of you. Tell Addie to give you some bread and honey before you go to bed, eh?"

Nicolas hesitated, then kissed Stefan's forehead before setting him on the floor.

"Addie!" Stefan shouted as he ran toward the kitchen.

"I heard!" Addie poked her head around the door jam. "Are you ready for supper?"

Nicolas clapped his hands and rubbed them together. "I believe we are." And to Sydney's horror, he did what any good host would do. "Mr. Kilbourne, will you join us?"

80 03

Dinner was excruciating.

The main dish was suspicion, sides included curiosity and speculation. The tension in the air was thick enough to be sliced and served with coffee for dessert. And everything was beautifully presented on a façade of politeness.

Through it all Sydney was silent, staring at her plate.

The three adults concentrated on their apple pie and fresh brewed coffee, for which Nicolas offered brandy as well as cream and sugar. In the midst of dessert came an urgent pounding on the front door. Addie lumbered past the dining room and Sydney jumped from her seat, eager to get out of the room. Before they reached it, the door opened and Rickard stepped in, soaked from hat to boot and dripping a pool of water on the polished wood floor.

"Is it raining?" Sydney asked. There wasn't a more ridiculous question to pose at that moment.

"Um, yes?" Rickard laughed.

Sydney stepped past Rickard to peer outside. "I didn't see lightening or hear any thunder."

"There isn't any. Just a good old Missouri summer downpour."

"Rick! What on earth? Is it raining?" Nicolas's booming voice filled the entryway as he approached his sopping friend. Rickard looked at Sydney and they both burst into gay laughter. Nicolas shook his head when he realized what he asked.

"Why are you on my doorstep, wetting down my floor, on a night like this?" Nicolas also looked out at the unexpected weather.

"I was in town until about half an hour ago. I thought I'd head home, but it started coming down hard. I almost got lost coming this far!" Rickard's home was another mile and a half down the road.

"Go on up to my room and get some dry clothes. Then come down and have some dinner. We've got plenty!" Nicolas offered.

"I'll make him a plate before Addie puts it all away!" Sydney grabbed Addie's arm and pulled her toward the kitchen.

Devin Kilbourne emerged from his isolation in the dining room and came down the hall toward the men. Spying Rickard's condition, he asked, "Is it raining?"

℧ ℥

The torrential rain prevented both Rickard and Mr. Kilbourne from going home to their own residences. Sydney was surprised when Nicolas gave the teacher the locked room across from hers; she had not seen that door opened once during the three months she lived in this household. Rickard, of course, spent the night in his regular room.

She sat in her bed, the lamp turned as low as it would go, and tried to discern why the presence of the teacher was so upsetting. And why her shifted gaze found him staring at her with a cold intensity that sent shivers slithering down her spine. Even though he had been nothing but polite, she didn't feel safe around the man.

A soft knocking at her door prompted her to climb from her bed and tiptoe across the floor. She wondered why Nicolas would choose this particular night—when the house was full of guests—to come to her. She opened the door, careful not to let it squeak.

But it was Devin Kilbourne that awaited her.

Sydney tried to shut the door, but he blocked it with his foot. "Do you want to tell me anything? Have you changed your plans? Can I count on your silence?"

"What?" she gasped. He repeated the questions.

Sydney narrowed her eyes. Her fingers gripped the edge of the door. She intended to keep him from pushing it farther open. "I don't know what you're talking about."

"I don't believe you."

"Leave me alone."

Sydney tried again to close her door, but Devin still stopped her. "Do you truly not remember?"

How did he know? She pushed harder on the door without gaining purchase.

"Your silence is worth your life, you understand that, don't you?" he whispered.

The threat terrified her, echoing through a part of her she didn't recognize. A soft sob broke away from her and she fought to shut the door. This was the second time in quick succession she wished it had a lock.

"Do you have business with her?"

Nicolas's deep voice quaked through the dark hallway. He stood in the doorway of Kilbourne's room, barely visible in the pale moonlight that seeped through the hall windows. He was a hulking, malevolent ghost. And the most welcome phantom Sydney could imagine.

"I—I thought she was someone else," Devin stammered. "I was obviously mistaken."

Nicolas stepped forward, becoming more visible. "Let me be crystal clear, Mr. Kilbourne. I hired you for one purpose, to tutor my son. You've done an admirable job in a very short time and for that I'm well pleased. But let me be clear about this as well."

Stepping forward again, Nicolas towered over Devin. "If you speak to her again, your position here will be terminated and I'll personally escort you from my property. Do you understand?"

Devin tilted his chin in a salvaged semblance of dignity.

"Stefan is an able pupil and a pleasure to work with. But considering that he is your son, and no relation to Miss Sydney, I see no reason for me to have any further discourse with her."

He stepped around Nicolas and returned to his room. Sydney closed her door.

The next day, there was a lock on it.

June 29, 1819

Half-a-week later, Nicolas announced at breakfast: "I need to go into Cheltenham. Will you be all right?"

No, of course not. How could she be? Until she regained her memory, she floated without an anchor through increasingly perilous waters.

"Sydney?"

She stood and shrugged. "I'm going to work with Sessa. I won't be near Mr. Kilbourne."

"Has he said anything more to you?"

"No."

Nicolas reached for her hand. She met his navy gaze, dark with concern. "You will tell me if he does."

She nodded, then left the kitchen without another word.

Sydney found the corral far too constrictive for her restless and hopeless mood, so she led Sessa almost a half mile into the forest.

Her thoughts meandered through the trees along with her path. What if she never, ever got her memory back? Or what if she created a new identity for herself—and then found the old one after it was too late?

"Oh!" she grunted in frustration, smacking the palm of her hand hard against a tree. She shook out the sting. "Stop thinking!"

In spite of her trainer's distraction, Sessa did very well. She let Sydney rest her body weight across her back for quite a long time without protesting. Sydney was tempted to try and sit her, but thought better of it.

No one knew where she was, and she most certainly couldn't take the risk of being thrown. It was best to head back to the estate.

As she approached the stable, Sydney heard urgent voices drifting from inside. Bits of intense confrontation were carried toward her on sporadic breezes.

She put Sessa in the paddock, disinclined to interrupt. Then she stopped outside the stable, a few yards from the back door, and waited.

"… doing here?"

"…to warn…St. Louis!"

"…big risk…know you?"

"…don't think so…"

With a start, Sydney realized she recognized the voices. One was Mr. Kilbourne. The other sounded like Dark Skinny, the man she and Nicolas met in St. Louis. Sydney's skin puckered in gooseflesh, standing every hair on her body at attention. The shadow of black, bottomless dismay invaded her soul.

"...care for me, Devin..."

"You know Rodger... no question..."

"Come... begging you..."

"... paid tomorrow... leave Cheltenham."

The voices stopped.

Sydney's heart trip-hammered in her chest and she began to shake. Something hideous, something familiar, something caustic, bore down on her. She lurched toward the stable door, drawn toward the horrible truth that she knew, without a doubt, waited inside. She stepped inside the doorway and forced her eyes toward the dreaded revelation.

Devin Kilbourne was kissing Dark Skinny.

On the mouth.

Sydney could not draw a breath. Her heart pounded so hard that her whole body jerked with each beat. Pinpoints of black and white threatened to overtake her vision before a surge of red did so. She was numb, yet she remained standing, rooted in place. She forced her lungs to inflate; the inhaled air seared her throat. Sydney heard screams, raw and primal. As her vision cleared, she knew that she was the one screaming.

And then it came.

Sydney's memory hit her with all the physical force of the flood waters that nearly took her life; the horrific awareness it brought pounded her with the same violence. She staggered with the impact and grabbed the stable door for support. The rush of knowledge exploded, excruciating and unbearable.

Devin Kilbourne was her husband.

And Skinny was his lover.

She remembered seeing them hold each other and kiss once before. In the back of the Cheltenham schoolhouse. It was the day that she forgot she was Siobhan.

She remembered running away in shock. She remembered heading into the woods, insensible of where she was going. She remembered the vicious argument with Devin on the footbridge and pulling off her wedding ring, saying she was leaving him.

And she remembered saying she would tell others the truth.

Then Siobhan remembered being hit in the chest and falling backward into the icy, rushing water. She felt her frantic struggle to reach air. She knew the burning in her lungs and the beating of the rocks. She remembered giving up, as the blackness of unconsciousness overtook her.

Then she remembered waking up in Nicolas' house, and the frustration and terror of not knowing. And she realized, with a loud sob, that Devin didn't come after her. That realization was what broke her spirit.

And once broken, she had no fear.

Devin and Rodger stared at Siobhan. Panic overfilled their eyes. Siobhan grabbed the hoof-trimming knife from a shelf by the stable door. She squeezed the unyielding curved wooden handle and held its arched steel blade and wicked hook in front of her. She was glad she wore the breeches; they allowed her to move freely.

Nicolas blasted into the stable with John in his wake. He shifted his gaze to the two men facing Sydney.

"What's going on?" he thundered.

"I remember." Sydney ground the words out between clenched teeth. "Devin Kilbourne is—was—my husband."

She adjusted her stance, crouched, and found her balance.

"And this man, Rodger," she jerked the knife, "is his—"

"SIOBHAN!" Devin shouted.

"Sho—vahn?" Nicolas repeated. "Your name is Sho—vahn?"

She didn't answer him. She remained in the ready position, the knife an unambiguous threat.

"You knocked me off the bridge, Devin."

Devin blanched. His gaze flicked away, then back.

"You didn't try to save me…"

Devin opened his mouth, wordless, red-faced.

"You knew I was here, didn't you?" When he didn't answer, she shrieked at him, "DIDN'T YOU?"

Devin nodded. He stared at her—the transformed apparition that was once his wife.

"That's why you're here now, isn't it?"

Devin didn't answer. He glanced at Rodger.

"LOOK AT ME!" she shouted again.

He did; his medium brown eyes sank into a bloodless face.

"For three months I've been here... And you never came for me! HOW COULD YOU DO THAT TO ME?" she screamed.

The force of it tore her throat, setting it on fire and turning her voice to a screeching howl. In the edge of her vision, she glimpsed Rodger moving toward her.

Nicolas leapt across the stable, flinging himself between her and Devin. He hit Rodger in the chest with his shoulder and slammed him against the wall. Nicolas grabbed the stunned man by the front of his shirt, pulled back and threw a punch into Rodger's face with all the force of his ample size. Rodger spun around and dropped to the floor like a rag doll. Nicolas shook out his hand and turned back to her.

"Rodger!" Devin cried out like the worried lover he was.

Rational bits of her mind cried, NO! God, no! Not *him!* What about *me? Your WIFE?*

Hatred born of anguish blotted out all further deliberation. With a feral cry, Siobhan lunged toward Devin. Blinded by insane anger, she slashed with the knife in wide, wild arcs. She pushed the blade toward him, cursed him, followed him, and tried to get around the huge blond obstacle that stayed in her way. She despised the man whose unspeakable infidelity turned her life inside out. And then left her for dead.

It was his turn to die today.

Siobhan went berserk with torment and rage. Thrust after thrust, she failed to connect with the personification of her pain. Grief-stricken, and exhausted by the effort, she glared at Devin as she crouched, panting, in the middle of the dusty stable aisle. Still, she would not give in. She shifted her balance for another swipe.

80 03

Nicolas saw the slide of Kilbourne's hand.

He perceived the next movements in horrified, dream-slowed motion as he tried without success to reach the man in time. The crack of the pistol deafened him. The explosion made his ears ring and lent an incongruently angelic quality to the hell around him.

With a raucous roar of denial that left him unable to breathe, he spun around to see if Sydney yet lived.

The force of the ball had tossed her back against the wall. Her right arm fell limp at her side and her hand relaxed. The knife dropped to the floor with a dull thump as her shirt bloomed bright red. The iron smell of blood mixed with the odors of hay and manure in the thick air.

Nicolas was at her side to catch her.

Devin stared at her, wide-eyed. "Oh my God..."

"John, take the pistol and lock Kilbourne in the root cellar until I decide how to deal with him!" Nicolas barked. "You can let the other one rot for all I care!" He cradled Sydney in his arms and tried to staunch the flow of blood with his palm.

He lifted stunned eyes to the housekeeper who had somehow appeared and knelt beside them. "Addie, we need to save her!"

"We'll do our best," Addie assured him.

"Sydney, can you hear me?" With obvious effort, she looked up at Nicolas. "Don't leave me."

Siobhan shifted her focus to Devin. He stared at her, his face taught and gray, arms hanging at his sides. The pistol lay impotent on the ground.

"Rodger has another lover," she rasped. "Ask him about the actor."

Her eyes closed and she was no longer there.

Chapter Twenty Two

*M*oving through a nightmare, Nicolas carried Sydney to her room and laid her in the bed. Addie pulled off her bloodied shirt and the disfigured corset without asking him to leave. The wound blazed angrily in the hollow of her shoulder beneath her right collarbone. It still bled and Sydney's face was a blue-tinged pale.

Gud, lar henne ikke dør, Nicolas prayed. God, don't let her die.

"Go find Maribeth and ask her to bring the laudanum," Addie told him, "Along with my needles and thread. And the pinchers. And a sharp knife." Nicolas bolted downstairs.

John waited for him at the bottom of the stairs. "That Kilbourne fellow is safe in the root cellar. What else you need, Nick?"

"Ride to Atherton's and bring Rickard straight away," Nicolas instructed. "And his housekeeper Betsy, if Rick will let you. She knows healing."

John nodded and left immediately. Nicolas found Maribeth and they rushed back to Sydney's room with Addie's supplies.

Addie leaned close and told Sydney she was administering the opiate. "I must get the ball out and it's going to hurt. This'll help."

Nicolas lifted Sydney's head and shoulders. She winced, grunting her pain. Addie poured the bitter liquid into her mouth. She tried to turn away, but Nicolas wouldn't let her. When she swallowed enough, her eyes rolled back and she went limp.

With the knife, Addie enlarged the wound, probing for the lead ball that could still kill Sydney. Nicolas held the lamp overhead and watched. He waited for Addie to tell him what she found. For once in his life, the housekeeper was enragingly tightlipped.

"Addie?" he finally ventured. "Tell me."

She looked up as if she was surprised to see him there. "It's cracked the bone, but it's not broke through. That seems to have knocked the ball sideways. I can feel it. Hand me the pinchers."

Nicolas did so. He held his breath. Addie chewed her lower lip, intent on retrieving the lead. Then she smiled. Slowly her hand retreated, the pinchers exited the wound, and the ball gleamed dark and bloody in the lamplight. She dropped it into his hand.

"Is it all together?" she asked.

Nicolas rolled it in his palm. The lead ball was dented—most likely from its collision with bone—but it was whole. A sigh cleansed his chest. "It is."

Addie nodded. "I'll flush out the wound and set to stitching it, then."

Even with the laudanum, Sydney jerked and twitched when the needle went into her skin. Nicolas held her as still as he could. When she whimpered, insensible, tears rolled down his tensed cheeks and dampened the blood-stained sheets. He experienced her agony so strongly, he wondered if his blood mixed with hers on the bed.

Rickard arrived with Betsy. Nicolas left the women to care for Sydney, painfully cleaving himself from her side. He met Rickard downstairs in his study.

"What the hell happened, Nick?"

"You know Devin Kilbourne."

"The teacher?" Rickard frowned. "What about him?"

"He was Sydney's husband, as it turns out." Nicolas poured them each a generous brandy, gulped his and poured another.

"Him? *Skitt.*" Rickard used one of Nick's favorite words. "Did he come for her?"

"No."

"So how'd you find out?"

"Sydney remembered, or so it appears." Nicolas swallowed half of the second brandy. It heated his belly nicely.

Rickard sat down, hard. "What brought it back?"

"I don't know. When I returned from town, she was in the stable holding a hoof-knife on him and the other fellow." Nicolas finished that brandy and poured a third. The heat of it coursed through his limbs.

"Other fellow?"

"This sodomite we met in St. Louis."

Rickard lifted his eyebrows and waited.

"He recognized Sydney and came to the hotel to talk to her."

"Did she know him?"

Nicolas shook his head.

"But he's here now?"

"Yes." Nicolas set the flask on the desk.

"Why?"

Nicolas turned to Rickard. "It looks as though Kilbourne, Sydney's husband, might be of the same... persuasion."

Rickard blanched. His tone carried his disbelief. "Sydney's husband is a sodomite?"

Nicolas finished the third brandy. "That seems to be the situation."

"Go easy, brother." Rickard put his hand on the flask. "I don't need you pissin' drunk at this time! You're barely making sense as it is."

Nicolas pulled a deep breath, capped the flask and dropped it in the desk drawer with a dull metallic clunk.

"How did Sydney get hurt?" Rickard asked.

"He shot her."

His mouth caverned. "Why?"

Nicolas's head fell forward, his puzzlement clear. "I don't know. Probably because she was trying to kill him." Then he slammed the glass down on the desk. "I need you to do something for me."

Rickard blinked his open-mouthed shock. Then he nodded. "Name it."

"I need you to go to St. Louis and see Nelson Ivarsen."

"Your lawyer?"

"That's the one. I need him to draw up a divorce decree between our Mr. Devin Kilbourne and Syd—I mean Sho-vahn—Kilbourne. *Skitt!*"

"What?"

"I don't know her legal name." Nicolas twisted and glanced around his study, patting his pockets. "You'll have to visit the root cellar before you go."

Rickard's eyes narrowed. "How many brandies have you had?"

Nicolas blew an exasperated sigh. "Kilbourne. He's in the root cellar."

"You're holding him prisoner?"

"I am. And he'll stay there until he signs the divorce papers."

"So, I'm to go to the root cellar and make a list of everyone's legal names," Rickard reiterated as he ticked off the tasks on his fingers. "Then ride to St. Louis and get Ivarsen to draw up the decree. I bring the decree back here and Kilbourne signs it, and then you'll let him go?"

"That sums it up fairly well."

"What are the grounds?"

Nicolas looked at Rickard; his disgust burned bitter in his mouth and roiled in his belly.

"Infidelity. On the husband's part."

Rickard nodded his agreement. "I'll leave off the reel."

A measure of relief melted through Nicolas's tense frame. "Thanks, brother."

Rickard headed to the root cellar before riding back home to prepare for his sudden trip to St. Louis. And Nicolas headed to the stable to deal with Rodger, the infidel.

ഇ ൙

When Nicolas entered the stable, Rodger lay on his back, knees up. His eyes were closed, one by choice. Nicolas approached him and intentionally towered over him.

"Can you stand?" He gave no pretense of caring.

Rodger's uninjured eye opened and swiveled to regard Nicolas. He grunted.

"That's not an answer." Nicolas prodded Rodger's ribs with his large, heavy boot. "Can you stand or not?"

Rodger rolled to his side and managed to get on his hands and knees. He pulled one foot, then the other, under him. Using the wall of the stall for support, Rodger eased himself to vertical. He turned an angry eye to Nicolas.

"Here's how it is." Nicolas's low tone spoke the threat very clearly. "You'll leave my property now. Alone. And you'll never return."

"Alone? What about Devin?"

It required every whit of self-control Nicolas could muster to keep from pummeling Rodger again. His gut begged him to do it anyway; his hands fisted on their own and his jaw clenched.

"I'm detaining Mr. Kilbourne for a bit."

"Wh—why?" There was a flicker of fear as Rodger's open eye dropped to the drying blood on Nicolas's shirt.

"That's no concern of yours."

Rodger glanced around the stable for a reason, a clue, a leg to stand on.

"Go." Nicolas indicated the stable door with a jerk of his head. "Before I do more damage."

"But is he alright?"

"He?" Nicolas frowned and looked down at his shirtfront. "The blood is hers."

"Oh!" Rodger let out his breath. "Thank God."

Nicolas froze for a heartbeat, disbelieving his ears.

"*Helvetet med det!*" He drove his fist so deep into Rodger's middle that he later swore he felt the man's backbone against his knuckles. Rodger folded in half and crashed to the ground. His attempts to breathe filled the stable with squeaking gasps.

"John!" Nicolas bellowed out the stable door. "Come harness the wagon!" Then he turned back and spat on the floor. "I need you to drive this garbage to town."

⁊ ℭ

Opium causes vivid dreams. While her nurses kept her sedated, Sydney dreamt constantly.

In some dreams, she was a little girl back in Kentucky, riding horses with her father. She felt the wind on her face as she galloped through golden fields. She felt the thrill of fear as her steed took a high fence. She threw her arms out and she knew she was flying. She saw the farm below her.

Sometimes she was a new bride helping to build a house in the wilderness. She smelled the pinesap as she struggled to lift logs into place and felt the burn of her overworked muscles; she tasted the salt of sweat that dripped into her mouth. Her eyes burned with the sting of wood smoke.

At other times she dreamt of her two dead baby boys, each one pushed from her body far too soon. She felt the pains of labor tear at her core. She cried out and begged God to make it stop. She curled into a ball and screamed at her husband to leave her alone!

And yet they emerged from her. Tiny, perfectly formed humans covered in vernix and smeared with her blood. She sobbed and held them and tried to make them breathe. When they wouldn't, she washed them; fragile, translucent, porcelain dolls. They made her put them in boxes in the ground. She dreamt she dug them up with her hands. Bloody fingers, broken nails, rotten wood, tiny skulls.

She screamed again.

She dreamt of drowning. And cold. And the terror of not being able to draw a breath. She dreamt about pain. She dreamt about abandonment and confusion and being completely and utterly alone. She dreamt about black. Empty, echoing, endless black.

July 2, 1819

Rickard returned three days later from St. Louis, his mission complete. He said once Nelson Ivarsen understood the situation and its urgency, he meticulously drew up the decree, assuring it would be legal from all aspects.

"It must go back to a judge after Sydney, or Siobhan, and the Kilbourne fellow sign it. Then it becomes final." Rickard laid his hand on Nick's shoulder. "I can take it back if you'd like me to."

"Thanks, Rick. I appreciate it. Let's go to the root cellar and get it signed."

Nicolas grabbed a quill and ink in his study, and then went outside to the cellar. Rickard held the writing tools while Nicolas unlocked the door and pulled it open. The stench of the chamber pot assaulted them.

After three days, Devin was not his previous cocky, well-put-together self. For those three days he lived in damp darkness, surrounded by barrels of flour, hanging onions and smoked meat. Once a day, John lowered him a sack of food and a jug of water. He didn't bother to empty the chamber pot. For those three days, no one talked to him. For those three days, Devin was in the hell Nicolas created for him.

"Come out, Kilbourne."

Squinting in the bright light of day, Devin climbed out of the dark cellar and wavered, blinded and disoriented. His clothes were filthy and reeked of sweat.

"Sign this."

Rickard handed Devin the quill and indicated the spot.

"What's this?" Devin fumbled for the document.

"A divorce decree."

Devin shot a nervous look at Nicolas. "On what grounds?"

"Today it only says that you are guilty of infidelity. Don't tempt me to change it."

Devin's hand shook, but he signed his name where Rickard indicated. Nicolas checked it, then handed Rickard the signed document. Then with both hands he pulled Devin up by the front of his shirt. He pressed his face close to Devin's. The man stank.

"I'm *asking* you to leave the Territory and never come back." Nicolas's voice cut like steel. "If you do come back, I'll bring you up on charges of sodomy. Do you understand me?"

Devin jerked his head in agreement. Pungent yellow liquid pooled in the dirt beneath him.

Nicolas twisted his hands and tightened his grip on Devin's shirt. His eyes narrowed.

"And if that woman upstairs dies as a result of what happened here, I'll hunt you down and kill you both, no matter where you've gone to." He let go of Devin's shirt with a push that sent him sprawling backwards on the ground.

"Now get out of here before I decide to stop being so nice."

Devin scrambled to his feet and stumbled toward the road without looking back.

When he passed out of sight, Rickard patted Nicolas on the shoulder. His attention reclaimed, Nicolas faced his friend and allowed himself a moment of weakness.

"Rick!" he gasped.

"She's strong, Nick. And she's feisty." His face was pale, and his normally affable personality, subdued. "I'm counting on it."

The men took the document upstairs to Sydney's room and Nicolas approached the bedside.

"Sydney? Sho-vahn?" Nicolas didn't know which name to call her.

"Siobhan's dead," she muttered without opening her eyes.

"I've a document for you to sign," Nicolas said gently. "But you have to sign it as 'Siobhan Bell Kilbourne,' can you do that?" Addie helped him prop her up. She whimpered in pain as her shoulder changed position.

"Stop…please," she whimpered. "I'll be good."

Rickard put his hand on Nicolas shoulder. "If she makes any mark at all, then you and I could witness it as her signature. Will that do?"

"With two witnesses who aren't related to her it would be legal. Good thinking, Rick."

Nicolas put the quill in Sydney's hand and held it to the parchment in the right spot. "Sign your name and Siobhan can go away. You can be Sydney."

That seemed to make sense to the injured woman. She blinked her eyes open and focused, squinting, on the paper. Nicolas supported her arm and she scribbled, *Siobhan B. Kilbourne.*

It was barely legible.

But it was completely legal.

Chapter Twenty Three

July 4, 1819

*I*t was past midnight on the fifth night. Nicolas sat by Sydney's bed to watch her sleep, and assure himself that her chest continued to rise and fall. She perspired and that was good. Fevered since she was shot, her three nurses forced her to swallow cooled tea or water whenever they could.

Nicolas's head jerked. He rubbed his stubbled face hard with both hands and combed his fingers through his hair. He stood and stretched, reaching toward the high ceiling. When he sat down again he was startled to see Sydney's open eyes. He peered at her to determine if she was in her right mind.

"Thirsty…" It was barely a whisper. She winced as he lifted her, but she drank the cooled tea. Nicolas lowered her back onto the mattress. Sydney frowned at him.

"I signed a paper?" she croaked.

"It was your divorce decree."

"How?"

"Rickard rode to St. Louis and had Nelson Ivarsen draw it up for me. For you, I mean."

"Devin?"

"I kept him here until Rickard came back. It took a couple of days. He signed it willingly enough."

Sydney lifted her left hand a few inches off the mattress. "Couple days?"

"Tonight is the fifth night since…" Nicolas's voice trailed off.

Sydney dropped her hand and closed her eyes. Nicolas thought she slept again, but her eyes opened.

"Devin. Where?"

"I told him to leave the Territory and never come back or I'll have him charged with sodomy." Nicolas thought it best not to reveal the accompanying duel death threat.

"I'm alone."

Nicolas didn't know how to answer her, so he just stroked the back of her hand. For a long time she focused on something not in the room.

Then Sydney reached toward Nicolas. Her fingertips brushed his shirtfront and she grasped at it.

"Tell me… about Lara."

"No, Sydney. Not now." That was the last thing he wanted to think about.

She struggled to swallow. Nicolas lifted the cup of tea to her lips. After she drank, Sydney tightened her grip.

"Need to know." Her eyes glittered with fever and desperation. "Please."

"Sydney, this isn't the time. Perchance when you're better?"

"No!" Tears welled and she held onto his shirt. "Tell me. How it was."

Nicolas acquiesced, in spite of his oppressive misgivings. "As long as you're awake, I'll talk. But if you fall asleep I'll not wake you. Is that clear?"

Sydney let go of Nicolas's shirt. He understood that to mean she agreed. He ran both hands through his hair. "Where should I start?"

"Married."

"I loved her, of course. When I asked for her hand in marriage, it was expected. We were married about three months later. Is this what you wanted to hear?"

Sydney's half-opened eyes stayed focused on his. She moved her hand to his arm. "Tell me about after."

"After?"

"The babies."

"Å min Gud." The recollection was imbedded, undiminished, in his core. "I couldn't believe it. I was in shock."

"Yes…"

"I kept thinking it must be a mistake." Denial and realization had taken turns tormenting him during those surreal days. "I wanted to turn back time and have things come out differently."

"Yes…"

"When I sat in the room with her body, I saw all of my expectations just disappear." As he spoke, Nicolas held up one hand, fingers cupped. He turned it over as though everything he held, including his very existence, was poured out.

"Yes…" Tears dripped down Sydney's cheeks.

Nicolas stared at Sydney's hand on his arm, but he didn't see it. His jaw relaxed, his breathing slowed. He stilled. "It seemed that my own life was taken from me."

Silence. Then a whispered, "Yes."

"I had no future, no life to live."

"Yes."

With a shock that jolted him back to the present, he realized why Sydney responded 'yes' to all that he said. He defined how she felt right now.

"Oh, Sydney."

Her eyes were dark and her pupils dilated with fever. Her only movement was the slow rise and fall of her chest. She closed her eyes.

Nicolas lifted her hand from his arm and kissed it. Her skin was hot and her palm calloused from tack leather, but he felt her steady pulse. He thought she fell back to sleep.

Then she opened her eyes and pegged him with a look so intense that he held his breath. His soul collided with hers. "What do you choose?" she whispered.

"Choose?"

"Life or death."

Nicolas shook his head, honestly confused. "What you are asking?"

"Which one?"

Nicolas felt like he should know, but he didn't. "I don't understand, Sydney."

"Yes, you do." Sydney stopped to catch her breath before she continued. "Since Lara died, you haven't chosen."

Nicolas frowned. Comprehension clambered up his spine and dug into his skull. His heart screamed at her to stop.

"Choose now." Sydney's challenge was almost too soft to hear. But he did hear her. And she was right.

"Do you still love me?" he hedged.

"I don't matter."

The possibility that she might no longer love him, now that she knew herself, her history and her husband, offset Nicolas's center. How could he step through that door without knowing?

"But, Sydney—"

"Choose."

She cornered him. He needed to make a decision and it had to be his own. Not for anyone else, and not because of anyone else.

Strained by days of worry and physically exhausted, Nicolas lost the ability to corral his emotions. He dropped his head on the bed and succumbed to his pain. Face pushed into the mattress, he muffled his sobs.

Nicolas had no idea how much time passed before his grief was emptied, but he felt it pouring out. Black and jagged, it ripped him, bled him, drained him. But it could not kill him. A thick fog lifted. Light moved in, faint at first. Gray, lavender, pink. A sunrise in his soul.

Hope.

Nicolas lifted his head. He pulled a shuddering breath of resolution. "I'll choose life, Sydney. I'm tired of death."

A faint smile. "I'll choose life, as well."

He lifted her hand and held it to his chest. "I was afraid you were going to leave me."

"I considered it." Her gaze flickered aside, then back. "But I do still love you."

Nicolas let his air out slowly. Relief cleansed him.

"Sydney, I…"

Sydney closed her eyes and turned her head away.

"Look at me."

"No."

"Please."

She pressed her lips together. Their corners twitched downward.

He was insistent. "Sydney."

"My shoulder hurts," she whispered. "I ache all over."

"I know."

"Nicolas, don't."

"Sydney! Look at me!" That startled her and gained her attention. His eyes bore into hers. "I love you as well."

Sydney blinked slowly. "You do?"

"I do. I love you, Sydney." Nicolas was amazed; once he shoved it out, it stopped fighting him. So he said it again, "I love you." Then he leaned over and kissed her perfect lips; hot, dry and cracked with fever.

Sydney laid her fingers on Nicolas's cheek. She opened her mouth to speak, but closed it again.

"Is something amiss, Sydney?"

She shook her head weakly and seemed to dissolve into the mattress. Her eyelids drooped as her strength evaporated. "Something to tell you."

"What is it?"

Her frail gaze pleaded for his understanding. "Couldn't help it. So sorry."

"What is it Sydney?"

"That night."

"Tell me."

"I'm pregnant."

80 CB

Sydney collapsed back into sleep as soon as the words were out of her mouth.

Nicolas was stone. Unmoving. Cold. Hard. His thoughts scattered everywhere and nowhere. He stared out the window and waited through the interminable final hour until dawn—the last of his watch. The moment Betsy appeared, he bolted from the room and flew downstairs to look for Addie.

He found her in the kitchen, in front of the stove.

"Addie, I need to ask you something. It's extremely important. And it's somewhat delicate."

"What is it, Nicky?"

"Since Sydney has come here, to the manor, has she had her monthly…" He hesitated, embarrassed to ask about something so personal. But he had to know.

Addie stopped her breakfast preparations and turned to face

him. Her eyes did not let go of his and her voice was stern. "She bled less than two weeks after you found her and not again since. The child is yours."

Nicolas was smacked speechless. How did she know?

Addie grabbed a bucket and left the kitchen. Nicolas followed her outside to the water pump. He held the heavy bucket while Addie raised and lowered the handle with more force than usual.

"How long have you known?" he asked.

"I figured it out myself around the end of May. When she got peaked and started sleeping in the afternoons."

Nicolas did some finger counting. He knew the night she conceived; it was the only night he entered her. It was ten weeks ago.

"What'll you do?" Addie asked.

Nicolas shook his head. "I don't know."

Addie frowned and pursed her lips. Her blatant disapproval buckled his knees.

Nicolas carried the water inside, then disappeared deeper into the house. When he returned, he carried his rifle and ammunition.

"Nick, you haven't slept!" Addie protested. "You're in no shape to go gallivantin' around the woods with a loaded weapon!"

Nicolas pushed past her and out the back door to the stable. He led Fyrste out of his stall and saddled him in the Cheyenne saddle. He tied his rifle and saddlebag behind the seat. Then he mounted the stallion while still inside the stable and kicked the startled horse, urging him to a full-out run when they cleared the building.

Chapter Twenty Four

July 5, 1819

*F*yrste's hooves thundered through the forest, hurling huge clods of dirt behind him. Nicolas leaned forward and the wind tangled his long, loose hair in Fyrste's charcoal mane. Man and stallion were one.

They followed a Mississippi River tributary upstream into the wooded hills. Nicolas pushed Fyrste for an hour, covering nearly ten miles before he slowed the laboring animal. He walked in slow, wide circles through the trees to cool him. Finally Nicolas hobbled the stallion, stripped off his clothes, and dove into the wide blue pond at the bottom of a twenty-foot waterfall.

Nicolas swam without stopping, crisscrossing the deep pool until his limbs ached and his lungs burned. Plunging to the bottom, pushing back to the top, he relished the water combing through his hair and sliding over every inch of his bare body. He wanted to wash away his worries. He wanted to indulge his physical desires.

Most of all, he wanted to stop loving.

He climbed out of the cool water and lay on a flat rock, breathless, warmed by the sun. The radiating heat on his back contrasted with the cold evaporation on his wet skin. The pleasant sensations soon evident in his private barometer, he stroked until it released, groaning with complete abandon. This was what he wanted, what he thought he needed. Relaxed, he slept.

Nicolas woke hours later, when the sun moved behind trees and the rock cooled. He was famished. He squirmed back into his clothes and wondered what he would catch. Rabbits and squirrels were abundant, as were birds.

"No feathers," he said aloud just to hear his voice. He loaded his rifle and searched for a likely hunting perch, settling in the fork of a nearby oak tree. In less than half an hour, Nicolas started a fire, cleaned and spitted the rabbit, and propped it over the flames. Satisfied, he sat back and watched the fire char the meat. Now, he would allow himself to think.

"*Gud forbanner det,*" he muttered. "*Gud forbanner det all til helvete!*"

Pregnant. With his child.

Not again.

Not again!

Nicolas's rage engulfed him. His heart threw itself against his ribs; his pulse thrashed in his ears. Was this some kind of cosmic joke? Was God finding it particularly amusing to toy with him? To see how much he could take?

Or not take? Was God searching for his breaking point? First it was his beloved Lara. When she breathed her last, Nicolas's world collapsed. He begged God to take him, too; but He wouldn't show Nicolas that mercy. So Nicolas was still here, pretending to live.

Apparently that wasn't good enough for God, because He turned around and dropped Sydney at his feet.

Sydney. Nicolas's heart eased against his will at the thought of her.

Beautiful, funny, strong, intelligent Sydney.

Warm, loving, giving, soft, sensual Sydney.

Desirable Sydney.

Fertile Sydney.

He rose to his feet, threw his head back and screamed as loud as he could, "*Gud forbanner det all til* fucking *helvete!*"

God damn it all to hell.

Nicolas stood, tall and defiant, and raised his fists to the sky.

"What do You expect from me? How much *skitt* do You care to dump on me? Just how strong do You think I am?"

Nicolas picked up a stone and threw it as far as he could. Then another and another. He threw until his muscles passed burning and went numb. Then he leaned his head back, threw his arms wide, and addressed the unfathomable Deity somewhere above him.

"I'm not that strong!" His voice echoed off the rocky cliff of the waterfall. "I cannot do this again! Don't ask this of me!"

Then from somewhere Nicolas couldn't place, he heard a voice. Not in truth a voice, because he didn't hear it with his ears; but he heard it just the same.

Trust.

What the *helvete* was that supposed to mean? Trust? Trust what? Trust whom? Nicolas trusted before. He was not impressed with the outcome.

He yelled back, "*Hvorfor skal jeg stoler på?*" Why should I trust?

He trusted that his love for Lara was strong enough to see them through a lifetime. He trusted that because he was a good husband, God would show him how to be a good father. That was not how it worked out.

"Are You laughing?" Nicolas sneered. "Your sense of irony is rather impressive! Or should I say, infinite?"

Less than an hour after Nicolas decided to let go of his pain, to open his heart again and let Sydney in, God turned the tables and put him back precisely where he was six years ago. Less than a *forbannet* hour! *Skitt!*

"I won't do it. I will not! I cannot, do You understand? I know there's a child. And I am sorry about that. But do not ask me to—"

Trust.

There it was again, that odd, disembodied voice that wasn't a voice. Clear, understandable and unmistakable, it chilled Nicolas to the marrow. A shiver skated up his spine.

The smell of cooking flesh diverted his attention. He looked at the fire as a piece of the rabbit meat fell into the flames. Nicolas rushed over and stabbed it with his dirk, then retrieved the spitted carcass and sat down on a log. He ate in silence and kept his thoughts to himself for the time being.

When he finished, he kicked dirt over the fire, staunching the flames. Nicolas stared at the smoldering ashes. Crazy as it sounded, he felt that by his unwillingness to trust, he paralyzed himself somehow. Like he was his own obstacle.

"Pure unadulterated bunkum!" he muttered aloud. He shook himself like a wet dog to rid himself of the feeling. He laid down on the flat rock again, head pillowed on his saddlebag. He must decide what to do next.

He did love Sydney. Just since the wee hours of morning, his feelings for her had solidified and become part of him. He would do everything he could to keep her.

But the child?

The child was a different story.

He hated the child.

The child would want to keep Sydney all to itself. To that end, it would do whatever was required to keep him away from her.

Including killing her.

In Nicolas's mind, that's what happened to Lara. The boy that died wanted his mother for himself, so he claimed her life to ensure she would be with him, and only him. But Sydney wouldn't understand the perilous situation she was in. She would love the unborn child; women were prone to such emotions.

This was going to be a balancing act of the greatest magnitude.

Nicolas knew that marrying Sydney was expected in this situation. After all, she would be divorced when Rickard returned from St. Louis with the signed decree. But marriage would place him directly in the jealous child's path.

It made sense within Nicolas's logic that if he and Sydney weren't married, then the babe wouldn't need to kill her. After the bastard child was successfully birthed, he'd be pleased to marry her. With luck and care, they could avoid conceiving any more children. Then he could be a husband without fear and live his life loving Sydney and being loved by her.

This appeared to be the perfect solution.

With a satisfied sigh, Nicolas stretched and groaned long and loud. He scratched his belly and considered another dip in the pond. The day's weather was definitely consistent with mid-July; hot and humid, with useless wisps of cloud striating the sky. The air was so heavy it couldn't move.

Nicolas stripped again and slipped into the cool water. He swam to the waterfall. Climbing the rocks behind it, he stood on a ledge, hands on his hips, as the water spilled over him. His hair washed around his shoulders; his legs and buttocks flexed to maintain his balance. His muscles were outlined by the glint of sunlight on his wet skin. The drenched hair on his chest grew darker as it narrowed to a trail leading to the nest of his manhood.

One last time, Nicolas released the lingering remnants of his tension, shooting his seed into the churning waters below him. Then he jumped in after it, submerging himself in the solitude of the deep, clear water. He held his breath as long as he could before he resurfaced and reentered his life.

ഇ ❧

It was dark when Nicolas arrived back at his estate. Eager to see Sydney, he took the stairs two at a time and followed the light to her open door.

"How is she?" he asked Addie as he approached the bed.

"Better. The fever's almost gone." She eyed Nicolas. "She asked about you today."

"Did she?" That made Nicolas smile. "I've a proposition for you, Addie, you old dear. I'll sit with Sydney if you'll bring me up a plate of food. I believe I could eat an entire cow!"

"I'll do it." Addie hoisted her bulk from the rocking chair and patted her surrogate son. "Just to make you happy."

Nicolas felt like a child waiting for Christmas as he watched to see Sydney stir. It didn't matter that her dark, tangled hair hadn't been brushed in days, nor her face washed or her bedclothes aired. Just to be near her and know she would recover was all he needed.

His diligence was rewarded when Sydney drew a breath and tried to stretch. Wincing, her hand went to her upper chest. Her eyes fluttered open. She turned toward the oil-lamp and Nicolas, food tray on his lap, laden utensils held in mid-bite, mouth open, eyes riveted on hers.

She smiled and his world righted itself.

"I missed you today." Her voice was much stronger.

Nicolas lowered the bite of food. "I had to sort some things out. You gave me quite a shock, you know. I had no idea." Nicolas set the tray on the bedside table and knelt by the bed. "I love you. We'll work it out."

"I didn't mean for it to happen. Not any of it."

"I know."

"Are you angry?"

"Not at you. Never at you." Nicolas brushed her lips with his. "But I believe it's best that we don't tell anyone about the child."

Sydney frowned. "Why?"

"You're recovering from a serious injury. You just got your memory back. You're not quite divorced yet, and your husband was—" Nicolas bit back the rest of the sentence.

"Oh." Her voice was very tiny.

"When you've done adjusting to all these things, we'll move forward. I believe that's the sensible way to go," he said, logically outlining his insanity. He lifted a stray lock of hair and tucked it behind her ear. "You won't have to do it alone. I promise."

July 6, 1819

"Would you open the windows? I feel like I'm in a tomb," Sydney said.

Morning's orange-pink rays and dew-freshened air swirled into the room, pushing aside sickroom mustiness.

"It's going to be another hot one." Nicolas eyed the cloudless sky. "I know my father built this house to withstand the twisters, but these thick stone walls are a blessing on days like this."

Sydney struggled to sit up. Nicolas moved to help, but she put up a hand to stop him.

"It hurts less when I move myself." She pushed the covers back and suddenly remembered she was naked. Mortified, she snatched the covers up to her chin. Nicolas laughed out loud.

"Sydney, you know I've seen—" He gestured along her body. "And not just looked."

"That's different!" Sydney was mortified at the untimely reminder of her indiscretions.

Addie entered the room and, with a sideways glance at Nicolas, hurried to Sydney's side.

"Whatever's the matter, child?"

She bit her lower lip and spoke a separate concern. "Will I be badly scarred?"

Addie patted her hand. "It's not that bad. Now the infection's gone, it should heal quite nicely."

Sydney gave her a look that clearly displayed her doubt.

Addie turned to Nicolas. "Shut the door. We'll take a look."

Sydney reached for his hand and her eyes squeezed shut. She reckoned it was best to confront this demon at the same time as he.

When the dressing was lifted away, no one made a sound. Sydney opened one eye to see Addie and Nicolas bending over her chest, frowning with interest, not revulsion.

"What do you think?" she whispered.

Addie squinted. "The stitches need to come out."

Nicolas left to fetch the scissors and tweezers.

Sydney steeled herself and looked. Multi-colored knots of thread puckered a four-inch line from her right collarbone to below her right shoulder. Deep pink showed along the edges and was evidence of healing. Sydney shuddered at what her husband had tried to do to her.

Nicolas slipped in the door and handed Addie her tools.

"How might I help?" he asked.

"Help her keep still. Though it's a lot less painful than putting them in, don't you know."

Nicolas sat on the bed next to Sydney. She gripped his hands. One by one, Addie snipped the knots and pulled the thread from her skin. She dug her nails into Nicolas's palms, but he didn't complain. When the torture ended, Addie laid a cool damp cloth over the wound to soothe her inflamed skin.

"You be careful now. You don't want to move too much and split that open, or you'll have a bigger scar for certain!" Addie gathered the bits of cut thread. "I'll send you both up some breakfast."

"Do you find it repulsive?" Sydney asked Nicolas when they were alone.

"No." Nicolas cocked his head to the side and fixed his dark-blue gaze on Sydney. "That wound signifies the end of one life and the start of another."

Sydney smiled faintly. "I love you, Nicolas."

"And I you."

"How do you say it in Norse?"

"*Jeg elsker deg.*"

"Yegg els-kerr dig?" she attempted.

"*Jeg elsker deg også!*"

With a gasp, Nicolas bounced off the bed. "I forgot! I have a gift for you. That's why I went into town that day." He was out of the door before Sydney could respond, and back in less than a minute. He set a large box tied with twine on the bed.

He untied the twine and lifted the cover to reveal soft buckskin. Sydney ran her hand over the leather and lifted the item from the box. It was breeches. In her size.

Sydney's face transformed into pure joy. "Where ever did you find these?"

"I had them made. If you're going to keep training horses, you should have your own clothes to do it in. There's more!" He wagged his finger at the box. Beneath the buckskin breeches was a coffee-colored canvas pair.

"Those are for summer. I picked the color to match your hair." Nicolas grinned like a euphoric hyena.

"I cannot believe you did this!"

"Keep going."

Sydney lifted a piece of paper and discovered two shirts of light-blue cotton chambray, tailored to her size and embellished with feminine tucks and pleats.

"Oh, Nicolas, this is the nicest gift I've ever received. Truly, it is." She pointed her forefinger at him. "And I have my memory back now, so I know what I'm talking about!"

Nicolas laughed. "There's one more article in there. Well, two."

Sydney lifted another sheet of paper and looked at him in disbelief. "How did you... where did you..."

"I drew the seamstress a picture and told her what they were for. She charged me triple because she thought I was joking with her."

Sydney lifted two short, boneless corsets from the bottom of the box. Each had rounded cut-outs that fit under her breasts and fabric that would cup and support them. They laced in the back like regular corsets.

"I honestly don't know what to say. I'm overwhelmed."

Nicolas out-beamed the morning sun. "I'm glad you like them."

The bedroom door swung open and Addie backed in with a heavy tray. Nicolas stepped to her aid and carried the food to the bedside table. Sydney held up her new treasures.

"Look what Nicolas gave me!"

"Huh." Addie examined the clothing, her expression a mixture of disbelief and approval. "Good stitching. These must've cost a pretty penny! They're odd, but they're practical, and I can't argue with that."

Chapter Twenty Five

July 6, 1819

*R*ickard returned with the signed divorce decree, along with a second document and a letter from Nelson Ivarsen.

"I would have gotten back yesterday if it wasn't for the other document there," Rickard pointed to the official paper.

"What's that for?" Nicolas squinted at the swirly script. "A name change?"

"Exactly so. That old fox persuaded the judge to sign it with the new name left blank. I reckon his argument—that it doesn't matter what name Sydney chooses—convinced him to go ahead and sign."

"It says here that Siobhan keeps both of these documents as proof." Nicolas looked at Rickard with one eyebrow raised. "It also says how much he's withdrawing from my account to pay for these bits of legal gold."

Rickard helped himself to a glass of brandy. "Good help doesn't come cheaply."

Nicolas considered the papers he held. "I reckon not. At the least, it's done."

Rickard downed the brandy and winked at Nicolas. "Speaking of good help, Rosie sends her regards."

Nicolas's mouth curled in a knowing smile. "Did she help you out, then?"

"That she did, brother." Rickard lifted his glass in a toast. "That she did."

Nicolas took the documents to Sydney later that afternoon. She wore a different nightgown and sat in the slat-backed rocker, her back to the room. He leaned in the doorway and watched Maribeth's nimble fingers work the snarls from Sydney's washed hair, restoring its glossy glory. She plaited it tightly to keep it neat. Only then did Nicolas make his presence known.

"How long were you standing there?" Sydney eased herself back into bed.

"Only a few minutes or so," he lied. "You have the most beautiful hair I've ever seen."

She pulled a face. "It's too heavy and straight."

"Why do you do that?"

"What?"

"You don't accept compliments well at times."

Sydney shrugged with her left shoulder. "I'm not used to them, I reckon. Devin didn't compliment me often."

Nicolas abruptly realized that Devin Kilbourne, as part of her past, would be part of his future. He wasn't at all pleased with that revelation. With a soft snort, he handed her the first document.

"Speaking of which, this is your divorce decree."

Her demeanor shrank. "So it's really over."

"It is." Nicolas waited while she read through it.

"What's the other?"

"A legal name change. I reckon Nelson got his answer about creating a new identity at the same time you found your original one." He handed it to her. Her brows drew together.

"If you want to change your name, you fill in your new name here," Nicolas pointed to the spot, "and it will be legal."

Sydney stared at the documents for several, silent minutes. "It's a strange thing to change one's name."

Though Nicolas couldn't imagine ever changing *his*—the Hansens of Arendal, Norway could be traced back for centuries, after all—he pointed out that, "Women do it all the time when they marry."

"But first names stay the same." She looked at him and he was captured by her gray-green gaze. "So which do I change?"

"To be honest, I'll call you 'Sydney' no matter what you decide," Nicolas confessed. "It's who you are to me."

"It's definitely who I've become, though I doubt my parents would agree should I be fortunate enough to see them or my brother again." She considered Nicolas. Her lips pressed and puckered. "I'll return to my maiden name. But I'll be Siobhan *Sydney* Bell."

She carefully filled in the paperwork and added both her previous and her brand new signatures. Somberly she handed the documents back to him. Her eyes lifted to his. "It's done."

July 17, 1819

The nightmarish confrontation that had uprooted, shattered and redefined her life was very nearly three weeks past. Sydney was contemplating her shapeless future in the drawing room when Rickard unexpectedly joined her for afternoon tea. He eased his long frame into the chair closest to her and grinned. He was as achingly beautiful as always.

"You look well, Sydney. How are you feeling?"

His dark chocolate voice thrilled her. She passed him the plate of biscuits and poured him some tea. "I'm getting stronger."

"That's good to hear."

She relaxed in the warmth of his smile. "Nicolas told me about your trips to St. Louis on my behalf. I owe you quite a debt."

"I was honored to be of service." Rickard tipped forward in salute. He inspected his half-eaten biscuit. "What will you do now?"

There it was, the unresolved question of her life dangled in front of her. A rather large issue was at stake, one that Rickard knew nothing about. And she certainly couldn't tell him. She sagged a little.

"I don't know."

"The papers are filed. You're no longer married." Rickard set his refreshments down and lifted her hand.

Sydney startled. He looked nervous; was his palm sweating? That wasn't like him; he was always so easy-going and confident. He smiled again and his chameleon eyes glowed golden in the afternoon light.

"May I court you?"

Sydney's brow plummeted and she examined Rickard's handsome face from beneath it. "What!"

Rickard shifted in the formal chair. "May I please court you?"

"Why?"

Rickard shook his head, obviously not anticipating that query.

His gaze pinned her. "Because you're interesting and intelligent. And beautiful." The next phrase came out one slow word at a time: "And I am very attracted to you."

Sydney sat back in her chair and scrambled for a response. There were so many reasons for her to say no. His friendship with Nicolas, her passion for Nicolas, the child she carried. Only the one irrefutable reason, the one she required from Nicolas, was missing.

"I'm very flattered, Rickard. I really am."

He deflated. "But?"

Sydney shook her head. How might she say it? "I must be honest with you. I'm not completely unattached."

Rickard frowned. "You're confusing me, Sydney."

Sydney picked up her tea, but her hand shook so badly she nearly spilled it. She set the cup down again and shoved her hands under her thighs.

"I mean, that I'm in love."

"Oh! You mean with your husband!" Rickard looked inordinately relieved. "Of course you are, sweetheart. Even after all he did, you can't be expected to stop loving him overnight. I understand completely."

Sydney nodded awkwardly. That was one pathway out of the conversation.

Rickard ran his knuckle up her arm. "Thank you for your honesty, Sydney. I do appreciate it. So yes, I may court you."

"Now you're confusing me, Rickard."

"I'm asking for the chance to—redirect—your affection." Rickard's eyes crinkled irresistibly.

"Oh."

"I won't pressure you, Sydney. We shall proceed at whatever pace you're comfortable with, and with no assumed outcome."

Was the room getting smaller? It was definitely getting warmer. She gulped the last of her lukewarm tea, then feigned wiping a tear.

"May I have a moment?"

"Of course!" Rickard graciously carried the jam jar and empty biscuit plate out of the room.

Sydney pressed her fingertips against her closed eyes. Since she told Nicolas about the baby, he hadn't said aught about their future together. In fact, he avoided the subject.

What if he didn't intend to marry her? Would he allow his child to be born a bastard? Sydney's acquaintance with Nicolas was less than four months old; and while she believed she understood his character, she could very easily be mistaken. In the meantime, might it be wise for her to explore other opportunities? And might Rickard's courting force Nicolas's hand?

One way or the other, I must provide for myself and the child. I've no other choice.

When Rickard returned to the drawing room, Sydney gave her answer, with the one enormous caveat.

"Yes, Rickard, you may court me. As long as you truly understand that my heart is presently occupied elsewhere."

"Thank you, my darling." Rickard lifted Sydney's hand and kissed it tenderly. His tongue brushed her skin sending shivers across her shoulders. "I don't wish to tire you so I'll call again in three day's time. Until then, I pray for your continued recovery."

Rickard leaned over and kissed Sydney goodbye. His lips parted, his tongue teased hers, and she was pulled into him. She had forgotten what an excellent kisser—*experienced* kisser he was. He stood, smiled his beautifully charming smile, and showed himself to the door, leaving her pleasantly dazed on the settee.

&) C3

That night at supper, Sydney was quiet and uneasy. Nicolas asked if something bothered her, but she insisted it was nothing. He didn't believe her. Later, when they sat in his study, he asked again, determined to get an answer.

"Rickard came to visit me today."

"Did he? What did he want?"

Sydney eyed her wineglass. "He wants to court me."

Disbelief skewered Nicolas. "Court you? What does that mean?"

Sydney rolled her eyes and tossed him a look. "It means what you think it means."

"What did you tell him?"

"I told him I wasn't completely unattached."

Nicolas waited, unsuccessfully submerging his discomfort. There must be more. Of course there was more.

"He got the idea that I'm still in love with Devin."

That unsettling thought was new to Nicolas and detoured his original concern. "Are you?"

"No." Sydney shook her head. "Not at all."

Prematurely relieved, Nicolas sipped his brandy. "So that was the end of the discussion."

"Well, no. It wasn't."

"He still wants to court you?" he asked, incredulous.

"He does."

Nicolas felt unexplained pressure in his chest. He drew a deep breath and rubbed his aching breastbone. "You didn't give him permission?"

"I have no reason to deny him." She stared at him then, and her eyes threw gray-green javelins aimed at his heart. "Do I?"

"No reason?" Nicolas was astonished. And angry. Very angry. "No reason! What am I to you, then?"

"You're the man I love. But—"

"But what?" Nicolas thundered as he leapt to his feet. He began pacing the room with quick, jerky strides. He needed to hit something. Hard. He punched his stuffed leather chair. "*Skitt!*"

Sydney stood and reached for his arms. When she grabbed him he rounded on her, the anger surging through him crackling dangerously in the charged atmosphere. *Why wasn't she afraid of him?*

"You and I haven't decided what to do," she declaimed.

Nicolas's frantic glance blew around the room, and then landed back on her.

She struck him with, "You've not made me an offer for the future. Perhaps you've no intention to do so."

Her eyes were intense, dark-fringed squalls and Nicolas was lost in them. He imagined he couldn't breathe.

"Until you make your decision, Nicolas, I cannot afford to ignore other possibilities." Sydney's voice lowered. "After all, there's the child to consider."

His plans rent by that bolt of lightening, Nicolas saw the gaping hole. When he decided to marry Sydney after the baby, he didn't consider that she might not wait for him. He was blown under again.

"Does Rickard know about the child?" he managed.

"No." An emphatic shake of Sydney's head punctuated the

denial. "That's between you and me, and shall stay that way as long as necessary. Or possible. As we agreed."

Nicolas gently pulled his arms from Sydney's grip and he sagged into his chair.

His choices were clear, then. Either offer to marry Sydney, or bide his time and let Rickard press his case. Judging by his past, Rickard wouldn't be in any rush to settle down. And when he does find out about the child, that will certainly cool his ardor.

At the least, it would buy Nicolas time.

Resigned to how he thought things must be for now, he pulled Sydney to him. He held her on his lap and dragged himself from the emotional whirlpool, breathing easier again. He wished he could feel differently, but he couldn't deny his loathing for the menace growing in her womb.

"I understand," he relented. "I don't care for it one whit, but I understand."

"*Jeg elsker deg,*" Sydney whispered thickly.

"*Jeg elsker deg også,*" Nicolas replied.

He hated that she meant it with the entire fabric of her being.

July 20, 1819

"I need to go home."

Nicolas gaped across the table at Sydney. "Go home? What do you mean by that?" he demanded.

"Carondelet. Where my house is. And all my belongings," she explained. Did he believe she was leaving him?

"Do you intend to live there?"

"Not unless you're throwing me out." Sydney hoped she was joking. "But I do need to go back and get my own clothes and things."

He relaxed then. "I hadn't considered that, but it's certainly a reasonable idea. We can make it there and back in one day if we get an early start."

"Do you mind?"

Nicolas covered her hand with his. His palm was a little damp. "Of course not. When do you wish to go?"

"Can we go tomorrow?"

"Are you certain you are recovered enough?" he asked,

surprised.

"I believe so. It's three weeks, now. And every day I linger only postpones the time when I can say this nightmare is finally behind me..." Sydney blinked back the sting in her eyes. "Can you understand that?"

Nicolas nodded. "Absolutely. We'll leave at sunrise."

As it turned out, the sun didn't rise. The morning dawned overcast and still, covered with clouds that held no rain, only humidity. Sydney sat next to Nicolas on the small bench of the wagon, and leaned against him.

"Now that you have your memory, I get to ask you questions." Nicolas slipped his arm around Sydney's waist and drove the pair of bays with one hand. "Tell me about your marriage."

She nodded, but didn't speak for several minutes.

"Devin was my teacher in Shelbyville, Kentucky. When I was seventeen, he asked my father if he might court me. He asked me to marry him when I was nineteen. We left Kentucky right after the wedding so Devin could take the teaching position in Carondelet."

"When your parents were none too pleased about you coming to Missouri," he interjected, remembering one of their early conversations. He saw her turn toward him from the corner of his eye.

"Yes. Yes, that's right. Then two and a half years ago, Devin agreed to hold classes in Webster Grove part of the time because they had lost their teacher."

Sydney reached behind the wagon seat for the water jug. She took a long swallow and hesitated again. She seemed to be pondering her story as she told it, reconsidering portions in light of recent events.

"Rodger grew up in Webster Grove and went back to teach there after finishing normal school. But Devin still made regular trips; he said it was to help Rodger get established." Sydney's voice caught. Nicolas knew she was thinking—the same as he—about Devin's recently revealed and much less altruistic motive.

"You were married eleven years but had no children?" he asked.

Sydney stared at the road ahead. "There were two babies. Both boys. Both born too early. They never breathed."

That revelation captured Nicolas and dominated his thoughts.

Was it possible the child she now carried might meet the same fate? He hated that the idea occurred to him, and hated himself even more for the sense of relief that accompanied it.

"I am so very sorry," he compensated.

Sydney turned to Nicolas. "Devin spent so much time in Webster Grove, the school board in Carondelet fired him. When he said we were moving to Cheltenham, I was so angry that I screamed at him, called him names. I accused him of caring more for Rodger's welfare than mine!"

Sydney drew a choppy sigh. "But he was my husband. I was wrong to belittle him the way I had. So I decided to ride to Cheltenham and surprise him with my apology and my support. I borrowed a mule from our priest and rode there as fast as it would go… Which wasn't very fast, in case you might wonder."

She glanced sideways at Nicolas. "And you know the rest."

The oppressive cloudy skies matched the mood of their conversation. Nicolas wracked his brain for another topic to divert her, but Sydney beat him to it.

"I wonder what happened to the mule?"

Nicolas laughed. "You only thought of that now?"

As they entered the town of Carondelet, Sydney shrank still and silent. Consisting of dirt streets, wooden boardwalks and variously constructed businesses, the town was very much like Cheltenham.

A few citizens ambled among the storefronts, but Sydney didn't greet them. She directed Nicolas west of town to the cabin and he felt her tension as it came into view. She turned concerned gray-green eyes to his.

"In all seriousness, though, I do wonder what happened to the mule."

℘ ℭ

The cabin door stood halfway open and a pair of chickens wandered out.

"I hope we haven't been robbed." Sydney climbed from the wagon without waiting for him to assist her. He jumped after her and grabbed his rifle. He caught her by the arm.

"Let me go in first."

Sydney stepped back and entered behind him.

The log and mud-plaster cabin was unoccupied, its simple furniture in disarray. Sydney stood in the center of the room and evaluated her surroundings. He could only image what was going through her thoughts.

"My dishes and pots are still here."

She opened a chest near the hearth and added the cookware to the items already in there. She asked him to carry that chest to the wagon and he readily agreed. Then she pushed open the door to the bedroom.

When he returned, Nicolas leaned in that doorway and waited. She looked puzzled, as if she was lost. "Several of my quilts are gone. Devin most likely took them. At least he left my wedding chest."

Sydney opened a plain pine wardrobe and began to snatch dresses and such. She stuffed them haphazardly into the large cedar coffer.

"Is there aught else?" Nicolas asked. "Did you have any animals besides the chickens?"

She looked at him, a little dazed. "We owned a couple of goats."

"They might be worth taking. If they're still here."

"They were in a pen behind the cabin." Sydney straightened and rubbed her lower back. "I'll go see about them. Will you take this chest to the wagon?"

Nicolas gripped the handles and grunted as he lifted the heavy chest. Straining with the effort, he carried it to the wagon, and rested a moment. He expected Sydney would reappear with or without the goats. When she didn't, he went to look for her. When he rounded the corner of the cabin, he saw her on her knees facing two small carved wooden crosses.

Reverently, he lowered to his knees beside her.

"I knew it would be hard to come back here," she whispered. "But I hadn't thought what it would feel like to leave them… I wasn't prepared for this…"

One of the crosses was etched with the name Colin and the year 1811. The second one said Robert, 1814.

"We named them after our fathers, you see."

Sydney stroked the markers, tracing the names over and over. She sucked ragged breaths that shook her whole body.

He slid his hand along her back and she collapsed against him, her rending sobs unleashed. He rocked her a little, stroked her hair, and felt like a complete ass. How could he be so selfish to wish she would experience this kind of pain ever again? What kind of monster was he?

A terrified one.

Nicolas murmured soothing words in Norse. Sydney lay in his arms, pain relinquished until she sagged, depleted. Then an idea came to him. It might help.

"Would you like me to bring them home with us?"

Sydney looked up at him with swollen, red-rimmed eyes and her curt words were a dagger through his heart.

"To whose home? It isn't mine. I don't have a home." Then she pulled away from Nicolas. "I have no choice but to leave them here. At least they'll have each other."

Sydney struggled to her feet and squared her shoulders. She crossed herself, wiped her tears, and rounded the cabin. She didn't look back.

Nicolas sat still a bit longer.

Dare he pray for his child to come early? In the same manner as Sydney's first babies, now buried beneath these stones? He shook his head. No matter the extent of his fear, he couldn't bring himself to ask God for that.

So instead, he climbed to his feet and followed the path of the broken woman he loved.

Chapter Twenty Six

August 7, 1819

*S*ydney appeared for breakfast dressed in her new work clothes. Pouring herself a cup of coffee, she was the recipient of several sharp looks from Addie. Sydney turned her back on the housekeeper and addressed Nicolas, sitting at the table with Stefan.

"Is this a Sunday that Father Mueller is in town?" Sydney blew on her coffee.

"Pastor Mueller will be here this Sunday, yes," Nicolas corrected.

"Good. I have much to talk with him about."

Nicolas pondered that uncomfortable tidbit as he stood and refilled his coffee mug. "Addie, I'm going into town for a meeting with Squire Busby. I'll be home for supper."

"Is something amiss?" Sydney sipped her coffee, then loudly sucked air over her tongue.

"Well, it seems the schoolteacher has gone missing." Addie snorted and Nicolas glanced at her back. "According to old Mrs. Ansel, he packed up his things and left the boardinghouse without a word. Busby wants to form a board to hire a new teacher." Nicolas considered Sydney over the rim of his cup. "Do you plan to work with Sessa today?"

"I plan to reintroduce myself to Sessa today." Sydney grabbed a biscuit. "I doubt that she even remembers who I am, much less what I've already taught her."

"Go easy," he admonished.

"Of course I will!" she snapped. Abandoning her coffee, she stomped out the back door.

Nicolas followed. His longer legs caught her easily. "Should you even work with that horse, considering?"

"If I don't do *something* with her, then everything up 'til now will be wasted effort." Sydney's mouth screwed sideways. "Not to mention the clothes."

"Clothes?" he repeated, confused.

Sydney stopped walking and grabbed his hand. She pressed it against her rounding abdomen. He wasn't expecting that and it shocked him out of language. She cocked one eyebrow at him.

"Clothes." Sydney forcefully threw his hand aside and walked on. Nicolas stumbled a pace behind her. She spun around and faced him.

"Why don't you want to talk about it?"

"About what?" he stalled. Panic turned his gut to water.

Sydney crossed her arms and narrowed angry tempest-gray eyes. "You have some time yet. But be aware, it grows shorter." She gave him her back and strode away with hip-swaying, braid-bouncing ferocity.

He scrambled for a response—any response. "Sydney!"

She kept walking. He trotted after her, plowing through ideas to get back in her good graces. "Sydney..." He grasped her elbow.

"What do you want, Nicolas?" she demanded.

He took a moment to choose his words. "I want to show you something special tonight."

"Oh?" Skepticism fractured her countenance. "Haven't I already seen it?"

He bit back a smile. "No. Not this."

She glared at him and bobbed a small nod. "May I go now?"

He kissed her forehead. And he refrained from reminding her to be careful again. It took more restraint than he thought himself capable of.

☙ ❧

Nicolas knocked on Sydney's door as soon as the sun was good and gone. He wore the drawstring breeches and held a blanket.

Sydney, clad in her shift, grabbed a pair of shoes and followed him downstairs and out the front door. "Where are we going?"

"Wait and see."

Nicolas took her by the hand. They walked about two hundred yards up the road that led north toward Cheltenham. A large boulder on the east side of the road marked a narrow trail into the woods. Nicolas and Sydney followed the trail another fifty yards and stepped into a moonlit clearing. Soft, mossy ground banked a clear spring-fed pool.

"Oh, how lovely!" Sydney exclaimed.

Nicolas spread the blanket over the moss. He dropped his breeches on the ground and walked naked into the water. He dove under the surface and reappeared about ten yards away.

"Come on in! The water's perfect!"

Sydney, in her shift, walked slowly into the unfamiliar pond; the water only came to her shoulders. She stepped into Nicolas's eager kiss. She tasted like the wine they shared at dinner, and her skin felt like silk in the water. He slid against her, separated only by her flimsy cotton shift.

"Lay back," he suggested.

Sydney closed her eyes and floated on her back as Nicolas supported her with one hand under her shoulders and the other under her hips. Her wet shift was transparent and her hair flowed like black ink spreading through the clear water. Nicolas took her mouth with his in a disembodied kiss that quivered through him.

"*Gud,* how I've missed you. I don't feel whole without you anymore." He carried her effortlessly out of the pond, and laid her on the blanket.

Sydney brushed Nicolas's wet hair out of his face. He kissed her again and pulled the hem of her shift above her waist. He climbed over her and worked his knees between hers. He lowered himself to enter her when she yelped, and scuttled backwards on all fours like a startled crab.

"What! What are you doing?" Her eyes were round as the moon behind him.

"I thought—I assumed—that we could join again."

"Why on earth would you think that?"

Nicolas sat back on his heels; the mast of his desire lowered.

"We've done it before. And we don't have to worry about making a baby. And you know for certain that you're not married to anyone. So…"

Sydney scoffed at his logic. "That's precisely the point, Nicolas! I'm not married. And I don't intend to do that particular act again until I am."

Nicolas stared hard at her. "Are you playing games with me, Sydney?"

Sydney slid forward and wrapped herself around him. He could feel the swelling in her belly and the heaviness of her breasts.

"Nicolas, I'm a thirty year-old homeless woman with no husband and a child on the way. I cannot be bothered with games. They're a waste of time."

Nicolas's thumb traced Sydney's jaw, dropped down her neck and traced the scar on her chest. Then it continued to her belly and circled the swell. He pulled his hand away.

"This is hard for me, you're sensible of that. I lost my wife. And if I lose you…" He looked away and heaved a ragged sigh. Sydney ran the back of her fingers down Nicolas's cheek. He grabbed her hand and kissed it.

"I need time to get my grit up, I reckon. It's not that I don't love you, because I do. But I've always been a private man, so perhaps you don't know what I feel."

"I know, Nicolas." Sydney rested her other hand on her belly. "I know."

September 5, 1819

Sydney was puzzled by a sudden and severe downward shift in Nicolas's mood. He grew irritable and distracted, barking at everyone over imagined inconveniences. Sydney asked Addie if she knew what was going on. She leaned close to Sydney and answered in a sotto voice.

"It's Stefan's birthday tomorrow. It's never a good day. At least Rickard will be here."

"Stefan's birth—oh!" Sydney's chest hollowed out with the connection. Stefan's birth. Lara and the other boy's deaths. Poor Nicolas. And poor Rickard.

"Why will Rickard be here?"

Addie tossed her a disgusted look. "To keep that danged fool from falling face down into the privy and drowning in his own piss!"

As surprising as her indecorous outburst was, the elder housekeeper didn't offer any more explanation. And when Sydney joined Stefan for breakfast the next morning, there was no sign of either Rickard or Nicolas.

"Happy birthday, little man!" She placed a wrapped package in front of his plate.

Stefan's eyes rounded. "What's that?"

"A birthday present! Go ahead and open it."

Stefan picked up the box as though it might dissolve in his hand. Inside was a fishing kit: flies, line and cork bobbers. Sydney found the items in the chest from her home.

"I like this a lot!" Stefan lifted the items from the box one-by-one. "I can go fishing!"

"Yes, you can! But you'll need help with the hooks at first. Your *pappa* can go with you."

Stefan picked up each item and inspected it, then placed it back in its spot.

"Can I show John?" he asked Addie.

"Are you done with your breakfast?" Stefan nodded and his auburn hair flopped forward. He brushed it back and waited for Addie's release. "Alright then, go ahead."

Sydney reached for his arm. "Addie and I'll bake you a cake today."

"Just 'cause it's my birthday?"

"Just 'cause," Sydney laughed. "You're six now and that's an important age." Stefan's face split with an incandescent grin before he disappeared out the back door.

"He didn't say thank you!" Addie scolded.

Sydney turned and smiled at her. "Yes he did."

Addie and Sydney worked to create a confection worthy of a sixth birthday, with Addie mixing applesauce, cinnamon, nutmeg, cloves and raisins into the cake batter. But when Sydney asked where Rickard and Nicolas were, she shrugged with her lips pressed, and stirred the cake batter with visibly more intent. Then Rickard appeared at the back door.

"Addie?"

She turned toward his voice. Pointing with her elbow, she said, "There by the door. The one with the torn label is yours."

"As always." Rickard lifted two bottles of brandy—one with a torn label—from the covered basket, then pawed through the remaining contents. "This suits. Thank you, Addie."

"Thank you, Rick."

With a wink at Sydney, he was gone. She turned to the housekeeper and waited. Addie angled a glance at Sydney but she just kept stirring the batter. She didn't speak. That by itself was uniquely unusual, in an already unusual day.

"Addie, what is going on?" Sydney finally asked.

"It's Stefan's birthday."

"Yes, it is." She eased her voice back. "And it's the anniversary of Lara's death. And the other boy. I'm sensible of that."

Addie poured the liquefied batter into the pans that Sydney prepared. Sydney placed them inside the three-legged cast-iron spiders in the fireplace and covered them with domed iron lids. Then she faced the older woman again, fists on her hips.

"Are you going to tell me?" she murmured.

Addie washed the mixing bowl, but she stared out the window. Her tone was resigned. "He doesn't want to remember…"

Sydney nodded. "I can understand that. So how does he try to forget?"

"Brandy."

"Oh…" Sydney's gaze rolled to the back door. "That's what Rickard came for."

Addie continued her task. "Not exactly."

Sydney walked to the older woman's side. "What did you do?"

"What I always do. What Rickard and I worked out the second year."

"And that is?"

"I water the brandy in Sir Nicky's bottle." A smile quirked the corners of her mouth.

Sydney crossed her arms. "And what is Rickard drinking?"

Adie looked at her now. "Tea and apple juice."

"Oh." Sydney struggled to control an inappropriate grin. "Doesn't Nicolas notice?"

Addie shook her head and her faint levity vanished. "Not after he's finished the first bottle. I don't touch that one."

Sydney walked to the back door. Somewhere out there, the rugged forested hills, lush green grass and pale azure sky scraped by wispy white blades cradled a man intent on wiping away the recollection of loss. It was a fool's endeavor.

"When will they come back to the manor?" she asked.

Addie appeared beside her. "At candle-lighting. Rickard's smart enough not to let him sleep out there."

§ ℂ

Sydney ate dinner with Addie, John, Maribeth and Stefan. They enjoyed the birthday spice cake before sending a blissful Stefan up to bed. The still-summer day was hot and sticky, and Sydney sat on the front porch hoping for a breeze. The last vestiges of the sunset dimmed in the sky.

Rickard and Nicolas emerged from the road and ambled crookedly toward the manor. Naked above the perilously low-slung waistband of his wet breeches, Nicolas did not acknowledge Sydney as he stomped heavily across the porch into the house. He reappeared with the pewter flask. He swallowed a long drink from the flask, lowered it, took a deep breath, and then another long drink.

"Were you swimming?" she asked Rickard.

Then Nicolas noticed Sydney.

"The spring pool," Rickard answered.

"Rick, go home." Nicolas did not take his unfocused eyes off Sydney.

Sydney glanced at Rickard, frightened by the very large, very inebriated man trying to stare at her.

"Don' look a' him!" he bellowed.

"Nicolas!" Sydney barked as she stood. Then a more calm, "Stop shouting."

Nicolas slowly wagged his head side to side. His expression was disgusted and excited, slack and tense, cold and hot. She had no idea what he was thinking, and no desire to find out.

"Rick go home. Sydney you go t' my room."

Her face burst into flames. Not that! Not in front of Rickard! She was afraid what he might do if she defied him, and just as afraid of what he might do if she didn't. Rickard's presence was the deciding piece. She'd play it out now, and explain it to him after.

Sydney leaned forward and gripped Nicolas's prickly cheeks

between her palms. He stank of stale alcohol and sweat.

"Will you go up and wait for me? After Rickard leaves, I'll come to you."

Seemingly satisfied, Nicolas downed the last drops from the flask. It fell to the porch with a loud clank. Rickard grabbed his elbow and the men disappeared into the house. Sydney sank in her chair with a sad sigh.

When Rickard returned, he sat next to Sydney and heaved his own sad sigh.

"Is it always like this?" she asked.

"Yes." They sat in silence for a while. The moon rose over the eastern horizon in a sky as dark blue as Nicolas's eyes.

"I'm not consorting with him," Sydney blurted. "After what just happened, I want to make that clear. I said what I did so he'd go to bed. Alone."

"Understood."

"Did he? Go to bed, I mean?"

"Yes."

"Do you believe he'll sleep the rest of the night?"

Rickard shrugged.

"You're staying tonight?"

Rickard nodded.

"I feel safer with you here," Sydney admitted.

Rickard reached for her hand and squeezed it gently. "It's been a long day, Sydney."

"I wish I could have known Lara. She must have been someone quite special for you and Nicolas to think so highly of her."

Rickard stroked her hand, staring at nothing. "She was."

Chapter Twenty Seven

*S*ydney slept later than usual, but even so there was no sign of Rickard as she descended the stairs to breakfast. When she reached the bottom, she glanced into the study and saw Nicolas sprawled on the floor, still half naked and snoring impressively. She shook her head, and wondered when—and how— he ended up there.

"Good morning, Addie," Sydney poured her usual cup of coffee. "Where is everyone?"

"John took Stefan fishing. Seems that present you gave him was a big hit!" Addie smiled. "But as for those two others, there's no life in them yet."

When breakfast was put away, Sydney helped Addie and Maribeth prepare a batch of tomatoes for canning. The back of the manor faced west, so the kitchen stayed cool in the mornings, a blessing on a sweltering day like this one was shaping up to be.

It was past noon when Nicolas's heavy, unsteady steps preceded his appearance at the kitchen. He gagged and stumbled to the back door where his body repaid him violently for yesterday's punishment. He moaned and leaned against the doorjamb.

"*Skitt*," he mumbled. He wove his way to the hall without another word. Sydney heard the door to his study slam shut.

After the canning, Sydney felt as cooked as the tomatoes, but her irritation with Nicolas had her too stirred up to try a nap. She had it in mind to go to the spring pool and cool off. She circled the house to let Addie know where she was going.

A hot breeze blew through the dappled clearing making the leafy shadows dance. Sydney laid her canvas breeches and work shirt over a bush, then walked into the water in her shift. The cool liquid surrounded and soothed her.

Sydney turned on her back, leisurely waving her arms to keep herself afloat. Eyes closed, she forgot Nicolas and his display of grief for now. She existed in the moment, aware of nothing more than the silk of the water and the confetti of sunlight flickering over her eyelids.

And then the child stirred.

Afraid to move, afraid she imagined it, afraid it might not happen again, Sydney pressed one hand over her swelling womb and waited. The baby shifted once more and she felt it against the palm of her hand. Hot tears leaked under her eyelids.

"Stay with me, little one," she whispered. "Please stay with me until it's time."

As if to answer her, the babe moved yet again. Sydney smiled. She knew nothing else that happened to her in this lifetime could be as significant as this first time Nicolas's child made its presence known.

Sydney stayed in the pool for nearly an hour, unwilling to end the magical moments she shared with the babe inside her. But even on that hot day, she began to chill in the cool water. She swam to the shallows and waded to the edge of the pool.

Her wet cotton chemise was nearly transparent and it clung to her like a second skin. She squeezed water from her thick, heavy hair. She ran her hands over her fecund body—heavy breasts and rounding belly—then turned toward her clothing.

With a feral growl Rickard stepped into the clearing.

She whirled to face him and crossed frightened arms in front of her bosom. He came toward her with an angry, distance-chewing stride. His features twisted into fury. Her eyes slammed wide and fear set her every nerve on fire.

She splashed from the water and grabbed her clothes from the bush but could only clutch them in front of her before Rickard reached her. He grasped her roughly by the arm and pulled her to him.

"Whose?" he hissed.

Sydney winced. "You're hurting me."

"Whose?" His voice was louder, his grip unchanged.

"Ni—Nicolas." Her cheeks flamed.

Rickard threw her arm away from him; she stumbled but regained her footing. She hurriedly pulled the shirt and breeches over the soaked shift. Rickard paced back and forth in the clearing. His anger flared and threatened to consume them both.

"You told me last night you weren't consorting with him! Have you played me false all along?" Rickard shouted at her.

"No! No, Rickard, it's not like that at all!"

"All this time I've been so careful not to push you, not to—but you have been warming his bed in the meantime!"

Sydney grabbed Rickard's arm, aware of the danger but needing him to understand. "No! I didn't want it to happen! You must believe me!"

The stricken look on her face gave him pause. His eyes burned into hers. "Did Nick force himself on you?"

Sydney let go of his arm and fell back. "Not precisely..." She swallowed thickly. "It was the night of the May Day Ball. I imbibed too heavily. So did he. And it hasn't happened since. I swear to you, Rickard!"

She looked him square in the eye. He must believe her.

Rickard considered the woman in front of him. "Why did you say I might court you?"

Sydney's chin quivered; she scrubbed her hand against it. Now was most assuredly not the time to fall apart. "I divorced a husband of eleven years who was unfaithful to me in the most unimaginable way. I have no promise from Nicolas. I'm alone."

"Nick knows?"

"Yes."

"And he hasn't offered to marry you?" Rickard's tone described his disbelief.

Sydney shook her head. "He's afraid to."

Rickard snorted. He stared hard at her for an eternity. He staggered his fingers through his auburn waves, laying them in molten rows. His eyes held every color she had ever seen there, then they dulled and darkened.

"Do you love him? Is that who you meant?"

Truth. It was time. Sydney nodded.

His chin jerked up a mite. "What about me?"

She touched his arm again. "I do admire you so much, Rickard. And I value your friendship very highly."

Rickard sagged and heaved a deep sigh. "Not quite the same thing, then, is it?"

After a moment, he gripped her hand. He turned to leave and tugged her along as she stumbled behind him, trying to keep pace with his long, angry stride.

"Let's go have a word with Mister Hansen."

&) C&

The front door to the Hansen manor flew open and Rickard strode inside. Nicolas sat at the massive desk in his study with the curtains drawn, his head resting on folded arms. The bang of the door hurt.

Rickard did not slow his approach.

"Stand up!" he demanded.

Nicolas raised his aching head and squinted up at Rick. "What?" he croaked.

"I said stand up!"

"Why? What's gotten into—"

Rickard grabbed the front of his shirt and yanked. "Stand up, damn it!"

Stunned, Nicolas stood. His head pounded and his stomach did somersaults. Backed by his considerable size and obvious anger, Rickard rammed his fist into Nicolas's midsection. Nicolas folded in half and dropped to the floor, unable to breathe.

"*Hva i helvete er De gjøre?*" He was shocked out of English.

"Get up."

Nicolas shook his head to clear it, but that only made it worse. He grabbed the seat of his chair and pulled himself into it. He peered at Rickard through pain and confusion. If he was in any better condition, he would have struck back, friend or no.

"Do you mind telling me why?" he wheezed.

Rickard bent over so his face was close to Nick's. "Hear me well, brother. You've started something and I intend to see you finish it."

"What?"

Rickard looked back at Sydney. Nicolas hadn't noticed she was there. But by the look on her face, he knew that Rickard knew. His stomach turned over again and he thought he would heave. He broke a cold sweat.

"Did you tell him?" Nicolas rasped, trying to figure out her motive.

"She did after I saw her."

Nicolas shifted his aching eyes back to Rickard. "Saw her?"

"She was swimming in the spring when I went to say good-bye. It was obvious."

Nicolas tried to swallow but his mouth was too dry. He rubbed his temples with the heels of his hands. "What do you want, Rick?"

"I'm giving you an ultimatum."

Nicolas narrowed his gaze. "And that would be?"

"If you don't marry her, I will."

"*Hva i helvete!*" he spat.

"And—I'll raise your bastard child as my own." Rickard's voice was hard as steel; it cut through Nicolas's skull like a blade. He waved his finger in Nicolas's face. "But you and I? We'll no longer be friends."

Rickard's eyes never left Nick's, but Nicolas's flickered to Sydney's and back. She was white as rice and gripped the doorjamb for support. It was a small comfort to see this was a surprise to her as well.

"And when do you expect me to do this?" Nicolas stalled as he tried to comprehend what just happened.

"Well, b-before the babe is born, to be certain!" Rickard sputtered.

"How dare you!"

Both men looked to Sydney, astonished.

"How dare you two discuss my future as though I were not in the room?" Red splotches highlighted Sydney's pale cheeks. Her eyes were dark, turbulent, dangerous. She let go of the doorjamb and stepped forward. "I'm standing right here!"

"You're carrying a child, Sydney. You and the child must be provided for," Rickard pointed out the obvious in a condescending tone.

"And the child is mine," Nicolas protested. "So I'll decide."

"No! After all I've been through, I'm not about to have my future decided for me. I'll have something to say about it!" Sydney glared at the two men, her fists clenched at her side.

"Sydney…"

"Hush!" she barked. Both men fell silent. Her gaze passed

between them.

"Gentlemen, I've conceived a child twice before in my life, but wasn't able to carry either babe past the fifth month." One pale hand gripped her belly. "It's very possible that I may see this one buried as well."

Nicolas flinched. Hope and guilt alternately smacked his chest without mercy.

"So you have another month and a half before you must choose which one of you might be forced into a marriage of pity and obligation."

Sydney pinned each of them with a defiant stare. "That's assuming, of course, that I'd choose to accept either one of you!"

She slammed the front door hard, rattling the manor. Rickard turned to Nick who dropped his exploding head back on the desk.

℘ ℭ

Sydney headed for the place she always found comfort: the horses.

She opened Sessa's stall, slipped inside, and latched the door behind her. She sank into a corner and curled around her baby. Sessa stepped to her, confused by her human sitting in her stall, and nuzzled her clothes for the telltale smell of an apple.

"I'm sorry, I've come empty-handed." Sydney stroked the filly's nose.

Sydney considered the options before her. Even if she was able to carry this babe all the way to her confinement, there was a very real possibility that Nicolas might not marry her. He was reluctant to even talk about the child. It was as though if he ignored it, then it would not exist. That bit of fantasy would be hard to maintain in the coming months.

Her new option was Rickard. If she accepted him, she would live comfortably with a man who would probably be a very good husband and father. Assuming, of course, that he was able to get past the fact that his ex-best friend was the child's true sire.

But that also meant she would live a mile and a half from Nicolas, raise the child he didn't want, and never see him again. Just the thought of that possibility brought tears to her eyes and made it hard for her to breathe.

Her second option was to return to her beloved parents' home in Kentucky. They would welcome her back, of that she had no doubt. There she would birth and raise her bastard child and make her way as best she could. She would have to give an explanation of why her marriage to Devin ended, but she could claim the child was Devin's and thereby erase the stigma of illegitimacy.

Unless the babe favored Nicolas.

There would be no way to explain how she, with her dark brown hair and green eyes, and Devin with his sandy brown hair and brown eyes, produced a tall, blond offspring with startling blue eyes. Her indiscretion would be laid bare for all to see. Sydney couldn't subject her child to that humiliation.

So that led to a third option: go somewhere new and create a respectable background story and live out the rest of her life as a complete and utter lie.

"Dear God," Sydney sobbed. "Have You forgotten me? How have I come to this point? And where shall I go from here?"

Sessa snuffled her hair, and Sydney pressed the filly's nose to her own.

September 8, 1819

At Addie's summons, Nicolas came down the hall toward the front door. When he saw Lily, his approach slowed. Addie passed by him without a word; but her seething disapproval deafened him. Nicolas concocted a smile for the girl and led her into the drawing room.

"Hello, Lily. To what do I owe the honor?"

"I wanted to see you." Lily batted her lashes as she closed the gap between them. "I worry about you, you know that."

"There's no need to worry about me."

Lily placed her hand on Nicolas's chest, tilting her face up to his, inviting a kiss.

Nicolas declined the invitation. "Was there aught else?"

Lily, always nimble when dealing with men, changed her direction. "Rickard told me some rather disturbing news. I wanted to talk to you directly about it and not rely on rumors." She stepped back and opened her fan, using it to insinuate her distress.

Nicolas remained stoically silent; he assumed to what news she referred and he wasn't in any mood to discuss it with her.

"Is it true, Nicolas, that it turns out our own Sydney was pregnant when you found her?" Lily neatly dropped the accusation into the question.

"No, Lily, that's not true."

"Oh! I'm so relieved! Can you imagine? Rushing to get a divorce and then finding out you're expecting his child!" Lily fanned herself furiously as if overcome by the thought.

"Lily."

"Yes?" She gave him her best innocent look. He'd seen it often enough to recognize it.

"Sydney is with child. But she was not with child when I found her."

Lily's brows drew together in a comely frown. "How can you be certain?"

Nicolas felt his cheeks heating, but honesty was required. "Addie told me she had her course less than two weeks after I rescued her."

Lily scoffed, "So just over a week after you discovered her—nearly beaten to death—she bled? Well! What else would you expect?"

Lily walked around the room, obviously intending to give Nicolas more angles to admire. "Did a doctor examine her? Is Addie certain where the blood was coming from?" The questions were blunt; Lily wasn't damping her weapons.

Before he could answer, she stopped and faced him with a look of incredulous disbelief. "You don't believe that story, do you?"

Nicolas rubbed his hands over his eyes. His headache finally subsided last night, but his eyes still itched. "In truth, I do. I trust Addie to know what she's talking about."

Lily tapped her perfectly shod foot on the carpet. She changed tactics once again. "Are you telling me that she tricked you into fornicating with her?"

Nicolas laughed. "Men would line up for that possibility! No, there was no trickery, Lily. It was fully my idea."

"A skilled woman always makes the man believe it was his idea," she scoffed. "So how long has that whore been spreading her thighs for you?"

"That's enough, Lily."

"No, Nicolas, it's not. My brother has been cuckolded. And I have been led to believe you wanted a future with me. I believe I have every right to ask!" Lily's voice was getting louder and higher in pitch. "How long?"

Nicolas raised one brow. "I'll tell you the truth. It was only the night of the May Day Ball. We both were the worse for drink and the evening progressed in a manner we didn't intend."

"And you expect me to believe that?"

"I don't care one way or another what you believe, Lily!" Nicolas threw his hands in the air and realized in a wash of relief that he truly didn't. "It doesn't change a thing!"

Lily's lip began to quiver and a tear formed in each eye. She placed one hand over her heart. "Are you saying that my opinion of you doesn't matter? You don't care what I think of you?"

"I reckon I am." His outlook brightened. "I don't care what you think of me."

"But, Nick! What about our future?" Lily's eyes widened and her cheeks hollowed.

"Lily, we don't have a future."

The blood drained from her face. "Don't say that! I love you!"

He delivered the death blow on a whisper, hoping to soften the impact. "But I don't love you. I should have told you sooner."

"But..." Lily scrabbled for words. "You might... You could learn to..."

"No, Lily. I'm sorry."

"Nicolas?" she pleaded.

"No."

Bursting into a torrent of tears, Lily lifted her skirts and bolted from the room. When she met the front door, she slammed it open. Nicolas reached the porch in time see her climb into her carriage without the footman's help.

She turned to him, her turquoise gaze as cold as the Nordic glaciers their color matched. "You will regret this, Nicolas Hansen!" she threatened. "Mark well what I say!" Then she slammed the carriage door.

"Go, GO, *GO!*" she screamed, pounding on the roof of the cab.

Once Lily's landau was out of sight, Nicolas spoke.

"How much did you hear?"

"All of it. I was in the kitchen when she arrived," Sydney answered from behind him.

"We need to talk. In my study. Now."

Nicolas closed the study door after Sydney and motioned her to a chair. "You heard her ask about the bleeding?"

Sydney blushed, but didn't turn away. "Yes."

"Might she be right?"

Sydney shook her head. "If I had conceived a child in March, before you found me, I would be six months gone by now. I would be a lot bigger, and the child would have moved by the end of July, not only this week."

Nicolas was surprised by both her words, and his reaction to them: hope buckshot with terror. "The child moves?"

"I felt it two days ago when I was in the spring pool. When Rickard found me."

Nicolas's eyes dropped to her belly. His fingers twitched. He willed his hands not to reach for her.

"Does it move often?" He hauled his eyes back up to hers.

"Yes. It seems strong." Sydney's wistful smile spoke of past pain. "I only hope that I can carry this one long enough."

Nicolas cleared his throat and purposefully changed the subject. "I, uh, understand that you made Stefan's birthday special for him. I wanted to thank you."

"It was my pleasure."

Nicolas pretended to organize items on his desk. "I don't recall much about the day. Did I—was I—rude to you?"

"No."

"No? Oh. That's good." He cleared his throat again. "I haven't had a house guest before on that day."

"On 'that day' Nicolas?" Sydney stood and moved to the study door. She fixed him with a glacial stare that disgraced Lily's effort and chilled him to his core.

"That day was immeasurably beneath you. You have entirely too much dignity for that sort of behavior. And you have far more strength than you give yourself credit for."

Sydney opened the door. "I pray a day like 'that day' never happens again. I also pray that your son will be able to enjoy his birthday from now on. It's the least of what he deserves from his *pappa*."

Sydney left the room, pulling the door closed with a soft click.

"*Gud forbanner det all til helvete...*" he muttered.

Chapter Twenty Eight

September 17, 1819

*S*tefan sat on the wagon bench wedged between his father and Sydney. The first day of school had dawned cool and clear. Birdsong echoed through the trees and squirrels darted overhead. Stefan's excitement radiated as he fidgeted, as much as space would allow, during the entire ride into town. Sydney smiled and patted his leg. His bright blue gaze tugged at her soul.

Nicolas guided the horses to the front of the school. Though two and-a-half months had passed since the return of her memory, the building still caused her heart to quiver.

I must go back to church. I must get over this, she resolved.

Nicolas turned to Stefan with a broad grin. "Here we are, son. Are you ready?"

He jumped from the seat and Stefan clambered after him. He handed Sydney down and they followed the bouncing boy into the building.

The new teacher, Miss Bronwyn Price, was a pleasant and attractive young woman, taller than Sydney's five-and-a-half feet by a few inches. Her hair was dark and wavy, and her eyes a warm sultry brown. She owned a dazzling smile which she turned on for Stefan.

"Welcome, young man. Are you ready to recite your ABCs?"

Stefan nodded with enthusiasm. "I can count to a hunerd!" he bragged.

"Can you now? Well that's wonderful!" There was that smile

again.

"Miss Price? I am Nicolas Hansen, Stefan's father." Nicolas extended his hand. "I'm afraid the boy's never been in school, and he only had a tutor for a short time. I hope he doesn't give you any trouble."

"I'm certain we'll get on fine."

"Well, please let me know if it turns out otherwise." Nicolas turned to Stefan. "John will pick you up after." Stefan threw his arms around Nicolas's legs and Nicolas ruffled his hair. "Be good, then."

Letting go of Nicolas, Stefan hugged Sydney. That was a delightful surprise.

"I'll have apple muffins for you when you get home," she promised. "Make your *pappa* proud."

"I will." Stefan waved and waded into the herd of chattering children.

"Mr. Hansen, Mrs. Hansen, it was a pleasure meeting you both." Bronwyn Price offered her hand once again.

Their awkward silence was brief, but it had substance.

Sydney took the teacher's hand. "I'm a houseguest of Mr. Hansen's. My name is Sydney Bell."

Miss Price's eyes dropped to the swelling below Sydney's waist before her eyes snapped back up.

"Please forgive me!" she blushed.

"It's an understandable assumption. Please don't give it another thought."

Nicolas led Sydney back to the wagon at a rather brisk pace. He was silent while she collected her purchases at the Brown's store. His hands fisted during the stop at the post office. His jaw clenched on the ride back to the estate. Sydney stared at the white scar on his cheek.

"It was an honest mistake," she ventured when they were almost home.

"She knows there's a baby."

Sydney scoffed. "It's going to be rather impossible to hide! In case that was your plan?"

Nicolas didn't answer her. The scar rippled on his cheek.

80 03

The next morning, Sydney woke in a bad mood. A realization insinuated itself into her consciousness yesterday and grew overnight.

Now she was just plain mad.

Sydney heaved the bedclothes aside, splashed her face with cold water from the ewer, and jerked into her breeches and work shirt. Even her clothing enraged her this morning. She dragged the brush through her hair and twisted it into a topknot as she hurried downstairs. She hoped to get a bite of food and be out of the kitchen before Nicolas came down.

Sydney was relieved to see only Addie in the kitchen. She poured coffee, added milk to cool it, and gulped it down.

"My, my!" Addie scolded. "What's your rush, dearie?"

Sydney grabbed a hot biscuit. She blew on it and tossed it from hand to hand, then broke it open and scooped honey onto it. As she stuffed it into her mouth, the back door opened.

Nicolas carried a newspaper. "I'm going to have to dig a new privy in the spring," he mentioned to anyone who listened. "I believe we can bide over winter if it all freezes."

Sydney stepped past him with no words of greeting. She needed to get away from him before she slapped him.

"Is there a fire, madam?"

Without a backward look, Sydney waved one hand and headed to the stable.

"That blasted, pompous, selfish man!" she muttered as she stomped across the yard. Wet grass tugged at her feet and dampened her ankles. She kicked a patch of dandelions, their fuzzy offspring grounded by dew.

In the stable, she climbed the ladder to the loft and dropped onto a rolled bale of hay. She felt it prickle the backs of her thighs through her canvas breeches. It crossed her mind that she should have worn the buckskin pair. She jumped up again.

"You expect too much, sir! As if I haven't enough to deal with as it is!" she yelled and paced in the small space. "You lost a wife? Well, I lost a husband! You lost one baby? Well, I lost two! *Skitt!*"

She kicked the closest bale, releasing a poof of yellowed straw dust.

"And now you ask me to play the role of wife and mother for

the world, but you cannot bring yourself to—to—Oh! How dare you? *Skitt!*"

She really liked that word. It suited her emotions. No wonder Nicolas used it so often.

"*Skitt!*" Sydney kicked the hay bales with all her strength. Bits of hay pirouetted around her and danced in a shaft of sunlight.

"*Skitt! Skitt! Skitt!*" She kicked and shouted with as much force as she could muster, satisfying her aggravated soul.

"Madam?"

Skitt. Sydney leaned over the edge of the loft and looked down into Nicolas's confused blue eyes.

"Yes?"

"Are you ill?"

Sydney shook fisted hands and hollered, "Why must you always ask if I'm ill?"

Nicolas's mouth opened. And shut.

"I'm fine. Fine! Do you hear me?" Sydney's voice grew louder. Her demeanor clearly negated her words. "I'M JUST FINE!"

"And your identical twin, the one with whom I usually breakfast in the morning. Is she 'fine' as well?" Nicolas raised one eyebrow, "Or has she been consumed in this inferno?"

Sydney's mouth opened. And shut. She stomped one foot. "Oh-h-h!" she groaned. "You're such a MAN!"

Nicolas frowned. "And your point, madam?"

"Leave me alone!" was all Sydney could think of to say. "Please! Simply go away and leave me the *helvete* alone!" She plopped down hard on the hay.

Sydney listened for Nicolas's booted step. Several minutes passed before she heard him leave the stable. She pressed her lips together as the corners of her mouth plunged. Her breath came in spastic gasps before she surrendered to her tears. She lay back and muffled her hopeless sobs in the crook of her arm.

Her situation overwhelmed her. At thirty, she was divorced, pregnant, homeless. Most women her age had children approaching their teen years. Many would have grandchildren in half a decade. And she was heartsick in love with a man for whom none of this appeared to matter.

What *i Gud's navn* was wrong with her?

October 28, 1819

Sydney stood in the kitchen door and breathed the crisp autumn air. "I love October."

Addie shuffled over to share her view. "It's God's glory, to be certain."

The Hansen estate was awash in yellows, oranges, reds, and purples as trees blazed their final glorious display. Their warm brilliance was complemented by a vivid backdrop of cool cerulean blue.

"Watcha lookin' at?" Stefan pushed between them.

"The leaves." Sydney rested her hand on the boy's shoulder. "Aren't they beautiful?"

"Uh-huh." Stefan looked at Sydney's stomach. "You're getting fat."

"Stefan!" Nicolas thundered as he ducked into the kitchen. "That's very impolite!"

"Why?" He looked at his father, truly puzzled.

"It's alright, Nicolas." Sydney squatted to Stefan's eye level. Uneasy yet determined, she laid out the truth to his son without bothering to ask his permission. "I'm getting fat because I have a baby growing inside me."

"You do?" Stefan's eyes got very round.

Nicolas coughed loudly. Twice. Sydney pushed on; it was too late to pull it back, even if she wanted to. Which she didn't. Lying wouldn't change her situation; it only allowed Nicolas to ignore it.

"Remember the white cat? She got fat and then the baby cats came out."

Stefan looked at Sydney with increasing interest. "Will the baby come out of you?"

"Yes, it will."

"When?"

"About four weeks after Christmas."

Stefan screwed up his face. "Will you have to lick it?"

Sydney laughed. "No! We'll use a towel."

Stefan looked relieved. "Can I watch?"

Sydney glanced at Nicolas then. His face was crimson, the scar a thin white danger sign. She turned back to Stefan. "We'll talk about that later."

Stefan nodded and scooped sugar onto his oatmeal.

Sydney moved to a chair and avoided looking at Nicolas again. He stood silent, looming, sipping his coffee. She chewed her lip and wondered precisely how angry he might be.

"How did the baby get in you?"

Nicolas choked. Coffee dribbled down his shirtfront. Stefan looked at him in curious expectation.

"I'll tell you after school," he answered. "Finish up your breakfast; it's time to get going!"

He mopped his shirt and poured himself a new cup of coffee.

"*Pappa*, can I play with Alex after school today?" Stefan asked suddenly changing the topic.

Nicolas frowned and Sydney was certain that was on account of her. "Who is Alex?"

"I met him at school. He's seven." Stefan shoveled his oatmeal.

"Has he a surname?" Nicolas snapped.

Stefan looked up at his irritated father from under his hair. "It starts with a 'muck' and sounds like boy."

"Muck-boy? Could it be McAvoy?" Sydney suggested.

"Yeah! That's it!" Stefan nodded.

"Stuart and Jenny's boy. He was born a year before... Yes, that must be him." Nicolas wrapped his hands around his mug. Sydney saw his knuckles blanche.

"Where is their home?" she asked.

"To the east of town, perhaps half a mile," he muttered.

"Alex wants me to see his puppies," Stefan explained. "He wants me to come over today after school. Can I, *Pappa?*"

"How will you get to his house?"

"His pappa will take us."

"And how will you get home again?"

Stefan slapped his forehead. "You will come and get me!"

Sydney laughed and Nicolas allowed a small smile. "How about this? I will come to the school this afternoon and talk to Alex's father. We will work something out so you two can play together. Perchance it might happen today, eh?"

"Okay." Stefan finished his oatmeal. He licked his spoon and hung it on his nose.

Sydney sat on the back porch with a cup of tea when a sudden movement by the paddock caught her eye. Nicolas hadn't said a thing to her all day since she told his son their secret. Now he came toward the house and she tried unsuccessfully to discern his mood by the long stride of his muscular legs and the looseness of his fists.

He dropped into the chair next to hers. "I spoke with Stuart McAvoy," he began. "He says Alex comes home each day with a new story about Stefan. Seems the boy's a bit outspoken."

Sydney bit back a smile as she considered the father. "If they get on well, you could set a regular time for them to associate," she suggested. "That would be good for Stefan."

He stared at his boots, eyes narrowed in thought.

Before he could say aught else, Sydney smothered her trepidation and asked, "Did you have a talk with Stefan about the baby?"

He nodded, but still didn't look at her. "I did."

"And did you explain how the baby got inside me?"

"I did."

"What did he say?"

He turned to meet her eyes. "I believe his exact words were 'that's yucky!'"

Sydney laughed nervously. "Better he believes that for now."

Nicolas grunted and relaxed in his chair. He seemed to have forgiven her.

Sydney pointed to a mature maple tree on the side of the yard. "That tree's so amazing, isn't it? Look at the color of those leaves!"

Sydney stared at the deep purples and scarlets of the foliage, set on fire in the setting sun. "I've never seen anything so absolutely glorious in all my life." Her hand dropped to her belly as the baby moved, wanting to add its weight to her opinion. She rubbed its bottom, pressed under her ribs.

Nicolas looked at her, not the tree.

"*De er slik vakker,*" he whispered.

"What?" Sydney turned her eyes to his.

Nicolas waved his hand. "Nothing."

Chapter Twenty Nine

That night, Nicolas opened Sydney's door—she had not locked it since she regained her memory—and slipped into her room. He hadn't visited her since Rickard punched him a month-and-a-half ago, but tonight he needed to be close to her. She turned toward him in the darkness and pushed back the bedclothes.

He dropped his breeches to the floor. "Should I light the lamp?" he whispered.

"If you'd like."

Nicolas lit a piece of tinder with the embers of the banked fire. He used it to light the oil lamp and turned the wick as low as he could. The pale yellow light bathed Sydney's body in a warm glow and soft shadows that enhanced her rounding shape.

Nicolas's breath caught in his throat as he looked at her. Her breasts were round, her bottom was round and her belly was round. He sat on the bed and lifted her nightgown to her shoulders, caressing the wonderfully curved sculpture that she was.

"*De er slik vakker.*"

"What does that mean?"

"You're so beautiful."

Nicolas's arousal engulfed him and he molded himself to her back. He cupped a warm breast with one hand and her belly with the other. Holding her heaviness with a reverence that bordered on worship, he buried his face in her hair and rubbed his erection between her thighs, imagining that he was inside her. When he finished, he didn't move, but simply lowered one hand. Sydney leaned into him. She put her hand over his and guided him. She was so hot, so damp. His fingers slid easily through the valleys of her quim. She turned her face into her pillow to muffle her cries of release.

Nicolas felt an immediate change in her belly. Her womb tightened, growing hard inside her abdomen. He could clearly feel its contours. Sydney held her breath and didn't move.

"Does that hurt?" he whispered.

"No."

"What is it?"

She didn't answer at first. "A contraction, I believe. But it's not labor."

As abruptly as it hardened, her womb relaxed. Sydney rolled over and looked at Nicolas, her eyes were wide and black as the night around them. She looked terrified. So was he.

"I'd better go." Nicolas retrieved his breeches from the floor, kissed her, then snuffed the lamp. "Sleep well *min madonna.*"

ഔ ❀

Sydney closed the door to Nicolas's study.

"We need to talk privately." She pulled a chair close to him.

His eyebrows raised in curiosity. "Are you well?"

"I believe so. But I feel we need to stop."

"Stop?" Nicolas stalled to re-group. He knew what she meant, but her words hit him harder than he would have expected. Loneliness of an unusual sort unfurled around him.

Sydney rolled her eyes. "Stop being together. At night."

"Why?" He knew the answer, but wasn't ready to concede.

"Because I'm afraid of hurting the baby!" she blurted.

Nicolas leaned back in his chair. He wasn't surprised by Sydney's decision, but he was surprised by his reaction to it.

He would miss her.

A lot.

Not just the physical release, he could do that for himself. He would miss her comforting presence in the dark, the warmth of her body as she wrapped herself around him. He would miss her soft moans and gasping cries as she abandoned herself to his touch. He was startled by his emotional response.

He felt like crying.

Nicolas swallowed the lump that choked him.

"I understand, Sydney. If you believe it's best." He couldn't look, just then, at her expressive face, her fertile rounded body, her transparent eyes.

"I do, Nicolas. I'm sorry."

"Don't be sorry. Your decision is the right one." He opened the drawer that held the flask.

November 6, 1819

Nicolas continued the unending task of chopping wood for the manor's ten fireplaces. Winter always approached faster than he expected, and frost had replaced dew for weeks now. The pile of logs on the back porch reached its roof, and the stack by the root cellar grew each day. In spite of the cool weather, his shirt stuck to him and sweat dripped from his brow. He paused to wipe it away and rest his arms on the long-handled axe. The autumn sun lowered in a hazy yellow sky. His stomach growled and he wondered what was for dinner.

"Nicolas!" Sydney called him from the house.

He walked out of the trees behind the stable. "Over here!" he answered and waved his arms.

"Have you seen Stefan?" she shouted. Stuart McAvoy was with her. Nicolas hefted the axe over his shoulder and trotted toward the house. Stefan was supposed to be at the McAvoy's home.

"What do mean, have I seen Stefan?" he asked when he was close enough to be heard. The look on Stuart's face made Nicolas's heart drop. "Isn't he at your place with Alex?"

"Aye, he was. But I went to find them and I couldna. I hoped that they showed up herre?" His mild Scots accent thickened to a full-on brogue when he was upset.

Nicolas turned to Sydney. "Have you seen them?"

"No." Sydney's eyes were dark hollows.

Nicolas looked at the sky. "It will be dark soon. Come on then, Stuart. Let's find our boys."

Nicolas recruited John to help with the search. Nicolas took his rifle, his hunting dirk, and tucked his pistol into the waist of his breeches

Sydney grabbed his arm as he turned to leave. "Shall I send for

Rickard?"

He paused, but need outweighed his irritation with the man. "That would be helpful. Thank you."

The search party spread out and headed east from the Hansen estate. They each took turns shouting the boys' names so they could hear any response, no matter how soft. Soon, Nicolas heard Rickard's voice to the south of him, and a little piece of his fear fell away. Bless Sydney. And Rickard.

The sun faded and allowed the half moon to assume the task of lighting the sky. The temperature continued to drop as the men made their careful way through the forest. Nicolas was skilled at tracking and his eyes swept back and forth for signs. He found none, but refused to panic. They would find the boys, as long as he remained calm.

And he strove to remain calm; but the idea that he might lose his only child twisted his belly until his gut felt like hot iron on a farrier's anvil. He knew he hadn't treated the boy the way a father should treat a son. Maybe this was his punishment. Or maybe it was a test. Either way, he mustn't fail.

It was his turn; he shouted Stefan's name.

Nicolas pushed aside a low-hanging pine bough. He felt sap on his hand and he tried to rub it off. Somewhere, a wood fire burned. He crunched a pine cone underfoot. Nicolas's ears stung with cold and his chest clenched with worry, wondering if Stefan had a hat. His eyes never stopped moving. A tiny forest creature scampered from the path of his heavy boots, clicking back at him in protest.

Nicolas stopped walking. He found the crackling leaves underfoot distracting. He closed his eyes and breathed through his open mouth. Clouds of steam formed around his face. He listened with every tightly-coiled inch of his frame.

He made out Stuart's faint voice far to his left. There was John, on his left, but closer.

There was Rickard to his right, God bless him.

Silence.

There was no breeze to rattle the trees. No canine howl, no flap of wings, nor hoot from any owl. Only cold, still air. Nicolas tilted his head back and slowly breathed in. His heart beat slow and hard. He could feel the vein in his neck throbbing.

"Stefan! Alex!" Nicolas's deep, thunderous call echoed off the distant cliffs. He waited, eyes still closed. Then Nicolas turned his head, did he hear something?

He put the entire capacity of his lungs behind the next shout. "Stefan!"

There was something. To his right and in front of him. Nicolas began to trot toward the sound. After he covered about forty yards, he stopped.

"Stefan!" His booming voice cut through the forest.

And he heard it; a very faint *Pappa?* from the same direction. Nicolas broke into a run and called his son's name as he moved. He heard Rickard, behind him on his right, crashing through the forest in pursuit.

Nicolas skidded to a stop on the damp, dead leaves carpeting the forest floor. "Stefan!"

"*P-pappa!*"

Nicolas turned in a circle and searched for the source of the voice. He saw his son, another thirty yards away, climb out from behind a fallen, rotting log. Stefan tilted his head forward and ran through the dim moonlight into Nicolas's outstretched arms.

"Where's Alex?" Nicolas demanded as he prepared to shoot his pistol into the air.

Stefan pointed to the log. Alex's pale face glowed in the dark above its edge.

"Come on out, son." Nicolas walked toward him. "You're not in trouble. Are you hurt?"

Alex shook his head. He hunched and covered his ears when the shot from Nicolas's pistol rang out. There were immediate answering shots from Stuart and John.

"We saw Indians, *Pappa!* We hid from them!" Stefan's eyes were huge and his grip dug into the muscle of Nicolas's thigh. Alex climbed over the log and made his tentative way toward Nicolas, chin down and hands tucked in his armpits. He did not appear to believe the claim that they were not in trouble.

"Nick?" John's voice was faint.

"This way!" Nicolas shouted. Rickard appeared, his breath coming in gasps. He leaned over and rested the heels of his hands on his knees. Nicolas grinned, though his own chest heaved. He turned his attention back to Stefan.

"You saw some Indians, did you?" He kept his voice calm.

Stefan nodded and looked at Alex for confirmation as he shivered and stomped his feet, "I think four."

"I only saw three," Alex stated with authority. He hugged himself for warmth and his breath made smoky clouds.

"Did they have horses?"

"They had one." Stefan frowned at Alex. This time, Alex did not correct him. Stefan screwed up his mouth. "They were real dirty."

"They *were* dirty," Alex confirmed. "And their horse was all bony lookin'."

"Alexander Stuart McAvoy!" Stuart's gruff voice was a mix of anger and relief. "What werre ye thinkin' of, laddie?" He stepped to his son and lifted him in one seamless motion. Stuart held his son close to his chest. He buried his face in the boy's neck, as Alex's arms circled his.

"I am sorry, da," Alex's muffled apology gave way to sobs of relief. "We got lost."

Nicolas looked down at Stefan as John joined the group.

"What were you about, son?"

"Alex w-wanted to go fishing and s-so I wanted to g-get the fishing box Sydney gave me for m-my birthday," Stefan's voice was very small and his teeth clacked from the cold.

"And you thought you could find your way home?"

"Alex said h-he knew a sh-short c-cut." His lower lip hid in his teeth and the corners of his mouth tugged downward. He sniffed and wiped his runny nose on the sleeve of his greatcoat.

Nicolas picked up his son. They were eye to eye. "Do not try that again, eh, Stefan? Do you hear me? Until perhaps you are eight."

"Yes, *P-pappa*," Stefan nodded, tears still in check.

Nicolas opened his greatcoat. Stefan slid his icy hands under Nicolas's arms and tucked his head under his father's chin. He wrapped his legs around Nicolas's waist. The woolen greatcoat covered him completely, and Nicolas's exertion-heated body leeched warmth. He sighed and closed his eyes.

"I don't want to lose you, son. I don't." Nicolas swallowed thickly and cleared his throat. "I love you."

Stefan hugged his father much harder than he ever had, as far as Nicolas could remember. "I love you, too, *Pappa*."

డి ౧౩

Sydney paced through the house.

No one ate dinner; the food was kept warm on the stove. Maribeth milked the cow and fed the chickens and sheep, as she did every night. Sydney fed the horses in John's absence. Addie puttered in the kitchen. And every one of them strained to hear the sound of voices outside.

Two hours after they left the house, Sydney heard Nicolas. She threw the front door open as the group climbed the porch steps. A cry of relief escaped her when she saw Stefan in his father's arms. Nicolas set him down and he ran to Sydney. She knelt to catch him and pull him close.

"Where were you, little man?" she asked past the lump in her throat. "We were so worried about you!"

"Me an' Alex got lost on the short cut 'cause we were trying to come get my fishin' box an' we saw Indians an' we hid from them an' it got dark an' we were real cold an' *Pappa* found us!" It all came out in one breathless rush.

"I see." Sydney brushed Stefan's hair from his face. "I bet you're hungry."

"I am. And so is *Pappa*! His stomach's makin' the most loudest sounds!"

"Well then you had better go wash up." Sydney stood and shifted her gaze to the owner of the 'most loudest' sounds. Nicolas rolled his eyes and blew a breath of relief from rounded cheeks.

"I'll be headin' for home now." Stuart still held Alex. "Jenny'll be a mite worried aboot the boy."

"Alright." Nicolas extended his hand. "God speed."

Stuart shook his hand, stepped down the porch steps and set Alex on the wagon seat. He waved as they pulled out of the yard. Nicolas waved back, and then turned to face Sydney, his voice low.

"The boys saw Indians."

A shock of fear slid through Sydney. "Is that a danger?"

"No... we're on good terms in the territory."

Sydney slipped her arm around Nicolas's waist. "I knew you would find him."

For a moment, he didn't speak. Then, "There was no other choice."

Chapter Thirty

November 10, 1819

"Go west?" Sydney set a basket of apple-cinnamon muffins on the table. "What do you mean?"

Nicolas grabbed one and dropped the hot pastry on his plate. "Every winter I make two hunting trips to the mountains southwest of here."

Sydney gave Nicolas a puzzled look that made it obvious his point was not clear.

"For pelts. To sell for income," he explained.

"Oh." Sydney sat in her chair and woodenly salted her eggs. Nicolas was leaving! "How long are you gone?"

"Usually about four weeks." Nicolas waved a hand back and forth. "Sometimes six."

Her stomach twisted. Sydney looked down at her eggs, though all she tasted was her bile's metallic bitterness. She counted weeks and months. She didn't dare look up again.

"How soon will you leave?" Addie asked.

"I reckon I could leave by the end of the week. It's a bit early in November, but that would get me back here around mid-December or so."

Sydney stood, her chair legs complaining loudly across the oak floor. Just as well—she couldn't find her own voice. She left the kitchen, abandoning her unfinished meal.

It was November and she began to believe the child she carried would be born at full term. Though she wasn't so confident as to consider names, she was no longer on edge, fanatically evaluating each twinge. That meant she needed to decide about getting married.

And the man she wanted to marry, the father of her child, was leaving and wouldn't be back for a month. Or more.

When Nicolas returned, assuming that all went well and he did indeed return in a timely manner and all in one piece, there would be a scant five or six weeks until her expected confinement. Sydney felt that was calling things a bit too close. Perhaps he truly had no intention of ever marrying her.

That afternoon she was huddled in the drawing room, pondering both the ramifications of this new development, and the late fall weather that matched her foul mood. A movement in the doorway diverted her attention.

Rickard had come to see her.

"I wasn't expecting company," she demurred, smoothing her hair and her gown. "Please, come sit."

"I hope I'm not unwelcome," he said with a twinkling grin.

"Of course not."

She served him tea and together they watched the dreary day outside the large window. A strong wind earlier in the week blew all the remaining leaves off the trees, and now the denuded branches formed stark webbed scars in the lowering sky. It would probably rain before morning, perchance even snow.

Distracted, Sydney met Rickard's various attempts to draw her into conversation with politeness, but no real engagement. After a while, he stopped talking. Ticks of the mantle clock measured the long silence. She sipped her cooling tea and wondered if Rickard knew that Nicolas was leaving.

"What's transpired, Sydney? You're not yourself today." The darkness of his chocolate voice startled her.

Sydney caressed the teacup in her diminishing lap. "Nicolas is leaving. For a month or more. It puts me in an awkward circumstance."

"Hunting for pelts."

"You knew he was going?"

"I hoped he wouldn't this time."

Sydney shrugged her lack of control over the infuriating man.

"I still intend to marry you if he doesn't," Rickard assured her.

Sydney's eyes snapped to his. "Are you in love with me?"

Rickard smiled softly and set his cup down. "Perhaps. I've never been in love so I can't tell for certain."

"Is the stallion truly reconsidering his track? " she prodded.

He shrugged. "I do admire you and value your friendship."

Sydney winced as she recognized her own words. "Is that enough?"

Rickard pulled his chair close to Sydney's. He lifted her hands and her skin tingled. "It's a good place to begin, I expect. And to be honest, the thought of marrying you hasn't filled me with terror."

"Your wooing skills are spectacular," she teased.

He looked adorably contrite. "Ah, Sydney, admit it. We're both reaching an age where our chances of having families are diminished."

Sydney offered the sacrifice. "What about Nicolas?"

"I know how much you love him, Sydney."

She straightened, startled. "You do?"

"You light up a room when you look at him. And he loves you as well. But if he's too much a scared, stubborn Norwegian jackass to do what's right, I won't allow you, or the babe, to pay for it."

Tears pricked at Sydney's eyes. "Thank you, Rickard. That's very kind."

"I won't do it out of kindness, Sydney. Don't misunderstand me." Rickard's eyes dropped to her lips, then blinked to her eyes. Her heart beat a little faster in anticipation of his kiss. "You're a beautiful, intelligent woman. I desire you. If it comes to vows, I'll be a very attentive husband."

Rickard leaned back, to Sydney's unexpected regret.

"But don't worry, we'll hold out as long as we can. We'll give that pompous, *skitt*-for-brains every opportunity to make his move."

That made Sydney smile. Then the baby kicked her ribs. Hard.

"Oh!" Her hand rested over the activity in her womb. "My little passenger seems to have awakened!"

"Could I?"

It was an unusually personal request. But he could very well end up being her husband and raising this child. Sydney flattened Rickard's palm over the spot. "It might take a minute."

Rickard didn't breathe. The babe obliged.

"Whoa!" Rickard's hand flew back as though burned. His eyes, round as mill wheels, lifted to Sydney's. "Holy—"

Sydney laughed. She reached for his hand and put it back. "Perchance it'll happen again."

They waited; it did.

"That's the oddest thing, isn't it?" Rickard's enchantment gave Sydney pause. He truly would be a good father.

"It's a bit disconcerting to have someone's body inside yours, to be certain. But every time it moves, I get a little more hopeful."

"Has Nick felt it?"

Sydney's smile faded. "No." They sat in silence and waited for another kick.

"Well, isn't this the delightful domestic scene?" Nicolas's earthquake shook them both. "If you two believe you might desist, dinner is ready."

Sydney faced him. "Oh, my! What on earth happened to your hair?"

Nicolas's long blond locks were chewed off right below his ears.

"I cut it every winter. It's easier to care for in the cold." He cocked an eyebrow. "Why?"

Sydney circled Nicolas and examined his destroyed coif. "Who cut it?"

"John."

"Well that explains it! After dinner I'll get Addie's scissors and fix it."

"Fix it?" Nicolas's hand went to the subject of scrutiny. "Fix it how?"

"Make it all the same length? Cut the ends to be even? Give it some shape? Pick one!" Sydney laughed as she slipped her arm through his, effectively altering his focus. "Meanwhile, I'm starving! Didn't you say dinner was ready?"

After dinner, Sydney searched out the scissors and a comb. In the study, she asked Nicolas to light the lamp and sit close to the fire. "I need illumination. I don't want to make it worse."

"Don't worry; you can't!" Rickard chuckled.

Sydney combed through Nicolas's thick hair, but he stopped her. "Let me take my shirt off."

As Sydney went about her task, she tried not to rest her hands too long on Nicolas's grooved back, muscled arms, or broad shoulders. His raw masculinity made her womb ache. It helped steady her hands to concentrate on Rickard's presence.

"So, Nick, you're leaving soon for your hunting trip." Rickard sipped his brandy. "How long will you be gone this time?"

"I reckon about five weeks. Why?"

Rickard looked pointedly at Sydney. "Have you made your decision?"

Nicolas shifted in his seat. "Um, no. Not yet."

"Isn't that calling things a bit close?"

"The child's not due until late January!" he protested.

"That's just five weeks after you get back. And many's the babe who made an early debut."

Nicolas looked startled. Rickard sipped his brandy and rolled it around in his mouth. Watching him, Sydney recalled the denied kiss earlier.

He lifted his glass in a salute to Nicolas. "She'll be married before the birth, Nick. I'll see to it. If the babe comes while you're gone, I want you to know, it'll not be born a bastard."

God bless Rickard. Sydney barely refrained from crossing herself.

He set his glass down and turned to Sydney. "It's been a delightful time, as always, but I believe I'll head for home." Rickard kissed her cheek, his lips warm and firm. "Sleep well, my darling."

He patted Nicolas on the shoulder and headed out the door.

Nicolas ran his hands through his repaired hair. "I'm sorry I didn't tell you I was going away. I honestly forgot you didn't know."

"Forgiven," Sydney sighed, staring at the fire. She had grown rather weary of his excuses and apologies.

Nicolas shifted in his chair. "I'm also sorry that I haven't—"

"I'm tired," Sydney interrupted and rose to her feet. "I'm going to bed."

She left the study without looking back.

December 1, 1819

Wrapped in pelts, Nicolas knew he looked as wild as the forest he disappeared into. He rode for seven days to reach the Sauk Indian village, and he stayed to enjoy their hospitality for three days more. He feasted on roasted venison and smoked the pipe with the men, sharing stories of personal prowess in hunting both game and women. And he slept with them in a log longhouse.

He dreamt that a young woman crawled under the furs that covered him. Nicolas was naked and her hand found him with accuracy. She readied him and he rolled onto his back. The girl lifted her tunic over her head and lay on top of him. His hands moved over her skin as she spread her legs.

And then he woke up.

He gripped the young woman by the waist and lifted her from him. He assured her it wasn't her fault; that he simply didn't care to do the act at this time. Nicolas pulled her insistent hands away from their upright target. It wasn't easy to make her leave.

It was customary hospitality for the chief to send a girl to him and in the past Nicolas took advantage of this particular offer and enjoyed himself well. Concerned that he might be ill, the chief brought the medicine woman to him the next day. How could Nicolas explain something to them that he, himself, didn't understand?

Lie.

"I asked my God for a special favor. I gave up this pleasure to show Him I'm sincere."

The chief frowned and nodded. He patted Nicolas on the shoulder. "I hope your God works quickly."

Tonight, Nicolas wondered why he felt it was wrong for him to enjoy one of the Sauk women. It would be merely to release sexual tension. He could do it himself, but it would be more interesting with a partner. And he wasn't married.

So why couldn't he talk himself into it?

Nicolas considered that question for the hundredth time as he tried to fall asleep. This was the ninth day since he left the Sauk village. The ninth day of eating what he could kill and cook. The ninth day of sleeping on the ground in the freezing air of early December. The ninth day of hunting, skinning and stretching the skins of his prey. He should be exhausted.

Nicolas hunted beaver. He came to find them in their winter coats, fat and glossy from a summer of feasting. And beaver were big, heavy creatures. In spite of the chilled air, Nicolas broke a sweat every day with the effort.

Some nights he cooked the beaver meat. Rabbit and fish were always available. But tonight, he feasted on a wonderful meal of pheasant.

Nicolas rolled onto his back and pictured the scene. The fat male strolled under the maple tree without a care in the world. Nicolas was downwind, undetected, and fired a clean shot. He particularly relished the liver he fried with wild onions.

The maple tree had a handful of purple leaves still attached. His maple tree at home was bare now. Sydney loved the way that tree looked in the autumn sunset.

Skitt!

There she was again.

A realization as shocking as ice water splashed Nicolas and chilled him as effectively. He never stopped thinking about her. He sat up and tried to recall a day, even an hour, when she wasn't in his mind. He couldn't do it. He carried her with him all the time. When he saw the maple tree. When he gave Fyrste a verbal command. When he ran his hand through his newly-shorn hair.

All.

The.

Time.

No wonder he wasn't lonely on this trip; he never felt alone! And of course he couldn't join with the Indian girl because Sydney was with him. Always with him.

Hellig skitt!

Nicolas clambered to his feet and began to pace. He listened to the midnight echo of dead leaves crackling under his boots. He relieved himself against a tree, and smelled the onions from dinner in the splatter of his water. He looked between the overhead branches and saw the moon with its icy ring. Nicolas sat on a rock, his legs bouncing. The chill of his frigid seat seeped through his leggings. His rapid breaths made steamy puffs in the dark.

She was always with him. What did that mean?

"I love her. I do. I love her," he said out loud.

Nicolas saw her dark hair hanging down her back in a braid, or blowing free in the breeze, or spreading around her on the bed or in the spring pool. He saw her eyes. Eyes that turned a stormy gray when her mood threatened, or glowed spring green when she was happy. Nicolas closed his eyes and remembered her rounded body glowing in the lamplight the last time they were together. She was the most beautiful creature he had ever laid eyes on.

Sydney cheated death twice in the eight months since he found her. She was feisty and had a mighty will to live. She buried two children and saw her marriage end in a devastating episode. Yet in the end, she challenged *him* to choose life or death.

She chose life.

Nicolas doubted Lara could have done the same. Unlike Rickard and Lily, who favored their father in their self-assured temperament, Lara resembled her mother. That mother high-tailed it back to the aristocratic comfort of her family's North Carolina plantation as soon as she was widowed.

Lara struggled through her pregnancy. The babies weighed her down, drained her. Though they were small, only about four or five pounds each, she was overwhelmed by their presence. Sydney, on the other hand, shone with health. She hardly even slowed the pace of her days, still working with Sessa and helping around the manor.

Nicolas rubbed his face hard, the crucial thought formed but not yet acknowledged.

The child was easy to dismiss when it was an unseen entity. When Sydney's belly was flat and there was no outward sign. But Nicolas nearly choked on his jealousy when he saw Rickard close to Sydney, his hands on her stomach and wonder on his face, as he felt Nicolas's child move inside her.

My child.

Not his.

Mine.

Nicolas sat very still. He barely breathed as the suffocating presence in his chest worked its way past his objections to his lips. He spoke out loud with growing determination, "I want my child."

Trust.

There it was again. That voice.

"Gud forbanner det!" he swore.

Nicolas jumped to his feet and kicked a smallish rock as hard as he could. He pulled a limb off the pine tree above him and used it to beat the trunk of that same tree.

"Trust what?" he shouted into the hollow night's void, disturbing the horses a considerable measure. "What guarantee do I get?"

There was no answer.

He destroyed the branch and threw the stub as far as he could. He fell on his knees, and pounded the freezing ground with clenched fists until they grew numb. Nicolas leaned back and considered the silent branches above him. He needed to decide. The time had come. Nicolas approached the decision with logic uniquely male.

He loved Sydney.

He wanted the child.

He was afraid that Sydney might die giving birth, because Lara did.

If she did, he would lose her.

But...

She was going to birth the child, one way or the other.

She would be married, with or without him.

If he didn't trust, and in that trusting, act, then his love and his child would belong to another man.

He would lose them both.

And his best friend.

That was his guarantee.

Nicolas stumbled to his feet. The realization didn't allow him to wait for daylight; he began to pack his camp by the icy moonlight. He fed the horses grain, himself cold pheasant, then he loaded the animals. He was four days from home.

Perchance he could make it in three.

Chapter Thirty One

*C*harming and gracious as ever, Rickard visited her often while Nicolas was away. Even though they had an understanding of sorts, that didn't make the man any less compelling. Sydney found herself wondering if what she was about to propose was, in truth, foolish.

He sat with her in the drawing room that snowy afternoon, watching the wind blow enormous snowflakes in a crazy dance outside the window. A fire beckoned in the fireplace and the sweet smell of Addie's sugar cookies filled the manor.

Sydney pulled a chair close, her heart heavy. "Rickard?"

"Yes, my darling Sydney?" His eyes warmed her in ways they shouldn't.

She strangled the anxiety that choked her. "I—I can't marry you."

Rickard carefully selected a warm cookie from the dish. "Why not?"

"Because." She hesitated, then charged through the obvious reason. "If I do, you'll lose your best friend, your brother, the one body on this earth whom I know you do love!"

Rickard leaned back in his chair. His hazel eyes reflected soul-deep sorrow. He looked at the snowy scene outside the window, then down at the floor, then back at Sydney. She poured tea and handed him the cup.

He stared into his tea. "Have you considered what alternatives you have?"

"Yes."

"And?"

Sydney shifted in her chair. "Might I ask you a favor, Rickard?"

"Other than my hand in marriage?" One corner of his beautiful mouth lifted. "Yes, go right ahead. You know you may."

Sydney looked down at the knot of twisted fingers in her lap. She drew a ragged breath and spoke quickly.

"If Nicolas doesn't marry me as soon as he returns, I'll go to St. Louis and birth the baby there. Afterwards, I'll book passage by riverboat to Louisville, Kentucky. Then I'll have my father take us back to Shelbyville."

Rickard gawked at Sydney. "Are you serious?"

"I am."

"Nick would be livid!"

"Quite."

Rickard reconsidered. "How can I help?"

"I need to borrow enough money to live in St. Louis for two months, and the fare for the riverboat." Sydney leaned forward. "But I'll pay you back. I'll send money once I get to my parent's home. I promise."

Rickard shook his head. "I won't loan you money."

Sydney deflated. Hopelessness pressed her back in her seat.

Rickard nudged her chin with a warm knuckle until she met his eyes. "I'll take you to St. Louis myself, and see that you're well taken care of. And when you and the babe can travel, I'll pay for your passage. But you'll not owe me one thing, do you understand?"

Tears threatened. She swallowed them. "No."

"My dearest, darling Sydney. Ever since we found you, you've brought excitement to our lives. While I've relished our flirtation immensely, you've truly brought Nick back from the dead." Rickard stroked his fingers along Sydney's arm. "If he's foolish enough to abandon you, that will be his loss to deal with. But I've every right to show you what you mean to me."

Sydney's composure fractured into a hundred grateful tears. Rickard pulled her into his embrace. He stroked her hair and held her close.

"You are the best friend I ever had, Rickard," she snuffled against his cologne-scented shirt.

He kissed her temple. "That's the nicest thing any woman's ever said to me."

෨ ෬

The snow slowed Nicolas down. Large flakes fell, paused, then melted and turned the ground to mud. Nicolas pushed himself and the horses hard, but the snow forced them off the road. In the forest, pine needles and dead leaves protected the ground; the horses didn't slip and their hooves didn't cake with mud.

Nicolas trudged on foot. Three hours ago, just before sunset, he removed his two-hundred-and-fifty pound weight off the exhausted Fyrste, and divided the comparable load of pelts and supplies between him and Rusten, lightening the horses' loads by half.

Nicolas reached into his pocket and felt the ring he traded for yesterday. When he came across a tinker on the road, he offered two prime beaver pelts for the piece of jewelry. The filigreed gold band with its rectangle garnet suited Sydney perfectly.

He hoped he wasn't too late.

Distracted, Nicolas found himself sprawled on the ground, his face buried in wet leaves. He had tripped over a root he should've seen, and fell forward without the protective roll he should've taken. As he considered how nice it would feel not to get up again, he realized he was too tired to continue. Only four hours from home, he knew he must rest.

Nicolas pushed himself up; it took more effort than he wanted to admit. Both horses were stopped, heads down. Their labored breath blew translucent clouds in the frigid air. Nicolas went to Fyrste and untied his pack. When he pulled it to the ground, the stallion sighed in relief. He then pulled off Rusten's pack and dropped it next to the first one. After hobbling the horses, Nicolas grabbed his blanket, rolled himself in it, and lay across the packs. He was asleep before he remembered lying down.

December 5, 1819

Weak winter sun pushed through the icy dawn and lit the crystalline landscape. Sydney gazed out the window at the pristine beauty. Blue shadows, pink snow, yellow sky and black branches. A soft, pastel palette etched with dark, angled skeletons; starkly beautiful and deceptively hospitable in appearance.

After the breakfast dishes were washed, Sydney and Addie

baked bread in the cozy kitchen. Without warning, the back door slammed open. A gust of ice crystals chilled the room as a huge, hairy beast filled the doorway.

Sydney cried out and glanced around for a weapon until Addie touched her shoulder. Sydney looked at Addie, then back at the creature, whose deep blue eyes burned into hers.

"Are you married?" it demanded.

Sydney recognized the voice before she recognized the man. Nicolas was dressed in fur from the hat he pulled off to the leggings tied around his limbs. Filthy, matted hair stuck out from his head and his month-old beard sprouted leaves and dirt.

She never saw a more beautiful sight. "N-no," she stammered.

He gave her a brisk nod and grinned, his teeth a row of small white eggs in a matted light brown nest.

"Addie, I need two or three solid meals packed straight away!" Then Nicolas turned toward the stable and bellowed, "John! I need the bays on the wagon as soon as you can harness them!"

With a wink, he was gone.

Addie started pulling out food to pack while Sydney went to the door. "Is he leaving again?" She turned incredulous eyes to Addie. "He just got here!"

"Seems so. Help me here, would you dear?"

Sydney helped Addie pack a basket with ham, chicken, biscuits, jam, beer, apples and pumpkin pie. Her hands shook, her legs felt like willow switches, and she wanted to laugh or cry but didn't know which. Or which to do first. She was a mess of shivers.

Nicolas returned to the kitchen. He didn't say a word to Sydney, but paused long enough to look her in the eye, lean down and kiss her forehead. He reeked of a month's worth of sweat, dirt, smoke, and the blood of animals.

He climbed on the wagon and straddled the basket of food with his feet. Slapping the reigns hard, he shouted, "Hah!"

The bays leaned into the traces and pulled the wagon through the shallow snow toward the road. They were soon out of sight.

Sydney turned to Addie and leaned backwards to counterbalance the somersaulting weight in her distended belly.

"Where's he going, Addie?"

The elder housekeeper shook her gray head. "I couldn't begin to reckon."

258 *Kris Tualla*

છ૭ ભ

Nicolas ate everything he could manage as he drove the wagon one-handed. After subsisting for a month on what game he caught, he was literally starving.

In contrast, Sydney looked rounded and glorious. Her skin was rosy, her hair shiny, and her eyes poured love all over him. He wanted to hold her and never let go. Thank goodness he could smell himself and knew better.

It took two hours to reach his destination. As people passed him, they gave the hairy, filthy, beast of a man wide berth. It required every ounce of his reserve to keep from growling at them. Starting a rumor about some hulking half-man, half-animal wandering the territory was quite tempting.

The cabin looked even more deserted than the first time he was there. No tracks marked the surrounding snow. Still, he pounded on the door and stomped around the building, searching for signs of life. When he found none, he returned to the wagon and grabbed his pick and shovel.

Though it was December, the ground wasn't frozen more than half-a-foot down; in Nicolas's powerful arms, the pick handled it with ease. When he passed the layer of crystallized earth, Nicolas switched to the shovel. He dug until he found what he was after, about three feet below the snowy surface.

Nicolas lifted the first tiny casket with reverence. It was so small it couldn't even hold his shoe. And it was so light. He clutched it to his chest and closed his eyes. The rough wood scratched his cold-reddened hands as he rocked on his knees in the snow.

He felt Sydney's grief at the loss of her boys. He also felt the loss of his own infant son. He saw the small blue and bloody body lying lifeless on the birthing bed. He relived the core-crumbling disbelief when the boy wouldn't breathe. He heard Lara cry out her grief that her birthing pain was insufficient to give him life. She died defeated.

Silent tears rolled down his cheeks, chapping his skin in the cold breeze. Nicolas crossed himself. Though not a Papist, he found the motion comforting.

He carried the dirty box to the wagon and laid it carefully in the bed. He returned to the burial plot and dug until he retrieved the second tiny wooden casket. He laid that one in the wagon as well, and then pulled up both the carved wood crosses.

The weak afternoon sun was hovering just above the hazy horizon when Nicolas finished. He slipped a feed bag on each of the horses and ate the remaining food in his basket. Then he stretched out to rest in the wagon bed beside his precious cargo.

Bright moonlight woke Nicolas several hours later. He stretched, stiff from the cold and exertion. Satisfied that this half of his self-appointed task was complete, he relieved himself, took the feedbags off the horses and started the bays on the return trip to his estate.

The air was cold and crisp, and the travelers' breath formed fairy clouds in the moonlight. It took three hours in the dark to get home.

Nicolas pulled the wagon under the maple tree to unload the caskets and grave markers. By the light of the moon, he re-buried the tiny boxes beneath the tree Sydney loved. When he finished, he walked to the south end of his property where Lara and Sven were buried.

Dropping to his knees in the dusting of snow, he asked their forgiveness.

He was sorry he had avoided visiting these graves. He was sorry he hadn't treated Stefan the way a father should treat a son. He was sorry he had turned his back on living, burying his zeal for life under a façade of stoicism.

He was glad Sydney came into his life. Glad she pushed him to be a better father to Stefan. Glad she was giving him a second chance at parenthood. Glad she encouraged him to be the strong and passionate man he was born to be.

I sent her to you, Nick.

Nicolas didn't know whose voice he heard. He didn't care. All he could do was raise his hands in the air and whisper, "Thank you."

December 6, 1819

The pale December sun snuck over the horizon before Nicolas walked back to the manor. Sydney and Stefan were eating breakfast and looked up in corresponding surprise as he ducked into the kitchen.

"*Pappa!* You're back!" Stefan jumped off his chair and ran to hug his father's legs. He backed away holding his nose. "And you're stinky!"

Nicolas's eyes locked onto Sydney's.

"Are you married?"

Sydney frowned as a smile tugged at her mouth. "No?"

"Addie! I need a bath!" Nicolas thundered.

The tin tub was dragged out and copious amounts of water heated on the iron stove. Addie gathered the comb, razor, mirror, soap and towels while Nicolas untied his stiff fur coverings. He removed his shirt and breeches only after Addie and Sydney left the kitchen.

He carefully placed the garnet ring in the center of the table.

Nicolas eased himself into the hot water and sank beneath its surface. The liquid heat rippled, luxurious and sensuous over his skin, raising gooseflesh. He ran his hands through his stiff hair to loosen the dirt.

Stefan grabbed a handful of that hair and pulled his father's head out of the water. "*Pappa*, you can't breathe under water!"

Nicolas's good-natured laugh filled the room. "No, son, I can't. But if I don't get this dirt off, no one else will be able to breathe once they get close to me! Will you soap my hair?"

Stefan scrubbed Nicolas's scalp while Nicolas washed the rest of his body. He ducked under the water to rinse, and then showed a very happy Stefan how to hold the mirror while he shaved.

Nicolas stood and let the water drip off his skin, bright pink from the heat. He rubbed himself dry with the towels. The golden hairs covering his body rose and curled.

It felt good to be clean.

After thanking Stefan for his invaluable help, Nicolas wrapped two towels around his midsection and grasped the garnet ring in his fist. Padding down the hall, he glanced at Sydney sewing in the drawing room, and then headed upstairs to get dressed.

℘ ℭ

When Nicolas announced his desire for a bath, Sydney vacated to the drawing room to sew in front of that east-facing window. She sank into the settee and picked up the half-finished baby gown she started the day before. As she sewed, she hummed to the child and tried not to think about the man she loved and the question she needed him to ask.

Soon.

Nicolas crossing the doorway caught her eye. A brief glimpse of his near-nakedness was enough to disrupt her composure. He had lost substantial weight in his absence. Her hands dropped to what remained of her lap as she closed her eyes and imagined how he looked the last time he stood naked in her room. Powerfully built, perfectly proportioned, covered in blond hair that got darker as it trailed down from his navel.

Stop that!

She opened her eyes, picked up her sewing, and concentrated on the stitches.

Chapter Thirty Two

*N*icolas wore the same clothes he wore to the May Day Ball: the dark blue velvet frock coat, brocade waistcoat, white lace shirt and fawn-colored breeches. His shortened hair was almost dry and combed back from his face. The ring was in his waistcoat pocket. He was ready. Nicolas opened the door to his room and called Stefan.

"Yes, *Pappa?*" He appeared, breathless, at the top of the stairs.

"Would you tell Addie and Maribeth and John that I want them in the drawing room with Sydney?"

"Why?"

"I have something to tell about my trip. About the Indians," came the sudden inspiration to divert suspicion, "and I want everyone there. It's very, very important."

Stefan's eyes grew wide at the mention of the Indians.

"Yes, *Pappa!*" He bounced down the stairs.

Nicolas paced the length of his room. His heart was full; it fought his lungs for space behind the bars of his ribs. It was fortunate both were securely jailed and their attempted escape foiled. Nicolas checked three times to make certain the ring was in his pocket. It was.

An excited Stefan topped the stairs. "Everybody's there now, and even *Onkel* Rick!"

"Is he?" Nicolas frowned. Well, no matter; his course was set. "Alright, then, let's go down!"

Stefan led the charge. Nicolas pulled a deep breath to quell a touch of stage fright. Fortified by his status—freshly bathed, clean shaven and dressed in his finest clothes—he stepped into the drawing room.

Conversation stopped as puzzled eyes considered Nicolas's elevated condition. But from his perspective, only Sydney was in the room. Nicolas's heart banged against its bone bars as he approached her.

"Are you married?" There was no demanding tone, no teasing tone now.

"No," she whispered. Her dilated eyes floated over pale cheeks, sunken and bloodless.

Nicolas lowered himself to one knee in front of her, reached for her hands and grasped them in his. "Then, would you consider marrying me? *Vil De gifter seg med meg?*"

Everyone in the room waited in stunned silence for Sydney to respond. Her blinking gaze caressed his face, but she didn't answer him

Had he waited too long? Had Rickard wooed her away from him? Nicolas's heart constricted, his mouth gone dry as straw. Somewhere he found a remnant of his voice. "Sydney?"

"Yes, Nicolas," she breathed. "Of course I will."

The room exploded. Nicolas retrieved the garnet ring from his pocket with a trembling hand.

"I traded pelts for your wedding ring." He slid it on her finger. It was a perfect fit.

"It's beautiful!" Sydney's gaze bounced repeatedly between her hand and Nicolas.

Nicolas straightened and pulled her to stand. He held her and the child close. She raised her lips and he kissed her with tenderness and promised passion. He hugged her again and waved the babbling occupants of the room to some semblance of quiet.

"Sydney, it's very fortunate that you said yes, for it would be quite awkward to return your wedding gift."

"Do you mean the ring?" Sydney looked at her finger.

"No. Get your cloak and come with me. Everyone come!"

Once the crowd was suitably attired to venture outside in the cold mid-morning, Nicolas wrapped Sydney's arm around his and told her to close her eyes.

"Don't open them until I tell you, do you understand?" Too happy, his voice failed to be stern. "I truly do want you to see this in in the right manner."

Sydney smiled, lifted her chin and closed her eyes. Nicolas led her to the maple tree, assuring she didn't slip on the crust of snow. He turned her and placed himself between her and the new graves.

"Do you remember when you told me you had no home?"

She nodded, eyes still closed.

"Well now you do. So, I brought them home to you."

Sydney gasped. Her eyes and mouth popped open. She stared up at Nicolas, disbelief and hope warring over her features. He stepped aside. Her gaze fell to the tiny graves under her favorite tree.

"Nicolas Hansen! You didn't!"

Her hands flew to her cheeks; they were much redder than the winter's chill might be blamed for. Heedless of the snow, she lowered heavily to her knees. Nicolas knelt beside her.

"Is it right that I moved them?" he whispered.

"Yes. Oh, yes." Her fingers traced the carved names. Tears spilled from her eyes and dripped down her cheeks.

Nicolas put one arm around her shoulders and rested a hand on her womb. "Now all of your children are with you." He leaned his head against hers. Their child moved under his palm. It was a strong, reassuring movement, and he cherished the moment.

Sydney wrapped her arms around his neck and buried her face under his chin. "Thank you. Thank you, thank you, thank you, thank you!"

"*Jeg elsker deg.*" Nicolas whispered.

"*Jeg elsker deg også.*"

"*Pappa?*" Stefan tugged on Nicolas's frock coat. "*Pappa!*"

"Yes, son?"

"When are you gonna tell about the Indians?"

Nicolas laughed and lifted his son to his hip. "Tonight. I promise." He planted a loud kiss on Stefan's cheek and set him back on the ground. He pulled Sydney close again. "Now let's go back inside where it's warm, shall we?"

Rickard stepped up and gave Nick a hearty back slap. "Brother, I couldn't be happier!"

"Truly?" Nicolas looked sideways at his friend.

"Truly. Sydney and I talked while you were gone. She refused my offer of marriage."

Nicolas looked down at the very pregnant woman tucked securely under his arm. "You did?"

She gave him a sheepish smile.

"I did. I told him that it would be disastrous for me to marry him considering I'm in love with his best friend. And the thought of raising your child without you, while living less than two miles from you, was something I couldn't do."

"So you planned to stay here, then."

"In truth, no." Sydney glanced at Rickard. "I'm packed to go to St. Louis, if you hadn't proposed. I arranged to have the baby there, and then return to my parents' home in Kentucky."

Nicolas stopped walking

"And how did you arrange all this?"

"Through me," Rickard confessed.

"I see." Nicolas was shaken to his core by their plans; he had come so very near to losing everyone, closer than he imagined. Thank goodness he came to his senses.

Thank God he *listened*.

Back in the drawing room, the wedding itself became the topic.

"I'd rather be married soon!" Sydney exclaimed, laughing. "The size of the occasion is of less concern to me than the size of my belly!"

"Shall we marry on Sunday? Pastor Mueller should be here this week." Nicolas looked at everyone and waited for an objection. None came.

"Done, then. Rickard, will you be my second?"

"I'd be honored. What can I do?"

"Make the arrangements at the church. We'll marry following the morning service."

"I'll plan the wedding dinner for here afterwards!" Addie offered, her face a puddle of happy tears.

"I reckon we could invite everyone at church on Sunday to stay for the wedding and come over for dinner. Is that too much work, Addie?" Nicolas looked to his housekeeper.

"No, no. Not at all! Truly, I wouldn't enjoy a thing more!" Addie dabbed her eyes with her apron.

"Then it's settled." Nicolas clasped his hands, grinning like a canary-stuffed cat.

December 7, 1819

"Stefan, Sydney and I are going to be married on Sunday. Do you know what that means?"

Stefan shook his head as he shoveled a spoonful of eggs into his mouth.

"Well, it means I'll be the husband and Sydney will be my wife."

Stefan rolled his eyes and slapped his forehead. "Like Addie and John. I know that!"

"Good. Yes." Nicolas nodded at his son. "That also means that Sydney will be the *Mamma.*"

Stefan's eyes got big and his brows disappeared into his hair. "I'll have a *mamma?*"

"And this baby will be your brother or sister," Sydney added.

"Do I get to pick?"

"No, son." Nicolas stifled his smile. "The baby's already a boy or girl. We'll find out which one when it comes out."

"Oh." Stefan took a disgruntled bite of breakfast.

Sydney laid her hand on Stefan's. "You can call me *Mamma,* or you can call me Sydney, but the baby will call me *Mamma.*"

"What will the baby call *Pappa?*"

"*Pappa.* He is the father of both you and the baby."

Stefan turned his gaze on Nicolas. "You stuck your prick in Sydney and made the baby?"

Nicolas coughed. "Um… yes."

Stefan looked around the kitchen for a clue. "Was I a baby?"

"Of course you were. Everyone was."

Stefan cocked his head to one side. "Who did you stick your prick in to make me?"

Nicolas shifted in his seat. Sydney rose and poured herself another cup of coffee.

"That was Lara, your mother. *Onkel* Rick is her brother and *Tante* Lily is her sister."

"Is she the one who died?"

"Yes. She died after you were born."

A wave of alarm washed over Stefan's face. "Will Sydney die after her baby is born?"

"No!" Sydney blurted. She sat down next to Stefan again. "I

already had two babies and I was fine."

"Where are they?"

"Well… Remember the white cat's baby? The one who was too little and wouldn't breathe? My two babies were born too soon. They couldn't breathe, either." Sydney swallowed several sips of coffee and didn't look at Nicolas.

"Is that what *Pappa* buried under the tree?"

She nodded.

"Will this baby be born too soon?" Stefan looked at Nicolas.

He chuckled. "It doesn't appear that way!" Sydney kicked him under the table.

"Did you stick your prick in Sydney to make the other babies?" Stefan was trying to fit all the pieces together.

"No, Stefan. She had a husband."

"Where's he?" Stefan looked back at Sydney.

Nicolas and Sydney exchanged glances. She said, "The man who was my husband died right before I met your father."

"That's when *Pappa* found you in the creek!"

"Yes!" Nicolas and Sydney said in unison.

"Do you have any other questions?" Nicolas asked his son.

"Will *Onkel* Rick be there?"

"He will."

"Good." Stefan went back to his breakfast.

December 12, 1819

Neighbors sat on every available flat surface in the Hansen manor, including the stairs and the floor. Well-wisher after well-wisher toasted the newly married couple, pumped Nicolas's arm and hugged Sydney. Stefan explained that Sydney was now his *mamma,* and when the baby comes out, he'll know if he's a brother or a sister.

Sydney smiled at his misinterpretation, marveling at how her life had changed. Six days ago, she was single and alone, her belongings packed for immediate exodus. Now, sitting on the edge of the drawing room hearth, a plate of food balanced on what small length of thigh extended beyond her belly, and trying to keep her tea cup out of the path of Erma Sinclair's exuberantly wobbling arm gestures, she'd never been happier.

Rickard arrived late, but with the teacher Bronwyn Price on his arm. Rickard's height was a good match for her five-foot-eight or so. Her dark hair and eyes contrasted nicely with his auburn hair and hazel eyes. Even her dress, a rich coffee brown with white lace trim, coordinated with his rust-colored frock coat. Sydney nudged Nicolas and nodded in their direction.

"They make a handsome couple, don't they?"

"They do." Nicolas grinned at her. "I hope she can run fast!"

"To get away? Or to catch him?"

"Does it matter?"

Sydney listened politely to yet another birthing horror story, and wondered why on earth this was the type of story most women felt compelled to share, when Nicolas gripped her arm. He interrupted, apologized for pulling her away, and then did exactly that. He led her to the kitchen, the only room not full of guests. Sydney sank gratefully into a chair.

"Are you exhausted, wife?" Nicolas sat on a stool and lifted her feet. He slipped off her shoes and rubbed her swollen feet. Sydney groaned with pleasure.

Nicolas's mouth curved. "Careful! Our guests might believe we couldn't wait to go upstairs to consummate our marriage!"

Sydney slapped her hand over her mouth, her eyes crinkled in mischief. The temptation to continue to moan, and loudly, tickled her more than the foot rub.

"You realize no one will leave until we go to my bedroom?" Nicolas's smile looked very different now.

Sydney dropped her hand to her semblance of a lap. "I suppose that's true, even in my condition."

"So I'm asking again, are you exhausted? Are you ready to end the party?"

"Yes and no. I'm so happy I don't want the celebration to stop. But, as you can see, my feet are quite swollen, and I can't eat another bite or drink another drop."

Nicolas lowered her feet to the floor. "Here's what we'll do. For twenty minutes more, you talk to who you want to and say what you need to say. Then I'll come get you and we'll take our leave, agreed?"

The twenty minutes blinked by. Nicolas pushed Sydney up a couple of stair steps and stood below her. He turned to address their guests, his voice carrying easily.

"Dear friends, thank you for coming on such short notice to celebrate our nuptials. Sydney and I would love to share your delightful company for longer, but find we must remove ourselves. Please continue to enjoy the food, and each other, for as long as you like."

He turned around, winked at Sydney, and lifted her enlarged body without discernable effort. She threw her arms around his neck, gasping her surprise. Nicolas ascended the stairs amid raucous whooping and hollering from their well-lubricated guests.

"Careful, Nick, or you'll be a father again before morning!" someone hollered, the comment followed by rounds of knowing laughter. Sydney hid her embarrassment in Nicolas's neck as he continued up the stairs.

"Not to worry!" someone else yelled. "When it sees what's comin' after it, it'll be frightened into stayin' put!"

Their guests articulated their mirth as Nicolas reached the top of the stairs. He smiled at the crowd over Sydney's shoulder, then stepped into his room. And his door always had a lock.

℘ ℃

A healthy fire removed the chill from the bedroom and the oil lamp glowed atop Nicolas's chest of drawers. Though it was but late afternoon, the approaching winter solstice left scant sunlight at this hour. Sydney lay back on the bed, arms thrown wide.

"Oh, I believe I had more wine than I realized."

Nicolas stretched out next to her. "I know I had my share of brandy toasts. That's one of the reasons I wanted to come up here. I didn't want to lose my ability to reason."

"What do you mean?"

Nicolas ran his knuckles over Sydney's cheek. "You're so beautiful in that green dress, the way the color goes with your eyes." He tangled his fingers in her pinned curls. "And your hair falling on your shoulders looks like a shiny, black waterfall. One more brandy toast, and I'd take you tonight, babe or no."

Sydney grasped Nicolas's hand and put it to her lips. She kissed it and tickled his palm with her tongue. Nicolas leaned over her and covered her mouth with his. Sydney held him close and whispered her confession.

"One more glass of wine, and I'd let you."

In an act of immense self-control, that certainly would earn him some kind of very large reward later in life, Nicolas rolled off the bed and rose to his feet. He offered his hand to his bride.

"May I help you undress?"

Nicolas unlaced her dress and lifted it over her head. Sydney shook it out and hung it on the wardrobe. She stood near the fire in her chemise, pulling pins and ribbons from her hair.

Nicolas removed his frock coat, waistcoat and shirt, and hung them in the wardrobe. He extinguished the oil lamp before he removed his breeches. He didn't want Sydney to see his unavoidable arousal. He slid into the bed and covered himself to the waist.

"Sydney?"

"Yes?"

"Might I see you?"

She looked down at her bulk. "I'm so unattractive right now."

"Not to me. Not at all."

Sydney hesitated. The fire cast a bronze glow over her body as she shrugged out of the chemise and let it drop to the floor. Nicolas drew a long breath through pursed lips.

Her heavy breasts rested on her perfectly rounded abdomen. Her skin stretched smooth over her womb. Her navel flattened. Though visible, the scar from the shooting had lightened over the past six months. The rest of her body was lean and slightly muscular.

"My God, you're beautiful," Nicolas breathed.

Sydney crossed her arms in front of her belly. "I'm scarred and misshapen."

Nicolas leaned across the bed and pulled her toward him. "You're beautiful. And I'm very proud to be your husband."

Sydney climbed into bed and pulled the covers to her shoulders, her back pressed against Nicolas. He curled around her and inhaled the heady scent of her freshly-washed hair. His hand moved over her body, exploring every swell, every curve, every crevice, concentrating on what his hand discovered as it traveled of its own free will over the landscape of her skin.

Hard as iron, he gasped when Sydney's warm hand closed over

him. He rolled onto his back as she stroked him, a whimper of arousal becoming a full-fledged groan until he could not hold back the flood. He winced and grunted as his body released. Then he melted to a heap of quivers and aftershocks. He could not have moved if a twister flattened the building.

Sydney whispered in his ear, and the heat and tickle of her breath promised to make him hard again. Quickly.

"That's only a taste of what's to come. After the baby, you're never going to want to leave my bed!"

"*Helvete*, Sydney! I don't ever want to leave it now!" Nicolas thundered. Then a much softer, "*De er slik vakker, min presang.*"

"What are you saying?"

"You are so beautiful, my gift."

"My gift?"

"You're a gift. My gift. *Min presang. Jeg elsker deg.*"

Sydney snuggled close to Nicolas under the covers. "*Jeg elsker deg også.*"

They did not move apart, even in sleep.

Chapter Thirty Three

December 24, 1819

$\mathcal{W}$hen Sydney awoke to her first Norwegian Christmas, Nicolas was already downstairs with John wrestling the huge pine Yule log into the drawing room fireplace.

"It's tradition," he explained. "Vikings used to celebrate the passing of the shortest day of the year with the longest fire they could burn. Now it's part of our Christmas tradition."

Sydney helped Addie prepare *pinnekjøtt* from lamb ribs that were salted and smoked last summer. They would steam for the next few hours in a pot with small stripped branches, until the meat actually fell off the bones. While the ribs cooked, Sydney propped up her feet and watched Addie make rice pudding. Nicolas kept coming to steal tastes and Addie kept smacking his hand with her spoon.

"Don't forget the almond!" he admonished. "Whoever gets the almond in their pudding will have good luck throughout the year!"

Nicolas stepped behind Sydney, leaned down, and wrapped his arms above her belly. "My year will be lucky no matter who gets the almond."

His soft lips, amidst the prickle of his beard, nuzzled her neck. Gooseflesh rippled down her arms. She wished she could drag him back to bed to play, even though her own pleasure was weeks in the future.

At a little past eleven o'clock that night, Nicolas descended the stairs with a sleepy Stefan in his arms. Sydney waited below in her cloak. She had just been to the privy—again—and still felt the chill of the December night.

"Is *Julenisse* here?" Stefan rubbed his eyes.

"I've not seen him yet. Are you certain you were a good boy this year?" Nicolas teased, setting him on the floor.

Stefan nodded, his auburn hair flopping in his face. "Real, *real* good!"

"Well, perchance he'll come while we're at church." Sydney suggested. She ruffled Stefan's hair. "Do you need to use the privy?"

Stefan yawned, shaking his head.

"Let's go then!" Nicolas herded his family out the front door.

A three-quarter moon shone on snow that twinkled with a million stars. Sleigh blades slid over the snow with a soft hiss, the team's hoofbeats hushed by the frozen fleece. The jangle of tack rang loud in the frigid air. Stefan snuggled between his *pappa* and his new *mamma*.

Tonight, entering the school and church building held no fear for Sydney. She considered her new Nordic-god husband and was certain it never would again.

"*Onkel* Rick!" Stefan bounced to his uncle as soon as they walked through the door. "Merry Christmas! Did you bring me anything?"

"Of course!" Rick pulled a bag of peppermint candies from his pocket. "Make them last, do you hear? And don't forget your *Tante* Lily!"

Stefan waved at Lily. She didn't seem to notice.

"Mamma, look what *Onkel* Rick gave me!" He showed Sydney the bag. "Can I have one now?"

Nicolas leaned over. "Did you say thank you?"

A horrified look came over Stefan's face and he bolted back to his uncle. "Thank you, *Onkel* Rick!"

His urgent voice pulled Rickard's rapt attention from Miss Bronwyn Price. "You're welcome, Stefan."

Stefan returned to Sydney, but his eyes slid sideways to his father. "Now can I?"

Nicolas answered him. "Yes. Sit down and be quiet then, the service is going to start."

Stefan sat next to Sydney and carefully unwrapped one piece of the precious candy. He slipped it into his mouth and his eyes closed in childish ecstasy. With a contented sigh, he pulled his feet up on the bench and leaned over. Resting his head on Sydney's stomach, he received a kick from his surrogate pillow. Unfazed, he patted her belly.

Sydney's composure quavered at his simple acceptance. She slid much more easily into Stefan's life than she had into his father's; now he casually comforted her unborn babe.

The immensity of being the only mother Stefan would ever know made her feel very small and very incapable. She closed her eyes and thought of Lara. Would she approve of Sydney as a wife for Nicolas? Would she trust Sydney to raise her son? She closed her eyes and crossed herself, finding the familiar motion reassuring.

With God's help I'll do my best for both of them, Lara. I promise.

The burden eased and a sense of goodwill infused her core the way candlelight infuses darkness. She ran her fingers through Stefan's hair as one tear rolled down her cheek.

Nicolas's finger brushed it away. "Is something amiss?"

She nodded toward Stefan.

His eyes dropped to his son, tunelessly humming as he rested against Sydney's bulge and patted its restless inhabitant. When his eyes returned to hers, they sparkled with moisture.

The last notes of the Christmas Eve service dissipated. Worshippers filed out slowly, calling 'Merry Christmas' to each other before dispersing to their far-flung homes. Rickard was one of the last to leave. He kissed the back of Miss Price's hand.

"He's smitten." Sydney held Nicolas's arm. "And he has a bad case!"

"It's about time. I was beginning to wonder about him." Nicolas helped Sydney into the landau.

"*Pappa*, do you believe *Julenisse* came yet?"

"Well, I don't know," Nicolas's mouth twitched. "Do you think he knows you forgot to thank your *Onkel* Rick for the candy?"

"Stop that!" Sydney laughed and smacked Nicolas on the thigh.

At the manor, Stefan jumped out of the carriage and ran to the door. He pushed it open and could not be bothered to close it.

Nicolas helped Sydney down and kept her from slipping as they mounted the porch steps. Stefan reappeared, radiating excitement.

"He came! He came!" Stefan bounded out the door. "Look what he brought me!"

Stefan held out a pair of carved wooden horses painted to look like Fyrste and Sessa. Nicolas looked down at Sydney with amazed appreciation. She gave him a self-satisfied smile.

"Did he?" He turned back to Stefan. "And is that all that you found?"

Stefan disappeared again. Nicolas and Sydney followed, closing the front door.

"Look at this!" Stefan held up two jointed wooden knights. They were painted like Knights of Norway. They were a little too large for the horses, but Stefan was already setting up a jousting match on the drawing room floor.

"Son, I'm glad *Julenisse* came tonight. But you'll have to wait until morning to play. Go upstairs and get into bed."

Reluctant to relinquish his new toys, Stefan did so without complaint only when Nicolas told him he could eat one more peppermint while he undressed. Sydney eased herself to the settee. The staircase was daunting when she was this laden and this tired.

Nicolas grinned at her like a lizard with a mouthful of cricket. "*Julenisse* brought something for you, as well. Wait here."

He strode from the drawing room. Once he was out of sight, Sydney awkwardly retrieved Nicolas's gift from her sewing basket on the floor and tucked it behind her back.

"Close your eyes!"

The command came from the hallway. Sydney heard the floorboards complain as Nicolas crossed the room. She felt something heavy come to rest in front of her. "You can look now."

"Oh, Nicolas! Did you make this?" Sydney ran her hands over the carved maple-wood cradle. It was large and sturdy, and it rocked easily.

"See this?" Nicolas pointed to an extra piece of wood on one of the rockers. "This is so you can rock it with your foot."

"I've never seen such a beautiful cradle! What are the carvings?"

"Norse mythology. I'll tell the child stories as he grows."

"I am certain she will love that!" Sydney laughed, reaching for Nicolas. "Thank you!"

Several lingering kisses later, Sydney pulled the pliable bundle from behind her back before his delicious attention made her forget it was there.

"Now it's your turn."

Nicolas untied the ribbon that held a roll of fabric. Two shirts of soft brushed cotton unfurled before him, both with elaborate stitching and pleating.

He wiggled the fabric between his fingers. "This material is so soft. Where did you get such a thing?"

"A peddler came by while you were hunting. I was only going to make baby clothes from it, but I struck a deal with him and got the whole bolt." She grinned up into his beautiful eyes. "You deserved to be pampered some as well."

"Thank you, *min presang*."

Nicolas kissed her again—very thoroughly—and she was transported. She inhaled the scent of him and nestled into his arms. She was so contented that she felt she could float up the stairs; her bulging womb would pose no impediment at all.

January 4, 1820

Nicolas reviewed his income and expense reports from Nelson Ivarsen. His investments were sound, though his income in 1819 was substantially lowered as a result of the country's depressed economy. So long as he didn't make any extravagant purchases—like another horse for Sydney—they would manage.

He was startled by urgent banging on the front door. Nicolas crossed the entry hall and opened the heavy portal. Frosted air from the overcast morning pushed through his new shirt.

Three men stood on his porch. The first was past middle age and sported white-streaked gray hair. The second looked enough like him to be his son. The third man held an important document, judging by the stamps and signatures Nicolas caught sight of.

The size of the one that answered the door seemed to give them all a moment of pause. So he straightened and looked down at them.

"Can I help you gentlemen?"

"Nicolas Reidar Hansen?" asked the man with the document.

"Yes?"

"I have a warrant here—"

Before he finished, the other two grabbed Nicolas's arms,

jerked him through the doorway, and threw him to the snow-dusted porch. Nicolas twisted his body, landed on his shoulder, and rolled away. He scrambled to his feet and turned as both men swung at him. He deflected the blow from the older, slower man, but the younger man caught him blindingly in his right eye, exploding fireworks in his skull.

While the young man shook out his cold-reddened hand, Nicolas's right fist cannoned past his pain and into that man's midsection, doubling him over. Nicolas swung his left forearm at the older man, crashed into his face and knocked him off balance. The old man's nose vomited blood.

"Stop this!" the man with the document shouted.

The younger man jumped on Nicolas's back and tried to choke him. Nicolas threw himself backward into a stone column. With a loud 'oof' and the crack of ribs, his assailant let go and fell to his knees, gasping. As Nicolas struggled to keep his balance on the snowy stone floor, the older man caught him in the chin with a surprisingly strong upper cut. Nicolas staggered backward and jolted down hard on his arse.

"This isn't how we do things in Missouri!" the third man bellowed. He pulled a pistol from beneath his greatcoat.

Nicolas blinked to clear the vision in his good eye. The older man jumped him, but Nicolas rolled and flipped him, landing him hard on his back. As he did so, the younger one swung back his heavy boot and kicked Nicolas squarely in the groin, paralyzing him instantly. With a roar of pain, Nicolas curled into a ball, unable to breathe, unable to see, unable to think beyond the blades of agony rending his core.

Third Man jumped forward as Nicolas moaned and cupped his crotch, and tied his wrists together.

Nicolas drew a loud ragged breath and wheezed, "What— what—"

With the pistol waving at the other two men, Third Man straightened and read from the document.

"Nicolas Reidar Hansen you are under arrest and charged with the crimes of kidnapping, rape and adultery."

Nicolas squinted through a swirling red-hot haze and stinging cold. What he heard made no sense.

Third Man continued, "You are hereby remanded into my

custody, and are ordered to stand trial for these crimes in St. Louis, Missouri Territory. The trial will be held seven days from today in order that you may prepare your defense."

"If he has one!" The older man might have sneered if his nose wasn't broken. The younger one was pale and stood crooked, favoring his cracked ribs.

"Can you stand?" Third Man asked.

Nicolas nodded, determined not to appear weak. He didn't know how he accomplished it, but he struggled to his feet in spite of the crippling agony radiating from his crotch. His shirt was bloodied and stuck to him where melted snow left wet patches. With effort that would make even Hercules envious, he straightened to his full height, towered over the other men, and glared at them through his undamaged left eye.

"Might I know who brought these charges?" he ground through a tender jaw clenched in pain.

Third Man looked back at his paper. "It was a third party seeking damages on behalf of a Mr. Devin Kilbourne."

"*Gud forbanner det all til* fucking *helvete!*" Nicolas rumbled. The three men exchanged troubled glances.

"Let's go." Third Man grasped Nicolas's elbow.

Sydney appeared at the door. Her eyes rounded at the sight of her bloody husband, beaten and tied, the man with the document looking haggard but official, and the battered father and son who stared at her, faces carved in horror.

"Daddy! Andrew!" she cried. "What on earth are you doing here?"

"Daddy?" Nicolas roared. He turned to stare at the older man.

"Siobhan, my darling! If only we'd known, we would've come sooner." The older man's distress bounced against them all.

"Known what?" Sydney shouted.

"We've come to avenge your honor," her brother stated with as much force as his cracked ribs would allow.

"Avenge my honor? Then why did you beat up my husband?"

"Husband?"

Nicolas raised the brow over his uninjured eye and glared at his attackers through a waxy halo of pain. The stone porch wavered under his feet.

"You're married to Devin Kilbourne!" Her father waved his

arms in punctuation.

"Not any longer, I'm not!" Sydney yelled back.

"Then he has corrupted more than your body, girl! He has corrupted your soul!" Andrew waved his finger at his sister. "And he'll pay for that, and pay well! Mark my words!"

"What do you mean?" Sydney's gaze ricocheted around the assemblage. "What's going on?"

"I'm being arrested," Nicolas managed, his voice hoarse and strained.

"Why? For what?" Sydney's horrified glance speared the man with the documents.

Third Man cleared his throat and read again, "…the crimes of kidnapping, rape and adultery."

"Against whom?"

Third Man squinted at the document. "A woman named Siobhan Kilbourne."

Sydney shook her head slowly. Splayed hands framed her face. "No. No! NO!"

"I'm afraid so."

"But *I'm* Siobhan Kilbourne! And I didn't bring any charges! You must let him go immediately!"

"I'm afraid I can't do that."

"Why the *helvete* not?" Sydney used Nicolas's word.

"These are serious charges, ma'am. I'm taking him to St. Louis today. The trial is in seven days." He tugged at Nicolas.

"I'll need my greatcoat." Nicolas resisted, sure he would topple at any moment. "Sydney, would you please get it for me?"

Sydney stared blankly at him. Nicolas tipped his head toward her and locked his gaze onto hers. "My greatcoat. I'm cold, Sydney."

She jerked a nod and stumbled into the house.

"Sydney? Who's Sydney?" Andrew looked at his father. The older man shrugged and held his nose, trying to staunch the blood. She returned and draped Nicolas's coat around his shoulders.

"Send for Rickard. Have him come to St. Louis and get Nelson straight away. He'll know what to do. And don't worry, *min presang*. I had the almond, remember? It's my lucky year."

Sydney's lips were tucked inside her teeth. Her chin dipped. She heard him.

"Let's go!" Third Man pulled Nicolas's arm again. This time he didn't resist, but walked erect and stiff-legged to the landau.

Sydney's father tried to say something to her that Nicolas couldn't hear; his throbbing injuries thundered in his ears. But he clearly heard her holler, "NO!"

Both her men were pale and quiet as the four of them squeezed inside the carriage. It was not going to be a comfortable ride for any of them.

Chapter Thirty Four

When the carriage pulled away, Sydney ran into the house shouting, "Addie!"

"What is it, dear?" Addie came in the back door. "Is it time?"

"No, I'm fine, but Nicolas isn't. Where's John?" Sydney pushed her way to the back door and screamed, "JOHN!"

John's head appeared at the stable door.

"Come here! I need you!" she yelled. He came at a run. When he reached the manor, Sydney related, as best she could, what happened to Nicolas.

"Oh, my Lord!" Addie dropped in a chair, clutching her apron to her chest.

Sydney ticked off points on her fingers. "John, go get Rickard. Tell him that Nicolas was arrested and what the charges are. Tell him we're going to St. Louis to get Nelson Ivarsen to defend him."

"We?" Addie's head snapped to attention.

Sydney ignored her and continued. "Then come back here and get me. I'm going to pack while you're gone."

"You're not going to St. Louis! Not this close to your confinement!" Addie's face ruddied alarmingly. "You've barely three weeks to go!"

Sydney faced Addie's objection; her backbone was granite and her determination, steel. "I'm going. I'll walk if I have to. No one can testify to what happened between me and Devin, nor between me and Nicolas, but me. I'm going to save my husband so he'll still be my husband when his child is born. Am I making myself clear?"

Addie frowned and loosed an indignant harrumph. "I'll go get a satchel and pack for you, then."

John touched Sydney's hand. "I'll get Rickard. Then I'll get you safe to St. Louis, don't you worry."

Rickard arrived at the manor in less than an hour with a bag tied to his saddle. He came to the front door and lobbed a warning at Sydney. "Nick would truly kill me if I let anything happen to you or the babe. I don't believe you should go."

Sydney laid her hand on Rickard's arm. "I'll be certain to tell him you performed your duty by attempting to dissuade me. But *I* know, that *you* know, I'm going."

Rickard was visibly distraught. "Sydney!"

"I'm going with you or without you, Rickard. Though truth be told, it would be a great deal easier with you." Her tone didn't betray the terror that she pummeled senseless and stuffed under her heart.

Rickard heaved an exaggerated groan of acquiescence. But he tied his horse to the back of her landau, and lifted her hastily bundled satchel. He nodded to John. "Let's go, then."

Sydney was quiet at first, methodically reviewing the charges and ways she could negate them, trying to find a logical counterpoint to each. She considered Rickard from under her lowered brow.

"When we get to St. Louis, I need you to find Rosie for me."

Rickard reacted like he had been shot. "Rosie?"

"Yes, Rosie. Do you know her? Nicolas used to 'visit' her regularly, is my understanding."

"Um, yes. I mean, I know her. I know where to find her, that is. Why is it you need her?" he sputtered.

"For the rape charge. A man whose 'needs' are being met doesn't resort to force."

"Oh. Of course." Rickard raked his auburn waves. "After we go to Nelson's, we'll go to the hotel. Then I'll find Rosie and bring her to you there. Is that satisfactory?"

Sydney nodded, curious to see Rickard so disconcerted. Did he 'know' Rosie the way Nicolas did?

Nelson Ivarsen was delighted to meet Sydney after the divorce and name-change decrees he prepared on her behalf. But as Sydney told him what she knew of the charges, his brow furrowed.

"I'll go discover what I can." He patted Sydney's hand. "We'll get this straightened out, dear. Don't fret; it's not good for the baby. When are you expecting, precisely?"

"In three weeks."

Nelson went ashen, though his lawyer's expression didn't change. "I'll go straight away."

John headed back to the estate, to return on the day of the trial. Rickard took Sydney to the hotel and, after she was ensconced in her room, went to find Rosie. Sydney collapsed on the bed, curled on her side, and sternly instructed her child.

"I need you to stay put, do you hear me? If you want to meet your *pappa* you can't come out early!"

Then she closed her eyes and refused to acknowledge the possibility that she and Nicolas had saved each other, only to lose each other. No god was that cruel. She lay still, breathed deeply and pretended to rest until the knock came.

Rosie entered Sydney's hotel room in a cloud of perfume and red organza ruffles. She claimed the only chair, chin high and unsmiling. Sydney sat on the bed's edge and Rickard stood.

"Thank you for coming, Rosie. Did Rickard tell you why I wished to see you?"

Rosie glanced at Rickard. "He said Nicky's in trouble and you want me to tell the court that, uh…"

"Well, I certainly don't expect you to say anything incriminating!" Sydney noticed a slight softening in Rosie's demeanor at that. "And I honestly don't know if we'll need you at all. But if it can help Nicolas's case in the charge of rape, I'm hoping you'll take the stand."

One eyebrow quirked. "What d'you want me to say, exactly?"

"I want you to tell the judge that Nicolas was a regular patron of your establishment for—how long?"

Rosie rolled her eyes. "Oh golly, let me think. Three, four years?"

Sydney hoped she hid her surprise well. She had no idea that Nicolas had been 'with' Rosie for so long. She forced herself to ask, "And how often did he visit?"

"Once a month, like clockwork."

"How long did he stay?"

"Usually two nights."

Sydney found this conversation much harder than she expected.

She tensed without being sensible of it. "Was he always with—with you?"

"Yes." Rosie had a challenging look in her eyes. Sydney was shaken. This was in his past; there was no reason for jealousy. Hissing, it snaked through her bowels even so.

"So would you be willing to say that in court?" When Rosie hesitated, Sydney added, "I'll pay you for your time, of course. To make up for lost income."

"Let me get this straight." Rosie leaned toward Sydney. "You want me to tell the court that your husband goes to a brothel?"

"Went," Sydney corrected. "Went to a brothel. As a regular. Yes."

Rosie leaned back and considered her. "What sort of wife asks that? Are you lookin' for an excuse to avoid his bed?"

Sydney hated the hopeful tone she detected in Rosie's voice. She pinched her own desire behind pursed lips. "No. I'm quite satisfied with my husband's bed."

Rickard coughed and pounded his chest. He blushed rather attractively. The women stared at each other. Then Rosie bounced a nod.

"I'll do it. For Nicky. And old times' sake." Rosie stuck out her hand. "And, I'll take the money."

Sydney laughed in relief and shook Rosie's hand. "Thank you, Rosie."

Rosie indicated Sydney's belly with her chin. "Is that his?"

"Yes."

"When's it due?"

"Three weeks." Sydney unconsciously rested her hand on the child.

"You know, our girls get caught now and again. I know a good midwife if you need one. She's clean and her ladies don't get sick after."

"Have you seen a lot of births?"

"My fair share, I suppose."

"I'll let you know, Rosie. Thank you again."

"Anything for Nicky." Rosie stood and walked to the door. "I'll be waitin' to hear from you. Rick, you know where to find me." She winked at him and closed the door.

Something in the exchange made Sydney believe her suspicions concerning Rickard and Rosie were true, but before she could say a word Rickard suggested they go back to Nelson's office. "We can take him out to dinner and see what he's learned."

Sydney put her hands on the small of her back and leaned backward. The babe was heavy and low enough to sit on her bladder. "Good idea. I'm starving!"

"Do you like fish? I know where to get the best fried catfish!"

Sydney laughed. And—as she assumed—it was the same place that Nicolas tried to take her on their trip to St. Louis. But now that Sydney was past the first nauseating months of pregnancy, the fishy smell didn't bother her one whit.

"So, Nelson, what did you find?" Rickard asked once they were settled at a table.

"Well, he's in jail. And that's not the nicest place to be spending your time. Tomorrow I can take him food and blankets; just give me what you want him to have and I'll see that he gets it."

Sydney leaned forward, hopeful. "Might I see him?"

Nelson shook his head. "I'll ask, but I wouldn't count on it." Rickard poured beer from a pitcher as Nelson continued, "I confirmed the charges are indeed kidnapping, rape and adultery."

"Who brought the charges?" Rickard asked.

"A man named Robert Bell. On behalf of Devin Kilbourne. Wasn't he the man you divorced?"

"Yes. And Robert Bell is my father. But I don't understand how he knew about any of this."

"Didn't you tell him about the divorce?" Rickard asked.

"Not at first… I waited until I knew how things would turn out. I wrote my parents a letter explaining everything the week after Nicolas and I were married. There's no way he could have gotten that letter and showed up here in that short amount of time. Someone else must have told him."

"Someone with an axe to grind!" Nelson snorted. "They painted Nicolas in the worst possible light in all of this."

"Do they want money?" Rickard addressed that question to Nelson. The barmaid set the food on the table.

The lawyer shook his head. "No, this is a criminal trial. No compensation will be awarded. The only outcomes are Nicolas goes free or goes to prison."

Sydney felt as though a dirk sank into her heart. She could not draw a deep enough breath. The walls became viscous, undulating toward the floor. Her body tingled and relaxed, and then she was looking up at Rickard and her head was in his lap. How did she get there? He brushed her hair aside, alarm sculpting his handsome features.

"Sydney? Don't worry, sweetheart. We'll get him out. The charges are unfounded. The judge will see that and let him go." But the confidence in his words had no impact on his expression. He looked to Nelson for confirmation.

"The problem is, Sydney, you're the only witness for the defense. You might not be allowed to testify because you are married to the defendant."

"They have to listen to me!" She sat up quickly, then grabbed the table edge and waited for the room to hold still. "I'm the only one who knows what happened…"

"And I'll use that, believe me. All other evidence against Nicolas is hearsay. In addition, the injured party—Devin Kilbourne—isn't appearing." Nelson took a generous bite of the fish and closed his eyes, chewing in ecstasy. "Dang good catfish."

"So, someone testifies on his behalf?' Rickard clarified. "Doesn't that take the wind out of his case?"

"It should."

Sydney felt Rickard's eyes evaluating her while she ate, but she avoided looking at him. If she saw panic in his eyes, she'd fall completely apart and be no good to Nicolas. Nelson didn't seem overly worried, and surely that presaged a good outcome.

Rickard escorted Sydney back to the hotel. He held her elbow tightly to keep her from slipping on the icy walkways. At her door he hugged her goodnight. "Don't worry, Sydney. Everything will be fine."

Sydney found comfort in her friend's embrace, but she couldn't trust herself to speak. Alone in her room, she crumpled on the bed and allowed herself to fall thoroughly to pieces.

&⳥

Nicolas lay on his back on a wooden platform, the only furnishing in the jail cell. He used his greatcoat as a partial blanket. The fire in the stove outside the cell died long ago, along with it all light, and the chill in the building deepened with each quarter hour. Rodent-sized feet skittered across the stone floor. The distinct scent of urine emanated from one corner. At least they untied his hands.

Once in the carriage, Nicolas hadn't resisted the arrest; he politely and proudly did everything they asked of him, presenting himself as civilized and above all this nonsense. Deeply relieved when Nelson appeared at his cell late in the afternoon, he was furious to hear that Sydney came to St. Louis as well.

"*Forbannet sta kvinne!*" he growled. Damned stubborn woman.

Longer than the bench, he bent his knees and shifted on the board to find a less excruciating position. His jaw was tender and he couldn't see out of his right eye. He figured the cold air would help the swelling go down.

It was his privates that worried him.

His balls throbbed and the sack was swollen to twice its normal size. He hadn't ever experienced such a direct hit in his whole life. He was alone, so he could undress and try to look at it, but there was not enough light to see aught.

"And there's nothing I could do about it anyway," he mumbled. His warm breath condensed in the frigid air.

Nicolas turned on his left side and pillowed his head on his arm. He couldn't put his legs together, so he leaned his right knee against the wall of the cell.

How did he end up in this place?

Someone trumped up accusations against him, that much was clear. The sheriff said it was on behalf of Devin Kilbourne. Why would he want to hurt Nicolas? Nicolas let him go after he shot Sydney! Did he want Sydney back?

"As if she would go!" he scoffed.

Nicolas closed his eyes and tried to relax, but as the cell grew colder, he began to shiver. He attempted to fit his whole body under his greatcoat, and wondered how much time would pass until the guard came on duty and re-lit the stove.

January 5, 1819
St. Louis

Sydney and Rickard bought a feather pillow, and two blankets. They also bought a double portion of roasted chicken, dried beef, biscuits and apples. Rickard suggested they take food for the guard to ensure Nicolas was allowed to keep his. He even added a small cask of beer to the larder.

The guard, whose mood was liberalized by his portion of food and beer, allowed them to deliver Nicolas's provisions themselves. Nelson led the way and Rickard carried the food.

Sydney followed. She wept openly when she saw her husband limp awkwardly across the cell, half of his beautiful face bruised and swollen. She reached through the bars. She needed to touch him. Until she did, he was only a ghoulish apparition. When she felt him, corporeal and alive, her nightmare lessened a tick.

"*Forbannet sta kvinne,*" he whispered. "Why did you come?"

"I had to. I'm going to testify for you," she whispered back and wiped her nose.

He shook his head. "You can't. You're my wife."

"Nelson said if they don't let me testify, then all the evidence is hearsay and the judge will have to dismiss the charges. Right, Nelson?" Sydney gripped Nicolas's blood-stained shirt tightly. It was one that she made him for Christmas.

"That's the idea, Nick." Nelson stood back, giving husband and wife some semblance of privacy.

Nicolas scowled. "The baby."

"Is fine. We had a talk. I told him he has to stay put until after the trial." That made Nicolas smile with the non-battered side of his face.

"Sheriff's comin'!" the guard called back. "Y'all need to get on your way now!" He stuffed his bribe into a saddlebag.

Nicolas leaned his head toward Sydney. "I'm still angry as *helvete* at you."

She leaned her head against his. "You may yell at me all you wish when you're out of here. I shan't even yell back."

"Take care of her, Rickard," he said in a louder voice.

"You know I will, Nick."

Sydney couldn't leave him. Her limbs refused to ignore her heart and obey her mind. Nelson and Rickard pulled her away from Nicolas just in time.

Chapter Thirty Five

January 11, 1820

*T*he day of the trial dawned cold and cloudy, threatening snow. Sydney sat with Rickard in the front row of the small courtroom. She shifted in the uncomfortable wood chair, and tried to relieve a persistent ache in her lower back. Worry jostled her all night and she had not slept much.

The rear door opened and Nelson Ivarsen appeared. Sydney sat up straighter to see Nicolas, her heart scrambling. His face was still bruised, but both of his eyes were open and functioning in tandem. Sydney noticed that his gait was still not normal and wondered what was amiss there. He looked scruffy with the week-old beard, but his hair was combed and his clothes were clean. Just to be in the same room with him calmed her.

When he saw her, deep lines of anxiety disappeared. He lifted the corners of his mouth in what she assumed was meant to be a reassuring smile. Nelson and Nicolas took seats in front of the railing that separated them from the courtroom audience. Sydney leaned forward and touched Nicolas's shoulder. He was still real. He leaned back and tilted his head toward her.

The lawyer for the prosecution, a tidy bald man with a large mustache, entered the room behind Nicolas. Robert and Andrew Bell entered through the court's front door. Sydney faced straight forward, her jaw set. As deeply as she desired to, she refused to acknowledge their presence. Reconciliation would come later.

If she still had a husband.

As the hour for the trial drew near, Rosie appeared in all of her unapologetic finery. She paused and perused the room. When Nicolas saw her, his eyes rounded under plunging brows. He looked at Sydney. Sydney raised her hand in greeting and flashed Rosie a grateful smile.

John Spencer entered the courtroom. He walked to the front and shook Nicolas's hand. If he was surprised by Nicolas's appearance, it didn't show on his placid face. A few other curious observers wandered in, before His Honor Judge Bernard Benson appeared and sat on his raised bench. He settled his spectacles on the bridge of his nose and banged his gavel, calling the trial to order.

The lawyer for the prosecution called Robert Bell as his witness. Robert testified that he received several letters containing information about his daughter, Siobhan, claiming she was lost on the property of Mr. Nicolas Reidar Hansen and, when he found her, he took her into his home and kept her there for several months. During that time, Siobhan was not allowed to leave Cheltenham.

"This is the grounds for the charge of kidnapping?" Judge Benson asked.

"It is, Your Honor."

The judge motioned for the testimony to continue.

According to the letters, it was during that time that Mr. Hansen forced himself on Siobhan, after taking her to a local ball, and plying her heavily with drink.

Hearing that, Sydney wanted to leap out of her chair and scratch her own father's eyes out. It was only Rickard's restraining hand on her arm, and the ache in her back working its way to her groin, which kept her in her seat.

"This is the charge of rape, I assume," Judge Benson clarified.

"Yes it is, Your Honor."

"Proceed."

The letters went on to relate that after the rape, Mr. Hansen continued to have intimate relations with Siobhan. It was during that time that her husband, Devin Kilbourne, discovered her whereabouts and came to rescue her. But Mr. Hansen held Devin Kilbourne prisoner for three days in his root cellar before ordering him off his property.

"And was Mrs. Kilbourne allowed to leave with her husband at that time?" Judge Benson asked.

Robert Bell looked at his lawyer, his face blank.

"That precise piece of information was missing from the letters, Your Honor," the lawyer answered.

"I see. Do you have aught else to present?"

Robert Bell shook his head. "No sir."

Judge Benson perused the papers which outlined the charges. "And after reading these letters, did you speak with Mr. Kilbourne?"

"Um, no sir."

"But you decided to bring charges against Mr. Hansen on his behalf?" Judge Benson peered at Robert over his spectacles. "Why?"

"I wanted to avenge my daughter, Your Honor. And Mr. Kilbourne."

"How noble." Judge Benson's comment splashed sarcasm over Robert's words. "Mr. Ivarsen, do you have any questions for this witness?"

"Yes, Your Honor." Nelson rose and faced Robert Bell. "Mr. Bell, is the person who wrote these letters in the courtroom today?"

"No, I don't believe so."

"You don't believe so? Tell me, sir, have you even met the author of these lively stories?"

Robert glanced around; he was trapped and under oath. "No, I haven't."

"In that instance, the evidence presented here is merely hearsay. Isn't that true?"

"But I had the letters."

"Are they with you?"

"No…"

The tidy bald lawyer jumped up and spoke with authority. "I saw the letters, Your Honor. I read them all quite thoroughly. I can attest to their contents."

Judge Benson raised his eyebrows. "Where are they now?"

"They were damaged." The lawyer stroked his mustache nervously.

"Damaged how?"

"Uh… an animal." He waved his hand in a gesture of dismissal. "Chewed them."

"I see." Judge Benson stared at the lawyer for a long moment.

"No more questions Your Honor." Nelson Ivarsen sat down next to Nicolas and folded his hands.

Judge Benson called for a short recess and banged his gavel. The prosecution's case had only lasted for half of an hour.

Sydney stood and stretched with her hands pressed against her lower back. Pressure was building in the lower parts of her abdomen from sitting so long. She excused herself to go to the privy. At Nicolas's look, Rickard followed her and escorted her back when she was done.

Nelson turned to her. "It's our turn now, Sydney. Are you ready?"

$\wp \, \backsim$

Sydney didn't look at Nelson. Her 'yes' was accompanied by a determined nod, but Nicolas saw something else in the set of her jaw that alarmed him. The judge re-entered the courtroom and ascended the bench. He gave a quick clack of his gavel.

"The defense may now present its case."

Nelson stood and in an authoritative voice called out, "Your Honor, I call Mrs. Siobhan Sydney Bell Hansen to the stand."

"What are you doing, Counselor? A woman cannot testify against her husband!"

"Mrs. Hansen is not testifying against her husband, she intends to present testimony on his behalf."

"Again, Counselor, I don't believe I can allow that."

"In that case, Your Honor, we respectfully request that all charges against the defendant, Nicolas Reidar Hansen, be dropped due to the fact that the only evidence presented against him is third-party hearsay."

"What!" Andrew Bell jumped to his feet, then winced and leaned to one side.

"Sit down!" The prosecuting attorney hissed and waved his hand at the young man.

Judge Benson glared over his glasses. "Kidnapping, rape and adultery are very serious accusations. It would not be prudent to simply throw them out."

Sydney pushed to her feet. "Your Honor?"

"Yes?"

"Might I have a word with you in private?"

"Mrs. Hansen, this is highly irregular!"

Sydney dipped her chin in deference. "I understand, Sir. But I have information that might influence your decision."

"Can you not state that information for the record?"

Sydney looked over her shoulders at the small crowd in the gallery, and then turned pleading eyes back to the judge. "I would rather not, Your Honor."

With an impatient sigh, the judge beckoned Sydney to approach. "Very well."

Sydney walked slowly to the side of the raised desk and Judge Benson leaned down to hear her. She raised her hand to shield her mouth. With a nod, then a smile, the judge thanked her.

"I shall allow Mrs. Hansen to testify," Judge Benson ruled. "Proceed."

The tidy attorney hopped to his feet. "I object!"

"Overruled!" the judge barked.

Sydney walked to the witness stand and was sworn in. Nicolas saw her grip the railing and lean on it. Her knuckles pressed white against her skin. Nelson approached her.

"Mrs. Hansen, tell me what happened the day Nicolas Hansen found you on his property."

"I fell into the creek and nearly drowned. I was unconscious when Nicolas found me. He took me to his manor where his housekeeper, Adelaide Spencer, nursed me back to health. He saved my life."

"And how did you come to fall in the creek?"

"I had an argument with Devin Kilbourne. I caught him in the arms of another… He was having an affair." Sydney closed her eyes for a moment. Her lower lip quivered. "He knocked me into the water."

Robert looked at Andrew.

"Were you held at the manor against your will?"

"No, I was not."

"Were you free to leave at anytime?"

"Yes, I was. In fact Nicolas brought me to St. Louis in June."

"Thank you, Mrs. Hansen. I believe that negates the kidnapping charge." Nelson Ivarsen looked to Judge Benson for confirmation. The judge nodded and gestured for them to continue.

Sydney shifted her weight from one foot to the other. Nicolas never took his eyes off her. He watched her breathing, her stance. His jaw worked and he scrubbed his chin with one hand. Something was very wrong.

"Now, Mrs. Hansen, let us address the charge of adultery. Can you explain the history of your marital status to the court, please?"

"When I first met Nicolas Hansen, I didn't know I was married." A murmur bubbled through the small crowd. The Bells exchanged shocked glances. "When Mr. Hansen found me, badly injured, half drowned and unconscious on his property, I wasn't wearing a wedding ring. I also had no memory of my identity."

Another murmur shuddered through the room. Judge Benson tapped his gavel. "Order in the court."

"I remained a *guest* at the Hansen estate while word was sent to neighboring towns to see if anyone knew of a missing woman."

"Was there a response?" Judge Benson asked the question himself, not waiting for Nelson.

"No, Your Honor. For three long months, not a soul came forward to identify me. I thought that if I had a husband, he would certainly come for me. Isn't that reasonable?"

The prosecuting lawyer jumped to his feet again. "I object! She's asking Your Honor to testify on her behalf."

The judge nodded. "Sustained."

Sydney continued, "In the meantime, I became a working member of the Hansen household."

"In what way?" Nelson asked.

"I train horses. Nicolas Hansen purchased a large stallion from Mr. Rickard Atherton—he's sitting right there behind Nicolas— because Mr. Atherton and his groom had not been successful in breaking the animal."

Sydney did not loose the railing to point at Rickard, but only tilted her head. Nicolas watched her uneven breaths and sought to set a steady rhythm by breathing along with her.

"And you were able to do so?" Nelson sounded deliberately skeptical.

"Yes, sir."

"With Mr. Hansen's help, I assume?"

"No, sir."

"Do you expect me to believe that neither of these rather large and imposing gentlemen," Nelson turned and indicated Rickard and Nicolas, "were able to control this stallion, but you did so all on your own?"

Sydney faced Judge Benson. "Your Honor, I'm under oath to speak the truth. Plus, I'm doing so in front of these men. If you still don't believe me, then by all means, ask them!"

Judge Benson looked at Rickard and Nicolas. Both of them nodded.

The judge cleared his throat. "Proceed."

"Three months after my rescue, I regained my memory. I realized that I was injured as a result of events that transpired when I discovered my former husband's infidelity. I had *removed* my wedding ring at that time and told him that I would divorce him."

Robert and Andrew Bell slumped stupidly with their mouths hanging open.

"The same day that I remembered these things, Nicolas contacted Mr. Ivarsen and had the divorce papers drawn up. I signed them and so did my unfaithful husband."

"You remember this situation, Your Honor, as you, yourself signed the decree?" Nelson prompted Judge Benson.

"Yes, of course." More throat clearing. "Proceed."

Nelson Ivarsen addressed the judge. "Your Honor, under the circumstances described here by the witness, it is clear that there was no conscious intent to commit adultery, the one and—I must point out, *only*—time actual congress occurred between Mr. and Mrs. Hansen.

"In addition, when it became apparent that the witness was, in fact, married, steps were taken immediately to rectify the situation. Furthermore, it's clear that the witness and the defendant were also victims, not only of an unfaithful husband, but of an unfaithful husband who purposefully hid Mrs. Hansen's identity and marital status from both her and Mr. Hansen."

Judge Benson nodded his agreement. "Is there anything further on the charge of adultery?"

"No, Your Honor."

"Then the adultery charge is dropped as well. Let's move on."

Sydney shifted her weight again and leaned on the railing, frowning at Nelson. Nicolas knew her well enough to deduce she was in pain. He leaned forward and dug his nails into the arms of his chair, legs flexed and ready.

"Now as to the charge of rape. Mrs. Hansen, were you raped?"

"No."

"Was the singular act which occurred between you and Nicolas Hansen consentual?"

"Yes."

"Have you aught more to add to that?"

"No." The crowd was silent, the Bells unmoving.

Judge Benson frowned. He pointed out Nicolas's size and rough appearance. "Mrs. Hansen, I have given you considerable dispensation to testify here. Let me assure you, Madam, if there was any force, of any kind, used against you, you may say so under the complete protection of this court."

"Your Honor, I don't mean to sound ungrateful or disrespectful in any way. You have allowed me to testify in this case and for that I thank you most sincerely." Sydney winced. Rickard reached over the railing and clamped his hands on Nicolas's shoulders.

"...But if I'm sturdy enough to break a stallion that neither of those men could handle, why would I marry a man who raped me?"

An excited murmur went through the crowd. The gavel came down again.

"Order!" Then turning to Nelson Ivarsen, Judge Benson asked, "Are there any last words, Counselor?"

"May I?" Sydney spoke. At Judge Benson's nod, she straightened; the effort it required was evident to everyone present. "If anyone here could be called a victim, it would be me. But I didn't bring charges against this man. Instead I'm here to testify on his behalf. He's my chosen husband and father of my child and I love him with all of my being. To find him guilty would only serve to leave me without a husband and our child—who will be born very soon—without a father."

Punctuating her words, Sydney gasped and doubled over. Water pooled at her feet. Nicolas threw off Rickard's restraint and shot from his chair. He picked her up, cradling her in his arms, and turned to face the judge. He would do what Sydney needed him to do, the court be damned!

Judge Bernard Benson banged his gavel and shouted over the chaotic crowd, "Case dismissed!"

Chapter Thirty Six

The courtroom churned with excitement.

"Take her to my landau out back!" Nelson Ivarsen directed Nicolas with a shove.

Sydney frantically tried to keep control, though it soon became apparent she had none whatsoever. She threw her arms wide and grabbed the doorjamb.

"Stop!" she shouted with all the effort she could spare.

Nicolas was trembling. "What's amiss Sydney?"

She leaned back over her shoulder and got an upside-down view of the courtroom. "Rickard! Rickard where are you?" she called out, desperate to find him.

"I'm here, Sydney!" She saw him push his way toward her. "Bring Rosie! To the hotel!"

"I'll get her and meet you there."

Sydney relaxed and let Nicolas carry her through the doorway.

"Why do you want Rosie, of all people?" Nicolas growled.

"It is a long sto—oh!" Sydney closed her eyes and breathed deeply. Her fingers dug into Nicolas's shoulder. He halted.

After a minute she opened her eyes. "That was a birth pain."

The bruises on Nicolas's face seemed to darken. He set Sydney on her feet. In the carriage, he leaned her against his chest. Nelson joined them and, once the landau was moving, articulated his praise.

"I've never seen anyone command a courtroom with such panache! Not only were you eloquent and rational, but, good Lord! What a finish!"

Sydney rewarded him with a lop-sided smile. "Anything to win, eh?"

Nelson laughed delightedly.

"Can you tell me why Rosie was there?" Nicolas demanded.

"I asked her to testify on your behalf, should it become necessary," Sydney said.

"And how, might I ask, would it have become necessary?"

"Rape. If your 'needs' were met, you didn't need to force anyone. Oh, *skitt!*" Sydney closed her eyes and concentrated on breathing. Her grip threatened to crush Nicolas's hand. After a minute she opened her eyes again.

"There was another one. How far apart do you believe they were?"

"I don't know, ten minutes? So, let me understand this. You, my wife, asked a whore to stand up in court and testify that your husband made it a habit of visiting a brothel?"

"Well, I offered to pay her for her time!"

Nicolas shook his head in disbelief. "I don't know what's worse! That you'd seek her out and discuss that sort of testimony about me, or that you'd even think of such a thing in the first place!"

Sydney leaned to the side and challenged him face to face. "And would you rather be in jail, sir? Because I'd much rather have you here! And if that means facing your past actions, so be it."

Another birth pain hit.

"Ouch! Damn it!" Tears leaked under her eyelids as Sydney tried to relax through the contraction, but her outburst at Nicolas made it impossible. Nicolas rubbed his fingertips over her taut belly.

"Don't worry, *min presang*. I'm sorry. Everything's fine. You did the right thing." Barely concealed panic colored Nicolas's tone.

Sydney drew a deep breath as the pain eased. "I couldn't bear it if they took you away, Nicolas, I truly couldn't."

The carriage stopped in front of the hotel. With one man under each arm, Sydney navigated the icy walk up the steps to the hotel's door. Nelson shook Nicolas's hand and congratulated him on both the trial's outcome and the impending birth.

Sydney walked into the hotel lobby under her own steam, but she halted at the bottom of the stairs. Without a word Nicolas lifted her in arms as strong as steel, and carried her to the upper floor.

When he set her down in the hallway, another pain came on her. She grabbed him for support, moaning softly as she waited for the intense pressure to pass.

Nicolas helped Sydney out of her dress and she climbed into bed, shivering in the chilled room. Nicolas set about coaxing the small banked fire to life. He lit the oil lamp as the winter's weak sun lowered behind the clouded sky.

Pulling the chair next to the bed, he asked, "Why did you send Rickard for Rosie now?"

"Whores have babies. It's bad business if they die doing so. If she recommends a midwife, that's a good midwife to have. And Rosie's been present at enough births to know what's going on. Besides, she's the only woman 'friend' I have in St. Louis."

Nicolas smiled at that. "My ex-whore is my wife's friend? Unbelievable."

"Keep saying 'ex" and we'll be fine!"

Another pain came, this one stronger than the ones before. Sydney held Nicolas's hand and breathed deeply, counting slowly to herself. When she reached sixty, the pain passed.

"You're so calm, Sydney," Nicolas ventured. "Does the screaming come later?"

"I don't plan on screaming." Sydney opened her eyes. "I've watched so many mares birth their foals that I did what they do. Of course, my last two babies were a lot smaller than this one!" She rubbed her belly.

Nicolas jumped to answer a knock at the door. Rickard was in the hallway with Rosie, now in a plain woolen dress and cloak. She crossed straight to Sydney's side.

"That was some great theatrics in the court, there! You brought the house down!"

Sydney grinned. "Thank you for being there. I'll see that you're paid for your time."

Rosie turned to Nicolas. "Did your wife tell you what she asked me to do?"

"Uh, yes. She did." Nicolas's blush was visible from the neck of his shirt to the top of his forehead. It flew out to the tips of his ears.

"This here's some little woman you got, Nicky." Rosie addressed Sydney. "So how're you doing?"

"The pains are getting harder and they're less than ten minutes apart. Might you fetch that midwife you told me about?"

"Let me time you for a pace, first." Rosie removed her cloak and sat down on the chair that Nicolas had vacated.

"I reckon this is when we leave," he said to Rickard, and turned toward the door.

"Oh, no!" Sydney reached for Nicolas. "Rickard needs to go, true, but you must stay!"

Nicolas was appalled. "Me? Stay? Here? You don't mean for the actual birth, madam?"

Sydney's eyes hooked his. "Yes."

"But—men don't—they're not—No!" he thundered. "I'll wait downstairs with Rickard!"

"Nicolas, I need you." Sydney swallowed the strangling fear straining her voice. "I can't do this alone."

"You're not alone," he protested, waving at Rosie. "Besides, you know I can't stay. And you know why."

"Nicolas, please? I was willing to do anything required when you were arrested and needed me. And now I need you." She tried to muzzle her fear. "Please don't abandon me. I'm so scared."

Nicolas was at the bedside so quickly, Sydney wasn't aware of him crossing the room. He kissed her and his beard pricked her chin.

"I'll never abandon you, *min presang*, never. If you need me here, I'll stay." His warm breath tickled her ear as his words flowed through her and calmed her panic.

Another pain came, the strongest one yet. Rosie produced a small clock from the pocket of her cloak which she wound up and set on the mantel.

"Alright, now we'll see how far apart they are. Nicky, you'll want to find a brace more chairs." Rickard volunteered for that duty. When he returned, Rosie asked him to see about supper for everyone except Sydney.

"Your body don't have time for food right now," she explained. "You'd just end up puking it on the floor." After supper, Rosie went for the midwife and Rickard made his exit. Nicolas and Sydney were alone.

"Thank you for staying," she whispered.

"Is there aught else I can do for you?"

"Count out loud during the pains. It helps me know that I can make it through them." Another one came. "Start now…"

Rosie returned an hour later with the midwife. Anabelle Graham was a tiny red-haired woman in her late forties, and she had an unmistakable demeanor of authority. Rosie warned her that Sydney insisted on Nicolas staying with her.

Anabelle's skeptical gaze blazed a path from his top to his toes and back again. "He can stay until he faints."

She gave him her rigid back. "I'll need the clean rags and a pot of hot water," she said to Rosie. Rosie nodded and set about the task.

Anabelle rinsed her hands and dried them on her starched white apron. She uncorked a small flask and poured oil on her fingers before she examined Sydney. Sydney gasped at the necessary intrusion. Nicolas averted his eyes.

"You're more than halfway opened up. When the water's hot, we'll begin softening your skin so it doesn't tear when the babe comes out."

The internal exam prompted another pain, and this time Nicolas counted to sixty-five before it ended. The next one came in four minutes and lasted until seventy.

Rosie pulled the sheet back and started the hot compresses at the opening to Sydney's womb. Anabelle rubbed oil on Sydney to help soften the skin there. She ran her fingers around the opening, pulling a little, her ministrations comforting Sydney between the intensifying pains.

80 CB

Nicolas was unexpectedly fascinated. His first surprise remained that Sydney wasn't screaming or writhing. Other than the occasional grunt or whimper, she didn't make a sound.

His second surprise was how much the midwife was able to ease Sydney's birthing. Had Lara's midwife taken the time to prepare Lara the way Anabelle did? Did she have hot compresses and oil? Was she calm and authoritative, inspiring trust? Nicolas didn't remember her that way.

Tucked inside that revelation was his assurance that Sydney would come through this fine. Within hours he would hold his second child. Nicolas could hardly contain his excitement. He leaned over and kissed Sydney hard on the mouth.

"Our baby is to be born!" he whispered.

Sydney opened one eye. "Yes it is. Now count."

Hours passed, and Nicolas marked them in his mind. He wasn't certain how long births were meant to take. Successful ones, that was. Sydney gripped his hand during—and wilted into the mattress between—every contraction.

"I'm so tired," she whispered. Nine hours had passed since her water broke.

"You're doing fine, *min presang*, I'm so proud of you." Nicolas was covered in his own sweat. Between worry for his wife, and straining through her labor pains with her, he was exhausted.

With the next pain, Sydney croaked, "I believe I need the chamber pot…"

"That's the baby." Anabelle and Rosie pushed the sheets out of the way. They pulled Sydney to a sitting position. "You," Annabelle pointed at Nicolas, "sit behind her and prop her up."

Too startled to argue, Nicolas slid one leg across the bed and straddled it. He winced at the pressure his breeches put on his groin, but there was no help for it. He rested Sydney against his chest.

"Hold her legs up," Anabelle instructed. "Now at the next pain," she spoke to Sydney, "you can start to push."

Sydney's face screwed tight and turned bright red. When the pain ended, she collapsed, panting, against Nicolas. The next pain came quickly and she pushed again. And again. And again.

And suddenly there it was: a small melon-shaped, sopping wet, blood-smeared, light brown hair-covered head. Anabelle wiped the nose and swept the mouth with her finger.

Sydney panted and whimpered.

"Easy on the next push," Anabelle instructed. "Let me work the shoulders out."

Nicolas stared, transfixed as she pulled first one shoulder, then the other. In one slick motion, the baby slithered out of his wife.

"It's a girl!" Rosie shouted.

Anabelle placed the baby on Sydney's chest and scrubbed her with a rag. Indignant at being squeezed out of her mother's warmth, she wailed her protest.

Nicolas could do naught but ogle the tiny creature who,

moments ago, had not existed in his life. Now there was no question that he would lay down that very life for her. Anabelle picked her up, cut the tied umbilical cord, swaddled her, and handed her back to Sydney.

"Put her to your breast," she instructed. "I'll help with the afterbirth."

As the babe suckled, she opened one dark blue eye, then the other. Her eyes rolled around, trying out their new function. She suddenly let go of the breast and looked at Sydney and Nicolas.

"Hello, little one," her exhausted mother whispered. Nicolas couldn't speak. He put his finger in her hand and she gripped it reflexively, cementing her grip on his heart.

"So what's her name?" Rosie asked.

"Kirsten Ciara Hansen, if that's acceptable to you?" Sydney twisted around to look at Nicolas. "After both our mothers?"

"I like it fine." Nicolas pushed Sydney forward. "I need to get off the bed."

Nicolas pulled a deep breath when the pressure on his groin was relieved. He stood and stretched, then bent his knees and shook out his legs to make room in his breeches. His scrotum radiated a deep, pulsating ache down his thighs.

"She looks so big. How much do you think she weighs?" he asked Anabelle.

"Eight or nine pounds. And she's long." Anabelle nodded toward Nicolas. "Like her father."

While the midwife packed her things to leave, she gave one last instruction: no intercourse for at least a month and a half. Nicolas nodded glumly and wondered if he would ever be able to have intercourse again. No point in worrying about that now.

He turned to Rosie and asked if she would mind telling Rickard he could come see the baby.

She patted his cheek, her smile wistful. "Not at all, Nicky." Then she tipped her head toward Sydney. "It had to be someday I'd lose your 'company' and I hoped she'd be worth it. You did good."

Nicolas's cheeks warmed, embarrassed by the woman's bawdy reference. "Thanks, Rosie."

"I'll send Rick in." She opened the door and followed Anabelle out, an afterthought returning her attention. "He's still unattached?"

Nicolas laughed. "For life, I'm afraid!"

Chapter Thirty Seven

*W*hen the landau pulled up in front of the Hansen manor, Nicolas climbed out first. Addie burst through the front door and started to bawl.

"Nicky! Oh, my Lord! I'm so glad to see you safe and home!" She threw her arms around him. Nicolas patted Addie's shoulder, his grin unrestrained.

"Thank you, Addie. When you gather yourself, might you carry the babe inside while I assist my wife?"

Addie pulled away and gaped at Nicolas. "Are you joking?" She pushed him aside and rumbled to the carriage. "Boy or girl?"

"Girl. Kirsten Ciara Hansen. Born past midnight last night." Sydney handed the infant into Addie's outstretched arms. Nicolas helped her out of the carriage. Then, over her mild protestations, he carried her upstairs to their room.

"*Pappa*? Is that you?" Stefan appeared in the bedroom doorway. Concern washed over his face when he saw Nicolas holding Sydney. "What's wrong with *Mamma?*"

"Nothing, little man!" she assured. "I'm just tired. The baby came out last night."

"But I wanted to watch!" Stefan's frown deepened. "Why didn't you wait for me?"

Nicolas set Sydney down. "We didn't have a choice, son. Your sister decided to come out and we couldn't stop her!"

"Sister? I'm a sister now?"

"No, the baby's the sister and you're the brother." Nicolas gripped Stefan's shoulder. "Do you want to see her?"

Stefan looked around. "Where is she?"

Nicolas led Stefan downstairs to see baby Kirstie, and left Sydney alone to see to her personal needs. By the time he brought his daughter upstairs, Sydney completed her toilette, changed into a nightdress and waited in his huge bed.

He laid the fussing baby in her arms. "What can I do?"

"Bring the cradle in here and put it by the bed. Then bring the chest of diaper clouts and gowns from the drawing room." She opened her nightdress and put Kirstie to her breast. She winced as her daughter latched on. "Ouch, ouch, ouch…"

He frowned. "Is it supposed to hurt?"

"It goes away."

Stefan leaned on the edge of the bed to watch. Nicolas carried the cradle into the room with the chest inside, setting them both on the side of the bed closest to the fireplace. Then he opened the chest and handed Sydney a baby gown and a diaper. Stefan turned to him with a serious expression.

"Can you put your prick in Sydney and make a baby again so I can see it come out?"

"NO!" Sydney and Nicolas's voices blurted identical denunciation.

"It's very hard on a woman to birth a baby," Nicolas explained. "We'll talk about it in a few months. Or more. Next year."

Stefan screwed up his mouth and smacked his chin into his palm. He watched intently as Sydney moved Kirstie from one breast to the other.

When she finished, Nicolas leaned over and kissed Sydney. "Now we'll let you two rest."

He took Stefan by the hand and led him to the door. Stefan pulled his hand out of Nicolas's and ran back to the bed. He kissed his sister on top of her head and patted her softly.

"I love you, baby Kirstie," he whispered.

He walked back to Nicolas, put his small hand back into his father's much larger one, and together they left the room.

℘ ℭ

Sydney laid Kirstie in her cradle. There was plenty of warm woolen batting in both the cradle cushion and the quilt to keep her warm on these frigid January nights. Even so, Nicolas stoked the fire before undressing for bed. Then he handed Sydney an envelope.

"What's this?" she asked, opening it.

"It was in the packet from the post office." Nicolas tried to look over the top of the paper, not even attempting to feign disinterest. Sydney frowned, and handed it to him.

> *My darling S,*
> *I have finally found you and my torment is over! I shall come for you soon. We will be able to complete our plans.*
> *As ever, I am completely yours,*
> *E.M.*

"E.M.?" Nicolas raised eyebrows at his wife.

She raised eyebrows right back at him. "There must be some mistake. This wasn't meant for me."

Nicolas reached for the envelope. "It's addressed to Siobhan Kilbourne in care of Nicolas Hansen."

Sydney rolled her eyes. "I'm still not acquainted with any 'E.M.'!"

"Hmm. Well, in case 'E' should appear, please don't open the door to any strangers when you're alone."

"Even so." Sydney tossed the missive into the fire and climbed under the bedclothes.

When Nicolas stepped out of his breeches, he forgot to turn away from Sydney. She flew from the bed when she saw his swollen scrotum.

"Oh my Lord, Nicolas! What happened?" She dropped to her knees in front of him and cradled his injury. "Who did this to you?"

"It happened when I was arrested."

Sydney rose to face him, furious. "The sheriff?"

Nicolas's voice was barely discernable. "No. It was the younger one."

She paled. "Andrew?"

"Your father went after me when I was down. I pushed him away, but Andrew caught me with his boot when I was vulnerable."

Sydney sat down hard on the rocker. She dropped her head between her knees.

Nicolas stood in front of her. "I'm sorry Sydney…"

"You're sorry? You're sorry! Oh, Nicolas!" Sydney's countenance liquefied. She pushed Nicolas's knees apart and cupped his wounded member; her tears baptized it with salt water.

Nicolas put his hands on either side of her face and tilted it. "Sydney, stop."

"But, Nicolas…"

"Stop," he whispered. He lifted her to stand in front of him and ran his knuckles down her arm. "You'll heal, Sydney. And I'll heal. There's nothing else to be done for it presently. Let's go to bed, eh?"

January 13, 1820

Two men sat in the drawing room, backs stiff and faces gaunt. After a delay of several minutes, intended to increase their discomfort, Nicolas walked into their presence, erect and unsmiling. He didn't sit. He didn't speak. He waited.

Robert Bell cleared his throat and stood to face his son-in-law. When he spoke, a Scots brogue rolled and tilted his words.

"Mr. Hansen, I've come to make reparation. I'm man enough to face up to my mistakes, and in the matter that passed between us, I was sorely misled. I've wronged you, to be certain." Robert held out his hand. "I pray you'll accept my apology."

Nicolas gazed at the proffered hand. He moved nothing but his eyes; they slid sideways to Andrew. Both men still bore the bruises he had bestowed on them. Andrew rose to his feet. He bobbed his head toward Nicolas.

"And mine." His voice was barely a whisper.

Nicolas's jaw clenched as he stared Andrew down for a solid, silent minute.

"Allow me to see if my wife is feeling well enough to join us." Turning on his heel, Nicolas left the men alone.

The atmosphere in his bedroom was a respite. Sydney sat in the slat-back rocker nursing Kirstie. When he appeared in the doorway, she looked up at him and smiled. Her smile faded, however, when he didn't return it.

"What's amiss?"

Nicolas pulled a chair close to the rocker and sat down. "Is she nursing well?"

"Yes, though my milk isn't in yet. Nicolas? What's amiss?"

"We have visitors."

Sydney raised her eyebrows in demanding question.

Nicolas drew a quick breath. "Your father and brother."

Sydney gasped. She stuck a finger in the corner of Kirstie's mouth and took her off the breast with a soft *pop*. She thrust the baby at Nicolas, pushed up from the rocker, grabbed her wrap, slipped it on over her nightdress and hurried to the bedroom door.

"Are you coming?" She didn't wait for an answer before disappearing down the stairs.

₮ ℞

Sydney strode into the drawing room and stopped, suddenly rooted. Part of her wanted to run to her father and be his beloved daughter again. And part of her wanted to scalp him bloody for having her husband arrested and beaten just before she bore his child.

"Da—"

"Siobhan, darling." Robert held out his hands. "I'm so very sorry."

Sydney crumpled into his arms.

Nicolas stood in the doorway with Kirstie. Stefan crept up behind him and slipped one arm around his tree trunk of a thigh. Four blue eyes observed the interaction in the room.

Sydney pulled away from her father and looked at him hard. "There are issues to settle between us."

"Aye," Robert agreed. "Shall we sit, then?"

Sydney took a chair while Robert and Andrew returned to the settee.

"You owe my husband an apology," she began.

Robert nodded. "Offered, but not yet accepted." Sydney glanced over her shoulder at Nicolas. It was clear to her that he wasn't ready. She turned to Andrew.

"Are you aware of the damage you've done?"

Andrew swallowed, shifted his gaze to Nicolas and shook his head. Sydney spared Nicolas the humiliation of explaining his condition.

"It's a blessing that we have our daughter, because after the caress of your boot, we may not be blessed with any future offspring."

Andrew blanched, horrified. His gaze toggled between his sister and her husband as understanding sunk in.

"Oh, God, Siobhan. I'm so sorry. Mr. Hansen, I had no idea." Andrew slid off the settee and knelt on the rug. "Please accept my deepest apology, sir."

Nicolas was silent, his mouth a grim, colorless line highlighted by the white scar. His chest expanded and deflated under the shirt Sydney made him. His soft voice rumbled through the room.

"I'll accept both apologies, under the assumption that the injuries I experienced were a result of misguided intentions. But I do hope that any future actions either of you engage in are more prudently considered." Nicolas further chastised both men with his steel-blue stare. "Especially if I'm to be the subject of any of your concerns."

Robert rose to his feet and bowed at the waist. "Thank, you, sir."

Andrew spoke from his spot on the floor. "Thank you."

Sydney looked at the three stubborn men she loved. "Might we begin again?"

"Aye, lassie. Let's do." Robert's voice was thick.

Sydney turned to Nicolas; her reach beckoned him to her side. Stefan followed, hidden under the hem of Nicolas's shirt as he gripped his father's leg.

"Robert McAuhl Bell, may I introduce my husband, Nicolas Reidar Hansen." The men shook hands. They were at least cordial. Sydney took Kirstie from Nicolas. "And this is your granddaughter, Kirsten Ciara Hansen."

Robert's wrinkled hand rested on Kirstie's silky head. "Hello, girlie. I am your grandda."

Sydney indicated the boy half-hidden under his father's shirt. "And this is Stefan Atherton Hansen, your step-grandson."

Robert's face paled and his eyes jumped to Andrew, who swallowed audibly. A curious look passed between them. Then he leaned over to see the auburn mop of hair and earnest blue eyes.

"And how old are you, then?"

"Six. I'm the brother."

"And so you are." Robert nodded at the solemn boy. "I reckon I'm your grandda as well."

Stefan looked up at Nicolas. "What's a 'grandda'?"

"It's a *bestefar*."

"This man is my father, Stefan," Sydney explained.

"Oh." Stefan looked again at Robert, eyes narrowed in consideration.

Andrew cleared his throat. Sydney gritted her teeth and turned to her brother. "This is my younger brother, Andrew. Sometimes he acts first and considers second."

"I said I was sorry," Andrew pouted. "I am, you know."

Stefan looked up at Sydney. "*Mamma*, can I show them my knights?"

"That would be nice."

As he trotted off, Nicolas said, "I'll ask Addie to bring tea and biscuits, Sydney. I know there's quite a lot to explain."

"Do you prefer me to wait until you return?"

"No, you go ahead." Nicolas's voice trailed behind him as he walked down the hall.

Andrew was confused. "Why does he call you 'Sydney'?"

"I needed a name when I couldn't remember," she began.

She told them about Lara, and Stefan's stillborn twin. She described Nicolas when she first met him and how much he changed. Then she pointed out the window to the maple tree and told them about Nicolas moving the graves.

Robert gazed pleadingly at his daughter. "Why did you no' tell us, lass?"

"I wrote you and Mother a long letter after the wedding, but you must have left Kentucky before it arrived. I should have written earlier, but I wanted to make certain of the ending." She adjusted her over-wrap. "As it was, I might have come home to tell you in person."

Nicolas returned to the drawing room and leaned against the wall, listening to her story. Stefan returned with his Nordic knights. Addie bustled in with tea and biscuits.

"I have a question for you, Robert." Nicolas's earthquake rumbled again across the room.

"Yes?" He turned to face Nicolas.

"The letters you received. Who wrote them?"

Robert shifted in his seat, distinctly discomforted. His glance bounced off Sydney. "Well, I don't rightly know, for certain, where they came from."

"Did you have occasion to reply?"

He turned to Andrew, but the young man's stark expression offered no consolation. "I was to send my responses to the post office in St. Louis."

"And was there a name?" Nicolas straightened.

"Part of a name, I suppose." Robert looked at Stefan.

"And that would be?" Nicolas growled. Robert slumped in his chair. Sydney held her breath, frightened by what the name would reveal. It wasn't like her father to be so evasive.

"L. J. Atherton."

The earth held still for a long, silent pause.

Then hell exploded.

"L. J. Atherton? Lily Jane Atherton!" Nicolas's fury resonated through the house. "*Gud forbanner det all til helvete! Gud forbanner det all til* fucking *helvete!*"

"The man who wrote those letters? He's a woman?" Andrew faced his father. Shock colored both men's faces.

"What *i Guds navn* was she trying to accomplish? *Skitt!*" Nicolas paced around the room, eating the carpet with swift, jerky strides. Sydney's intense stare tracked her irate husband.

"Who is she?" Andrew asked.

Nicolas didn't respond, so Sydney spoke. "She's the younger sister of Lara and his best friend, Rickard."

She rose to face Nicolas, her attention still pegged. She laid her palms lightly on his arms. He glared over her head and let loose a powerful paragraph of Norse curses. His fists clenched and unclenched; the scar on his cheek was a bolt of lightening in the storm red of his face.

"Go punch the pelts."

"What?" He looked down at her as if surprised to see other people still in the room.

"Go out to the stable and punch the pelts. You can't hurt them and they can't hurt you." Sydney grabbed Nicolas's elbow to turn him toward the door.

He remained still for a moment. His jaw was set and his brow rolled. His pupils were so dilated that his eyes were nearly black. He looked down at his hands and slowly unfurled them. He shook his head, and then he shook his hands.

Without a knock, Rickard burst through the front door and froze.

"Oh, God! Nick!"

With understanding born of over twenty-five years of friendship, Nicolas croaked, "We know."

Chapter Thirty Eight

*R*ickard was a pile of misery, shoved into the corner of the settee. Nicolas handed him a tall brandy.

"What do I do, Nick? What do I say? I can't presently bear to look at her, much less share a residence with her."

Awkward silence reigned as the four men stared at the floor, at the walls, out the window.

"I've a suggestion. It's fairly harsh, but it's sensible," Sydney ventured. Tightness in her chest warned her of the risk too late; the statement was out in the room.

"Please, tell me." Rickard's disconsolate features begged for hope.

She nodded. "I suggest we make public what Lily did."

Stunned silence absorbed her words.

Confusion narrowed Rickard's hazel gaze. "You mean to tell everyone?"

"Yes. We talk about what happened to Nicolas and who brought it about, including her motive."

"Which was what? To get back at me for choosing you?" Nicolas's ocean eyes looked dangerous, like a storm at sea.

"It seems so. Do you remember her words that day you turned her away?" Sydney shuddered. "I do."

"She threatened me, said I would regret my actions." He snorted. "Those were merely the overwrought words of an angry girl."

"Angry *woman*, Nicolas, and a scorned woman at that."

The storm in his eyes darkened as the truth filled them. Rickard pulled a long hissing breath. She displayed her last weapon.

"If we do so, Lily will be forced to face what she's done."

Sydney waited for the men to steep the idea in possibilities. Either they would vilify her, or laud her; she honestly didn't know which to expect, nor which she deserved. She looked at each of them in turn, trying to predict her prospects.

"She'll have to apologize." Rickard downed the brandy. "Grow up a little. Or a lot."

"Or she'll turn tail and run to North Carolina and her mother," Nicolas outlined another possibility.

"Either way, we don't have to do anything 'to' her," Sydney finished the scenario.

"It's brilliant," Rickard handed his empty glass to Nicolas for a refill. "Consider it done."

Nicolas went to his study to fetch Rickard another brandy. Sydney stood and followed him into his sanctuary.

"Would you consider inviting my father and brother to stay so they might get to know you?" she whispered.

His lips pressed to a grim line and he didn't look at her.

She kept her voice soft so they wouldn't overhear her. "Please, Nicolas? I haven't seen them in—I don't know how many years."

Nicolas drenched her with his sea-storm gaze. "For how long?" he groused.

"A day or two?" Sydney rested her hand on his arm. "How long can you bide?"

Nicolas grunted and eye-rolled a sigh. "Even so. A couple days, then."

Back in the drawing room, Nicolas rested his elbow on the mantel. His tone wasn't as hospitable as his words, but Sydney was grateful for any purchase he might give.

"Robert. Andrew. My wife and I would be honored if you would be our guests for the next few days."

Robert's gaze hopped to Sydney, then back to Nicolas. "We were planning to go back directly."

Nicolas raised flattened palms in front of his chest. "Oh. Well, then. If you must."

"Might you stay until Sunday? We're having Kirstie christened," Sydney announced her sudden plans.

Robert shrugged. "In that circumstance, we would be happy to accept."

"Addie?" Sydney called to the kitchen. "Can you show my father to Rickard's room and Andrew to my old room? They'll be staying with us the next two nights."

The housekeeper approached, grinning. "Well, God bless us! Come along, then. Look sharp." Robert and Andrew followed Addie from the room.

Still hunched in the settee, Rickard swirled the unfinished brandy in his glass. "I believe I'll go to St. Louis for a day or two."

Nicolas finally lifted his heavy gaze off Sydney. "And let Lily stew a bit, eh?"

"Has Miss Price been to St. Louis?" Sydney planted the idea.

Rickard's demeanor brightened. "Why, I don't know. Do you think I should I ask her to accompany me?"

"You could do with the diversion." Sydney let the statement hang.

Rickard rose to his feet with a soft smile and a rerouted purpose. He patted his pockets absently and glanced around the room. "Yes. Well, if you'll excuse me, then, I'll be on my way. But I shall be back before the christening on Sunday!" He shook Nick's hand and left the Hansen manor, whistling as he did so.

Nicolas assessed Sydney with suspicious eyes. "Have you ever done that to me? Changed the subject to twist my intent?"

She smiled and slid her arms around her husband's waist, her head against his solid chest. She heard his heartbeat, steady and strong. "Of course not."

January 18, 1820

Robert and Andrew left on Monday morning. There were back-slaps and hugs, and Sydney sent along a lengthy missive for her mother.

"I'll try to visit sometime soon," she promised.

"Nicolas and I talked quite a bit about breeding horses out here. Perchance we'll go into business, aye?" Robert hugged his daughter one last time.

"Goodbye, sir," Nicolas offered his hand first to Robert, then to Andrew. "*Kan Gud er med De.* May God be with you."

The men climbed into Nicolas's landau for the ride into Cheltenham, and John slapped the horses into motion. When the carriage disappeared from sight, Nicolas enveloped Sydney in his embrace and held her until, with a hiccough and a shudder, her mourning stilled to silence.

When John returned that same afternoon, he carried a letter addressed to Mme. S. S. B. Hansen. The return was Mr. N. Ivarsen.

"It's probably a bill for services rendered," Nicolas grumbled.

"And why would he send that to me?" Sydney broke the wax seal and unfolded the parchment. She laughed as she read the barrister's words:

My Esteemed Madam,

Please accept my heartfelt congratulations to you on the birth of your healthy daughter. I am most pleased to know that your confinement was not hindered by the lack of a husband.

My purpose in writing you this day is twofold, however. I am afraid that curiosity has eaten at me these many days and it is my hope you might assuage it. Pray tell, what words did you share with The Honorable Judge G. Benson that encouraged him to hear your testimony?

It is my intent that, by sharing your secret with me, you will provide me with as yet another valuable tool in my profession.

I remain, as ever, your Faithful Servant,

Mr. N. Ivarsen, Esq.

Sydney sat at Nicolas's desk. He leaned over her shoulder as she penned her response at the bottom of Nelson's letter.

My dear Mr. Ivarsen,

The information, which I rightly believed to be of assistance to Judge Benson, was also information which, due to its sensitive and personal nature, I did not wish to share with the family members and strangers in the gallery. The statement was, in itself, quite simple.

Since exchanging our marital vows in December, Nicolas and I had not consummated those vows because of my delicate condition. So by law, we could be considered not yet legally married. Therefore, my testimony would be allowed by law.

Judge Benson was wise enough to understand that making such a statement in court, and on the record, could render our child a bastard. So he allowed my testimony, rightly, while preserving the status of our daughter.

While I sincerely hope you never need use this tactic, I expect that this response will assuage your peculiar state.

Respectfully,

Mrs. S. Sydney Bell Hansen

Nicolas laughed so hard, he nearly wet himself.

February 10, 1820

Kirstie awoke early, long before the household stirred. Outside the window the winter wind keened through leafless trees, moaned over the tops of the chimneys and clattered the shutters. Sydney drew the heavy curtains back and tried to peer out. The horizontal flurries were so thick it would be dangerous to go outside, even to the privy.

She brought Kirstie into the big, warm bed to nurse. She lay on her side, her bottom pressed against Nicolas's hip, and tucked the babe to her breast.

Nicolas turned and curled around her, not completely awake.

Sydney smiled to herself and whispered over her shoulder. "Congratulations, husband."

"Hmm?"

"You're not gelded." Sydney arched her back and pressed her bottom against his groin.

Nicolas came awake instantly. He rolled onto his back, lifted the covers. His flesh stood, strong and hard, for the first time since he was kicked. He circled it with his hand and breathed a sigh of relief so huge it seemed to empty the room of air.

"Thank God. I wasn't certain…" his voice choked. "It was such a hard hit."

Sydney said her own silent prayer of thanks. "I'm quite relieved as well. While I shall love you no matter what, I hated to think of that particular activity falling aside."

"Perchance we should test it? Just to make certain, you know?" He groped for her hand under the covers and wrapped it around his exigent member. He curled against her again and nuzzled the nape of her neck, sending pleasant shivers over her skin that had nothing to do with the room's chill.

Sydney turned her head and lifted her lips to his.

"Ask me tonight," she murmured, shifting Kirstie to the other breast. "As for now, I desire a few more hours of sleep."

When she awoke later, that morning's sun shone on a recreated landscape. White drifts blinded, sparkling with the pristine purity that only an unspoiled snowfall can own. Bare tree branches glistened with crystal coating. The intense sky turned shadows into sapphires.

Sydney threw back the curtains and let the sun's smile light up the manor. She stood in the upstairs hall, Kirstie snug against her shoulder. Nicolas stepped up behind her and slipped his hands around her narrowing waist. He kissed the top of her head.

"It's a beautiful day for a thirty-third birthday, isn't it?"

Sydney whirled to face him. "Today's your birthday? What day is it?"

"February tenth in the year 1820."

"Why didn't you tell me? I would've gotten you a gift!"

"You mean, besides marrying me and giving me this little beauty?" Nicolas stroked Kirstie's hair as her blue-gray eyes explored his face. "I'm quite satisfied."

"Even so, it's the principle."

"I don't seem to recall you having a birthday. Or did it happen before you got your memory back?"

"On March fifteenth I'll be thirty-one."

"The Ides of March? Good thing I'm not Caesar!" Nicolas teased. "You're a good age, well suited to me."

Sydney shook her head and turned back to the window. "We're old parents. I'm afraid Kirstie's friends will believe we're her grandparents."

"If someone mistakes you as that, I'll inform them that you're the most desirable 'grandmother' I ever met!" Nicolas pressed his hips against her back. "See?"

Sydney laughed suddenly and startled Kirstie who began to cry.

"Let me take her." A grinning Nicolas lifted his daughter. "That was my fault."

"Half a month to go," Sydney sighed.

ಬಿ ಛ

After dinner, Nicolas handed another letter to Sydney without any comment or explanation. He turned his back and poured his brandy, listening to her unfold the paper.

"I didn't write to Nelson," she stated.

He half-hoped she'd give the opposite answer. Because somebody did.

"You believe me, don't you?"

Nicolas dropped into his favorite chair and rubbed his hand over his face, then through his hair. He didn't look at her as alternatives shuffled through his consideration, none of them good.

"Of course I believe you, Sydney."

"Nicolas?"

"Yes?"

Her glare was pewter and just as cold. "I've no interest in your money, your lands, or—what else did the letter say?—your heritage. I don't even know what that means! I trust you to take care of me and the children. It never occurred to me to consult your lawyer about putting a portion of your income into an account for my access!"

Nicolas sipped his brandy and gazed into the fire, pondering ramifications. He shifted in his chair. "Have you any ideas, then, who contacted Nelson?"

Sydney shook her head. Her gray gaze slammed into his. He felt it best to change the subject.

"Your idea worked. Lily's gone."

She hesitated before biting. "Gone where?"

"Back to her mama in North Carolina."

"For good?" she queried.

"Definitely for 'good'!" he quipped and finished his brandy.

Chapter Thirty Nine

February 26, 1820

*N*icolas threw the front door open and slammed it shut with a grunt that shook the windows.

"Sydney!"

"In here." Sydney appeared through the kitchen door. "What's amiss?"

Nicolas strode toward her and thrust a package at her. "It's addressed to Siobhan Kilbourne in care of Nicolas Hansen. Again."

Sydney hefted the package then sat at the kitchen table to open it. When she saw what was inside, she looked at Nicolas, her features gone to chalk.

"What is it?" he demanded.

Sydney shook her head and hid her face in her hands. Nicolas grabbed the package and lifted out a pink silk chemise trimmed in expensive lace.

He was beyond livid.

"Who the *helvete* is sending my wife French lingerie?" he bellowed.

Sydney shook her head again, her face still hidden. Nicolas fumbled for a note and found one in the bottom of the wrapping.

" 'I can't wait to see you wear this, my darling, though the beauty of this simple garment pales in comparison to yours. We shall once again experience Cupid's blessings...' *Gud forbanner det!* What the *helvete* is going on?" Nicolas crumpled the shift in his outstretched fist.

Sydney jumped up and pushed past Nicolas. He heard her feet on the stairs, and a moment later, the heavy clunk of their bedroom door. Nicolas stood in the kitchen and stared at the silky garment in his calloused hand. He pulled a deep breath and dropped the shift into its wrapping. He rolled it up and tucked it under his arm, then trudged toward the stairs.

Someone was either playing a cruel joke, or Sydney was hiding something from him. Would she do that to him? He couldn't see how. She wasn't that sort of woman.

What if she hadn't regained all of her memory? With Devin gone from home so much, had Sydney turned to another man for comfort? And not remembered?

Nicolas pushed on his bedroom door, relieved that it wasn't locked.

"Sydney?"

The door to the adjacent nursery was open. He crossed to that once-locked room and stopped in the doorway. Sydney knelt on the floor, diapering Kirstie. She sniffed and wiped her nose with the heel of her hand.

"I'm sorry, *min presang*," he whispered.

Sydney lifted their daughter to her shoulder. She sat cross-legged, her cheeks marked by tear trails.

He dropped to his knees next to her. "I don't believe you've played me false. But something's greatly amiss, is it not?"

Sydney nodded and patted Kirstie's solid little back.

"Might I ask you some rather difficult questions?" Nicolas ran his knuckles up and down her arm. "I don't mean to suggest any wrong-doing. I'm merely attempting to figure out the solution to this puzzle."

"Yes," she whispered.

"Fine, then." Nicolas regarded his wife with the kindest expression he could muster. "First off, are you certain that you've regained all of your memory?"

Sydney's brows dipped. "Yes. I don't have any gaps in time that I can't account for."

"I only thought that, while Devin was absent from your home so often—"

"No. Absolutely not. No."

"How can you be so certain?"

"I simply am certain, Nicolas. There've only been two men in my bed. I've been married to both. And one is preferable."

Nicolas allowed the corner of his mouth to lift. "And the letter to Nelson Ivarsen?"

"The only letter I ever addressed to Mr. Ivarsen is the one you watched me write."

Nicolas's bowels constricted. "So we're being toyed with. For what purpose, then?"

Sydney shrugged. For a pace, Kirstie's contented gurgles were the only sounds in the room. Then, "Do you consider me to be a practical woman?"

Sydney's words found Nicolas off his guard. It took him a moment to respond. "How do you mean?"

"Do I ask for frivolous things? Am I overly sentimental? Or do I seem to you the sort of woman who is sensible in her choices?"

Nicolas smiled broadly at that.

"This question comes from a woman who stated that a pair of breeches was the best gift she ever received? I'd say that qualifies you as most practical." He leaned toward her, wary. "Why?"

"Well… the chemise is beautiful. And obviously expensive." Sydney paused. "It would be a shame to waste it."

"Are you *serious*, madam?" Nicolas blurted. He unrolled the bundle burning under his arm. "You would wear this?"

Sydney grasped the silk and lace garment. "Someone ought to enjoy a garment so beautiful. It might as well be you and me!"

She lifted it to her cheek. "Does the color suit me?"

Nicolas raked his hand through his hair while he tried to conjure a proper objection. But how could he? She reasoned like a man.

The color did indeed suit her. And the garment was finely made, the silk of the highest quality. The thought of running his hands over her body and feeling her curves through the thin fabric stirred him strongly.

He wished he'd bought it for her.

"Again your logic's irrefutable. Whether I'm glad to be married to such a sensible woman remains to be seen. In the meantime, I can't state a logical reason why you shouldn't enjoy the shift."

March 1, 1820

Nicolas was late for supper and his stomach chastised him for the delay. But instead of food, the empty table held a note: *Come up to our room.* He considered searching out sustenance before going up, but curiosity beckoned like a siren and he followed, helpless.

In the bedroom, a naked Sydney nursed Kirstie on a quilt spread by the hearth. A picnic dinner and an open bottle of wine waited beside her. Firelight undulated over her skin. Her loose hair veiled her shoulders in striated shadow. Nicolas closed the bedroom door behind him. And he locked it.

"What's this?"

"Kirstie is six weeks old. And, after she suckles, she'll sleep for at least three hours. I thought we should celebrate." Sydney's smoky green eyes met his, and the corners of her mouth lifted in conspiratorial promise.

As if on cue, Kirstie's mouth let go of Sydney's breast and her head rolled back in smiling, satiated sleep. Sydney carefully handed her into the cradle and laid her on her side.

Nicolas unfastened his breeches and dropped them to the floor. In one swift movement, his shirt joined them on the polished wooden planks. As he stepped forward, he pulled his feet out of his shoes and stockings so that he was naked by the time he reached his wife.

He lifted Sydney to her feet. As he lowered his mouth to hers, she whispered, "Aren't you hungry?"

"Oh-h-h, yes." His hunger stood straight and hard between them.

Nicolas lifted Sydney and she wrapped her legs around his waist. He pressed her to his chest and walked to the bed. He laid her on her back. Her hand felt cool against his arousal as she guided him to her. She gasped as he pushed inside.

He paused, not at all sure he could stop. "Did I hurt you?"

"No-o-o…" she sighed and lifted her hips. "At last we can… Oh, my!" She shifted under him, adjusting her position. Her eyes were closed; little moans slid from her lips.

Nicolas tried to move slowly, worried that he might do harm after the birth. But he hadn't been inside any woman—and in particular *this* woman—for over ten months. His body advanced his purpose much faster than his mind intended.

"Sydney—I can't hold—" he grunted.

"Go ahead," she panted.

Nicolas released with a loud groan that started in his belly and ricocheted through his chest before it roared out in a throaty explosion. His entire body shook in long, joyful spasms. He was weightless, spinning.

Emptied out and completely filled.

Physical and phantom.

Floating.

೮೦ ೮೪

Sydney stroked her fingers through Nicolas's hair, and strummed them over the taut muscles in his back, while she waited for him to return to full awareness.

He lifted his head and kissed her, breathless. "*Å min Gud...*" he moaned. "I promise I'll take more care next time."

"Yes, you shall!" Sydney laughed, her voice bubbling with delight. "But right now, I'm starving."

They sat by the fire, naked as snakes, and fed each other with their fingers. The full bottle of wine was empty by the time their supper was finished. Sydney felt the effects; her eyelids were heavy and relaxation flowed through her.

She also warmed with desire for her half of the bargain.

She led Nicolas to the bed and pushed him back. His prick pointed toward the ceiling, a pulsating spear. She straddled his hips and settled herself over the considerable length of him. Her sigh of pleasure escaped long and low. She felt his girth as she tightened.

Sydney rested her hands on Nicolas's shoulders. Her hair formed a dark curtain around them as her hips moved with the angle and rhythm that pleased her well.

Then Nicolas began to move with her; their speed and intensity increased in increments. She arched her back. He sat up and gripped her waist. Her fingers dug into his shoulders. Pulsing waves of pleasure radiated outward from their joining.

She cried out and pushed against him. Her world condensed to a tiny ball between her thighs that exploded, throwing her into the heavens.

Nicolas watched his smiling wife descend the stairs. She slept rather late this morning and he didn't wake her. Yesterday for her birthday he gave her a beautifully tooled and feminine saddle; light enough for her to handle with ease. She thanked him very well last night.

Twice.

Consummation. Consummate. Consume. He was consumed by consummating with her.

Grinning at his private joke, he opened the front door in answer to a polite knock. A slick-looking man in his late twenties stood on the porch. He was neatly made, with dark mustache and combed-back hair, and dark brown eyes. His clothes were impeccable, as was his speech.

"I'm sorry to disturb you, sir, but I'm looking for Siobhan Kilbourne."

Sydney stopped at the bottom of the stairs.

"Siobhan!"

He leapt toward her and trapped her in his embrace. His lips landed on hers in spite of her surprised and explicit resistance. Nicolas clamped his hand on the man's shoulder.

"I'll thank you to unhand my wife!" His fingers drilled into the man's flesh. The man winced and let go of Sydney, who leapt back and wiped her mouth with the back of her hand.

"Your wife?" The man looked sorely stricken. "Siobhan is that true? You're married again?"

"Who *are* you?" Sydney's tone broadcast her near-panic.

"I heard of your situation, but I wouldn't believe you could ever forget me! Nor what we mean to each other!"

"I believe my wife asked for your name?" Nicolas angrily emphasized the words 'my wife.'

"Edward Macken. Siobhan? Please assure me you remember!"

Sydney shook her head. "I've no recollection of ever meeting you. I'm sorry."

"Did you receive my correspondence? And my gift?"

Sydney glanced fearfully at Nicolas.

"And even still you don't know me?" Edward looked as though he might swoon. He staggered to the stairs and sat down heavily. He dropped his head into his hands and mumbled between his fingers, "No, no. After all this time!"

"Mr. Macken, would you care for a cup of tea?"

Nicolas's mouth opened to protest when Sydney lifted her hand to beckon him. "I'm certain Mr. Hansen could add a drop of brandy, if you believe that might be of help?"

Edward Macken lifted his head and looked at Sydney with damp, sorrowful eyes. "Yes. Yes, thank you."

Sydney pointed to the drawing room. "Nicolas, would you escort Mr. Macken to the drawing room and bring the baby to the kitchen for me?" Sydney turned and headed down the hall without waiting for his answer.

Nicolas scowled, but did as he was bid. When he entered the kitchen with Kirstie, he stepped close to Sydney and rasped in her ear, "What game is *this* now?"

Sydney placed her index finger in front of her lips and set the teapot on the stove to heat. "I don't know this man," she whispered.

"Fine, then. So why are we serving him tea and brandy in our drawing room?"

"Don't you care to know who he is? Or why he's here?"

Nicolas paused, strangling his jealousy and allowing sanity to live. "I suppose if he's attempting to claim you, he might be involved with the letter to Nelson."

Sydney's eyes rounded. "But he can't claim me if I'm married."

"Yes, well. He was none too pleased at that bit of information."

The two were quiet for a moment.

"I'll invite him to stay for lunch," Nicolas decided. "See what we're able to draw out of him."

Sydney put the teapot and cup on a small tray. "I'll let Addie know we have a luncheon guest. Give me Kirstie." She accepted the squirming pink bundle. "Might you take the tea in to Mr. Macken?"

Nicolas picked up the tray with one hand, and reached into a cupboard for a bottle of brandy. "I'll be generous. Might help loosen his tongue a bit, eh?"

Chapter Forty

Nicolas and Sydney faced each other over the midday meal and placed Mr. Macken at the end of the table.

"Please, call me Edward," he shifted his gaze to Sydney. "Or Eddie."

Nicolas's jaw clenched as he passed the platter of meat. "Tell us, *Edward*, how did you become acquainted with Mrs. Hansen?"

"Mrs. Hansen? Oh, you mean Siobhan. Yes, well. She lived in Carondelet with her husband Devin Kilbourne. He was a teacher."

"And did you live in Carondelet as well?"

"No, my home was in Afton. I worked for the post office there, and made regular trips between the towns, you see."

Sydney's shrug gave no indication of familiarity, so Nicolas continued. "Under what circumstances did you make her acquaintance?"

"We met in church. Don't you remember, dearest?" Edward's brows dipped with obvious concern.

Nicolas calculated that he could break the man's neck in two quick moves. *Go ahead, Eddie. Tempt me.* "I'll thank you to keep personal endearments out of your conversation. Eddie."

"I beg your pardon, sir." Edward appeared sincerely contrite. "It was the fall of 1817 that I first saw you. You were so beautiful in that green wool dress with the white collar and cuffs. Do you still have it?"

Sydney shook her head.

"Pity. It looked so well with your eyes. I did not speak to you until December. We had dinner together at the boarding house on a

Sunday. And every Sunday after that, when Devin was away."

Nicolas reclaimed the man's attention. "It seems as though your relationship entailed more than simple meals on Sundays, Eddie."

"Siobhan was lonely, and she needed help at the cabin. I came to her aid quite often."

He lowered his gaze, then blinked at Sydney like a love-struck girl. "And in personal matters as well."

Sydney faced her dinner plate and cut her meat into tiny pieces. Her face pulsed from red to white to red again. Still, Nicolas pressed for information. "When did your relationship become physical?"

"In the fall of 1818. October. I'll never forget it. Siobhan planned to leave Devin this past September, after school pulled him away from Carondelet again. We were going to be married." Edward gazed, moon-eyed, at Sydney. "But then in March we realized that Siobhan was with child."

Sydney coughed, choked and grabbed her wine. She swallowed several times. Then her watery eyes met Nicolas's in tight-lipped, outraged, denial.

He drew a deep breath and slid his gaze back to Edward. "How did you find her here?"

"There were notices in the post offices."

"Those notices are nearly a year old. What took you so long?"

"I didn't connect the missing woman with Siobhan. Devin said she had gone to see her father in Kentucky. He said Mr. Bell was quite ill. But when Devin moved away from Carondelet, I grew suspicious."

Nicolas leaned back in his chair and made a great show of swirling his wine glass, holding the glass to the light and sniffing the bouquet. "What are your plans now?"

Edward's mouth flapped open and shut. "I—I hoped to make Siobhan my wife. Was that our child?"

"NO!" The response exploded from Sydney. Edward's eyebrows dipped in confusion.

"My wife conceived in May. The child was born at the end of January." Nicolas fudged a little to make his point. "So you see, if she knew she was with child by March, the child would have come at the end of October, three months earlier."

Edward's shoulders fell and he nodded his reluctant agreement.

Nicolas leaned forward. "The question remains, sir. What are your plans now?"

Edward stared at his plate. His hands fell to his lap. Then he straightened his back and faced Nicolas with a level gaze.

"I don't suppose you would set her free, under the circumstances?"

Nicolas was aghast at the man's bold-faced impudence. "What circumstances?"

"She and I, we had a commitment. We enjoyed a physical relationship. We made arrangements to be together. We had a child."

Sydney cast the iron refutation: "There was *no* child!"

Edward stood and rested his fists on the table as he leaned toward Nicolas. "Then on the basis of ethics, sir! She promised me first!"

Nicolas rose as well and stretched to his full height. He leaned forward. His razor stare sliced Edward. Edward flinched and fell back into his chair.

"No."

"But—"

"I said no. I meant no."

"Sir, if I may—"

"No."

Edward turned his plea to Sydney. "Siobhan?"

Lips drawn in a tight pucker, she didn't acknowledge him.

"I'll drive you into town." Nicolas dropped his napkin over his plate. "Let's go."

Sydney stood, then, and addressed the suave interloper. "I'm married to Nicolas. The child is his. None of that will ever change. Good—"

A pistol clicked.

She froze, her startled eyes aimed below the table's edge.

Nicolas felt his anger begin to rage. Edward's warning slithered over the remains of the meal.

"Don't try to be a hero, Hansen. Sit down." Two pistols appeared above the tabletop. One was pointed at him. "I hoped it wouldn't come to this."

Nicolas remained outwardly calm. He sat slowly. "What do you want?"

Edward stood. "Won't you sit down Mrs. Hansen?"

Sydney lowered into her chair.

"There's no reason we cannot be civil." Edward flashed an ingenuous smile. "A little business among friends."

Nicolas cocked one brow and shot each syllable of his challenge like a lead ball. "What do you want."

"Well, Hansen, it seems you owe a debt. A generous payoff to compensate for my broken engagement will suffice."

"What!" Nicolas huffed. The man had some kind of nerve, even if it required a pair of pistols for it to materialize.

"Breach of promise. Clear cut."

"But I don't know you!" Sydney objected.

Edward shook his head. "You have suffered from a well-witnessed memory loss. Any judge would rule in my favor."

"Interesting angle, Eddie." Nicolas chuckled and wondered how to reach his rifle in the hallway, only fifteen feet from the table. "My compliments on your creativity."

The man dipped a small nod. "I was hoping we might dispense with the legal fees and settle this as gentlemen."

Sydney's head swirled to face his. "Don't pay this lying snake a penny, Nicolas."

"Now, darling," Edward drawled.

"Don't you dare to call me 'darling'!" Sydney snarled as she rounded on the man. If he wasn't holding her at gunpoint, Nicolas might have let her at him. That would serve him right.

"My apologies. Sweetheart." He lifted the pistol and shot a glance at Nicolas. "Shall we discuss an amount?"

Nicolas chuckled again and shook his head.

"Something funny?"

"Yes, actually." Nicolas scooted his chair back, and leaned on the table to disguise the distance. He tossed Sydney a look that he hoped said, *sit still*.

"Enlighten me."

"Well—Eddie—a gentlemen's agreement requires more than one gentleman."

The man blinked, then sneered as he grasped the insult. "Watch yourself."

He didn't. He continued to press the hooligan. "And, in light of the fact that you have fabricated this whole story for the purpose of extortion, I'd say the amount I owe you would be precisely nil."

Nicolas leaned back in his chair and stretched his legs.

"I have a legitimate legal claim!" Edward barked.

"And I say you don't. But I'd be pleased to call on the sheriff if you feel a crime has been committed."

All pretense of politeness fell away. The pistols wavered. "I'm not amused, Hansen."

"Neither am I. Now get out of my house."

Sydney coiled and jumped sideways out of her seat. *Skitt!*

Edward leapt after her. His chair upended and banged against the wood floor. Nicolas jumped to his feet, whirled toward the dining room door and stretched his arm. He almost reached the gun rack.

The pistol fired. Sydney screamed.

Nicolas spun to see a shower of ceiling plaster, Sydney cowering, and Edward Macken with the second pistol pressed against her neck.

"I'll not waste another shot," he warned.

Nicolas calculated the time and distance it required for him to kill the man. Right now, Edward had the advantage. He'd have to play Eddie's hand. "I don't keep my money here," he stalled.

Edward shook his head. "Hansen, you must take me for a fool."

Of course I do, you lying piece of skitt. He was eight feet from the rifle rack in the hall, hidden thus far from Eddie's perspective.

He spread his arms wide. "You have me there." Five feet more.

"The safe is in my study." One step toward the door. Three feet.

"Stop!" The pistol sagged a little. He shoved Sydney forward. "Get away from the door."

Nicolas twisted and pointed toward the hall. "My study is in the front of the house." So close.

"Get away from the door now!" Edward shouted. He jabbed the barrel of the pistol deep into Sydney's neck.

"Ouch!" she yelped.

Then she swung one foot in front of her and rammed it backward with so much force that she tumbled forward. Edward tumbled with her. The pistol hit the floor and discharged. A spray of plaster burst from the wall close to Nicolas's right.

Nicolas grabbed for his rifle and cocked back the hammer. He aimed at the surging mess of limbs and fabric. When he was able to separate Sydney from Edward, he fired.

Sydney screamed again, and curled into a ball, her hands over her ears and her eyes squeezed shut. Edward bellowed and rolled away from her, gasping for breath.

"Oh, God! Oh, God!" He coughed. Blood bubbled from his mouth.

"Sydney!" Nicolas dragged her away from the dying man. "Are you hit?"

"N-no. No." She tried to stand but fell back to the floor.

Nicolas laid his rifle on the table and slid bladed hands under her arms. He lifted her to her feet and guided her to a chair. "Are you certain? You aren't hit anywhere?"

"I've been shot before, and I'd know if I was shot again!" she snapped, her voice much less commanding than completely unnerved. "There's a hole in your shirt."

He looked down and stuck his finger through the opening. "In the front and out the back. That was close." He turned his attention to Edward as Addie appeared in the doorway.

"N-n-nicky?" she warbled. Her face blanched to the color of her ever-present apron.

"We're fine, Addie."

He crossed the room and knelt by the imposter. "Do you have any last words?"

Edward's skin was rapidly losing color. Blood frothed pink and airy from his lips but stained his waistcoat burgundy around the ragged hole.

"Tell... Rodger..."

Rodger?

With a blast of nauseating recognition, Nicolas realized this was the actor from St. Louis. Dark Skinny's *other* lover. Skinny—Rodger—must have concocted this whole extortion scheme after Nick banished Kilbourne from the Territory. Retribution, it appeared, for exposing Rodger's duplicity.

Apparently Macken wasn't the jealous type. Just the greedy type.

Nicolas turned a stunned gaze to Sydney. By the set of her features, she realized all this as well.

"Tell him what?" Nicolas managed.

He turned back to Edward, but the man was gone.

Chapter Forty One

April 1, 1820

*O*ne year had passed since Sydney tumbled onto Nicolas's land and into his life. In his study after supper, as if in commemoration, he held a parcel between them. She saw that it was rather battered. It must have come a long way.

"What's that?" she asked. Even the arrest warrant was less official-looking than this.

"I'm not certain. I wanted you with me when I opened it." Nicolas hefted it in his hand. "If heaviness signifies importance, we have a packet of some magnitude here."

She gripped her wine glass tightly; the liquid inside rippled. "Are you expecting anything?"

"No."

Something in his expression made her ask, "Are you afraid of something?"

His brow dipped. "No..." That sounded less certain.

Sydney pulled a bracing breath. "Waiting won't alter it."

Nicolas gulped his brandy, and then untied the twine. The soft leather unfolded to reveal a stack of thick parchment scribed in black ink. Some had multiple signatures. And all were in a language unfamiliar to Sydney.

It was the gilded wax seal displaying a castle that caused her gooseflesh. "Can you read it?"

"*Ja, jeg kan lese Norse.*"

Sydney saw his hands begin to tremble as he read the

documents. "What is it?"

"It's a summons."

"For whom?"

"Me."

"You? Who's summoning you?"

"The royal family in Norway."

Sydney sat back in her chair, incredulous. Her inflection carried her blatant disbelief. "The royal family of Norway has summoned you."

"Apparently."

"Why?"

Nicolas shifted in his chair. He shuffled through the papers, then downed his brandy. He stood and jerked his fingers through his hair. He put his hands on his hips and looked at Sydney. He looked away. He looked back again.

"There's something about my family that I, perhaps, forgot to tell you."

His words punched her in the chest. Sydney didn't know if she would laugh or cry. What now?

Nicolas screwed up his face. "It concerns my heritage."

There were those words again: his 'heritage.'

Sydney set her glass down and stood. She spoke with more assuredness than she felt. "Nicolas, whatever it is, we'll face it together. I love you and I'll stand by you. You're sensible of that, aren't you?"

"I am."

She took his huge, calloused hands in hers. "Tell me."

He lifted her hands to his lips and kissed the back of one, then the other. His worried blue eyes pinned hers. "Sydney?"

"Yes, Nicolas?"

"It seems—well, I was already aware, of course—I simply never mentioned to you, specifically—that I, uh…"

Sydney held her breath at his heart-pounding pause.

"I'm a prince.

Following is an excerpt from:

A Prince

of Norway

by Kris Tualla

Coming in November 2010
from Goodnight Publishing

"You're a *what?*" Sydney blurted.

Nicolas Hansen's wife of fourth months gaped at him and her dark brows plunged dangerously. He stroked a forefinger across his lip, calluses rasping his stubble.

"A prince."

Nicolas lowered himself onto the leather ottoman in the event his feisty spouse's shocked response involved impromptu fists. His gaze flickered around his dark, mannish study, and landed back on her.

"It's on my mother's side. Her grandfather was King Christian the sixth of Norway." He cleared his throat. "And of Denmark."

Sydney's expansive gray-green eyes did not leave his, though her hand flailed to the side in search of a seat. Nicolas shoved his favorite leather chair toward her with his foot.

She submerged between the worn, over-stuffed arms as if she hoped their bulk could block out the bizarre reality he had just doused her with. "So those portraits in the stairwell…"

"…look royal for a reason," Nicolas finished the sentence.

Her stunned expression had not altered. *"Skitt."*

Nicolas laughed at her imitation of his scatological Norse.

Sydney—decidedly *not* laughing—pressed palms against her violently flushed cheeks. "Why didn't you tell me?"

"To be truthful, I forgot. It's not as though we live in Norway." Nicolas scuttled his fingers through his hair and shrugged. If he acted unconcerned, perhaps she would take his next words well.

"Nor am I in any danger of becoming king, I don't believe."

"You don't *believe?*" she shouted. Her dilated pupils obliterated any trace of color in her eyes. "Nicolas! You're an *American!*"

As if he was unaware.

He dragged his gaze away from hers and hefted the package of letters which—after an eighteen month, multi-continental sojourn—arrived at his estate that day. The missives very strongly demanded his immediate appearance at the royal court in Christiania, Norway or he would suffer the penalties of his disobedience.

"Nicolas?" she squeaked. Her cheeks hollowed and lost their bloom. "What is this all about?"

He exhaled, resigned. There was no point in trying to delay the telling. It would only anger her and postpone his preparations for departure. He fixed his gaze on hers and arranged his features in a deliberately calm set.

"Norway has been under the control of Sweden since 1814, after Denmark's unfortunate decision to side with Napoleon. So the royal family has decided to pull together their various members and test the viability of regaining the country."

"And choose a king of their own?" It was an accusation more than a question. Sydney looked desperate as a drowning cat in spite of his attempt to downplay the summons. She leaned back—and away from him. "Is there any wine?"

Nicolas pushed up from his perch and poured her a glass. Her hand trembled as she reached for the crystal goblet. He knelt beside her chair while she gulped the burgundy liquid in a very un-ladylike manner. He stroked his fingers through her straight, dark hair; that action usually soothed her mood.

"Don't worry, *min presang.*" Nicolas had called her *my gift* since the day he confessed he loved her. He kissed her temple and inhaled the warm, rosy scent of her. "Other than my trip to Norway and back, nothing about our lives will change."

Sydney wagged her head and fixed her gray-green eyes on his. Mossy pewter shards pierced his fantasy and it shattered with irrevocable finality.

"I love you, Nicolas. You are sensible of that. But you are so very, *very* wrong."

Also from Goodnight Publishing:

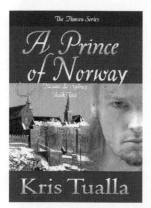

A Prince of Norway

The Hansen Series:
Nicolas & Sydney
Book Two

November 2010

A Matter of Principle

The Hansen Series:
Nicolas & Sydney
Book Three

January 2011

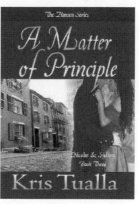

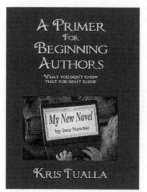

A Primer for Beginning Authors

What you don't know
that you don't know.

Available now!

Kris Tualla is pursuing her dream of becoming a
multi-published author of historical fiction. She started in
2006 with nothing but a nugget of a character in mind and
absolutely no idea where to go from there. She has created a
dynasty -
The Hansen Series - with six novels currently
in line for publication.

For more information and release dates visit:
www.GoodnightPublishing.com

For inquiries about publication, contact:
info@GoodnightPublishing.com

Kris Tualla is an amusing, enthusiastic presenter and
available for workshops and speaking engagements.
Please contact her at any site listed below.

http://www.KrisTualla.com
http://kristualla.wordpress.com
http://www.facebook.com/KrisTualla
http://www.youtube.com/user/ktualla
http://twitter.com/ktualla

Made in the USA
Charleston, SC
02 February 2011